"Let your plans be dark and impenetrable as night,
and when you move, fall like a thunderbolt."
— Sun Tzu

Books in *The Blood Dagger* Trilogy:

Volume One: *The Outcasts*
Volume Two: *The Watchers*
Volume Three: *Tree of Souls*

Ascended Guardians Series

BOOK ONE

SHIELD & SHADE

MISTY HAYES

Shield & Shade: Guardians Ascended Series: Book One by Misty Hayes

Paperback Ingram: 978-1-7321405-7-8
Paperback KDP: 978-1-7321405-8-5
Hardback: 978-1-7360862-0-9

Dedication

*For the dreamers. The survivors. The brave souls fighting
their own personal battles. You are not alone.*

1

ZOEY

I'd gotten lost when I was five years old. Just up and wandered out of our unlocked house during the night. A mistake my parents still blamed themselves for. But our household was a full one, and it could have been any of my older siblings who'd left the door open and unlocked.

A mistake that haunted our family, even to this day—ten years later.

There was a patch of wooded area within a mile of my house—not enough acreage to call it a forest but big enough to call it home to coyotes, the occasional bobcat, deer, and snakes. And it was where I'd ended up. I shuddered, thinking about a five-year-old drifting through the woods alone at night.

No wonder I had nightmares.

Those few days were a massive blank in my life. My lost time. I didn't remember anything except for the frightening visions that assaulted me in the middle of the night.

Nighttime. The time when my bad dreams rose up, unwanted and unbidden, like stomach acid in the throat, to assault me. My heart would burn. My lungs would clog. And my mind would race. It happened often. Even when falling asleep with the light on. I'd tried sleep aids, playing white noise in the background, and deep breathing, falling asleep with earbuds in, listening to music, but nothing ever stopped the dark visions from creeping back in.

They were always the same: I was trapped in a dark, cramped space, terrified and blind. I couldn't breathe. The air was too thin. There would be a flash of red, like fur, or hair, or blood … and then sharp, feral teeth snapping—a wild animal attacking me—eyes flashing with eyeshine, and I'd wake up panting and sweating, my own blankets smothering me, holding me hostage.

Tonight was no different.

I woke, sitting up ramrod straight in bed, with a cold hand pressed to my forehead.

"Shh, shh, shh, Zo. I'm here. It was only a bad dream. You're okay."

I blinked, my vision sliding in and out of focus, gulping in a lungful of air, willing myself to fully wake up out of the foggy haze, the last of the flashes passing across the backs of my eyelids. Dark eyes. Red hair. Sharp teeth.

"You were screaming again."

My mother. She was sitting next to me.

You're awake, Zo.

I could see her worried and strained face in the soft golden glow coming from my bedside table lamp. The creases around her eyes had deepened. She looked so much older and more fragile, and for a second, I felt bad that I'd woken her up. And then her smile returned, and she was sitting back, her facial features softening. It was one of the only times I'd ever let her comfort me—when I was half out of my mind from the lingering aftereffects of a vivid nightmare.

I was fifteen, too old for being coddled or tucked into bed, and yet I was still terrified of being left alone—to be sucked back into those chilling nightmares all over again. Taken. Drifting into the scary black void, feeling helpless and afraid.

"How bad was it this time?" my mom asked. Her voice was soft and low. "You need anything?"

I shook my head as I raked a hand through my hair, sweeping it off my damp forehead. "I'm okay. Thanks."

I felt the full weight of her concerned gaze on me. "Do you want to talk about it? Was it the same nightmare?"

When she tried to slip her hand into mine, I pulled away, feigning an apologetic grimace. I just wanted to go to sleep. I wanted to forget about the debilitating fear and solitude. I didn't want her to psychoanalyze me. I didn't want anything from her. This was her fault.

I thought I saw a flash of hurt cross her face as I tried to explain. "It's just late. I'm going to try and get some sleep. It's nothing new … the same thing over and over again. A strange creature and a flash of red hair, like fur … I'll be fine. Now that I'm awake, I know … it's silly … it's nothing."

Those words sounded hollow in my own ears.

She didn't quite look convinced, and I could tell she wasn't going to drop it. After a second, she cast her eyes down and pressed her lips into two thin lines, seemingly thinking. "If you do ever want to talk about it … about that night—"

"I'm good." I let out an angry breath of air. That was all we'd ever done: talk about it. "I don't want to talk about it anymore." And with that, I rolled over and left her sitting on the side of my bed.

2

ALASTAIR

On most days, Alastair Iszler found the forest an extremely calming place. Peaceful. Serene. Perfect. The birds above him would normally be chittering to one another as he sprinted by, out on his morning run. The squirrels would already have been winding their way around tree limbs, acorns pelting down from above.

Today, though, the woods felt ominous. Too quiet. There were no animals, or insects, or even wind. A heavy fog clung to everything. A warped fairy tale. The entire land placed in a deep sleep—like an enchantment. Every living thing affected by it but him. This odd feeling was what gave Alastair pause. He couldn't see more than ten feet in front of him in any direction. It was eerie, and the sun hadn't yet started to rise to burn the fog away.

As soon as he'd raced to the crest of a steep hill, he halted, winded and perturbed, a nagging feeling hitting him right in the pit of his stomach. Foreboding.

Something was wrong. Trail running was usually meditation for his soul. Not this morning.

A niggling intuition at the back of his mind told him to be on guard. There was still a little over ten kilometers left to go on this route, but now he was only thinking about turning around and going home. The top of his scalp prickled—a feeling he got when he was being watched.

Alastair had learned to listen to his intuition after over a hundred and fifty years' worth of fighting experience. He used to be a preternatural creature—a vampire—and he possessed over twenty different black belts in various martial arts to prove this skill.

Alastair had a PhD in heightened awareness.

He took in a few deep breaths, the smell of pine and earth strong in his nostrils, and something else: *Sulfur.*

Alastair had been around enough weird in his life to recognize that portentous feeling immediately.

Someone could spin him around blindfolded, and he'd still be able to find his way back home unassisted. After all, he'd been hiking, and running these woods for the better part of seven years. His cabin—well, technically, the cabin belonging to his wife, Larna Iszler—sat just five kilometers to the east of where he'd stopped. It was nestled in woodland, bordering northeast London.

The forest could be a peculiar place as well as a tranquil one. Nature was fickle. If you weren't cautious around her, she could wipe you off the face of the planet in one fell swoop.

The mist thickened unnaturally before his very eyes, and his skin prickled again. Someone was definitely out there, watching him.

Things had been much simpler since he no longer retained the mantle of vampire, which was fine by him. Alastair's life was perfect without any world-ending crisis or supernatural bad guy to worry about.

Like Gabriel Stanton.

It had been ten years since the battle at the Tree of Souls—an epic, world-ending war between angels and vampires. It was a miracle he'd survived, and that was only because of his best friend and half human, half angel: Corinth Taylor. Nephilim. Elite warrior. The Watchers, a team of angels and guardians who took care of anything preternatural or demonic that popped up on their radar.

Alastair was retired. For him, there were no more threats. No more bad guys to worry about. No supernatural battles to fight. Except that wasn't true. Not at all. He just didn't deal with it now.

He'd gone about his life, occasionally hearing stories about Corinth, Leo, and the rest of the Watchers over the years. Even Corinth had a day job—telecommuting professor for a college in Texas, so he could stay close to his family but also pick up and travel whenever he needed to, which, technically, was the best cover to have for a part-time superhero gig.

Larna Iszler, formerly Collins, had graduated medical school, and shortly after that, she'd gotten married—to the luckiest man in the world: him. She was now a well-respected doctor in London. But she was on leave back home in Fort Worth, Texas, visiting her mother and family for the upcoming Thanksgiving holiday. He missed her already.

Alastair had been trying to open his own deli and

bakery in central London, and there had been a lot of unexpected holdups and red tape, which had delayed him from joining his wife right away. Actually, she was probably still sound asleep, he mused. The difference in time was six hours. While it was 6:00 a.m. in London, it was 12:00 a.m. in Texas.

He regretted leaving the warmth of his bed, and not being with his wife right at this very moment. She usually joined him on his early morning runs. They'd just celebrated their seventh wedding anniversary in Italy a few weeks ago. The topic of having kids had come up on more than one occasion.

A branch broke close by, pulling Alastair fully out of his reverie, and an icy sensation settled between his shoulder blades.

He jerked his head around, scanning the area, suddenly alert. It didn't help that he couldn't see anything past the dense haze, which had started to feel more and more like a swampy bog than England.

Alastair knew he had felt something peculiar: a tug of sixth sense. His heartbeat quickened as he listened to his surroundings.

A resounding crack sent some crows flying from their roosts overhead—he couldn't see them, but he could hear the beating of wings as they fled, their caws loud. It wasn't out of the norm to hear these kinds of things in the woods. Dry, brittle branches broke all the time—whether it was caused by the wind or wildlife or just the passing of time. Except this felt different.

He knew the sound of someone trying to conceal their own footsteps—and someone trying *not* to. The hairs at the nape of his neck stood up as stiff as wires.

Cold air hit the back of his neck—an instinct told him to run.

Alastair pretended to check his heart rate monitor on his smart watch as he took in his surroundings. All he had to do was press one little button, and Corinth Taylor would show up *instantly*. The Nephilim could travel through lightning.

A teleporting skill Alastair wished he now possessed.

But he didn't want to cry wolf too early. He hadn't needed to call for backup in *years*. And the first sign of something paranormal wasn't going to change that fact. Besides, he could wait until the lurker revealed themselves to him at the very least—that way, he would know what he was dealing with.

Alastair still kept in close contact with Corinth, and he knew there hadn't been much activity of late, or if there was, Corinth hadn't shared it with him.

Oh well, time to check in anyway, he decided.

As Alastair started to press the emergency signal to alert Corinth and transmit his location, a deep boom broke through the quietude, sounding a lot like a cross between a gunshot and a cannon being fired. More startled birds flew from the roosts above him, squawking madly as they went.

Something whizzed past his head, sharp and biting, and the next thing he knew, his ears were ringing and he was rolling down the wrong side of the hill he'd just sprinted up—the side where there was no path, only trees and a short drop-off to another path below that, like a switchback. Dirt and dust billowed out behind Alastair as adrenaline tore through his veins, sharpening his focus. Several branches poked and scratched his face and neck. Bits of sharp rock impaled him. He clawed wildly at the dry leaves, trying to find purchase, and on his slide, about halfway down the slope, a rope coiled around his wrist, and a hot, agonizing pain tore up his arm at the same time as he was jerked to an abrupt stop. Fire lanced through him like a lightning bolt, shocking his system into submission; air left his lungs in a violent, ragged gasp.

He couldn't see his attacker, only knew that they were standing above him at the top of the incline he'd just fallen down.

Alastair craned his neck to see something coiled around his wrist—the same wrist his watch was attached to. He caught a glimpse of brown braided leather.

No, not a rope. *A whip.*

Alastair let out a gurgled cry as he reached for the tiny red dot flashing on his watch like a beacon—

The deep crack came again, sounding a lot more ominous this time.

In the next instant, the cord uncoiled and tore the watch clean off his arm, and his last chance at calling for aid went soaring through the air, out of sight. And because the whip was no longer holding him in place, he finished plummeting down the hill backward, hitting rocky outcroppings and prickly brush on his way down, until his breath was knocked free of his lungs as he finally landed flat on his back with brutal force. Pain exploded through his body, immobilizing him.

Vaguely Alastair was aware that someone was coming. There was movement off to his left, a sleek shadow darting toward him, but he could do nothing but wait for it to greet him.

"Can't have you calling for help, now, can we?"

The voice sounded raspy and deep and odd, as if from disuse.

Move, Alastair. Move your ass.

Out of the heavy fog strode a shadowy figure, a sharp outline of a body—as lithe and ethereal as a half-erased pencil sketch. Alastair blinked a few times, his senses scattered, trying to figure out what he was looking at right as his attacker hauled back on the whip again—

Knowing he only had a fraction of a second to react, Alastair flipped himself back to his feet and lunged into the shadow thing, barreling into a half-solid body. A surprised grunt came from the creature, as if it hadn't expected Alastair to be so bold.

The smoke spiraled up and around the shadow thing as it took on a more humanoid form. A strong smell of rotten eggs burned his nostrils.

And then the thing materialized fully, taking on the shape of a man—at least, Alastair thought it looked like a man. It was bald, and had unnaturally polished onyx skin, and those *eyes* ... Alastair shuddered. They were ink black, like obsidian marbles. No white in them whatsoever. Thick silvery veins snaked up its arms and the sides of its neck, looking a lot like liquid mercury.

Alastair had never seen a creature like this before.

He struck out several times in rapid succession, hitting the shadow thing in its abdomen, chest, and torso, and in the same fluid movement, he twisted around and attempted to land a roundhouse—except his foot connected with *nothing,* only smoke as it sailed right through the thing and he lost his footing.

The creature, seeing an opening, rematerialized in front of Alastair, jerked its head back, and headbutted him across the bridge of his nose. Blood burst across Alastair's vision, blinding him and pouring down his throat.

Alastair flew backward, rolling across a carpet of dead leaves and grime before fetching up against the side of a giant oak, stars shooting across his vision. Dirt and leaves ground into his back as he tried to move. Dammit, he'd gotten slow. And that thing was inhumanly strong.

For a long-drawn-out moment, he couldn't see or hear; he only felt the thudding of his blood slamming through his veins. Alastair swiped a hand down his face, trying to clear the salt out of his eyes. It stung.

"Alastair Iszler … you can't fight us."

Us?

Alastair was brutally aware of the brown braided whip wrapped up in the shadow thing's grip. The notches and plaits were interlaced with worn leather. Aged, cracked leather. He studied the weapon like someone might study a guillotine in startling detail right before being beheaded.

Get up. Get up. Get up.

Alastair stumbled to a knee, a hand going to his head as the oppressive fog turned into something dark and sinister, filling the forest, wrapping around his chest, almost choking him. It looked like night had suddenly fallen in the span of mere moments. There came a chill in the air, and his sweat crystallized on his skin. Now Alastair's tremor was caused by something else entirely: fear.

The thick, black smoke seemed to have a mind of its own as it formed a wide circle around him, solidifying— and evolving into a … *Holy hell.*

A darkly clad army.

Where was his watch? He cast a furtive gaze around, licking his dry lips, assessing.

The creatures all looked alike. Like the monster standing in front of him. Same liquid metal marks in place of veins, tracking lines up and down their arms and necks. Same bald heads and ink-black skin—disturbingly ugly.

And one horrifying word popped into Alastair's head: *Demons.*

3

ZOEY

Mondays sucked. Especially when you were a freshman in high school and you were taking Advanced Placement courses for college already. *And* you'd spent your entire weekend studying.

I had a study hangover, which was as unpleasant as it sounded. I'd already taken one placement test in May. I scored a three out of five in AP English Literature and Composition. A three was passing. A five was the best you could get. *A three is not good enough.* My plan was to take the AP World History test next year. It was not my best subject, which was why I had to study. And study some more. *Blech.*

It was T-minus three days until Thanksgiving break.

Most kids my age liked breaks. I couldn't stand them. Maybe it was because I couldn't concentrate at home. My brothers, Pete and Jimmy, never let me study in peace. They were a whirlwind of chaos and sound and burps and immature jokes and … just *boys*. There was never a time when they sat still—even in sleep.

This break would be especially bad, since my oldest brother, Corinth, would be back from his vacation for the holiday, and they all liked to gang up on me, especially him. He traveled quite frequently. Being a professor—online—gave him the freedom to pick up and go whenever he wanted. Lucky.

I turned the page on my microeconomics book and yawned. Graphs and charts and data—oh my. I couldn't see straight. My eyes glazed over for a second. With my back wedged up against a tree, I found that the bark had started to dig painfully into one of my shoulder blades. This was my usual spot in the lunch courtyard at Grover Heights in Fort Worth, Texas.

My parents had wanted me to stay in private school, but I had begged them to let me go to GH instead. All my brothers had gone the private school route, but I felt the need to branch out on my own. It was not exactly easy growing up in a household full of older siblings.

I felt a slight tug on the braid at my back and smiled. It came again, more insistent this time.

"Trevor," I said without turning around. "To what do I owe this well-timed interruption?"

When he didn't answer, I twisted around to see creamy skin, auburn hair, and wide, wide chocolaty eyes staring back at me from behind square-rimmed glasses. Gosh, he was startlingly breathtaking. Almost to the point that it hurt to look at him. He was the kind of hot where I knew he was so out of my league that I didn't even consider dating him. Not once. Okay, maybe once. But that was what had solidified our friendship, why we were so close. He knew I didn't care. We both knew we were destined to be best friends and nothing more. I was far too busy for boys, anyway.

Trevor gave me a dazzling smile and then bounded around the other side of the tree I was leaning against. He flopped lazily onto his stomach on the grass in front of me, resting his chin in his hands, his mouth shaped into a perfect bow as he gazed up at me.

A dark lock of his hair fell into his right eye, under his glasses. He had this childlike wonder on his face, like he always did. There was something so arresting about that grin, and those angular cheekbones. The guy was popular. I was not. Well, I guessed I was somewhere in the middle. He was the kind of person who got along with everyone. And he flirted with everyone too. It didn't matter who you were—boy or girl. People liked him.

"I thought you were taking a break from studying." He smoothed his floppy hair back into its usual sideswept style and tilted his head to the side, giving me a hard glare. "Why do I always have to be the voice of reason? It's really quite annoying. You know how I hate reason. Look at this gorgeous day." He gestured around us. "Wasting away while you're under a tree … ignoring it."

"You mean, ignoring *you*," I corrected.

"Exactly."

I slammed my heavy textbook closed and sighed. Enough was enough. "What do you have in mind?"

"For starters, ditch class at the end of the day—computer science—it's super easy to do," he explained, as if I had never had this conversation with him before.

"You know I can't skip. I have way too much going on. Besides, my brother is back in town after being gone for months, and when I get home, there will be no time to study. He'll annoy me and make me hang out with him. He is so *not* cool. And I'd much rather hang out with you."

Trevor sat up, crossing his legs underneath him on the dry, prickly grass. He picked at it, giving me another look from under those glasses. A devilish look that made my heart flutter. *Stop it, heart.*

"Your brother Cory is in town? He's … uh, a strange one. Remember that time at your place, the night of that big storm? He had just walked into the dining room, and then there was a commotion—thunder shook your house and lightning struck—and he was just … *gone.* Poof." He waved his hands in the air for dramatic effect. "I ran in there, and, like, he'd just *vanished* into thin air—right along with the storm. I swear he's a sorcerer or something."

"Don't let him hear you call him Cory," I said, ignoring his theatrics. "And you never saw him walk into the dining room. He didn't vanish into thin air. Besides, I don't see your fascination with him, anyway. He teaches *physics* at Westchester College. His idea of fun is trivia night at the local coffee shop."

He threw his hands in the air. "What about the weird electrical storm?"

I shrugged. "We live in Texas; the weather changes on a dime."

My brother did have his secrets though. I still had this vague memory of Cor coming home ten years ago with a half brother, Leo, in tow. I mean, what was that about?

None of us had ever known about a half brother. Family drama 101. I had only been five years old at the time, but I'd still noticed the marked difference in his appearance after he'd been gone for eight months.

Corinth had been skinny and lanky when he'd left, and when he'd come back, he'd had muscles in places I didn't even think you *could* have muscles. London had transformed him. He had calluses on his hands and somehow he knew martial arts. He'd claimed it was by taking CrossFit or something. He was a gamer and a geek and a softy at heart, and I had never known him, pre-London, to want to work out or be athletic in his entire life. Ever. People changed when they got older, I guessed.

And he'd had this strange sort of glint in his eyes when he'd gotten back from his trip. Not quite sad, but not quite happy either.

My guess was that he'd gone after his high school sweetheart, Larna, in England and she'd rejected him—*big time.* That kind of loss could mess with your head—I mean, I wouldn't know from personal experience, but still. Larna, his best friend and love of his life, had come back from England with a boyfriend in tow, Alastair Iszler, leaving Corinth behind in the dust. *And* she'd transformed herself too.

Talk about muscles. Goddess goals.

Then she'd crushed my brother's heart into a million tiny pieces—with those muscles, probably. I still thought Corinth and Larna should have gotten together. But she'd married Alastair Iszler instead. Dreamy Alastair. Good-looking Alastair. Okay, I didn't blame her there.

"Your entire family is strange," Trevor pointed out,

interrupting my rampant thoughts as if he'd read my mind. He took his glasses off. When he pulled his shirt up to clean them, I caught a flash of golden, tanned skin and flat stomach. "I love them. Please tell me I can come over tonight and hang out. Are they all going to be there?" He stared at me with wide eyes, and with his glasses off, his irises looked like pools of dark liquid. He threw his glasses back on again, and I could see a hint of light-brown flecks swimming in his eyes.

I rubbed a spot at the center of my forehead. "You only like my family because it's like watching a train wreck. You can't look away. There's always drama on Thanksgiving."

"Exactly. Free reality TV." He shrugged in concession. "It's not my fault my parents are always out of town on business. Your family is blissfully hectic. There's something that makes me want to stick around and watch all of it in action."

I waved a hand toward a cadre of girls across the courtyard who were all ogling Trevor, casting furtive gazes in his direction and giggling. His skin was clear; he was athletic; he knew how to dress; and he had a confident way about him that was magnetic. He was comfortable in his own skin, which was, like, ninety percent different from the rest of us poor saps still trying to figure it out.

He was definitely an anomaly at this school.

It was not known for its amazing football team, or good-looking people, or its wealth. Trevor's parents were rich. Mansion rich. And they'd enrolled him in just about every extracurricular activity out there: karate, gymnastics, Latin, and drama club. He'd quit every single one of them, some after only trying them out for a few days. That was his one and only downfall: he just couldn't seem to finish anything he started. Not that I didn't like Trevor, but he was the kind of guy who would never settle down, always looking for the next big thing. I didn't expect us to get together, *ever*. Heck, I didn't even know what *settle down* really meant. I was not his type, anyway, and he wasn't mine. He was outgoing, energetic, and I was the exact opposite: bony, introverted, and shy.

We'd met last year at the local library. He'd tripped over me. I'd been sprawled out on the floor by a shelf in a back section of no-man's-land, near the encyclopedias, sound asleep. The lights had been not quite dark, but right on the verge of dimming out altogether. The temperature had been perfect. I'd passed out while studying. Most days, I was invisible.

On that day, I was *especially* invisible—because he tripped over me and twisted his ankle. I ran away, horrified, without making sure he was okay.

As I said, introvert.

To make matters worse, he tracked me down at the end of school one day, pretend limping. Surprisingly, he was checking to make sure *I* was okay and not the other way around, which I thought was kind of sweet. He was glad he'd had the excuse not to go to karate practice.

"Your life is perfect," I said, smiling at the distant memory of how we'd met for the first time. "Everyone loves you, and I wish my parents would leave me alone, by the way."

Trevor laughed softly and pointed at the pile of books by my right leg. "You could have just as many friends."

He snapped his fingers as if he were trying to remember something. "What about the guy who works at Sweets and Stuff? What's his name? His crush on you is so big I'm pretty sure he's already bought a ring to pop the question—"

"Cruz!" I cried, my face reddening all of a sudden. "The guy with the scars? He smells like cooking grease and stale french fries." I screwed my face up in disgust.

"*Zo*," he crooned. "I realize it's hard to get out of that shell of yours, but it might be good for you to put down a book once in a while and meet new people."

"You sound like my mom," I said, half-annoyed with him, except I liked the way my shortened name sounded on his lips, like a soft caress upon my skin. My cheeks started to flush even more, so I glanced away, brushing at a stray piece of hair that had escaped from my braid. I flipped it back over my shoulder. We might not be meant for each other, but he was still really hot. And it wasn't against the law to admire him.

My lifted mood didn't last long. I kept thinking about the fact that he was the one who didn't ask me out. *Would I say yes?* My eyes raked over those dark eyes and light lashes hidden behind his glasses, and I thought, *Maybe. Maybe I would. No, Zo. No you wouldn't.* I admonished myself in the same thought. *Too hot is a thing.*

The bell rang one shrill toll, ending our conversation and our lunch period at the same time. I started picking up my things, scattered across the lawn, tossing books into my backpack as Trevor said, "So, I'll see you tonight at Sweets and Stuff—at around six?"

I let out a quick huff before nodding, unable to say

no to that face. "Yeah, I'll see you then."

Sweets and Stuff smelled like vanilla and waffles and baked sugar. Three of my favorite things. They were well known for their freshly made waffle cones. The birthday cake ice cream tasted like heaven. Not to mention, the burgers and fries were out of this world. The inside of the place was set up to look like a 1950s shake shop. Checkered black-and-white linoleum floors, mint-green countertops, and red stools lining the front counters.

I had decided to get there early to wait on Trevor—and study.

I grabbed one of the last corner booths available and unloaded my backpack.

Thoroughly entranced by the law of demand, and enjoying a vanilla milkshake, I almost jumped clean out of my skin when someone cleared their throat beside me.

I glanced up to see Cruz holding a tray full of food. A golden crinkle-cut fry hung precariously off the edge of the tray. As always, my eyes found their way to his hands. There were a bunch of white half-moon scars scattered across the backs of his fingers and knuckles. I wondered how he'd gotten them. My imagination kept coming up with wild, unbelievable scenarios, like he was a lion tamer or a snake charmer.

He was wearing his usual uniform attire: an off-white apron, stained with grease and ketchup—and who knew what else—a purple T-shirt, khaki pants, and cream-colored tennis shoes with purple laces. I could see the collar of a white tee underneath and a glint of gold at his neckline, a chain he'd shoved under his work shirt. He had caramel-colored skin and a crown of dark curls hidden beneath a purple baseball cap. Considering he seemed like he wanted to crawl out of his own skin, I assumed he did not like his work attire.

He tugged at his collar in annoyance with his free hand. "Hi, Zoey. I brought you some … uh, food." He gestured at the table, full of my textbooks, papers, and notebooks, and flashed me a small, shy smile. "If you have room, that is."

"Oh, I didn't order that," I said with an apologetic grin. "Sorry."

"It's on the house," he whispered, glancing around. "Just don't tell my boss."

I shoved my books aside so he could slide the tray across the table. "Free food?" I said, smiling. "Your secret is safe with me. Thank you so much … You must have heard my stomach growling from all the way across the restaurant—" He leaned across me, effectively shutting me up. A strong whiff of fried food, hair gel, and something like cloves or mint hit me. "But you didn't have to do that. I have dinner with my folks tonight. They're probably already waiting on me …" I let my voice trail off as soon as I saw the look of disappointment cross his face. "This looks way better though," I finished awkwardly, plucking a stray pickle off the tray and popping it into my mouth.

"You must be studying for something important," he said, tipping his head at my books. "I see you in here a lot … with that guy with the black-rimmed glasses … your boyfriend."

My eyes caught his briefly. They were chestnut brown, almost bronze in the afternoon light that glinted in from the set of wide windows behind me. I'd never noticed his eyes before.

A flush of heat hit the tips of my cheeks as I smiled again, embarrassed. "Oh, Trevor isn't my boyfriend. He's just a friend." I held my book up to show him the cover—*Economics*—and said, "I'm studying for a test."

He perked up as soon as I told him Trevor wasn't my boyfriend, I noticed.

Someone shouted from behind the counter, "*Cruz Saldivar! Where are you? ORDER UP!*"

Cruz pulled his baseball cap down, as if he was trying to avoid being spotted by the guy yelling. I glanced at the man behind the counter. He was dark-skinned, middle-aged, and thicker around the middle—like he sampled everything he served. What little hair he did have on the sides of his head was damp with sweat. I could see why Cruz might want to avoid the man—he had a permanent scowl on his face.

I didn't know what made me do it. I hadn't really been in the mood to socialize—except with Trevor. I hated small talk, and I wasn't done studying yet, but Cruz had this desperate look on his face, so I took pity on him and gestured to the opposite side of the booth I sat in. "Quick—sit down before he sees you."

As if it was the invitation he'd been waiting for all day, Cruz quickly slid in across from me and shoved his back against the wall, stretching his legs out on the seat in front of him, looking both thankful and relieved to be off his feet.

When he glanced back up at me, I met his gaze. For

a second, it was just him and me in the overcrowded ice-cream parlor. The loud, raucous voices from the next table over seemed to die down to a small buzz. I kept replaying Trevor's words over and over again in my head: *His crush on you is so big I'm pretty sure he's already bought a ring to pop the question.*

I didn't think we'd ever really had a full conversation before. It was always "Hi. How are you?" "Fine. You?" "Great, goodbye." Small talk was always wasted on me.

"Thanks a lot," he said, sounding relieved. "That's my boss, Edgar. Sometimes he can be a real jerk. If it's überbusy, like today, I'm not able to take a break until *after* we close, which makes no sense."

"Take your break now," I suggested. "You can help me eat some of this food."

Cruz plucked a fry from the tray and threw it into his mouth, beaming from ear to ear, and on instinct, my eyes flickered back over to the scars on his hands. There were so many. Across his knuckles. On the backs of his hands. Even on his fingertips. Had he tried to fight off a pack of wolves?

He must have seen me staring at them, because he pulled his hands back under the table, out of my line of sight, his cheeks flushing. "So, this test you're studying for … why's it so important?" he asked between chewing.

I took a small sip of my milkshake, thinking about how much I wanted to share with him. Finally I said, "It's for a college aptitude test. I'm trying to graduate early."

"Really? Wow. Aren't you like a freshman or something?"

I nodded, wondering how he knew that.

"Yeah. What about you?" I asked.

"Sophomore," he answered, grabbing another fry from the tray and dipping it in ketchup that was in a small white cup. He must've been hungry, because he seemed to have forgotten about hiding his hands as he ate with reckless abandon. I watched as he tore open a salt packet and dumped it into the ketchup cup, and then he did the same with a pepper packet and, using a fry as a spoon, stirred it all together.

I raised an amused eyebrow, and he laughed. It came out guttural sounding, from the back of his throat, most likely because he'd seen the look on my face. "What?" he asked with a sniff of indignation. "I like salt."

"I can see that." I covered my mouth to stifle a grin and then picked up the knife to cut the cheeseburger in half. I pushed one of the halves across the table on a napkin for him. "You know you can overdose on salt."

"A lack of salt can be fatal too," he pointed out, grabbing the burger and taking a big bite. "Did you know salt used to be a precious commodity? It used to be so valuable that people called it white gold. Right up to the early twentieth century, one-pound bars of salt were still used in Ethiopia as the basic form of currency. I wish that were still the case …" He let his voice drift off, as if he wasn't used to having any sort of attention on him.

"I did not know that," I said, surprise coloring my voice. "How do you know so much about salt?" I asked.

He cocked his head to the side. "You're not the only one who studies."

Something about that answer in combination with the way he was looking at me—like I was the most interesting thing on the planet—made my heart rate kick up a notch.

He paused for a beat to finish swallowing and then continued. "So, why are you trying to graduate early, Zoey?"

I cleared my throat, not sure where to begin. I instinctively wanted to give him my generic answer— "I like to torture myself"—but something about his undivided attention on me made me want to open up to him. Argh. Conversing. Small talk.

"I'm the youngest in a family filled with way too much drama," I answered with a shrug. There, not too much information. Just enough.

Except he had paused, holding the almost-finished burger in front of his face, his mouth hanging open. There were only a couple of bites left at most. After a moment, he said, "I'm listening."

"There's an opportunity for me to go to college in England—to study abroad—so, I guess I really want to take it." I took a sip of my milkshake and then picked up a fry.

I hadn't even really told Trevor any of this stuff. Or my parents … *yet*. I mean not all of it.

"I get family drama," Cruz said, glancing down at his hands. I couldn't quite interpret the look on his face as he chewed on the inside of his cheek. Maybe sad. Maybe he was absorbed in his own head. "It's the reason I work so much—it's just me and my mom. I take care of her." He lowered his head but didn't elaborate any further. The emotion in his voice surprised me. I was a perfect stranger to him, and he didn't have to share anything personal with me. I wondered if I'd pressed too much, or stared too hard at the marks on his hands. There was a story there that I felt he wasn't going to open up about. But suddenly I found I really wanted to know more about him.

After he was silent for another minute, I said, "Are we trading sob stories? Because I feel like I might give you a healthy dose of competition."

At that, his head snapped up. He was grinning again, all white teeth. At least we were beyond small talk.

"So, what's your family drama?" he asked.

"My mom had an affair, which led to a half brother I never knew about until ten years ago," I blurted out. Dang, I had no idea why I had to vomit out *all* of my dysfunction. *Double argh. Argh. Argh.* Something told me I'd regret that later.

One of his eyebrows arched as he held up his hands in surrender. "Whoa. Okay, okay. You win."

"I told you," I said with a shrug.

"Where'd you get that key chain from?" Cruz pointed at my backpack, on the seat beside me, quickly changing the subject. "I've noticed it before, and I've been meaning to ask you about it. That's a shield, right? It's cool."

I looked down at the key chain clipped to the strap of my backpack. I carried it everywhere. Corinth had given it to me. I could see why it had drawn his interest. A shaft of sunlight refracted off the shiny metal and hit me at eye level, momentarily blinding me. A pocket-size shield made out of polished gold. A simple souvenir.

"A gift from my oldest brother," I told him. "When he got back from his trip from England."

I knew it was probably bought at the airport on his way back from London, but it was my good luck charm.

I unclipped the key chain and reached across the table to show it to him. He took it from me, his fingers brushing mine so he could study it more closely.

"This is heavy," he said, his eyes still focused intently on the metal. "I think it's real gold. This is like a trident or a three-pronged shield. It looks like a medieval knight's shield or something. But there's no coat of arms on it. Do you know where he got it from?" he asked, seemingly intrigued and lost in thought at the same time.

I was surprised at seeing him so interested in it. "No idea. I thought he just bought it at some souvenir kiosk."

He licked his lips, gazing at the small trinket in his palm.

"How'd you get those scars on your hands?" I burst out. I couldn't help it, the question had been eating me up alive. *Real smooth, Zo.*

He looked up from the key chain, and his face transformed completely. His smile vanished, and he went a little pale, and then he stood up quickly, almost falling out of the booth in his haste to get away from me. I cringed, realizing I'd asked the wrong question.

Oh yeah. This was why I was an introvert.

"My, um, break is over …" he all but stammered, and then he set the shield back on the table and turned on his heel before I could respond, sticking his hands deeply into his pants pockets, practically running to get back to work.

Oh no. Lame, Zo. This is why you don't make friends easily.

"I'm sorry—" I started to say, but right at that moment, Trevor walked up behind Cruz and stepped around him, scooting me over and cutting off my dreadful attempt at an apology.

What a dope. I felt awful. My chest constricted.

Cruz was already behind the counter, helping another customer, who'd stepped up to the register to order. By the way he hunched his shoulders and avoided my gaze, I knew I had offended him.

"What was all that about?" Trevor asked, eyeing me up and down, dark eyes glittering behind his glasses. "Everything okay? You look rattled. Did he propose? Was it something that guy did? Because—"

"Everything's fine," I reassured him quickly, rolling my eyes. "He was just bringing me my order."

Disappointment hit me hard for some reason. I'd really been enjoying our conversation, and I'd messed it all up. I was good at that. My mood had started to sour, so I gathered my things and shoved them irritably into my backpack. I had just been trying to get to know the guy.

"Hey, I just got here," Trevor said, his mouth falling open. "Where are you going?"

"I have dinner. My parents will kill me if I'm late again." I had only eaten a fraction of what Cruz had brought, but I just didn't want to deal with Trevor's endless teasing if he found out Cruz had given me free food.

I grabbed the rest of my things and left Trevor sitting at the table. Apparently unfazed, he didn't seem to mind my disappearing act. To be fair, I did this to him a lot.

As I was bolting through the doors, I saw him eating the other half of untouched burger on the tray and chatting with some girls across the table from him, all smiles.

Boys were trouble. Every single one of them.

4

ALASTAIR

Alastair ran as fast as his legs would carry him, back through the thicket of trees, fog, and heavy smoke that kept re-forming into bodies all around him, dark shapes—so many he wasn't going to stick around to count them all.

No matter how swift he was though, he couldn't lose his pursuers. He darted to the side at the last second as something heavy, a branch probably, slammed into the trunk of a tree near his head. It broke apart in a loud *BOOM* that echoed over the foliage high above him.

A dark hand came out of nowhere, latching onto his arm; the thing tried to jerk him off-balance. Alastair wrenched out of its iron grasp, ignoring the searing pain in his wrist, and using his forward momentum, he bounded up the side of an oak.

He flipped himself backward, landing behind the shadow creature—the thing that had grabbed him—and he was already on the move again as it shouted to the others, "*He's quick!*"

With his heart hammering a million beats per second, Alastair was sure it was going to give out on him, but he kept going. Breathless, he sprinted up the rise of another incline, toward the main path he knew would lead right to his cabin. Not much further, and then he'd have backup, and more weaponry—

Something barreled into Alastair's chest hard enough to bruise his ribs as rough hands seized him around his middle.

They went down, and his full weight, along with his attacker's weight, slammed onto his right kneecap; he collided with something solid, a stone, earth, hard soil, and a body. A second later, a terrible pain ripped through his head as he hit something, a sharp rock, and his vision blurred. The throbbing was livid—angry and alive, like it wanted to rip his soul from his body.

More hands snaked around his throat and chest and legs. Shadow figures materialized out of thin air, crushing him, forcing his face down into the hard-packed earth, trying to wrench his arms behind his back, all of them inhumanly strong. His nostrils filled with the scent of soil. Snorts and grunts of effort came from the forms around him. A weird keening noise made him want to cover his ears.

Alastair didn't have his usual weapons on him.

Stupid, Alastair. Stupid.

He fought with renewed energy and adrenaline, shoving, kicking, and struggling against the horde piled on top of him, until finally they started to move, to give.

Inch by bloody inch, he managed to wriggle his way through the press of bodies on top of him, until eventually he emerged on the other side.

Cool air hit Alastair in the face, and he almost collapsed in sheer relief. He leaped to his feet, but as soon as he did, a tidal wave of agony struck him so violently his vision clouded over, and then turned fire-engine red. He howled in misery and folded in on himself, his legs buckling out from under him, grabbing blindly at his kneecap.

Curling onto his side, he thought, *It's shattered.*

Alastair tried to fight his way back to his feet, but instead, he let out a choked cry mixed with dread and rage and frustration.

"Keep him alive. Bind his hands."

The brash voice that spoke overshadowed the sharp stabbing sensation right in the center of Alastair's chest, and a new bout of energy tore through him as his need to get away increased exponentially, taking with it some of his torment.

They wanted him for some dark purpose, so he forced himself back to his feet to get away, bracing for the pain—

There was a shift in air pressure, and he rolled to the right as something zipped past his face again: the whip.

Alastair crashed into a dark form. He seized hold of an arm and shoulder, and threw the shadow thing's body out in front of him like a shield. There came a sharp *SNAP*, and the whip struck the monster instead of Alastair, and it dropped like a stone at his feet, landing facedown.

Too late. It didn't matter. Alastair wasn't fast enough.

The wicked whistle came again, and this time there was no avoiding it.

The leather dug into his skin as it looped around his neck, cutting off his oxygen. He gasped, blood-slick fingers clawing at the noose as his assailant yanked back on the grip in its hand, dragging him forward, and throwing him off-balance. Alastair slammed onto his already-battered knee, the burning so intense he wasn't able to move or breathe or think.

All he could do was stare at the canopy of trees above him, their scraggly branches drooping and swaying in the wind. The fog had started to lift as soon as the sun had emerged.

It might have been a beautiful morning had the shadow thing not been standing over Alastair, gazing down upon him with the truest form of loathing on its face.

His chest was heaving as he gasped, trying to get air into his lungs, scrabbling at the leather.

The thing smirked, and its face cracked open like day-old shoe polish as it spoke. "I've never seen a human move that fast before. Guess that explains why the boss wants you so badly. You tried, Alastair Iszler. I'll give you that. It was a valiant but wasted effort."

The dark figure moved closer, and as it did, it took up the slack of the whip, forcing Alastair to roll onto his side. He cringed and groaned in pain, feeling something warm and sticky sliding down his neck.

The creature studied Alastair. He had seen that look before, more times than he cared to admit. This was something that thrived on seeing pain in others. It regarded Alastair with wide all-black serpentine eyes. Up this close, it looked like someone had doused the creature's entire body in thick oil.

Alastair managed to hiss between his teeth. "What … are you?"

"A demon," it answered, bending down to peer into Alastair's eyes. His pulse quickened as the demon continued. "I have no name, but you can call me Gray. Like the color of an impending storm. You run almost every morning. Same route. Same time. Same distance. Predictable. No armor or fighting gear, just jogging pants, a long-sleeved thermal, and tennis shoes. No cell phone." It made a tsking sound, adding, "But the *watch*, I knew that was going to be my biggest problem. No calling for help from those pesky angels. That's why I have this." Gray gave the whip a tug, and it tightened around Alastair's throat. He panted, struggling to pull in a deep breath. "It was perfect timing, your wife, Larna, being gone. Where's she at now? Visiting family?"

Alastair did not like the sound of Larna's name on its tongue. Or the fact that it knew his *and* Larna's schedules. This was bad. Very bad. She was in trouble. That thought was enough to give him a renewed bout of strength.

Sitting up, he grabbed the slack in the whip, surprising Gray, and the cord around his neck loosened. But Gray was already snapping the weapon back as several more demons grabbed hold of him, shoving their feet into his back, forcing him facedown into the muck. He cried out as the leather went taut around his neck, and a moment later, they were binding his hands behind his back.

"Don't you know when to stay down?" Gray asked, shaking the coiled whip in its hand, yanking Alastair viciously back to his ruined knees once he was restrained.

"*You'll … find that … to be … one of my more annoying … qualities,*" Alastair growled, anger lacing his voice. "What do you want?"

"I don't want anything, but the boss does." Gray's smirk widened, revealing pointy white teeth. "*He wants your soul.*"

5

CRUZ

ruz Saldivar's tiny efficiency sat on the north side of Fort Worth, in the general vicinity of the Stockyards, one of the oldest historical districts in the city. But back in the early twentieth century, the Stockyards had been the place to sell and buy cattle by the millions. Hence, Stockyards. Now, though, the area mainly consisted of entertainment venues, shops, hotels, and old-timey-looking saloons. Cruz's apartment was tucked back into an older neighborhood that was well past its prime.

This was where the tourists came to sightsee—*not* where the West began, as advertised. The history behind the Stockyards was pretty cool though, Cruz had to admit.

Fort Worth was the only city to have real cowboys on its payroll—they tended to the herd on the Chisholm Trail, near the Trinity River. Downtown used to house gambling parlors and saloons. *Also cool*, he thought.

Outlaws used to hang out in this area. *Bonus.* There was something enthralling about outlaws—rogues and pirates. The idea of being able to do what you wanted, when you wanted, was so foreign to him that he was attracted to that kind of living. He imagined it had been a rough neighborhood back in the day. You had to get by on your grit and wits alone.

Cruz respected that, except he couldn't afford to get in trouble with the law now—not with a sick and dying mother to take care of. There had been many times when he could have gone that route—should have taken that route. He needed money. His *madre* needed him. She needed medicine they couldn't afford.

Just then he heard coughing coming from his mother's bedroom.

There was only one bedroom in the tiny place. Cruz slept on the couch, in the living room. He could hear her trying to get the phlegm out of her lungs again. Always coughing and wheezing. A heartbreaking sound. If she got pneumonia one more time, she'd probably have to be hospitalized … *again* … and he didn't want to think about that. His mother's fit was particularly bad this time around. She seemed to be getting weaker with the passing of time. His heart ached. Useless, that was how he felt. He glanced back down to the scarred notches on his hands. Ugly reminders of his past.

"Dinner's ready in a few minutes."

It was past 10:00 p.m.

He heard her speak softly. "*Sí, mijo.*" Yes, my son. "*Estoy bien.*" I am fine. "*Deja de preocuparte.*" Stop worrying.

His *madre* suffered from lung disease. Antibiotics, inhalers, and meds were all expensive. So he worked to help with bills, which rarely left him any time to study. School was an afterthought. His life was an afterthought. Friends were nonexistent, and the idea of actually having a girlfriend anytime soon was preposterous. Cruz's thoughts strayed to Zoey. He felt a pang of regret at leaving her at the table the way he had. He'd ruined the great moment they'd been sharing.

He couldn't help thinking about her. Those rosy cheeks, her long, pretty hair the color of a sandy beach. She always wore it in a braid down her back. And that thousand-watt smile could buoy his spirits for days. He liked the way one of her cheeks dimpled when she talked. And also the cute pattern of freckles across her nose. He thought about connecting the dots.

His eyes once again flickered back to the palm-sized gold shield lying on the coffee table. She'd forgotten it at the restaurant. Her friend Trevor Malcolm must have missed it before he'd left too. Trevor's attention had been elsewhere—like, on every single girl in the place.

Cruz did not like that guy.

Trevor was always in there with a different girl. He saw how Zoey looked at him. She liked him. Trevor was everything Cruz was not. Confident. Carefree. Rich. *Spoiled.*

Cruz had found the shield charm as he'd been cleaning up the table for the next group of kids.

A comforting warmth had radiated off it as soon as he'd picked it up. The weight was reassuring in his hand. Even now, he could feel the strange pulse of heat. He pulled it close against his chest. Cruz didn't remember picking it up. Most likely his imagination, but still ... there was something about it. Something that kept drawing him back to it. Bizarre. Maybe it was just because it belonged to his crush.

Zoey's gift from her oldest brother.

He wasn't going to keep the souvenir—he'd return it, of course, on his day off. The one and only day he didn't work: Thanksgiving. But for now, it was a nice reminder of Zoey Taylor. He could hold on to it for a few days. Cruz was a firm believer in talismans. He had one of his own. A pendant he wore every day. Saint Peregrine Laziosi, the patron saint of people suffering from incurable illnesses, like cancer. Like his mother. He pulled the chain out from under his shirt and kissed it. *Healing.*

He could hear the sizzle and hiss coming off the burners as the pozole rojo started bubbling over the top of the pot.

"*Crap!*" Cruz shouted. "The stew's burning!"

He jumped up and flew to the kitchenette to turn the heat off, tugging the overflowing pot off the flame, burning his hands in the process.

"Ow, ow, ow ..." he muttered crossly as he placed it in the sink.

His mother was laugh-coughing from the bedroom. "Told you you'd burn it again."

A minute later, she was shuffling into the living room, her slippers sliding across the cheap shade of brown carpet as she moved, hunched over from fatigue and pain.

She was wearing her favorite purple robe, and she had a hand pressed protectively to her chest, holding it closed.

She looked so frail. Her hair was the color of ash, streaked through with darker strands the shade of charcoal. He noticed the caramel shade of her skin was no longer healthy. In fact, it looked waxy in the moonlight that spilled in through the open window in their tiny apartment.

It was muggy this evening. A warm, humid air had hit in November. But they couldn't afford an astronomical electricity bill, so they kept the AC off—and the Texas heat in—even in November.

Cruz's concerned gaze took in his mother as he started to clean up the mess he'd made. "No need to get up, *Mamá*. I was going to bring it to you."

"I can still walk," she said, a light chiding tone in her voice. "Besides, it's good for me to get up and move. I can't be confined to a bed all day."

Right as she said this, though, she broke out into another bone-rattling cough, chest heaving. She looked so slight under the fluffy robe, her ribs practically poking out of her back. She needed to gain more weight. This worried him greatly.

Cruz was beside his mother in an instant, his hand on her back as he helped guide her to the couch to sit down. "Did you take your antibiotics? Your nebulizer?"

After the fit passed, she nodded and gently clutched his hands in hers. "Always, *mijo*. You're a good boy. You work too hard. And … you're sticky." She pulled her hand away, shaking it in mock disgust. "You still have ice cream on you. Go get cleaned up. Take care of yourself for once."

Cruz looked down at his forearms. She was right. His skin was perpetually sticky, both from caked-on ice cream, from scooping it out of the cartons all day, and from grease from the fryers. He had washed his hands but had missed his forearms. He'd have to scrub down like a doctor before surgery to get it all off. Even his hair smelled like grease.

"I'll go take a shower right now," he said evenly. "Do you need anything else before I do?"

She started to shake her head, but then her eyes caught on the key chain clutched in between his fingers, the gold glinting bright. "What is that?"

Cruz glanced down at the shield still in his hand. "Oh, uh, it belongs to a friend. I have to return it to her."

"Her?" His mother's eyes sparkled with amusement. "It looks expensive." She reached out and plucked it from his grip, her fingers cold on his. They left smudges on the polished metal. She closed her eyes momentarily and then opened them again, a small smile playing across her lips.

"Since when do you have friends?" she teased lightly. "Would this be a *girl*friend?"

He eyed the small trinket in her hand and gave his mother a dazzling smile. "I'm full of surprises," he said, thinking about Zoey. Maybe he did have time for *one* girl.

6

ZOEY

The house was full when I got home. Pete was sitting on the couch, a loose arm hanging around his girlfriend's shoulders.

I threw my backpack down beside the couch. I swore this was how I'd *finally* gain muscle—or break my back—by carrying around my book bag all day, every day. It weighed a ton. I was all arms and legs and knees and elbows and awkwardness.

Pete was the second oldest of my siblings—twenty-three, to be exact—and he still lived with our parents. Well, technically, when he wasn't hanging out at his girlfriend Carlie's place. But she had two roommates, and they took up a lot of the space with their art projects. She was an art major herself. I was positive she only dated Pete for the food she stole from us. She was twenty, the same age as Jimmy, my other older brother, and she had dark skin and light, curly auburn hair. Today it was styled in a high bun on the top of her head. Pete had said her family came from Hawaii. She had on an oversize tan wool knit sweater and brown leggings, and her bare feet were perched on the edge of the glass coffee table. I noticed her perfectly pink manicured toenails.

Why my parents let everyone hang out at our house, I had no idea. It felt more like a subway station than a home. This was why I didn't get any studying done. This was why I needed out of Texas.

I glanced at the TV to see what they were watching. Entertainment news—*again*. A show featuring up-and-coming popular singers, business moguls, and movie stars. Carlie made Pete watch it instead of sports.

The anchor was in the middle of saying, "... humanitarian and Nobel Peace Prize winner Gabriel Stanton has done it again. As his nonprofit, Global Reach, celebrates huge success in England, being recognized by the queen herself ..." A picture of the billionaire popped up on-screen.

The first thing I noticed was that jagged scar running down the left side of his face. The guy wasn't exactly a supermodel, because he was old, but he did have a headful of thick, wavy dark curls and olive-toned skin, and I supposed, with those high cheekbones, maybe in his younger years he could have been hot. The salt-and-pepper stubble on his cheeks and chin only made him look more regal. What really struck me, though, were his eyes. Deeply set and pitch-dark. A cold chill crept down my spine.

There was something decidedly familiar about that face. Déjà vu struck, and in my mind's eye, I saw a flash of bright red hair, like a flame, and a bright light and sharp teeth. I shivered past the visceral recollection—like one of my nightmares. Great, now I was having them during the day too.

The anchor said, "Having built well over one hundred free schools around the country, poverty-stricken kids can now receive affordable private education …"

I'd seen him on TV before, on magazine covers, advertisements—he was a household name: Gabriel Stanton. One of the wealthiest people on the planet. Still, the strange feeling lingered. Maybe some people just rubbed you up the wrong way. *Yet …*

Pete glanced up from the TV, as if he'd just now noticed I'd walked into the room. "Hey, chicken legs." He twisted around on the couch to get a better look at me. "You look like the undead. You need some sun—you're way too pale. Also, Mom's going to kill you for missing dinner again."

I rubbed the cold from my arms and pulled a face at him as the program switched to something else. "Don't call me 'chicken legs.'"

I heard my mom shout from the kitchen, "*That better be Zo I heard coming through that door! You're late, young lady!*"

Carlie coughed out a laugh. "You're in trouble again."

There came the sound of heavy footsteps, and then the wind was ripped from my lungs as I was hauled into the air.

My legs went out from under me.

The room spun, and I smelled soap and oranges and aftershave. *Jimmy.* He wasn't much taller than I was, but he was stocky and built like a steel rod. And he loved to play fight. He wound an arm around my head, effectively putting me into a headlock before I had the chance to fight back.

"What are you going to do now?" he whispered in my ear, already sounding winded.

"*This!*" I said, jabbing a sharp elbow into his ribs. He doubled over with a grunt of surprise, but the shot didn't hurt him. Instead, it only seemed to egg him on. He took me to the ground in a jumble of arms and legs and grunts.

From somewhere in the back of the house, I heard my dad shout, "*No rough housing!*"

Jimmy liked to pick on me, but I was no stranger to tussling, and even though I was petite and built like a reed, I had learned how to hold my own—at least for a minute. It was sink or swim in this household, and with three older brothers, I'd had to learn real quick how to handle myself. Another reason I didn't want to come home.

He put a wet finger in my ear and twisted it around. "Wet willy!"

I thrust another elbow—the best weapon I owned— into his nose, and he let out a cry of pain, but then he pulled my arms down by my sides, trying to pin me so he could put me back into a headlock. He rubbed the top of my head with his forearm, messing up my braid. I was breathing heavily now as I tried to wrench myself out of his grasp by sheer force of will. But he had me on weight and muscle and skill. I wriggled and struggled against his hold, the carpet burning my skin in the process. My face was red. I was starting to get angry. I seized hold of his foot, which only had a sock on it, and bit down hard on his big toe. Not enough to draw blood, but enough to hurt him.

He screamed and instantly stopped trying to put me into a headlock, and then I felt the crushing weight roll off me, and I could breathe again.

He grabbed his foot in pain. "You win," he gasped. "You win. And *gross*."

I splayed myself out on the carpet, spent. "You say gross to that," I rasped, "but not to putting one of your fingers in your nose?"

"The undefeated champion!" Pete crowed from his position on the couch, seemingly unfazed by our play fighting. "You gotta toughen up, Jimmy—letting a fifteen-year-old beat you like that is just sad."

"Y'all's family is strange," Carlie said emotionlessly, still glued to the TV, chewing on one of her fingernails.

Jimmy put his hand out and helped me into a sitting position. "No skill whatsoever, but you're tough; I'll give you that."

A flush of pride went through me as I got back to my feet. I complained a lot about my brothers, but I loved them.

My dad came wandering in from his bedroom at the back of the house and saw me, my face red and hair standing on end. He had a huge grin on his face, but his hands were on his hips, so I couldn't tell if he was angry or amused—probably a little of both. "Did you break anything?"

Pete piped up. "Not today—"

The front door swung open, interrupting Pete.

All our heads swiveled in the direction of the door

right as my oldest brother walked in. He was so tall he had to duck down in order to get through the entryway. I'm sure the way he styled his hair, piled on top of his head, untidy chic, didn't help either.

Corinth's sharp gaze took in the scene around him, ticking over each of us in turn, assessing. Always assessing, it seemed. There was something about the way he scanned the room, as if he were searching for unseen enemies, that made me laugh. I noticed it every time he entered a room or went out in public. He was just a little too guarded and on edge. He didn't like crowds. I missed carefree Cor.

But then, as if he'd decided everything was all good, he shut the door behind him and ambled the rest of the way into the living room, towering over me. "Hey, kid."

I shot to my feet and threw my arms around his waist. It had been two whole months since I'd seen him last. He had been vacationing in Egypt, visiting one of his friends—Imani, I thought her name was. I'd never met her before, but Corinth had a lot of friends in a lot of places because he traveled so much.

"Where's Leo?" I asked, eyeing the door as if he were about to walk in right behind him.

Corinth extracted himself from my arms. "He's got some work to do, but he'll be in town by Thanksgiving." He ran a hand over my hair, mussing it up. "I've got some gel that might tame this bird's nest."

"Shut up, Cor" I said, but I couldn't wipe the grin off my face. It was good seeing him again.

Dad turned and regarded me. "You know, Zo, you should talk to Cor about taking self-defense lessons— what we talked about."

I snorted, amused by that idea. *Please.* Like he could teach me self-defense. I was not interested. And I was also wondering why my dad always jumped to the self-defense talk as soon as he saw Cor. I had absolutely no interest in physical sports or activity or moving. I liked books. Books liked me. End of story. Of course, looking Corinth up and down now, I realized he probably could take care of himself in a fight. There were the usual calluses on his palms; his chest was broad, his forearms well developed, and he was leaner than I remembered, his waist tapered. He was wearing a dark gray hoodie, jeans, and a pair of gray Converse.

"Actually," Corinth corrected, "if you *really* want to learn self-defense, you should talk to Al. The guy has, like, twenty different black belts. He taught me everything I know. I could ask him for you if you'd like ... He'll be in town, visiting Larna's mom soon."

Pete said, "Oh, I bet she would *love* Alastair to show her some moves ... Isn't he the one you have a major crush on, Zo? Or is that Trevor? The guy with the glasses?"

I felt my cheeks start to heat up right as Mom finally ambled back into the living room, a frown affixed to her aged face upon seeing me. Her hair was cut short, angled at the chin, and dyed strawberry-blond, but her natural color was closer to Corinth's dark brown. I was late again, and she was about to start scolding me. I saw her open her mouth, but as soon as she saw Corinth, her frown disappeared and she gave him a grin from ear to ear. *Figures.* Before I knew it, she had him wrapped up in a hug, standing on the tips of her toes to give his cheek a peck.

"Hey, Mom," Corinth said, gently pulling back.

She pursed her lips in thought, studying him. "How was your trip? We were worried about you …" She let her voice trail off, giving me a quick glance. "I mean, with the passport issue you had."

"Everything's all good, Mom. I took care of it. Nothing to worry about."

She let out a visible sigh and patted Corinth on his arm affectionately. "Good. I'm glad it worked out."

There was something special about the way they greeted each other, as if they'd never get the chance to do it again.

Corinth gave my dad a nod in greeting from across the room. "Dad."

My dad wasn't exactly Corinth tall. He was five feet eleven, with sandy-blond hair, closer to the color of straw, like mine. I couldn't see the resemblance in him to Dad, not as much as I could with me, Jimmy, and Pete. He took more after my mom, for sure. Auburn hair, long limbs, sharp jawline.

"How come we don't get that kind of welcome from y'all?" Jimmy complained, flicking a glance to my parents and then back to Cor again.

I shot him a look, sticking my tongue out at him before saying, "Because you literally *never* leave."

"Want some coffee, son?" my dad asked Corinth, ignoring our comments and snide remarks and everyone else in the room.

"You know my answer is always yes to that question," he said gratefully. "Hey, Carlie," Corinth said as he moved past everyone to follow Dad into the kitchen. "Good to see you again."

"Hi," she said in her deadpan voice, her eyes never leaving the TV, zombielike.

Seeing my chance to escape, I relocated to my room, quickly slipping inside and shutting the door behind me before my mom could get onto me for being late. Maybe she'd forgotten about it. Two bright emerald eyes met mine as soon as I turned on the lights. An orange-and-white tail flicked in approval, and then I saw pointy ears pop up on my bed.

"Hello, Biscuit," I cooed, moving over to my bed to drop my heavy load. I scratched his head, right behind his ears, and he closed his eyes in contentment. "Did you miss me?"

He purred his response: *Yes.* Biscuit had so much fur that I thought if he were ever groomed, he might disappear completely.

A sharp rap came from the outside of my door. I closed my eyes briefly. No alone time. *Ever.* Knowing who was on the other side, I growled, *"Come in."*

My mom shouldered her way through the door, glancing around the messy room in disapproval. The scowl was back on her face. I could see two dimples, one on either side of her mouth. She closed the door behind her and glanced around, unable to make eye contact with me. "You were late again. We talked about curfew, didn't we?"

I threw my hands up in frustration. "Curfew? At seven thirty? That's not a curfew; it's a prison sentence. This is ridiculous. All of my friends get to stay out later—"

"Don't argue with me, young lady," she said, interrupting my tirade and finally meeting my gaze. Her eyes were hazel: green, mocha, and gold flecks. "Your friends are welcome to come here, but out there" —she gestured toward my window— "I don't know what's going on. I can't control anything that happens. It's not safe."

I rolled my eyes up to the ceiling. "Seriously, you are *so* paranoid. Nothing is going to happen. You have to give me some space, Mom. I'm suffocating here. I hate this. I need out."

"Zo, ever since you got … *lost*"—she faltered on that word—"when you were five years old, things haven't been the same. If you could only remember what we went through as a family … if Corinth hadn't found you … I can't go through that again."

"*I was five!*" I shouted. "The point is, Corinth *did* find me. You gotta let the past go." We'd had this same argument over and over again, and I couldn't take it anymore.

She swallowed hard before pressing her hands together. "Curfew is at seven now. If I catch you coming back late again, you're grounded."

"That's not fair—" I started to argue, but she slipped out of my room before I could finish, slamming the door shut behind her.

I turned to Biscuit, who was curling himself around my feet. "I get no respect around here."

$$7$$

ALASTAIR

A sharp, insistent pain pulled Alastair back to reality. He was disoriented and groggy—and his *knee*. Nagging. The discomfort kept coming—building to an excruciating degree. He bit the inside of his cheek and tasted blood. A warning bell went off at the back of his mind.

There was something seriously wrong with him.

He couldn't move.

The thick edges of fuzzy-headedness still clung to him though. His mouth was full of cotton. He was thirsty, but when he tried to lick his lips, to moisten them, his tongue hit something solid, and he tasted salt and copper, and the scent of leather and sulfur was strong in his nostrils.

Alastair's eyelids fluttered all the way open.

He was lying on a smooth, hard surface, and someone was trying to smother him—

On instinct, he tried to sit up, to rip whoever, or

whatever, was attacking him off, only to realize he was pinned down, unable to move. Panic sliced through him, sharpening his focus; his heartrate lumbered along at a good pace the more alert he became.

Alastair squinted down, his vision still blurry. The thing over his face was not a hand. It was leather strapped around his mouth and chin.

No one is attacking. Breathe.

With his restricted range of motion, he managed to glance at his hands, which were still in his field of view. Thin wire encircled his wrists, cinched down so taut his fingers had gone numb, and leather bands had been buckled around his forearms and strapped down to the table. Also, he noticed he was shirtless, wearing nothing but the black athletic pants he'd had on when he'd been grabbed. His bare feet and ankles were bound by thin razor wire too. And his calves were strapped to the table, much like his forearms. Torture rack. *Great.* Par for the course. They weren't taking any chances on him trying to escape. By the looks of it, that was exactly what they wanted him to try and do.

Alastair's chest heaved up and down as he struggled to pull in oxygen. *Don't panic. You can get out of this.* He couldn't quite catch his breath. Couldn't quite get enough air into his lungs. The thing on his face was suffocating him.

Breathe. In and out. In and out. In and out. In and out.

Once his breathing had returned somewhat to normal, he made himself look around—as much as his restraints would allow, anyway. That was when he realized he wasn't so much in a room as in a cavern or chamber—

at least, that was the closest thing he could think of to call it. The shadows slunk and flitted unnaturally wherever he looked. Things … *alive*. Demented things. Dark and evil things. He could feel the despair of this place clawing at him, leeching all the warmth from his body, seeping all the way down into his bones.

What is *this place?*

His vision swam out of focus again, and when it cleared, he could just make out formations above him. Rocks? Pillars? No, not rocks, spikes. They glowed orange, like embers in a fire—abnormally so. He was in hell. He'd been transported to hell. His stomach bottomed out at that thought. *Demons.*

Gray's voice came slamming back into his skull as he remembered what it had told him its boss wanted: *He wants your soul.*

Some of the formations protruded up from the floor, curling, winding, and creeping like vines toward what had to be a twenty-foot-high arched ceiling above him. Some of the stalactites stabbed downward, looking a lot like spears. And the more he studied the ceiling, the more he realized exactly what he was seeing: Faces. Hands. Legs. Bodies. Hundreds of dead people, reaching down toward him with silent screams on their faces.

He shuddered.

Sharp barbs protruded out of the bodies, pinning them in place. All of them were on display. It reminded Alastair of insects preserved on a setting board. Except in this case, the human bodies had been stabbed through their torsos, much like the insects' thoraxes, their hands and legs extended out like limbs and wings.

The floor was made of obsidian-colored stone, too iridescent and too glossy to be natural. There was a charged energy to the air, a snap and electric sizzle of ozone. Angel energy, but *not*. Something else—demonic.

He'd seen this type of orange energy before. It reminded him of looking through a stained glass window, like back when Angela had erected a barrier around the white throne at the Trembling Giant, in Utah, ten years ago—a barrier meant to keep angels out—and *in*.

Even though Alastair knew it was useless, he pulled against his restraints. Gently at first, in order to test their strength, and then harder, more desperate, as a deep-seated terror started to set in. His ankles and wrists burned as the sharp cable, like piano wire, bit into his wrists, sinking into his flesh.

Sucking in a breath and holding it, he twisted his hands in slow circles, causing the restraints to dig deeper into his flesh, drawing blood. He just needed enough slack to slip his hands free. Maybe he could break a thumb to give him more room … He was no stranger to pain.

Alastair had been injured on countless occasions. He'd seen war. Seen men's heads separated from their bodies. Attended to grievous wounds. Knife wounds. He'd seen vampires and angels vaporized by lightning. Hell, he'd dealt many of those wounds to others. Alastair had been vampire—alive for over one hundred and fifty years—and during that time, he hadn't exactly treated his body like a temple, because he hadn't needed to.

He'd been able to rapidly heal himself in seconds. For once in his life, Alastair missed being a vampire. He missed the way his torn skin had stitched itself back together again when he'd been injured. He missed superstrength and supersenses.

A vivid memory of Wrentmore, the vampire who'd turned Alastair, popped into his head, and his stomach heaved. Wrentmore was someone he hadn't dredged up in ten years. No, he'd never go back down that road again. Never. *Don't go there.*

But there was something about this dark prison that raised his hackles and set his nerves on edge. An innate malevolence waiting to pounce on his insecurities and fears. Maybe this place amplified fright, took away people's center of calm, brought out terror in agonizing detail. Or maybe it was just because he was mortal now, and he had a wife. His death-defying days were over.

An image of Larna being attacked by the same demons who had attacked him flashed across his vision.

Was she one of those poor souls pinned to the ceiling above him? Dead?

Alastair let out a snarl of fury at the thought. *Please let her be safe.* He struggled against his bonds again, but the leather and wire would not budge. His muffled scream behind the mask over his face was infuriating. He tried to shove the mental image of Wrentmore down, tried to ignore the helplessness washing over him—at not being able to check on his wife. He needed to be free of these restraints. Acid hit the back of his throat.

There came harsh laughter from somewhere off to his left, and he froze.

"This table has held much stronger and deadlier than the likes of you, Alastair Iszler."

The male voice startled Alastair into submission.

Alastair could feel the warm blood dribbling down his wrists and ankles. He could hear the starkness of it hitting the polished stone. For what seemed like an eternity, it was the only sound in the place, until the voice spoke again.

"You're only going to make it worse, struggling like that. You can't break those bonds … *or* your thumbs … if that was your plan." A sharp, cruel laugh echoed around the cavernous space again.

Alastair tried to hold his breath, and he had to work extremely hard to make his face a blank mask. Not that it would matter anyway—half his face was covered—but it was his eyes he was worried about the most, in case they gave anything away.

Don't show fear.

A dark form materialized out of a swirl of black smoke, darting forward, agile—another demon. Soundless. The shadow stopped next to Alastair's left side, the air shimmering around it like magic, and then the coil of smoke and fire coalesced and took on the shape of a human.

At least, that was what Alastair guessed it was, because the form was swathed in black robes, a hood hiding its face from view. For all he knew, it could be a grotesque beast under there.

"I love watching people come fully awake on this table … Seeing that look of abject horror on their faces is exquisite."

The voice didn't sound deep. No discernable accent. Youngish. And familiar. They'd crossed paths before; he was sure of it. *Where?*

"Fear is priceless, you know." The hooded figure gave a tiny shrug. "Darkness is bleak. Lonely. Some people who get put on this table get the blindfold. The anticipation of being tortured is much worse than actually being tortured. Some get manacles, while others get chains. But you, Alastair Iszler … I know what frightens you most." He paused for dramatic effect. "No guesses?" he said flippantly. "Okay, fine. Since I have you on the edge of your seat. You get the muzzle—like a dog. Only the most stubborn and strong-willed get collared. If you're a good boy, I'll take you for a walk later."

If the demon wanted to get a rise out of Alastair, he would have to work a hell of a lot harder than that. He had been through worse mind games—he'd pretended to work for Gabriel Stanton. He'd seen combat on more than one occasion.

Dark, unblinking eyes glittered from underneath that black hood. Alastair could not make out a face, but the eyes seemed fathomless. *Pure evil.* Not like the demons who'd attacked him earlier. This one was calling the shots. The boss. Now he was getting somewhere.

His captor reached out from the deep sleeves of his robe to touch Alastair's cheek. There was a flash of pale skin. A human hand. Smooth. No black oil or silver veins. "Your distress is rich and intoxicating, a rare delicacy around here." The hand was beyond icy, and it made Alastair want to jump out of his own skin. "Do you know how long I've been waiting for this moment?"

Silence stretched on until, "Nothing? No reaction to that, Alastair? It's almost as if you've been put through something like this before … You look positively bored."

The demon paused briefly, tilting his head, waiting for Alastair to do something. Even if he could have spoken, Alastair wouldn't have. After a few more drawn out seconds, the demon continued. "The way you fought off my legion of Shades was impressive. *Very* impressive. Nonhuman impressive. Of course, I already knew that about you."

Shades?

The cloaked demon traced a slender finger along the edge of the table near Alastair's head. "You could saw off both your hands at the wrists, but you still wouldn't be able to slip out of this contraption." Slowly he reached out and patted the thick leather securing Alastair's forearm down. "This piece keeps you from yanking too hard on your restraints in order to break bone. Now, these wires"—he pointed at Alastair's bloodied right hand—"around your wrists are designed to cinch down tighter the more you struggle. That's for torture."

Alastair resisted the urge to move his hands, to get the feeling back in them, and he also resisted the urge to try and shrug the mask off his face. The itch to cough rose up inside him, but he held it in. He was dehydrated after all that running and fighting … and his knee was still aching with a vengeance.

There was a flash of white teeth as the hooded form smiled behind his hood. "My name is Ephrem. It is the name you will use to beg for mercy." Alastair let his eyes follow Ephrem to the end of the table, where he stopped at Alastair's feet. "Boy, those are some penetrating blue eyes. If looks could kill right now …" He held up his pale hands as if in mock surrender and laughed. "You see,

Alastair, some people have *too* much fire in them. *Too* much spirit. *Too* much life running through their veins. Those are the best kind of people to break. Believe it or not, you *can* still hear someone's screams just as loudly from behind a muzzle. I liked hearing yours."

Dread and fear clawed at Alastair, relentless, but he shoved those feelings back down, trying to keep his face and eyes emotionless. *We'll see about that.* So, this thing didn't want information from him. It wanted him dead. Torture. Definitely. Revenge? Something much worse? *His soul.* If he could have talked, he would have told Ephrem to get to the point.

The demon's hand shot out, and he lifted Alastair's right pant leg all the way up to his injured knee.

Alastair's eyes narrowed in anger and rage at this thing touching him. Even though his muscles were screaming at him to take action—to rip this demon's head off and fight with every ounce of strength he had left in him—he stayed stock-still, locking his jaw. *Patience.*

Ephrem cracked a grin, whistling softly. "I guess we won't be taking that walk after all. I hope you're not very attached to this leg. It looks nasty. Discolored skin. Dislocated knee. Constricted blood flow."

Alastair knew something was seriously wrong with his knee. The pain was persistent and debilitating. The blood in his veins seemed to thicken, and his stomach felt leaden. Ephrem wanted inside his head. That was what demons did, right? Mind games.

Ephrem slammed his hand down on Alastair's already-injured knee, and it felt more like a mallet than a hand. Alastair screamed at the same time as he heard the deep crack of bone breaking. Fire tore up his thigh, and bright splotches exploded across his vision as a sharp stitch knifed its way through his belly, stealing the breath from his lungs.

His heart was beating way too fast. Reflexively he strained against his bonds, causing the wire to cinch down, cutting deeper into his skin. He bit his tongue, suppressing the urge to cry out again.

Ephrem let out a derisive laugh at seeing his pain. "I can make you suffer for an eternity by keeping you dangling between life and death, Alastair Iszler."

Alastair *was* pretty attached to his leg, but there was nothing he could do now but ride out the unendurable amount of torment he was in. His breath sawed out of his nose, and sweat glistened on his forehead. He closed his eyes, unable to look at Ephrem or the ceiling above him any longer.

How had his day gotten so turned upside down?

By now, Larna must be worried sick about him. Would she send up flares? Ask Corinth for help? Was she in trouble? Would they go after her? No one knew where he was, but Corinth might be able to track him down using his angelic abilities. Icy panic sliced through him again and he gasped—this wasn't like him. Fear didn't rule him, but something at the back of his mind kept telling him, *Yes, it does.*

"Well, now, *that's* irreparably damaged," Ephrem said coolly, cracking his knuckles. "Shall I move on to the other leg?"

The demon's words drifted away from Alastair, and the world spun behind his closed eyelids. He was going to pass out.

"I know what you must be thinking ... Someone must be missing you by now. Maybe your pretty wife. Maybe your friends. Maybe the *Nephilim*. Unfortunately, Alastair, time works differently in here. In this place—the dark realm—you've really only been gone for a few hours. Out there, though, in the real world, you've been gone for days."

Alastair clung to those words, *dark realm*, and his eyes flew open again. Through glassy vision, he could make out Ephrem reaching into the deep pockets of his robe to pull out a cell phone, wallet, and keys. *His* phone and wallet and keys.

"I've been texting your wife all day. She's very charming. I'll meet her soon. Add her to the collection." The demon pointed above him, to the dead pinned to the ceiling, like it was a trophy case containing his most prized possessions.

At this, Alastair couldn't help but let out a low, guttural growl of warning at the back of this throat.

Ephrem said, "Aw, finally, a sore spot. Your wife. Loved ones. You don't have to lose your leg, you know," he insisted. "We'll get to that later, but I admit, it would be an interesting turn of events if you did."

Alastair remembered leaving his cell phone and wallet at home, on the kitchen counter. How could they get by security cameras and alarm systems without being noticed? Not surprising, since angels could travel through lightning ...

Would Larna be able to tell it wasn't him texting her? Was Ephrem lying? Could she trace his cell? At that, Alastair's pulse started to slam behind his eyeballs.

Doubtful. He didn't think there would be phone service in this place. He didn't want to put her in danger. His head was pounding in tune with the deep throbbing in his leg. He couldn't think straight.

Even though his hands were brutally numb, and the restraints were cutting into his skin, he could still feel his wedding band on his left hand. Feel the ring's comforting weight. A reminder. Alastair took security in it. It was all he had left.

He thought about Larna. She would be able to tell something was wrong. His eyes popped open, and he stared daggers at Ephrem, setting his jaw.

This *thing* would not scare him. He would not yield or bend.

"Well, then," Ephrem cooed. "You are going to be a lot harder to break than I originally thought."

At that, he whirled around and disappeared in a swirl of black smoke, leaving Alastair alone once again to his endless suffering.

8

ZOEY

The rest of the short week sped by, to make room for Thanksgiving break. And because I had a new curfew, thanks to Mom, I didn't get a chance to see Trevor or go to Sweets and Stuff. I thought about how upset Cruz had looked when I'd asked him about the scars on his hands. *Stupid, Zo.*

Trevor I hadn't seen in a few days, which was rare for him, since he hated being all alone in that huge house of his. I felt *so* sorry for him.

He probably wasn't alone. He probably had a million people over at his place right now, throwing a huge party. I wasn't invited because I had a curfew …

In my room, I searched for my key chain. I'd realized it wasn't on my backpack strap, where I normally kept it. The last time I'd had it was when I was showing it to Cruz. I didn't know why I'd felt the need to take it off my backpack. I had called Sweets and Stuff and was advised that no one had turned it in.

I was absolutely gutted.

The trinket had been a gift from Cor—and now it was just *gone*. I texted Trevor, to see if he'd seen it, but he'd promptly texted me back with a *No* and a frowning emoji, and then he'd asked me to meet him at Sweets and Stuff, and I'd responded with *Curfew* and also a frowning emoji.

How was I going to break it to Corinth that I'd lost it?

I was in the middle of cleaning my room, one wireless earbud in my ear—I'd lost the other one—listening to Billie Eilish, trying to see if it was hidden under a pile of clothes or lost in my closet, or stuck in the Twilight Zone, when I heard a soft knock come from the other side of my door.

"Come in," I said distantly, picking up a pillow and tossing it aside in frustration. *Where is it?*

Speaking of the devil, Corinth slid into my room as silently as a phantom, shutting the door behind him. It was as if he knew I'd lost the key chain, and was here to heckle me about it. The guy had an uncanny sixth sense about everything.

"Hey, kid, whatcha doing?"

I glanced up right as he perched himself on the edge of my bed, grabbing his knee with one hand, as if he were planning to stay for a good long while. I shut my music off and sighed. "Oh, uh, cleaning," I said with a one-sided shrug. "You know, all the fun stuff teenagers do these days." Could I tell him it was lost? *Not with those big puppy dog eyes staring at me.*

"Sounds riveting," he said with a lopsided grin. "But

how 'bout we slip out of here and go for trivia night instead? I'll have you home in time for more ... *studying*." He picked up my economics textbook and wiggled a teasing eyebrow at me.

I shot him a glare. "Aren't you a professor? Shouldn't you be encouraging me to study more?"

"I could help you study, if you'd rather, but it *is* Thanksgiving break."

I barked out a huff that sounded like a half laugh, half snort. "What about Mom?" I asked.

"Let me handle Mom," Cor said conspiratorially. This was why I loved my oldest brother.

"Troublemaker," I said, rubbing Biscuit's ear and smiling.

Corinth stood back up, but his eyes homed in on my backpack, and then they flew back to land on me, probing. *I knew it.* "Where's your key chain?" he asked quickly.

My heart fell into my stomach; guilt gnawed at me. "I ... I ... Okay, so, don't be mad ... but I seem to have misplaced it. But I'm going to find it!"

He raked a hand through his tousled hair and frowned. "You lost it?"

I shrugged, grimacing. *Maybe. Maybe not. I hope not.*

His large amber-colored eyes seemed to bore a hole right through me. I hated to see them filled with so much disappointment. "That was ... a one of a kind," he said, and I heard the regret in his tone. Gosh, I was starting to think Cruz had been right about the trinket.

"I'm so sorry, Cor. I think I lost it at the ice-cream place."

He tilted his head to the side and flashed me a

lopsided grin, a dimple popping up on his left cheek. "I'm sure it will turn up."

"How are you so darn levelheaded *all* the time—?"

The doorbell rang, interrupting me. Biscuit's head popped up, and his ears swiveled around at the sudden disruption of his beauty sleep. He hopped off my bed and padded to the closed door, waiting for me to open it, his tail high in the air, haughty, so he could inspect the newest arrival himself.

Corinth rose from my bed and gestured at the closed door. "You might as well go ahead and get it—we all know Pete and Jimmy won't. Mom and Dad are out at the store."

I flew past Corinth, passing Pete and Jimmy, who were both lounging on the couch, just as Corinth had predicted. I didn't think they'd get up even if a tornado were circling over the house.

Breathless, I pulled the front door open to see Larna Iszler standing on the front porch, her mouth turned down at the corners in a frown.

When she saw me though, she gave me a quick smile in greeting. Her hair had grown out since the last time I'd seen her. It now hit the tops of her shoulders and was cut at an angle that framed her jawline nicely. Dark brown hair made her hazel eyes stand out. A swirl of olive and chocolate mixed together. I hadn't told her this—I didn't want it to be weird—but I'd always marveled at her physique. She was wearing a dark brown rawhide trench coat. Underneath her unbuttoned coat, I could see a knee-length navy blue dress and brown ankle boots the same color as her jacket. *Stylish*, I noted.

How could someone with such a demanding day job have the time to work out *and* get biceps like that? I mean, she looked like she could put Corinth down, and that was saying something, because she was so much shorter than he was.

If I were going to ask anyone for self-defense lessons, it would have to be *her*. She must spend hours in the gym. Fierce female.

"*Zo*," she breathed, throwing her arms around me and hauling me close, squeezing the stuffing out of me. "It's really good to see you."

I returned her near-death grip on me in earnest, looking over her shoulder to see if Alastair was right behind her. "It's great to see you too. Is Alastair with you?" *Please let Alastair be with you.* Alastair was a hunk, and I would only admit it to myself, but I had *the* hugest crush on the guy. He could fill a white T-shirt out for sure. I hoped he'd be with her. They came over for dinner every Thanksgiving holiday, along with her mother. Our families had been close for a very long time.

"No, he's not with me." Her brow furrowed as she moved around me so I could pull the door closed behind her. When I turned around, she had her hands locked together, her knuckles bone-white. She toyed with the wedding ring on her finger, and I noticed she looked a little chalky; the tips of her cheeks seemed to be the only coloring left in her face. I idly wondered if it had gotten chilly outside, or if she had a cold. It hadn't felt cold out when I'd opened the door.

"Are you okay?" I asked slowly. "You don't look well. There's a bug going around—"

"Is Corinth here? I really need to talk to him," she said quickly.

I nodded and screamed over my shoulder, "*Cor! Larna is here to see you!*"

"I'm right behind you," he muttered, placing a hand on his right ear. He'd appeared as if out of thin air. Sometimes he was as stealthy as a stalking cat. He dragged Larna into a tight embrace, laying his head on top of hers. "Collins *hyphen* Iszler," he said, emphasizing the word *hyphen* with a lopsided grin. "It's good to see you."

Larna wrapped her arms around Corinth and leaned into his chest as if she might be blown over by a gust of wind. "It's really good to see you too." She drew back, and the pinched, strained expression returned to her face. "I really need to speak with you though." She gave me a quick glance, and then her gaze darted to both my brothers. "In private."

Corinth swept an arm out toward the back of the house and stepped aside. "Of course. We can talk outside." With that, they disappeared quickly out the back, the storm door clapping closed behind them without another word or any preamble. *That was shady.*

I didn't know what had hit me—maybe it was the conversation I'd had with Trevor about Corinth, or about that night of the lightning storm, or a weird intuition, or Larna's anxious mood—but something had me incredibly curious about why they needed privacy. And so suddenly. I couldn't help myself.

It wouldn't be that bad of me to check and see if they were okay.

I darted out the front door, rolling down the sleeves

of my sweater against a sudden cool breeze, slipping through the side gate beside the house. The weather had turned on a dime.

As I tiptoed through the backyard, barefoot, padding silently along, their voices started to become louder. They were standing behind the garden shed, near the back fence line, so it made it easier for me to sneak up on them without being detected. *This is so wrong.* But to be fair, they were acting really strange. I was better than this. Well, sort of. They'd always been so close … Maybe this concerned my family. Eavesdropping wasn't *that* wrong. I crouched down on the other side of the shed from them, and listened, only feeling slightly ashamed at my invasion of their privacy. If they were doing something they shouldn't be, I was going to kill Cor.

This was just me keeping them in check—or so I told myself.

Larna was in the middle of saying, "… checked in an hour ago. Something's not right. Listen to this text he sent me: 'The permit issue put me behind. Hitting snags left and right. I don't think I'll be able to make Thanksgiving in time. Send my love to your mom. Love you, and I'll call later. A.'"

"It's kind of weird that he didn't ask about me," Corinth said, sounding half-serious, half-playful. "But everything else sounds legit … except for maybe the part where he didn't send me his love too. Of course, I'd have a nickname for you, something like Sugar Plum or … Puddin'—"

I could practically hear Larna's eyes rolling as she said, "He wouldn't cancel coming to Thanksgiving. And even if he did, he wouldn't cancel via a *text* message. He would call to give me bad news. He's old-fashioned that way." She repeated, "Something's not right. I can feel it."

"Does he have his watch?" Corinth asked. I didn't hear a response, but I assumed she had nodded, because he continued. "He'd press his panic button if something were really wrong. Did you check the video footage? Any alarms go off?"

Panic button, I thought. *Video footage? Paranoid much? Were they doing something illegal? Selling something illegal?* I kept thinking about the TV show *Breaking Bad* …

Larna said, "No alarms were tripped. It's just a funny feeling …"

"He *did* say he'd call you later. Maybe he wanted to let you know as soon as he could, so you wouldn't be expecting him on the next flight out. Of course, there's a simple solution to all of this … Why don't I just pop on over there, scoop him up before he has a chance to argue, and bring him back here without giving him a choice?"

There was a long pause, and then Larna said, "Let's do that. I'm coming with you."

Pop on over to England? I must have misheard him, he probably meant call Alastair to check in on him—

But right as I thought it, there was a horrendous clap of thunder. A flash of light flared up so brightly from behind the shed that my heart skipped a beat, and I fell backward onto my rump, my heart tripping along, trying to play catch-up.

A moment later, I jumped to my feet and ran around the corner of the shed, expecting to see them both flat out on the ground, having been struck by lightning or worse, but there was only a lingering crackle to the air, and it smelled like rain … no, inclement weather … I glanced up at the cloudless sky, bruising the soft color of a peach at dusk, my mouth hanging open.

No rain … What the heck just happened? They're both gone. Vanished. Where did they go? What the actual …?

9

ZOEY

I'd gone and had a mental breakdown. It had to have been from too much studying. My breath was shallow at the back of my throat as I darted back inside the house, heart hammering, because I just knew something terrible had happened to my brother and Larna.

I half hoped I'd find them talking to Jimmy or Pete, inside again. Maybe I'd missed them. They were playing a trick on me. Whatever the case, there had to be a logical explanation for their disappearance, and that lightning show. *There has to be.* But at the back of my mind, there was a tiny niggle of doubt. And that niggle of doubt gave way to something else: A flash of red hair. Sharp teeth. Glowing eyes. The vision was gone before I even had the chance to make sense of it. Suddenly I felt sick to my stomach.

I'd had strange flashes like these since I was five years

old. A distant memory trying to take shape, perhaps. Something that had happened to me when I'd gotten lost, and I'd shoved it way down deep in the recesses of my mind. Goose bumps pebbled my flesh at the thought. A part of me, the greater part, didn't want to know what had happened to me. Maybe my mom and dad knew more than what they were telling me. Corinth knew. I was positive.

What had Trevor said about Cor? How there had been a clap of thunder, and then he'd just vanished into thin air. I shivered at the thought.

After I'd searched the entire house and hadn't found them, I stopped in front of Pete, who was asleep on the couch, snoring.

I smacked his arm, and he startled awake with a grunt.

"What are you doing?" he asked, bleary-eyed and peeved.

"Did you see Cor and Larna come this way?"

Pete stretched out, yawning at the same time as he gave me a peculiar sort of look. "Beanpole, I haven't exactly been keeping track of them." He ran a hand through his curly hair. "Why? What's wrong?" He sat up, suddenly looking more alert.

"You didn't notice any … strange lightning—?" As soon as I said *lightning*, the back door flew open and Larna and Corinth came traipsing back inside, frowns marring both their faces—they were alive and not fried by lightning.

"See," Pete said. "They're right there. You're obviously seeing things."

My mouth fell open. I let out a deep breath of relief,

unaware that I'd been holding it in. They were okay.

"Where the heck did y'all go?" I asked, almost frantic. "I … I … went outside and then … saw lightning strike … I thought you'd been hurt, and then you were gone!"

Larna had something clutched tightly in her hands. A watch with a thick band. It looked like a smart watch. She quickly tucked it into her pocket and glanced back at Corinth, a grimace appearing back on her face.

Corinth said, "Lighting? What lightning? We just went for a walk."

On the tops of Corinth's shoulders, I could see a light dusting of moisture glittering on his hoodie. *Odd.* There had not been rain. My stomach bottomed out again. *Liar.*

"Then why are you all wet?" I asked him, suspicious.

Corinth brushed a hand across his shoulder, his eyes darting to Larna's before they swung away from mine, evasive. "Some sprinklers must have doused us on our walk," he mumbled under his breath.

He's lying.

It was the way he avoided eye contact. I didn't think he'd ever lied to me before. It was so out of character for him. My heart leaped in my chest, and I swallowed hard. I was onto something. I was about to argue with him, to try and pry more information out of them both, when the front door flew open, and my parents came traipsing inside, stomping their feet on the floor mat. I heard a toilet flush from the spare bathroom, and Jimmy came walking out.

My mom trudged past, precariously clutching four full paper bags in her arms as she said, "Zo, help me put groceries away, please."

My dad was cursing under his breath as he almost dropped the frozen twenty-pound turkey wrapped up in his arms. Cor was there in a heartbeat to help, pulling the bird out of his hands, making it look like it weighed nothing at all as he took it from him. He disappeared into the kitchen, looking a little more noticeably relieved to be out from under my scrutiny, I thought.

"Pete, Jimmy," Dad wheezed, planting a hand against his chest. "Can you grab the rest of the groceries out of the car?" His eyes landed on Larna, and they widened in surprise. "Larna, dear, it's so good to see you. We didn't think you'd be here until tomorrow afternoon. Will Alastair and your mother be joining us for dinner again this year? We have plenty of food."

Pete popped to his feet and brushed past me to go outside, his curly hair poking up in all different directions. My mom called my name from the kitchen, but I ignored her.

Larna shook her head and said, "I'm so sorry, Mr. Taylor. Not this time. I have some pressing business in London that I must get back to right away."

I knew something was wrong, and now she'd just confirmed it.

I texted Trevor as soon as Larna and Corinth left again. They said they were going to Larna's mother's house. I didn't think that was where they were going at all. I thought they were going back to London. Our conversation went as follows.

Me: *I think you might be onto something.*

Trevor: *Oh, cryptic. I love cryptic. What might I be onto?*

Me: *About Cor and his strangeness. We should speak in person.*

Trevor: *Aren't you under house arrest?*

A GIF popped up on my phone with an adorable white cat behind kennel bars. It was standing on its hind legs, pawing at a latch, trying to free itself from its cage.

I rolled my eyes but smiled. He was a jerk, but at least he was a cute jerk.

Me: *This is important, so screw my curfew. Can you meet?*

Trevor: *Where?*

Me: *S&S.*

Trevor: *I'll pick you up a block down from your place. See you in 10.*

I shoved my phone into my back pocket, then pulled on my blue Converse, grabbed my red sweater and threw it on over my head, and lastly, ran my fingers through my hair, finger combing it. I usually wore it in a braid, but I didn't have time to fix it. My hair was a lot wavier than usual because I'd just taken it down.

My room was Corinth's old room, and I remembered how he'd told me Larna used to sneak over and slip into his bedroom undetected. I'd never snuck out before. I'd never had a reason to. This was all new to me, so, ever so gently, I popped the lock open and slid the window up, thankfully on well-oiled hinges.

A cool breeze hit me full in the face, and I shivered, more from the thrill of doing something I wasn't supposed to be doing. *This is important*, I kept reminding myself. I had to tell someone about my discovery. My parents would never believe me, and clearly, Corinth wasn't going to tell me the truth. *I'm not just seeing things.* I had to speak to someone who would understand, and that was Trevor. He would help me get to the bottom of this.

I pulled myself through the window and turned back around to shove it down, leaving a small gap so I could get back inside without making any noise. On the other side of the glass, I could see Biscuit jumping up onto the windowsill to peer out at me. It gave me the mental image of the cat trying to paw its way free from the kennel. Free. *Free at last*, I thought.

It didn't take long for Trevor to find me. I was waiting on the curb for him, my hands wound around my knees, when his red Challenger pulled up. A beautiful machine. He revved the engine and rolled down the window, giving me that playful smile of his, dark eyes glittering from behind black-rimmed glasses. "Get in."

I shot forward, threw open the door, and jumped inside as if someone were right on my tail. "I'll never get used to how cool this car is," I said breathlessly, slamming the door closed. "You are unbelievably lucky." The interior was all red. It smelled like new leather, and the gears looked as fancy as a spaceship's.

Trevor gunned it, and the tires spun for a minute before gripping the road and taking off like a rocket. My head slammed into the headrest, and I gripped the seat belt tighter and laughed, feeling thrilled and excited and a wee bit rebellious.

Trevor matched my laugh with one of his own. He

reached a curve and slowed down, wheels right on the yellow line. The car performed like a dream, and he was surprisingly skilled behind the wheel.

"My parents sent me to a driving school last year. It was the *only* class I was able to finish—that I *wanted* to finish. Passed it with flying colors," he mused. "Guess I should be a race car driver."

"Why does that not surprise me?" I muttered, giving him a sideways glance. "You've been driving for a year, and I've never even been behind the wheel of a car."

His auburn hair was piled on top of his head and swept to the side with styling gel. He gave me another grin, his teeth flashing, and shrugged. "You want to drive?"

My heart skipped a beat. For a second, I studied him to see if he was joking. Trevor only raised one eyebrow in question. I *did* want to drive. Very much. For once in my life, I wanted to do something slightly reckless. My parents wouldn't let me near a car. They wanted to keep me as controlled as they possibly could. I suddenly wanted to know what it would feel like to … just *go*. Anywhere. There was something about being with Trevor that made me feel so carefree and alive. Invigorated.

He merged over to the wide shoulder on the right, put the car in park, and turned to look at me expectantly, his eyebrows still raised in question, teasing and cute and flirty. "You can drive the rest of the way if you want. It's only two blocks down the road."

My cheeks were burning. The car sat idling, and the growl beneath the heated seats was almost like the car was giving me its permission to drive it too. I wanted to get behind the wheel. I wanted to prove to myself that I could do it. Prove to everyone that I wasn't just boring and predictable. Be a nonconformist for once in my life.

After another minute, I nodded, pushing a lock of stray hair behind my ear. "I want to drive."

Trevor laughed softly at that, eyeing me behind those glasses of his. "Bold choice."

Without another word, he got out of the driver's seat and came around to my door before I had the chance to open it. He gave me a crooked smile as he pulled it open and held a hand out for me to take, which I did. His fingers were cool in my warm palms.

Behind the steering wheel, the rumble of the car beneath me sounded like it was in surround sound. Trevor leaned across me, his feather-soft hair hitting my face as he pulled the seat belt out for me and snapped it into place, *oh-so* very close now.

"I think I could have figured that part out on my own." I was grinning at him like an idiot though—and definitely not complaining at his closeness. He smelled of spearmint and cologne and a hint of ash and smoke, like he'd been at a bonfire. Maybe he had been. I recalled he had a pretty nice firepit at his place. A thrill of excitement tore through me, and my stomach fluttered in anticipation.

Adjusting the rearview mirror, I could still feel his lingering body heat radiating between us. "You can adjust the side mirrors too. Check all your mirrors before you pull out into traffic. Keep your foot on the brake when you switch to D—for drive," he instructed. "And then give it some gas."

I shook my head and cleared my throat, nervously

shoving the car into gear to drive, foot on the brake. "Like this?" I asked.

"Yeah." He turned his head to look behind us, throwing an arm over the back of my headrest. "You're all clear."

Gently I took my foot off the brake and pressed the skinny pedal to the right of it, and then, feeling confident, stomped my foot down on the accelerator. The car, being the monster that it was, jolted forward, and my head hit the headrest as we shot forward like a bucking bronco.

My stomach flipped, and confused by the sudden adrenaline coursing through me, I slammed my foot on the brake instead of the gas, and we came to a shuddering halt in the middle of the—*thankfully*—empty street.

Trevor had both his hands clutching the dashboard, his head hanging down, dark russet locks obscuring his face. His shoulders were shaking along with his entire body. And at first I thought he was mad. I mean, seriously irate.

"I'm sorry. I'm so sorry. *Oh—my—gosh!*"

But then he looked over at me from under his bangs, and I could see that he was laughing so hard nothing was coming out of his mouth. Trevor clutched at his stomach. Finally, after he was able to somewhat recover, he wheezed, "Seriously, Taylor, have you never even driven in a mall parking lot before?"

I didn't even give him a chance to say anything else as I pushed down on the gas again and floored it. That shut him up.

We'd surprisingly made it to Sweets and Stuff without me causing any major accidents. It had been exhilarating. Sitting in a booth at the back of the almost-empty restaurant, I realized it was well past my curfew—7:30 p.m.—and the day before Thanksgiving. I guessed most people were at home spending time with their families. Unlike Trevor and me. His was out of town again, and mine I was just tired of. A Sprite sat in front of me, and he had an untouched Dr Pepper sitting in front of him.

I craned my neck to look around the restaurant to see if Cruz was working. He wasn't behind the counter or in the dining area. He must have had the day off for the holiday. My stomach dropped in disappointment. I had been hoping to at least get a chance to apologize.

Trevor was chewing on the end of a toothpick, and I kept staring at the perfect shape of his lips, so when he spoke, he took me completely out of my reverie.

"So, how did you like the *joyride*?" He wiggled his eyebrows at me.

Heat spread across both my cheeks. Man, he knew how to flirt. I wondered if he knew he was doing it. I couldn't help it. I knew we were nothing more than friends, but he'd let me get behind the wheel of one of his favorite things on this planet. There was a sense of trust between us that hadn't been there before.

"I think I should break curfew with you more often," I said shyly, glancing at a couple across from us, who were holding hands.

He was giving me a lopsided smirk when I looked back at him. "Are you flirting with me?"

"No," I said hoarsely, dying inside. I took a long, slow

sip of my drink to hide my red face. "I'm not."

Trevor held his hands up in surrender. "Okay, dropping the subject. I do want to know more about you though. Tell me something personal—that I don't already know."

I tugged at my ear, thinking this sounded more and more like a date to me. This was where it got awkward. "Like what?"

"Liiiiike …" He drew the word out, contemplating. "Like, why do you feel the need to study so much?"

I glanced down at the Styrofoam cup I had clutched in my hands. "I don't know. I mean, everyone has their own thing. I'm good at it, I guess. And I feel stifled at home. I think I just want a chance to get out and see the world. Travel. Explore. Read books in different places."

Trevor leaned back in the booth, pushing his glasses up the bridge of his nose. "That's understandable. I mean, I'm not good at anything. My biggest fear is disappointing my parents. There's a lot of expectation with them, you know. They think I'm lazy."

I knew his mom was an international aid worker, and his dad was a CEO for a major airline. They both traveled a lot for their work. I felt a pang of sympathy go through me at him being left all alone on Thanksgiving again. I mean, not that much sympathy—the guy had a lot going for him.

"What about you, Zoey Taylor?" he asked softly. "What's *your* biggest fear?"

A lot of things flitted through my mind. My family being one of them. Their health and safety. Not having the trust and approval of my mother. Blowing my aptitude tests. Not getting into the college I wanted. The prospect of disappointing my dad by not doing well in school. Clowns. Rabid animals. Sharks. Things with sharp, pointy teeth. Then that led to the flash of red hair and white fangs. The same vision that had given me the willies since I was five—*the dark*. I hated the dark. The dark held all my insecurities and doubts and anxieties.

"The dark," I whispered hoarsely, averting my gaze. "Since I was a little kid … I never liked it." I sighed and then said, "Don't laugh, okay, but I still sleep with a night-light on in my room."

There was a long silence, and I expected him to laugh or make fun of me, but when I looked back up at him, he had a funny look on his face that I couldn't quite interpret. "No judging," he said, taking a sip of his Dr Pepper. "So, Zo, what's all this mystery and intrigue about your brother?"

I turned to regard him, biting my lower lip in thought. Maybe I was making a bigger deal out of this than I should have been. My thoughts drifted to that strange crackle of energy I'd heard when Larna and Cor had disappeared. *They'd disappeared!* I reminded myself. *No.* There was definitely something going on.

"There's something strange going on with my brother. I think you were right about him."

Trevor ran a hand through his wavy locks. He glanced around the restaurant, even though we were almost all by ourselves, and then leaned across the table on his elbows. "What happened?"

Our server came up to the table before Trevor could respond. He looked to be about seventeen, with obvious dyed white hair, and acne covering his chin and nose. His name tag said his name was Toby. "Can I get you anything else besides soda?" he asked in a monotone voice, like he'd done this a million times over, and he was just done with the day and really wanted us to leave.

Trevor spoke up first, before I could tell him that I didn't want anything. "Two chocolate shakes and two orders of fries."

My stomach was doing weird somersaults.

Toby nodded and sauntered off without another word.

"Thanks," I said, rubbing a hand across my forehead. "I wasn't going to order anything … I forgot my money." I didn't tell him that I didn't have any money to forget.

"My treat." Trevor's dark eyes were glittering behind his glasses. "So, what happened?" he prodded again.

"I overheard him talking to his best friend, Larna. She was saying something about her husband not joining her for Thanksgiving. Maybe she's worried about Alastair cheating on her or something … That would make more sense, right? Anyway, she was suspicious of this text he'd sent her—then Cor said he could go and check on him …"

"So—" Trevor started to say.

"In *England*, Trevor." I raised my eyebrows. "And before I knew it, lightning struck right where they'd been standing. I mean, my hair was practically standing on end there was so much electricity in the air—and then they were just … *gone*. Poof. But it doesn't make any sense. How can that be possible? There wasn't a cloud in the sky."

Trevor perked up at hearing this bit of information and crossed his arms over his chest. "Did you see them disappear? What did it look like?"

Again I shook my head. "I just heard it."

"I knew something was up with your brother," Trevor said thoughtfully. "It makes perfect sense. He lived in London for a while, right? Maybe he went to Hogwarts. That's where all wizards study wizardry, right?" He tapped his forehead knowingly, smiling, teasing. "Have you found his wand yet? I bet he keeps it in his back pocket. If we search his apartment, I bet we'll find it."

I rolled my eyes at him, clearly hearing the mocking tone in his voice. "Okay, now you're just making fun of me—"

He was sitting across from me, but then before I could finish speaking, he slid over to my side of the booth, using his body to scoot me all the way into the corner against the wall. He was so close now, squished up against me like that, I could feel his body heat.

I was certain my entire face was the same shade as the barstools: strawberry red. And I was also certain he noticed me blushing, because his face lit up. He had this flirtatious smirk that made him look so much younger than he actually was. It was the face Peter Pan would have made right before flying off to Neverland. He leaned down close to me and whispered, "If you wanted to go out with me … all you had to do was ask."

Toby came back with our order, plunked our shakes down, and then set the tray of fries in front of us. "Enjoy," he said without meaning it, and turned back around to leave us alone.

Trevor reached a hand out and tucked a lock of hair behind my ear. His skin felt cool to the touch, and I shivered. "You should wear your hair down all the time. I like it like this."

He smelled like spearmint and a hint of after-shave and also … woodsy. *Is he hitting on me?*

"What if we catch him on camera doing … something *magical?*" Trevor pushed his glasses further up the rim of his nose, playful. He looked cute, so earnest, like this was the distraction from life he so eagerly needed. I knew he was messing with me, but in this moment, it felt adventurous and fun and espionage-ish—to pretend. Honestly, I was sure there was a reasonable explanation for how my brother and Larna had vanished. But this sounded way more exciting—and I'd get to spend more time with Trevor. *Do I like him?*

Flurries erupted in my stomach again. *Yes. Yes, I do.*

"What do you think?"

I cleared my throat. "I think it's brilliant. What are you doing for Thanksgiving dinner?"

"It just so happens I'm a free agent. My parents are out of town for a work conference in Tallahassee. We have a dinner planned when they get back … Until then though …"

I pulled a couple of fries off the tray and threw them into my mouth. When I was done chewing, I said, "Would you like to join me and my family for dinner?"

He flashed me a wide grin of understanding. "I would love to."

10

CRUZ

It was uncanny and miraculous. Elena Saldivar was getting better. Cruz's mother was in their kitchenette, cooking and singing lightly to herself, a spring in her step. Her skin did not look quite as waxy as it once had. Her cough had almost cleared up, and he could see darker, healthier strands of hair on her head shining through.

Cruz pulled his necklace up from beneath his undershirt and kissed the pendant. *Healing.* Something had happened to her to improve her condition this rapidly. He didn't want to look a gift horse in the mouth though. Sunlight streamed in through the open window, and it hit the little golden key chain, drawing his eye to it immediately. A sudden warmth and happiness filled him to his core, and his blood started to sing in his veins.

Something strange …

The shield flashed brightly from the kitchen

countertop, almost as if winking at him. Again Cruz felt the odd sort of pull to pick it up and pocket it. And then he found himself standing in front of the counter, staring down at the trinket in equal parts bafflement and awe. He couldn't blink; he could only stare at it, letting his eyes fill with water, his vision blurring. The shield seemed to be emitting a comforting sort of hum.

"You've been staring at that thing for over half an hour," his mother said, as if from very far away. Her warm hand on his shoulder startled him into finally looking up at her. He had kind of just zoned out altogether.

"Are you sure you feel well enough to cook?" he asked her distantly.

"*Sí, mijo.* I'm wonderful," she answered in a sing-song voice, again from a million miles away. "I haven't felt this good in ages. Dr. Heathcliff said she's never seen a recovery like it."

"Are you taking a new supplement or medication?" he asked, still half-transfixed by the shield. "I haven't seen you well enough to make tamales in a long time."

His mother's eyes flickered with delight and gratitude and something else—and then she was shooing him out of the kitchen. It wasn't big enough for the both of them. "Don't you have something better to do right now? Like hanging out with a certain pretty girl—the one who gave you that little golden charm?"

Feeling flustered all of a sudden, Cruz shook his head to clear it and spluttered, "I … I'm sure she has better things to do on Thanksgiving … I barely know her at all … Anyway, it would be weird …"

"*Here.*" Cruz's mother tutted and then turned to the

fridge to pull something out. When she twirled back around, he could see she was holding a round tin dish with a piece of foil covering the top of it. "I think it's high time you get to know her, then. Besides, girls like it when boys make an effort."

"What's in the dish?" he asked, eyeing it suspiciously.

"My special tres leches cake. Tell your friend … What's her name again?"

"Zoey Taylor," he answered gruffly. His tongue felt like it weighed a thousand pounds. Even her name felt rich.

"Tell the Taylors that the Saldivars wish them a happy Thanksgiving." She gave him an all-knowing grin and patted him on the arm. "And, *mijo*, never go visit a pretty girl empty-handed. Also, dinner will be ready by eight o'clock."

Cruz didn't need to be told twice.

He was already shrugging into his favorite parka— well, technically, his *only* parka. The color was somewhere between blue and gray, and it reminded him of autumn and fall and colder weather.

"You sure you're feeling okay?" he asked, zipping it up, not really giving her time to answer. She chuckled and nodded as he gave his mother a quick peck on the cheek.

Don't over think it, he reprimanded himself, his mind already taking him to places it probably shouldn't.

Why am I so nervous?

Cruz really did need to get a life. Suddenly all he wanted to do was talk to Zoey and apologize for his behavior. Maybe he'd even open up to her about his scars.

"Thank you, *Mamá*." He plucked the key chain up

into his palm and had grabbed for the door handle when his mother clucked at him again from the kitchen.

"Aren't you forgetting something?" She pointed at the cake, still sitting on the countertop.

He *had* forgotten it. Cruz picked the tin up and pulled the door open, giving his *madre* a quick wave goodbye.

Cruz knew where Zoey lived. She had entered their rewards program, and he'd looked it up in their system so he could return the key chain to her in person. It wasn't weird, he tried to convince himself. He'd been trying to drum up the courage to ask for her phone number first, but this was the perfect opportunity to thank her—and also question her about the key chain *and* return it at the same time. He knew how she felt about it.

For the first time in forever, he felt excited about something, and it made *all* the difference in the world.

11

ALASTAIR

lastair had stopped struggling. He had only been hurting himself, and that was exactly what the hooded figure, Ephrem, wanted him to do. Dread filled him to his core, wriggling its way through his gut like a sickness. How was he going to get out of this?

Ephrem was standing motionless at the end of the table Alastair was strapped to, holding something in his hands. From Alastair's prone position, he couldn't tell what that object was. Something told him he probably didn't want to know.

Get on with it.

His mouth was dry, and his lips were cracked. The uncontrollable urge to mouth at the leather covering his face hit him strongly again—he needed it off, but the gag was buckled at the back of his head, restricting his movements.

He wondered how many people had worn it before

him. *No.* No good would come from that line of thinking, so he shut it down immediately.

Blood still leaked from the open wounds at his wrists and ankles. It was the only thing keeping him slightly warm. He could no longer feel his injured leg, which he knew wasn't necessarily a good thing. He just felt numb all over.

The demon gave a sniff from under its hood. "You smell like one of them. Did you know that? Like an angel. I knew you were different. Maybe you'll look different too …" The demon placed the object he was holding into his flat palm and held it up so Alastair could see it. In his hand sat a clear, capped vial the size of his pinky finger, containing what looked like a shard of glass—almost needlelike. The thing was pulsing a faint reddish-yellow hue.

Alastair's heart was thudding in his ears, deafening. *This can't be good.*

"Ah," Ephrem cooed. "*Now* I have your undivided attention. You've stopped thrashing against your restraints, which means you're ready." His eyes glittered like liquid mercury as he studied Alastair. "I told you I would break you, Alastair. And this is just the beginning."

Anger stirred in Alastair's chest, sending fire shooting through his veins. He didn't move, but he really wanted to, just to shut this demon up. Ephrem wanted to get a rise out of him. *Still not going to happen.*

"I have been working on this dark realm for ten years." He gestured around them. "Lots of souls have been taken in this very spot. Yours will be next. The Nephilim set my work back eons when he drained Angela dry."

The demon noticed Alastair's surprise, and his hood moved up and down as he nodded in affirmation.

This is about Angela. The demented angel hell-bent on killing all Nephilim—Corinth included—and subjugating the entire human race. *Psycho.*

"Do you remember the shield Angela erected at the throne? I helped supply it with dark energy. I thought that if the Nephilim were separated from the angels, he might be easier to kill. We needed something to draw Corinth inside and keep him there, and also prevent any of the Watchers from entering to help him. At the time, I had been supplying Angela with my strength and power, so she could create a barrier only Corinth could pass through. It was meant to drain him of his powers—but I didn't account for him being part vampire." He let out a derisive laugh. "That was my fault. His compulsion and thirst for blood were just too strong. I admit when I'm wrong. Corinth ended up destroying Angela—well, sort of—*and* the throne. The Nephilim destroyed *vampires.*"

Alastair detected a hint of derision and awe in Ephrem's voice, like he still couldn't believe what had happened.

He fixated on the words *sort of.* He really hoped Angela was gone for good.

"The entire virus … eradicated by his hands, and that stupid blade," Ephrem continued. "Thousands of years' worth of work, and the Nephilim managed to destroy it in mere minutes. And now I have something much worse than death planned for him. I can see that look on your face, Alastair. You think I might be planning on resurrecting vampires. No. That's over. But this"—he rattled the container, and the object inside hit the glass with a delicate clink—"will be used to create something better. Something only *I* control. A dark army. I was working with Angela on creating the means to convert mortal souls, but Corinth set me back quite a bit. I owe him for that. I owe you for that. Which is why I chose *you* for this special experiment. I need your angelic blood."

Angelic blood? Alastair knew he had been altered somehow when Corinth had brought him back from the dead, but he was still human … wasn't he?

"This shard is charged with demon blood, vampire blood, and something darker. I bet you want to know how it works." Ephrem stepped closer to Alastair, dropping his voice ominously as he leaned in. "Once in your bloodstream, this shard will eventually make its way to your heart—at which point, it will pierce it, and then make you into something else. Something better. Mine to control. A Shade."

Ephrem was going to create a new race of evil beings. Worse than vampires? Alastair's mind was playing out every horrible scenario that could transpire if this were to be let loose upon the world. *Great. Just great. He wants your soul.* That was what Gray had said he'd wanted from Alastair. Everyone's.

I am the bait. Alastair's eyes widened in understanding. Ephrem *wanted* Corinth to find him.

"I'm sure you're well aware of what I plan to do with *this* particular shard, Alastair Iszler." He shook the vial again.

Ephrem was planning on turning Alastair into one of them. *A Shade.* He shuddered at the thought of being at this demon's beck and call.

"This shard here will kill a full-blooded angel—I couldn't quite get the formula right without Angela's help. But if a *human* or … *Nephilim*, for instance, were to be infected with it, it turns them into something else entirely. You were brought back from the dead by Corinth. You had angelic blood in your system when you died. You see, I needed to test this out on an angel, but I couldn't just go and grab one off the streets … They stick together like glue. And since you're the closest thing to a half angel and mortal … *well* …" He uncapped the glass ampoule and flipped it upside down. The small sliver of glass landed in his open palm. "You're the test run, and the bait at the same time."

Alastair's head was swimming now. His whole body went rigid with tension and—dismay. Corinth was in trouble. He had to get out of here.

"Fortunately, I had someone else willing to give me all of this knowledge about you after Angela was slain. An innovative genius who knows you quite well." Ephrem jutted his chin out and nodded. "You were right, Stanton, Alastair *will* do quite nicely."

A tall, dark figure materialized out of the shadows, and Alastair's heart stopped beating in his chest. His blood began to boil at the sight of the person standing in a shadowy alcove.

The world around Alastair was whittled down to a tiny pinprick of light as stars of rage exploded across his vision. He would know that dark profile anywhere. The traitor had his arms crossed over his chest, a scowl on his face.

He'd dreamed of killing this man often enough. Upon hearing his name, Gabriel Stanton inched into the dim lighting, the soft orange glow from the shard illuminating his face.

Stanton was wearing an expensive-looking suit with a blue-and-white striped tie. Gabriel had aged. Not considerably, but his hair was more salt-and-pepper than black, and he had a short, well-trimmed beard now. He looked to be about forty instead of thirty.

It had been a nice long ten years since Alastair had seen Gabriel Stanton last—at least in person. He had seen his endeavors in the corporate world through the media outlets. The billionaire had made quite the name for himself as a humanitarian. *All bullshit.* Alastair had known Gabriel Stanton wasn't legit in anything he did. Especially not his morals.

A zing of fury made his levelheadedness instantly dwindle down to nothing. He needed at Gabriel Stanton, to wring his neck.

To kill him.

To wrap his hands around his throat and squeeze.

This is all my *doing.*

Alastair couldn't help himself; he jerked hard at his restraints, kicking—and then he screamed in pain and frustration and fury, even though he knew he was doing himself more harm than good. His cries and shouts came out sounding inaudible and frantic. He was going to lose his mind. His breaths were shallow, and his chest rattled. Stars filled Alastair's eyes with blinding light as the wire buried itself deeper into his flesh, but still, he kept fighting with every ounce of strength he had left, not caring about the excruciating fire running through him, or that his hands were slick with his own blood, or that his head was pounding. *Get free!*

A fiery warmth spread through him, and he glanced down to see that his body had started to glow golden, almost crimson. Power and energy uncoiled in his chest. He felt the pull of something supernatural taking hold. Red ran down his ankles in rivulets, and his muscles screamed just as much as he did—

Rough hands seized hold of him out of nowhere, dragging him back down.

The Shades that had grabbed him were extraordinarily resilient, but Alastair thrashed against their iron hold, unable to control the madness roiling through him. His entire body was shaking. He was going to rip all of them limb from limb, like he had done to Wrentmore.

There would be nothing left of Stanton. Nothing left of Ephrem. Or his Shades.

More arms and hands and bodies jumped on top of him, forcing him back down onto the table, and black bled into the edges of his vision.

Ephrem whistled. "He really doesn't like you, Stanton, does he?" The demon reached out to Alastair's left hand and plucked his wedding band off his finger as he continued to fight. "Won't be needing this anymore, will you?" Ephrem pocketed his wedding ring.

Larna.

There had to be a way to prevent this from happening.

Ephrem held his palm out, and the shard lifted into the air all by itself. Magic. Alastair watched in horror and fascination—it looked like when Leo used telekinesis to control his weapons—as it raced toward him in a blur, a silver thread of light.

Too late.

The shard slammed into Alastair's left side, lodging beneath his ribcage. White-hot, excruciating pain struck, and he went rigid and stiff all over, and then the power drained completely out of him and he went slack.

How something could be so small and do so much damage, he had no idea. Like a bullet. He'd been shot before. This felt like that, except infinitely worse. Torturous metal twisting through his insides. Alastair's body was agony—burning or melting, he couldn't tell which.

His back arched up off the table as the scent of copper and sulfur hit his throat.

Ephrem leaned in close to Alastair, his hand held out so he could see what the demon held in it. His wedding ring. The demon closed a fist around the band and squeezed until his knuckles turned white, and then a moment later, Ephrem turned his hand over and opened it.

All that was left of the silver was powder and pulverized metal. Ephrem blew on his palm, sending the shavings drifting to the floor in an eerie tableau.

And it reminded Alastair of human ashes rather than the remains of a wedding ring.

12

GABRIEL

Gabriel knew the change was happening inside Alastair. He could practically feel the evil coming off him, clawing at his own mind—like an animal scratching at a cage—and he couldn't imagine how it felt to be the one suffering through it.

Alastair was still writhing in torment, his bare chest glistening with sweat, moaning behind the gag over his face, his eyelids clenched tight.

Gabriel glanced down to see the spiderweb of thick black lines creeping out from the spot where the crystal shard had entered at his left side, snaking up toward Alastair's still-beating heart. The pallor of Alastair's skin had a grayish-blue tinge to it. He looked terrible. A bloody mess, really. His flesh was torn at his wrists and ankles— and that leg. Gabriel was not squeamish, but still … he felt like he might be sick. There was no way Alastair wasn't walking away from this without a limp from now on.

Gabriel carefully removed the wire entrenched in Alastair's skin at his wrists, working with all the care of a surgeon. And once he was done with his hands, he moved on to Alastair's bloodied ankles—all the while, Alastair's eyes stayed closed, his breathing shallow.

It must have been the contact with his injured knee, but Alastair finally jerked awake, his pain-glazed eyes locking on Gabriel like twin missiles. The look of revulsion on Iszler's face as soon as he saw Gabriel touching him was priceless.

Alastair struggled and tried to kick out at him, but the restraints shuddered and held, and he bit back a muffled cry of pain. That earlier display of power had been something else. Gabriel wondered if Alastair could tap into it again. His body had turned golden, and he'd almost ripped right out of his restraints.

"I'm trying to help you … Stop struggling or you'll make it worse, Iszler."

Alastair's gaze was guarded, and he went incredibly still, like a snake right before it struck. He obviously didn't believe Gabriel.

Gripping Alastair's injured leg with one hand, just above his knee, and placing the other on his calf, without warning, Gabriel heaved down on it as hard as he could. Alastair's leg made a sickening pop, and his eyes rolled to the back of his head as he went incredibly still. It had been a bad dislocation.

For a moment, Gabriel thought he'd killed him.

But then Alastair screamed bloody murder, and even though it wasn't exactly coherent, Gabriel got the gist of the sorts of names he was calling him.

Everything in the book.

Gabriel edged his way over to Alastair's head and reached out toward him, but then he stopped himself short, his hand hovering over his face. "Listen to me, Iszler. I tried to get you out of here before Ephrem did this to you, but I couldn't get past his Shade army. Let me help you," he beseeched. "Nod and tell me you understand. If you don't try and kill me, I'll free you of the rest of these restraints."

When Alastair did not nod, only glared at him, with squinty, suspicious eyes, Gabriel sighed and tried again. "You cannot alert them to my presence. If you do, I can't help you. Nod that you understand, Iszler. Think about Larna."

Finally Alastair did nod, if only slightly.

Alastair's gaze tracked Gabriel's hand as he slowly reached over to free him of the restraint over his face.

Once it was off, Alastair coughed and blinked, his eyes glassy, and then, ever so slowly, they drifted closed once again, and Gabriel could see that his chest barely lifted.

Gabriel grabbed Alastair's face with one hand and shook it. "Don't give up on me now, Iszler. It doesn't suit you."

Alastair's eyes popped open, and his rage seemed to bring him crashing back to reality. Only then did Gabriel inch back, letting Alastair recover. He licked his lips, probably trying to coax the moisture back into his mouth again.

Alastair spoke in a raspy voice. "I am … going … to … *kill* … you, Stanton."

"Better," Gabriel said, sounding satisfied. If he was strong enough to threaten violence, he was strong enough to move. "I can't carry you out of here. You're going to have to get up."

"You planned all of this … from the … beginning. You're working with that *demon*," Alastair spit. "You're a … *dead* … man. Once I get free, I will rip you to shreds."

"Don't be an idiot. I'm here to *help* you." Gabriel said the word *help* like a curse as he shook his head and ran a hand through his hair, aggravated. He opened his mouth to say something else but then stopped to listen. He could almost feel the air thickening around him. He had been around enough of the Shades to recognize the cold spell and sulfur that accompanied their arrival.

"It's too late. You can't move quickly enough on that leg." Stanton reached back and snapped the restraint back over Alastair's mouth, tugging the strap down taut before he had a chance to give him away. "They're coming."

"*You son of a—*" Alastair tried to shout.

Gabriel took a step back, and then another, before vanishing into the shadows, leaving Iszler alone once again. He had been too late.

13

ZOEY

The aroma of turkey roasting in the oven was more than mouthwatering. Mom made the best stuffing on the planet.

Jimmy and Pete were in the living room, planted in front of the television, watching *Temple of Doom*. My parents were both in the kitchen cooking. Dad was finishing up his famous pumpkin pie while I nervously awaited Trevor's arrival. He was late. *Is this a date?* My stomach turned over in anticipation and nervousness.

He'd come over plenty of times in the past, but this felt different. Something had changed between us ever since he'd let me drive his car. I had no idea what that meant.

Larna, her mother, Corinth, and Leo had yet to arrive too. Larna was sort of like my older sister. Maybe I'd ask her advice about boys. I hadn't even had my first kiss yet—

"Honey, can you set the table in the living room?" Dad yelled from the kitchen.

There were so many people coming over we had needed to set up a card table in the living room, behind the couch. It was still folded, disassembled—we'd put it up at the last second so as not to block the pathway to my room.

I ambled into the kitchen and was immediately met by a waft of hot air as my mom opened the oven door to baste the turkey.

The plates were already piled high on top of the counter. I stepped around Mom to grab them, but she was already finishing up and turning to face me, her cheeks mottled from the heat and exertion of bending over. "Zo, will Trevor be joining us for dinner? Do his parents know? I'd really like to talk to them again—once is not enough ..."

"Mom," I said with a sigh, "don't give him the third degree. They know."

I was going to grab the plates, to put them on the table when she stopped me with a hand on my arm. "How's studying going? Making any progress?"

I pulled away from her touch and shrugged. "It could be better. I can't study here—there's too much noise and distraction. It would be nice not having such an early curfew. Like, I could be spending more time at the library in the evenings ..." I stopped when I saw the look on her face. This wasn't going to go well for me. It never did. We always went round and round on this subject. She didn't trust me. She never would.

She bit her bottom lip in thought. "What if I take you

to the library tomorrow? We could spend all day there and come back before they close. Maybe grab some ice cream afterward."

"I'm not seven anymore, Mom. How about you drop me off at the library and then pick me up later?" I countered.

Dad walked up behind my mom and put his arms around her shoulders affectionately. "That sounds like a good compromise to me." He gave me a quick wink in support.

Mom was shaking her head though. "I'm sorry. Not after the stunt you pulled coming home late. I'm coming with you, or no library at all. End of story."

Dad gave me a look over her shoulder that said, "I tried." Mom's word was always final.

"I guess no deal, then." I heaved the pile of plates into my hand, turned on my heel, and went back into the living room before she could argue or stop me. Argh. I didn't need a chaperone.

As I finished setting the table for all our guests, the doorbell rang. I wiped my hands and went to get it.

Outside, dusk had fallen, painting the sky burnt orange, like pumpkin pie, and the clouds looked like whipped cream. I was pretty hungry.

My jaw practically hit the floor at seeing who was standing on my porch. *Cruz.* He was there with a sheepish grin on his face, holding a covered dish in his hands. How the heck did he know where I lived?

I gave him the once-over, noticing how different he looked out of work attire. Like way hotter than I remembered. Really hot. His short dark hair was neatly styled on top with gel to a fine point. Cruz's dark jeans accentuated a lean, athletic waist I'd never noticed before, because he'd always been wearing an apron. His silver-blue parka seemed to enhance the amber hue of his eyes, and he had on a pair of dark brown lace-up boots.

Cruz is … good-looking?

He cleared his throat and held the dish out to me, the tips of his cheeks ruddy. I tried my best to ignore the white scars on his hands, not wanting to get caught staring. "This is from my mother. Tres leches cake." As an afterthought, he added, "*Feliz Día de Acción de Gracias!*"

I reached out and took the cake from him, too stunned to find words to say anything. Socially awkward, table for one. Feeling mystified and flustered, I finally managed to mutter out a "Thank you, and happy Thanksgiving to you too.

How do you know where I live?" I blurted out, still feeling bamboozled by his sudden appearance.

He hung his head, looking embarrassed. "Oh, uh, you put your name and address on the reward card program at the restaurant, and I, uh, sort of looked it up." I raised an eyebrow as he threw a hand out. "Now that I say that out loud though, I realize how ridiculously weird it really sounds. But I wanted to return something important to you—"

I heard my dad shouting from the kitchen. "*Who's at the door? Don't keep it open. Let them in, for heaven's sake.*"

I cocked my head to the side, ignoring my dad to close the door slightly so he couldn't see who I was talking to on the other side. I didn't need my family butting in and humiliating me any more than they already had.

"You came all this way just to drop off a cake your mom made and return something to me?"

He held his hand out and uncurled his fingers to show me what he was holding. In his palm sat my gold shield key chain. The metal glinted in the porch light, sparking his eyes like a flint.

I sucked in a surprised breath.

"I thought I'd lost it," I said slowly, feeling winded.

"I found it at the restaurant … at your table, when I was cleaning up. I took it home with the intention of returning it to you as soon as I saw you again, but something happened with my mom—"

"Is she okay?" I asked quickly, suddenly worried.

His eyes lit up, and he broke out into a wide grin. "She's more than okay, actually," he said breathlessly. "That's what I needed to talk to you about."

I didn't think I'd ever seen him so happy before. In fact, I was used to seeing him sort of grimace when he was at work. The way he smiled at me now made my stomach do a little flip.

"Can we talk? I mean, if you have some time before dinner. It's important, or I wouldn't be bothering you on Thanksgiving."

"You do remember I have family drama, right?" I opened the door all the way and stepped aside. "So enter at your own risk."

Cruz gave me a wider grin and came inside, brushing past me and handing me the dish, his mouth hanging open as he looked around. "I'll take my chances."

Biscuit came out of nowhere and wrapped himself around Cruz's legs, his way of saying hi, which was rare, because he usually hated everyone else.

In the living room, Jimmy and Pete glanced up from the TV at the same time as Cruz shuffled around Biscuit and then bent down to give the cat a scratch behind the ears. Biscuit actually purred.

Jimmy said, "Who's this?"

"Uh, hi," Cruz said, standing back up. "I'm Cruz."

"Wow, Zoey, you invited not one, but *two* boys over today?" Pete piped up. "I think that's a record. When's Trevor arriving?" He raised a teasing eyebrow.

An awkward silence settled between Cruz and me as my stomach bottomed out. *Oh, crap.* Trevor would be here any minute. I'd almost forgotten I'd invited him over. Nothing to be concerned about. Right?

My dad came wandering into the living room from the kitchen. When he saw Cruz, he gave him a warm smile and extended his hand as he strode over to us. "I'm Zeke."

"Cruz Saldivar," he said timidly, shaking my dad's extended hand.

"Cruz's mom made us a cake for Thanksgiving," I said quickly, holding it out to my dad.

He took the dish from me, his chestnut eyes sparkling. "You tell your mom thank you very much. We sure are looking forward to trying this." As an afterthought, he added, "Would you like to stay for dinner, Cruz?"

"I can't stay, Mr. Taylor. Thank you. My mom is expecting me home by eight o'clock."

"Zeke," he corrected Cruz. "I understand. Thank you for dropping by—but we'd love to have you if you change your mind."

"Um, Dad," I said, "we'll be in my room if you need us. He just needs to grab some homework from me …"

My dad glanced between us and then nodded, giving me the stern "behave yourself" look. Like he had anything to worry about. "Dinner's ready in twenty—" Suddenly his eyes flitted to the watch on his wrist and he shouted, "The turkey!" He twirled on his heels and yelled, *Hon, the turkey!*

I took Cruz by his elbow and guided him toward the back of the house, in the direction of my room. We scurried through the first door on the left, and I started to shoulder it closed right as Biscuit darted through at the last second. My brothers had multiple ways of embarrassing me, and I didn't want to expose Cruz to any more of their antics if I didn't have to.

His dark eyes zipped over my unmade bed to the soda cans on my desk, which was littered with paperwork and textbooks and my laptop. Biscuit hopped up onto my bed and arched his back as he stretched out on top of it.

"Uh, sorry about the mess," I said, glancing around, mad that I hadn't done a better job of cleaning my room.

He put his hands in his coat pockets and stood awkwardly behind my desk chair. "It looks great. Way nicer than my place."

I sat down on the end of my bed, deeply troubled by the fact that he smelled delightful. Like warm cinnamon, dry cedar, and mint citrus. *Nope, not awkward at all.*

"Nice room," he reiterated, his eyes drifting down to my fluffy pink rug and then back to my lavender flannel coverlet.

"So … uh, what did you need to talk to me about?" I

asked. "Sorry about that homework thing. My dad can be so weird and overprotective sometimes."

"That's okay. I understand." Cruz opened his palm to show me my key chain again. "This shield … where did you say your brother got it from again?"

"I've never thought to ask. Probably at a gift shop, I think." The way Cruz was looking at it with something akin to reverence made goose bumps pebble up my arms. "Why?"

He shook his head and then set the charm down on top of my desk, near my laptop. "I know how much it means to you, so I wanted to return it … and apologize for the way I stormed off the other day—when you asked about … my … my scars." His voice sounded low and raspy.

My eyes shot to his hands on instinct, but they were already shoved back into his coat pockets. He hung his head. Maybe I didn't want to know how he'd gotten them. This might be way too heavy a topic. Dark and twisty roads that I probably didn't want to go down. I was intrigued though. There was probably a reason he didn't like talking about it—and I'd way overstepped. I didn't plan on doing that again.

"You don't have to explain yourself," I said, my heart squeezing in empathy. "It's none of my business—"

"I know, but … I mean, I—" His voice was so hoarse. "I want to … talk about it … with you, I mean." Cruz bit his lip, the tips of his cheeks turning bright pink, before saying, "My, uh, mom, she was very sick. For a long time … like … like terminal sick, and I had a hard time dealing with it. I have been her primary caretaker for years. I'm only seventeen. And every day, my scars remind me of how poorly I've handled it. I've … I've never really been … in another girl's—" he swallowed hard "—bedroom before."

I took in a shuddering breath, feeling *all* the feels. I mean all of them. *Oh, man.* Guilt swelled up inside me, and also sorrow and empathy and regret. I felt bad for him, but I felt privileged he'd decided to open up to me in this way. The moment felt special.

"I'm so sorry," I whispered.

"That's just it though … She's getting better. And it was only *after* I brought your key chain home, which is why I asked about it. It's … it's a talisman … Well, whatever it is, I know one thing for certain: it brought me and my mom some much-needed good luck."

It was like a bolt of lightning hit me out of nowhere, jolting my entire system. It made me think about Corinth and Larna and my half brother, Leo. The strangeness of my family. The way Corinth and Larna had disappeared without a trace. I wasn't exactly sure what to tell him, and I didn't know where this fit in with the scars on his hands. There could be a million explanations for why his mom seemed to be getting better.

"You should keep it, then," I said on impulse, feeling the need to help.

Cruz swiped a hand under one of his eyes, snapping his head up. "Really?" he asked, surprise coloring his voice.

I nodded. "Absolutely."

"My mom's not doing anything different with her medication, and her doctor says it's … it's a miracle."

"I—" I started to say, but my door popped open a

crack, and I jumped in surprise at the interruption. I thought it was my brother coming to bug me, and I was starting to get irritated, until it opened wider, and I saw that it was Trevor, inching his way into my room.

"Guess who just sweet-talked your mom into letting me sample some turk—" Trevor slid all the way inside, half-closing the door behind him, but his mouth fell open the minute he saw Cruz standing in my bedroom. He suddenly looked thrown, which didn't happen often.

Why were my cheeks burning?

We hadn't been doing anything, and Cruz was on the opposite side of the room from me, but dang if it didn't feel like we'd been caught making out. Awkward.

Trevor was wearing a baby-blue button-down shirt, untucked over form-fitting black athletic pants that tapered at the ankle. His brown hair was tousled, making it look disheveled like he'd just gotten out of bed. There was a tamed sort of messiness to it.

He took in Cruz, his mouth corkscrewing up on one side. "Heeey, Tom."

I hopped off my bed, clasping my hands, unsure what to do with them as Cruz's eyebrows drew together in annoyance at Trevor calling him the wrong name. It felt super uncomfortable having two boys in my bedroom, sizing each other up.

And they must have felt it too, because the room was quiet for a second longer before Cruz muttered under his breath, "My name is Cruz ... *not* Tom."

Trevor waved a hand in the air, as if his name should have been Tom—like Tom Cruise or something—in the first place. "That's what I meant. So, Zo, you invited someone else over for dinner too? I thought …" He shook his head, pursing his lips. "Never mind."

My stomach gave an unsettled flip. *Does Trevor like me? Is he jealous?*

I opened my mouth to speak, to defend myself, but Trevor plopped down onto my bed like he owned the place, and Biscuit sprang up to his haunches, his hackles raised. He hissed at him and bounded off the bed, shimmying through the crack in my half-closed door like he was running for his life.

Trevor stretched his legs out, making himself comfortable, and then put his hands behind his head. "Have you been on this bed before, Cruz?" Trevor braced his back against the wooden headboard, looking smug. "Because I have. Like, dozens of times." And then he had the audacity to wink at me. "I think you're a little out of your league. I saw Cruz's bicycle out front. Maybe he'll give you a ride on his handlebars, Zo. Are you going to tell him about the joyride we took in my *car?*"

My mouth fell open, and my eyes almost bugged out of my head. *What the actual—? What is he insinuating we do in here?*

I threw Trevor a mortified glance, offended. Apparently, I'd offended Trevor first. I hoped the face I was making conveyed exactly how upset I felt. I couldn't speak. All the air had vacated my lungs. He might as well have punched me in the gut. I'd had no idea the guy could have a mean streak. Sure, he was arrogant, and kind of spoiled, but not *mean.*

Finally I said, "Excuse me?" My surprise was rapidly changing to anger.

"I mean *studying*, of course," Trevor said nonchalantly, pulling at a loose strand on the end of his shirt. "What did y'all think I meant we do in here?"

"Trevor," I said, aghast. "Why are you being so … rude?"

Cruz's eyes hardened around the edges, and the mood in the room shifted completely. He stepped closer to the bed, his hands balled into tight fists in his pockets. The tension was building to an unbearable degree as his eyes slid to Trevor and locked on him, narrowing.

In that moment, I was positive Cruz was about to pummel Trevor.

It made it all the worse with what he'd just confessed to me about not having been in a girl's bedroom before.

"I think you should leave," I said, refusing to meet either of their stares, hoping to defuse the situation. Just what I needed—two alpha males knocking each other out in my tiny bedroom. I could feel the moisture on the back of my eyelids, scalding. This was not how I expected this evening to go.

Cruz blew out a deep breath, and then took two more, his chest heaving, and then he turned around to leave.

I let out a shaky breath. "Not you, Cruz. Trevor."

No one said anything.

And then finally Trevor lifted his shoulders as if to say, "Whatever."

"Seriously, Zo? I was only kidding. Jeez. Take a joke, why don't you?"

I opened my mouth to speak, but my bedroom door cracked open all the way, and my oldest brother Corinth popped his head inside, glancing around. I'm sure my face was still beet red.

He gazed around at each of us in turn, the corners of his mouth turned down as he did. It was almost like the guy could read the tension in the room, because his eyes lit on me and then flitted to Cruz standing uncomfortably by my desk, and then eventually halted on Trevor. They narrowed down to slits as he observed Trevor so casually stretched out on my bed.

I cracked an uneasy half grin as Corinth said, "I hope I'm interrupting something."

"As a matter of fact—" Trevor started to say.

"No," I blurted out at the same time.

I pointed at Trevor. "He was just leaving."

Corinth nodded at Cruz in greeting before his eyes settled on Trevor once again. His frown deepened. "Dinner is ready, kiddo," he said. "I'm supposed to tell you to come join the rest of the family in the living room."

Cruz glanced between us and only shook his head as Corinth shoved himself all the way into my messy room, looking around with an eyebrow raised. He was wearing a blue-and-white-checkered button-down shirt with denim jeans and gray Converse.

"When did you get here?" I asked, my throat still constricted. "Is Leo here too?"

Corinth's eyebrows drew together and met in the middle. "Only just, and yes, he's here too, but ... uh, I can't stay. I've got something urgent I have to do. I just wanted to tell you to listen to Leo—and Mom and Dad—until I get back. Okay? Promise me, Zo."

I shot forward on instinct. "You're leaving? During

Thanksgiving *dinner?* Cor, what's wrong?"

He held his hands out, looking around. "Larna, she, uh, needs my help. She's got some marital problems to work out."

Marital problems? That's what's been going on?

"You're telling me she's having trouble with *Alastair?*" My voice rose in incredulity. "*Alastair?* The perfect couple is having problems?" I repeated. "Isn't he in England? You're telling me you're going to England, like, now? Like, right now?"

Corinth ran a hand down his face. "It's an emergency. I'm catching a red-eye out."

I glanced between Trevor and Cruz again. Trevor took his time standing back up, I noted, looking tense and annoyed. "Well, this has been fun, but … I gotta go, anyway. I'll see you around, Zo," he said casually before squeezing past Corinth and walking out of my room. I didn't stop him.

I hadn't ever gotten the creep vibe from Trevor before. Never. But now an alarm in my head was blaring bloody murder. Maybe he was just being defensive and insanely jealous, which I did not find an attractive quality. At all. It was overbearing and weird.

I marched over to Corinth and craned my neck to meet his eyes. He threw his arms around my shoulders, pulling me close, and whispered in my ear, "Take care of yourself. Please stay here and listen to Leo. It's important."

I pulled back suddenly, trying to search his eyes for answers I knew wouldn't be there. "Are you in some kind of trouble?"

"No, no trouble." Corinth glanced back at Cruz,

smiling. "It was nice meeting you, Cruz." And then he turned around and walked out.

"See," I said, turning to Cruz. "Family drama."

Back out in the living room, I noticed Trevor had already left, and the card table had been set up.

Jimmy was standing at the head of the dining-room table. Pete was sitting at the opposite end, tapping a finger nervously on his empty plate. Larna was speaking quietly to Leo, a hand under her chin in thought, her eyebrows drawn together in concern.

I didn't think I'd ever seen Larna look so serious. She was imposing, even standing beside Leo, who was so much taller than she was. There was a hardness in her eyes I didn't recognize. Corinth had already grabbed his coat and thrown it over one arm as he moved up beside Larna, ready to leave. I guessed he'd jumped over the couch—which made sense—he had superlong legs.

Cruz stopped beside me. "I should be going too …" He let his voice trail off. "*That's* your half brother?" he whispered out of the side of his mouth. "I can see what you mean about the guy. He *is* tall."

Leo was about six feet five or six. Taller than Corinth. His eyes were the palest shade of blue I'd ever seen. Dark hair. Fair complexion. And he had on a full-length tan trench coat. He resembled Corinth in stature and bone structure, and he commanded the attention of everyone in the room. I rarely ever got the chance to see him, he was always so busy. Leo was some high-ranking investment banker—he traveled a lot for work. He wasn't a talker, like Cor, either. He was the opposite. Stoic and reserved. And he had a light and airy perfectly British lilt when he spoke. Polite and British.

My dad was carving the turkey at the main table, and my mom was putting serving utensils in the mashed potatoes. I watched her move on to the salad, stabbing tongs into the bowl. My stomach rumbled, but not in hunger. Trevor had put me in a sour mood. A weird sort of tension buzzed around the room.

My mom seemed like she was in a mood too as she shoved a serving fork into the ham. When she saw me, she said, "Ah, Zo, why don't you and your friend sit down? There's plenty of food for everyone—"

The doorbell rang, interrupting my mother. Her eyes snapped toward the sound, and she quickly turned to give Corinth a glance. "Get the door, will you, Cor?"

Corinth nodded without a second thought, striding over to it. After a second, he reached out and swung the door open wide. His entire body went rigid, and his fingers flexed down by his sides. Suddenly I was all too curious about who could make him react in such a way. Especially on Thanksgiving evening. I edged closer to the card table, which blocked my path to the entryway, to see who was standing on the front porch.

A dark stranger wearing an onyx-colored suit and a black fedora stepped inside. When he took his hat off, I got a full glimpse of his face, and a jolt of recognition tore through me. My heart lodged itself in my throat.

The man standing in the hallway had a trimmed black beard, a headful of salt-and-pepper hair, and a raised scar on his cheek. His irises were what stood out most though. They were jet-black. Dark as the night sky. Maybe darker. I knew, as soon as I saw them, that I'd seen this man before. On television.

I jerked back a step, bumping right smack into Cruz. He staggered backward too, surprised by my reaction—that is, until he started to recognize the man at the door too, his mouth falling open at the same time as mine.

"*Holy smokes* ..." Cruz breathed. "Is that—" he let out a stunned exhalation "—who I think that it is standing in your foyer?"

I didn't answer him. All I could think about was flame-colored hair and pointy white teeth. The image crashed over me as a memory surged to the surface of my consciousness. Being crammed into a really dark space, my only company the sound of my rapidly beating heart. I remembered the feeling of being terrified of ... of *what*? Monsters. Real-life monsters? Not make-believe ones that hid under your bed. A flash of a boy's face flared up in my mind's eye. Flame-red hair. Bright eyes. Not a rabid animal. The tall, scary boy with the strange flashing eyes and the ... fangs?

Only in my darkest imagination.

Except this wasn't my imagination. It was a recollection.

It had been real. I felt ill. Like someone had thrown me right into the deep end of an ice-cold pool and told me to swim. My breath was coming in shallower and shallower. I was going to sink to the bottom. Sweat popped up along my brow.

I'd only seen the stranger on the television and on my

social media feeds. Or so I'd thought. I'd been wrong this entire time. He was one of the most famous and richest people on the planet. A household name: Gabriel Stanton. And he was standing in my hallway as if he'd been invited over for dinner.

The man who'd kidnapped me when I was five years old. Gabriel Stanton.

14

ZOEY

Gabriel Stanton had been the one responsible for my disappearance. I hadn't wandered off and gotten lost in the woods when I was five, like my family had told me. I had been grabbed by a younger-looking kid with red hair and … and *fangs*? A vampire. Okay, maybe not a vampire … Maybe I'd mixed my nightmares with reality. But I did recall Gabriel Stanton standing over me, incredibly scary. I shivered, trying to cling to the fragment of memory, but then it was gone—only leaving behind a prickly feeling on my scalp as chill bumps pebbled my flesh from head to toe.

My eyes swung to my oldest brother. I knew one thing for certain: Corinth had been involved in my disappearance. He had been the one to find me. He knew the answer to this puzzle, and he had been keeping it from me my entire life.

No one moved for an incredibly long, stretched-out

second, and then Larna and Leo were behind Corinth in a fraction of that time, both of them squaring up, their chests pushed out and their shoulders thrown back, like they were about to break out into a fight at any second. They seemed to know the danger this man brought with him. Danger practically oozed out of his pores.

Cruz fidgeted nervously beside me—I could tell he felt it too.

Leo placed a hand at Corinth's back. A familiar sort of gesture communicated by touch alone. Corinth gave him an imperceptible nod, like they were used to interacting without words.

"You realize how incredibly dumb it is for you to be standing in my family's living room, don't you, Gabe?" Corinth said icily. But instead of Corinth asking him to leave, which would have made more sense to me, he shut the door behind the creepy business mogul—and kidnapper—and came back around to stand in front of him.

My chest constricted, and the blood in my vessels seemed to thicken. The air pressure in the room compressed around me, like I was in a hyperbaric chamber—I guessed being in one would feel exactly like this. It smelled like an impending thunderstorm. In fact, the room filled with so much static electricity that a spark popped between Cruz and me, and we both yelped in surprise.

Gabriel Stanton?

I blinked rapidly in confusion as my scrambled brain tried to play catch-up.

Gabriel Stanton's onyx eyes slid to Larna, and then

amazingly, they softened as soon as he caught her gaze. "Larna." He nodded in greeting. "It *is* good to see you again."

Larna jumped in front of Corinth before he could stop her. "You know where he is, don't you? Where is he, Gabriel? Where's Alastair? Tell me now."

Alastair is missing?

The room went incredibly still—as if it could get any quieter or tenser or scarier than it already had.

I heard Cruz say, "What the—?"

Gabriel Stanton turned back to glower at Corinth, with the rest of my entire family slow-blinking back at them both in confusion and fear. It was the first time a guest had actually looked unwelcome in this household.

Finally he spread his arms out wide, a mocking sort of gesture. "Don't bare your fangs at me, Mr. Taylor." He broke out into a predatory grin, his own teeth flashing as if what he'd just said was an inside joke meant only for the two of them. I shuddered at the feral look on his face as he continued. "Oh, come now. Don't tell me you lost your sense of humor. I'm sure your family knows what you are by now. And who I am—what *I* used to be."

Vampire.

My vision plunged into black for a second as a trill of alarm went through me, and the world rocked, shaking me to my core. *Who is he?* I knew what he was. But it couldn't be. It was impossible. *Don't bare your fangs at me, Mr. Taylor.*

Vampire.

Corinth's hand twitched down by his side, his whole body tensing. I could see the hard outline of muscle on his back even through his long-sleeved shirt. "Assuming you're not here for my mother's turkey, *Gabe*, you had better have a very good reason for coming to my family's home," he hissed.

Cruz leaned over to whisper in my ear, "Your brother is on a first-name basis with one of the wealthiest people on the planet."

Gabriel Stanton raised a dark eyebrow at that, and his eyes flitted to Larna's wedding ring, on her left hand. The diamond seemed to sparkle brighter, and his superior grin faltered. "I know where Alastair Iszler is."

Gabe? Corinth was on a first name basis with *Gabriel Stanton?* And he'd never told me.

My gaze snagged on my parents, who were both standing at the head of the dinner table in the dining room. They didn't look as surprised as I thought they should be—but they were both incredibly pale. I was pretty shell-shocked. Pete and Jimmy stood at attention by their side, their eyes wide in alarm. Everyone was on edge.

Cruz stiffened beside me, but he didn't say anything, only shifted on the balls of his feet, clearing his throat. "I think, um, I should be going now," he squeaked. And when every eye in the room swiveled to him, he sucked in a sharp breath and whispered, "Uh, never mind. Not a good idea. I'll just be over here … minding my own business …" He let his voice trail off.

"Zo, take your friend and go back to your room and shut the door," my dad commanded, his voice firm. "Now." He gestured at me to go. We were on opposite sides of the room from each other, and the card table was blocking my path to them, butted up to the back of the couch. I supposed I could jump over the couch and refuse to leave, but something told me that was not a good idea. I'd never heard my dad speak to me in such a manner before, so gruff. There was a flicker of fear in his eyes. He was scared. No, not just scared—petrified.

I stayed rooted to the spot by indecision a moment longer. There was no way I was missing out on this conversation, but I was also deeply anxious and afraid. Something inside me knew this was when I'd finally get the answers to a lot of strange questions—answers that had been hidden from me for so long.

Gabriel Stanton's lip curled up on one side as he moved to stop in front of Corinth, forcing Larna to back up a step. Even she looked spooked.

"Gabriel, where—the—hell—is—Alastair?" she said, enunciating each word as a threat, clear and angry.

He sniffed at the air as if disgusted, and glowered around the room at everyone staring at him. Dad moved to stand protectively in front of Mom. My father was not a fan of his, apparently. No one in this household was, which made me even more curious about this strange man.

Gabriel Stanton's eyes narrowed, and as if he'd just read my mind, his gaze slid over to me, as slick as cooking oil, and then stopped. That stare gave me the willies. I shivered, not at all liking his attention focused on me.

"Zoey Taylor." He nodded at me as if he knew me. "How you've grown since I saw you last."

I swallowed hard at hearing that, my throat feeling raw and thick and achy. *He does know me. I'm not crazy.*

"Gabriel Stanton *knows* you?" I heard Cruz echo my unspoken thoughts from behind me. "You really were right about your family drama. Do you think you could get us a ride in his helicopter?"

A weird tug in my gut struck. I was pretty sure my face was salt white as I glanced at my mom, hoping she would provide some answers, but she only shook her head, silently pleading at me to stand down. She knew what was going on. She knew, and she'd never told me. They all knew. Everyone except me. My gaze glided from my mom to my dad's worried face, and then back to Corinth, Larna, and Leo once again. Leo was standing at attention, his shoulders thrown back, but he didn't move. He looked as still and silent as a placid lake.

"You're a vampire." I didn't know why I said it out loud. The words were on my tongue before I could even stop them, or think them through.

The tension was like a live wire writhing with electrical currents, and it seemed to spread to me too. My limbs felt heavy with apprehension.

Gabriel Stanton laid his hat down on the entryway table and cocked his head to the side, clearly annoyed at being addressed in such a manner. "Ascended being," he corrected, moving further into the room, closer to me, appraising. "Once upon a time. And it appears you remember—when you shouldn't … Strange," he said, a hand going to his chin.

My gaze shifted to Corinth again right as he threw an arm around Gabriel Stanton's shoulder. "I'll explain everything later, Zo," he said with a minute shake of his head.

"What do you mean, I remember when I shouldn't?" My gaze halted back on Corinth and then Gabriel Stanton. "What is going on? Explain what, Corinth?"

He kidnapped me.

Deep in my soul, I knew this stranger standing in our hallway was telling the truth. *Is my brother a vampire?* But as preposterous as that sounded, in a weird way it made sense. His strange vanishing acts. The beefing up on an unnatural scale. His odd twitchiness. All those late nights with little to no sleep. He could go outside in the daylight though. He ate garlic on his pizza …

Leo followed them at a distance, looking menacing and dangerous. *Cor just threw an arm around the shoulder of one of the richest men on the planet.* It didn't seem friendly to me though. It felt the opposite. Like a warning. And I was sure Stanton thought the same thing, because he flinched as soon as Corinth touched him.

"Gabe, I should have given you a warmer welcome. Come in … Have a seat. We're friends, right?" Gabriel Stanton stared uncomfortably at Corinth's arm around his shoulder. "Because if we're not friends … that makes us enemies, and if we're enemies … well …" He let the sentence hang in the air for a second. "Not—good."

Enemies?

My dad jumped in quickly. "Cor, what do you want us to do?"

Corinth's eyes flickered to my dad, and then to my mom and to his brothers. "Nothing yet."

Larna joined them in the living room, folding her arms across her chest. *So, who is she?*

"Where is Alastair?" Larna repeated.

"He's in trouble," Gabriel Stanton said. "I need Corinth to come with me. Now."

Larna looked like she was two seconds away from throttling him, her chest rising and falling rapidly now as Gabriel pulled something out of the inner lining of his suit jacket and held it out for her and Corinth to see. A small round device with a toggle switch. "If you want to save Alastair's life, Mr. Taylor, you will stop asking me questions and come with me right now. He has little time left—"

"Stanton, you really do disappoint me."

A voice spoke from behind me. Not Cruz's. Not Jimmy or Pete's. Someone else's. I implicitly remembered no one standing there a moment before.

Everyone's head spun in the direction of my room toward the back hallway.

A thick wall of smoke rose up, looking, oddly enough, like a pillar of black sand, crackling with blue flames as it shot up toward the ceiling. It smelled like sulfur and burnt wood. A sliver of icy panic tore through me as my heart gave a painful jolt in my chest.

Cruz smacked my arm in surprise and shock. To be fair, he looked just as stunned to see the supernatural occurring right in front of him as I probably did. Actually, scratch that. He let out a bellow and fell right on his butt, gaping back up at the cataclysmic event happening in our hallway right in front of us. *Holy smokes.*

I froze, my legs feeling like lead weights.

"*Demon!*" Leo cried, but it was so hard to hear the rest of what he was shouting over the ruckus of wind and ash raining down around us.

Did he just say demon?

And then, just as magically as it had started, the gust died down, and the smoke took on the shape of a body. It looked like a dark cape settling over a human form, and then the dark cape's face sharpened and came fully into focus: Glasses. Chocolate eyes. Auburn hair. Recognition hit me like a wrecking ball.

Trevor.

He had on some sort of hooded black cloak, making me think of clothing an assassin or a cult leader might wear. And then I knew it. I was being pranked. They were messing with me. I wanted to tell them Halloween had already passed, but the words stuck in my throat like cement. They couldn't have faked that black smoke effect … There was no way.

My blood thudded oddly through my veins, and I swayed a little on my feet.

"*Gabriel Stanton,*" Trevor Malcolm snarled. "It appears I have put way too much trust in you as of late."

Trevor had left. He'd gone. *Trevor?* In a split second, I'd already played out our entire year together. How we'd met. How he'd acted. How he'd let me drive his car. All the ice-cream sundaes we'd polished off together. His incessant flirting. What if he was possessed? Possessed by a demon. I'd seen the TV show *Supernatural* enough times. I mean, I guessed there was no rationalizing anything now. What was the point? But why? Something told me it wasn't so he could be crowned homecoming king.

Prince of Hell, more like it.

Trevor pushed his glasses back up the bridge of his

nose and shrugged, tilting his head to the side. "I never would have guessed you'd go behind my back like *this*. To the *Nephilim*." He laughed, and it was a distressing sort of sound that grated on my ears, and then he lifted a hand, and to my surprise, it was glowing like molten metal. It looked like he could melt someone's face off just by touching them.

"Trevor?" I finally managed to croak out. "W-w-what are you doing?"

Trevor's dark eyes glittered behind his glasses as he flicked an amused glance my way, and he had the audacity to wink. "Nephilim," he said with a sneer, staring daggers at Corinth. "Move, and I'll cut down your entire family before you can even pull up a portal." He held that same radiant hand out toward me, clenching it into a tight fist. "Surprised, darling?" he all but purred. "Your boyfriend is a demon."

There was movement off to my right, in the dining room. *Leo.* A gloriously golden light burst out of his body and spread out like an exploding star.

I was dead.

No, *he was* dead—someone can't just spontaneously combust like that and live. But then the flames were gone, and I was left blinking back the sting of tears, staring at a man I didn't recognize.

Wearing golden armor.

Leo's breastplate was polished to a shine so bright I could see my dad's pale face in it. And to top it all off, he was holding a short sword high above his head, at the ready. His irises were still their usual shade of pale blue, but now they were ringed by a thin circle of indigo. I'd never seen eyes like his. Last I recalled, humans didn't have purple irises.

Jimmy and Pete were standing pretty darn close to Leo too, but I noticed they didn't flinch. They didn't look surprised that Leo had just magically transformed himself in two seconds flat. They seemed frightened, sure, but not surprised.

They knew.

This whole time.

"Oh, for the love of all that's *holy*," Corinth snarled.

Dazzling blue and gold sparks lit up his entire body like a human firecracker—in much the same way as had happened to Leo—and the blazing light spread outward behind his back, forming ... *WINGS*. Like, almighty biblical, the-world-is-ending wings. *Can he fly?*

I threw a hand over my face to shield myself from the sudden intensity and tried to scream, "*Cori—*" but I choked on oven-hot air as it hit the back of my throat. My mouth went bone-dry, and the room filled with the smell of ozone and rain, and a thunderclap erupted throughout the house, rattling the walls, knocking picture frames off.

When the light finally dissipated, I had to blink past the tears and bright spots to try and focus on my brother again.

He was wearing a gold-plaited chain mail vest, which had an unnatural sheen to it. Strapped to his lower thigh and hip, was some sort of high-tech black holster. A bluish sort of energy traced patterns up and down his arms, illuminating his veins—like lightning. In his hand, he clutched a dagger, and white sparks shot from the tip of the blade, which he pointed at Trevor.

I was the only one who hadn't known. Gutted. That was how I felt. So many emotions were flooding through me all at the same time. There was so much I didn't know about my family. I doubled over as everything hit me all at once.

Corinth had never looked so terrifying.

He wasn't a vampire. He was something else entirely.

15

ZOEY

The room had gone devastatingly quiet, and I was still shaking like a leaf.

Gabriel Stanton was standing behind Corinth, the weird device he'd pulled out of his pocket clutched in his hand. All I could think about, though, was my brother. *My brother is a Nephilim.* Half angel. Half human. Holy.

His cheeks were shadowed and contoured by the contrasting light as lightning danced in pools of empty sockets where his eyes should have been. But then in the next moment, they flickered back to their normal honey-colored hue.

The wings at his back were as impressive a sight as I'd ever seen in my entire life. He'd just been my oldest brother, who really liked coffee … but not anymore.

The knuckles on my mom's hands, which she had clenched together, were bone white. Dad mashed his lips into two thin lines. He put a hand on Jimmy's arm, and then his gaze locked on me from across the room, his eyebrows knitted in concern. He tried to mouth a word at me, but I couldn't tell what he was trying to communicate.

Gabriel Stanton's eyes darted to Corinth. "You don't have warding for these types of situations, Taylor?"

Corinth eyed Trevor more warily, stalking forward, his flaming blade still pointed at him, and then he motioned to Leo. "This *kid* is a *demon*? You didn't know?"

Leo shook his head. "Did *you*?" he asked, clearly agitated. "I couldn't tell until he used his powers."

Angels and demons and vampires and Nephilim.

I mean, I hadn't believed it. Not really. This was crazy.

Cruz swore under his breath, gazing up at Corinth from his prone position on the ground, his face puckered in the most peculiar way, seemingly captivated and shaken. "Trevor is a *demon*?" He reached under his shirt and pulled out his pendant, clutching it in his hands. I was pretty sure he was praying under his breath in Spanish. "Actually, that explains a lot …"

Trevor gave a theatrical bow. "I'm very good at misleading fools, Cruz. And so is Stanton, I suppose. Pretending you don't like Corinth Taylor—" his eyes lit on Corinth briefly and then swept back over to Gabriel Stanton "—that was convincing. Now, give me the device, Stanton. I won't ask again."

Stanton took a hesitant step back, looking anxious. "I-it's not what it looks like, Ephrem—"

"Zoey!" My dad shouted. "RUN!" And the sheer

terror in his voice shattered my trance completely, and reality came slamming back into me full force—back into all of us.

This time I listened.

I started to turn to leap over the card table—my right arm lifted, one leg hiked up—but I froze in place midmovement, a scream stuck in my throat. All that came out instead was a gurgled whimper. I couldn't move a muscle. My limbs were held frozen in place by some invisible force.

"Where do you think you're going, *darling*?"

Out of my peripheral vision, my distressed gaze caught a blur of black, and then someone was standing right behind me. I knew it was Trevor. I could feel his body heat radiating off him.

Every single one of my nerves felt like it was on fire.

Why couldn't I move?

I tried to order my brain to move my limbs, but nothing would work.

My terrified gaze drifted to Cruz on the ground, his eyes wide and face incredibly ashen. Trevor didn't seem to pay him any heed, like he was no threat to him whatsoever.

Corinth lifted his blade, and sparks shot out of the tip.

I couldn't quite see Trevor, but I heard him speak behind me; his breath rustled my hair.

"What did I say about moving, Nephilim?" he snarled. "You want me to snap her neck like a twig?"

The thumping of my pulse was deafening. No matter how hard I tried to get my legs to work, they—just—

wouldn't. *I can't move!* I tried to speak, to cry out for help, but nothing would come out of my mouth. It was absolutely terrifying. A waking nightmare.

I'd never done anything to Trevor, but the way he was talking about snapping my neck, the derision in his voice, made me think I'd mutilated his entire family—and his pet—right in front of him. It left me feeling light-headed.

His riches. His car. His hobbies. He was too good to be true. His parents were always out of town. The guy—*demon*, rather—was a fraud. And he'd flaunted it right in front of my face. I felt sick.

Your boyfriend is a demon.
Your boyfriend is a demon.
Your boyfriend is a demon.

Those words Trevor had said to me were on constant replay in my head.

Finally, after what seemed like an eternity, I was able to form a full sentence. "You are *not* my boyfriend." It came out sounding strained and odd even to my own ears.

Trevor gave a scornful grunt behind me. "You think I'd ever be interested in someone like you, little girl?" I could practically feel his eyes on the back of my head, dissecting. It felt like a thousand ants crawling over my skin, chilling me to the very bone. "I mean, have you looked at yourself in a mirror lately? Pathetic."

In the background, I heard my dad shout, "*Let me at him!*" but everything else faded into the distance. My ears were ringing too loudly; my heart was beating way too fast; and my breathing was a little too ragged.

Trevor had only wanted to get close to my brother. *I*

had brought him in here. *I* had confided in him. I squeezed my eyes shut. *None of this is real.* The room started to spin. I couldn't catch my breath. I couldn't *move.*

Suddenly Cruz bolted back to his feet, boldly throwing himself between me and Trevor, his hands balled into fists in front of him, and to my extreme surprise and satisfaction, he took a swing at Trevor. "You leave her alone, douchewad! Go back to hell or wherever it is you came from—"

I craned my neck around as far as it would go to get a look at them, right as Trevor made a flicking motion with his hand, like a slap, and Cruz went flying off his feet, careening over the back of the couch, then landing in a heap at its base, motionless. Trevor threw his head back and laughed, a deep belly laugh.

"No—"

My throat clamped tight, and I felt the veins in the side of my neck pop out. I'd gone looking for this. *So stupid. Stupid, stupid, stupid.* I'd shared things with him … This was my fault. I'd let a demon in my bedroom. *Oh—my—gosh.* A demon had sat on my bed.

"*Trevor,*" Corinth whispered, inching closer, his blade dripping white-hot sparks. "You are in my family home. Big mistake." His voice, even lowered still carried around the room like a shout. "I am going to give you to the count of three to let Zoey go and vacate the premises—or I will make you."

Larna was behind Corinth, just off to his right, and armored Leo was standing to his left. She had a hand at his back as she wedged herself between him and Leo and

Stanton. Two thin blades were ejected from buckled bracers at her wrists. Holy crap, she looked fierce. *Who are these people?*

"One," Corinth said evenly.

Trevor spoke only to me, a smirk plastered across his face, ignoring Corinth's countdown. "So, Zo, you didn't know your brother was a Nephilim?" He chuckled. "You really are dense. I bet you didn't even know Corinth is only your half brother ..." He took a step closer behind me. Now all he had to do was reach out and touch me. Not that it really mattered. Apparently, the demon had telekinesis. My heart was racing; I felt like it might give out on me at any moment.

My half brother?

Corinth lifted his hands, I could see them crackling with some kind of weird, dark energy. "Two."

My tight throat tried to work past a swallow.

Trevor rolled his head from side to side, stretching his neck as if getting ready to make his move—and then suddenly I *could* move again. I was free.

And because I'd been tense for so long, I'd forgotten I was already in the forward momentum of running, so as soon as I started to move again, I went sprawling right into the edge of the card table—

Trevor was there, already wrapping a strong arm around my throat and pulling me flush against him before I could even take in a deep breath. He smelled like wood and smoke and metal.

"*Watch this,*" he whispered in my ear, sounding amused, at the same time as he extended a hand out and flung something small and wicked sharp at my mother.

There was a flicker of movement as whatever he'd thrown at her rippled through the air—a sliver of silver metal. Leo threw his hand out at the same time, motioning at the object, sort of like Trevor had done.

And just like that, the shiny object stopped midflight. My mom sucked in a shocked breath, her face waxy as the thing hovered right in a direct path to her heart. Light glinted off the object, making it look like a broken shard of glass from a mirror. Thin and needlelike. My mom went stiff, and my dad tried to pull her out of its path, but she seemed stuck, rooted to the spot by invisible chains— I guessed it was like the same invisible force that had stopped me from moving.

Leo's extended hand shook, and I could see sweat beading on his forehead. "I …" He licked his lips, turning to give Corinth a quick glance. "I can't hold it, Cor—"

Corinth started to move, his body teeming with cobalt electricity—fire *and* ice.

Trevor hauled me off the ground by the crook of his arm, the one he had circled around my throat, chuckling in my ear and choking the life out of me. His hot breath hit the side of my cheek as he flexed his bicep, cutting off more oxygen flow. I gripped his forearm with both hands, trying to pull down on his iron grip. I couldn't get air into my lungs. All I could do was make a weird retching noise, gasping, hoping he wouldn't kill me in front of my entire family. I tried to kick out behind me, but it was like hitting a stone wall, which only seemed to make him laugh harder at my expense.

"All I need to do is squeeze, Cory … Lower your weapon," he hissed into my ear.

Corinth obeyed, lowering his blade, his eyes flashing dangerously. "You hurt my family, and what I did to Angela … I'll make that look like a cakewalk compared to what I do to you. *Let—her—go.*"

"You don't know what you're up against, Nephilim," Trevor cooed.

I couldn't breathe, and by this point I was plummeting down into darkness, scary darkness, as my eyelids drifted closed. And then Trevor relieved some of the pressure on my jugular, and sweet air flooded back into my lungs.

"No passing out on me now," he whispered. "I need you to witness this."

Jimmy yelled something and rocked forward, and Pete opened his mouth to speak, but all that came out was an "*Oomph!*" on his exhalation as he jumped in front of my mother. And then he was sinking to his knees, into both Jimmy's and Dad's arms.

My mother screamed. I couldn't keep up. A part of me, the terrified five-year-old, was back, stuffed into a dark place, and I didn't want to. The world was spinning, falling far, far away.

I knew the thing Trevor had thrown had unstuck and then struck home, sinking deeply into flesh. I let out a strangled sob at realizing whose flesh it had sunk into. Not its intended target. Not my mother, but Peter. *Pete.*

A clap of thunder rolled through the house, so loud my teeth shook in my skull. Light engulfed us and exploded outward in a giant sphere, blinding the entire room; Leo disappeared in a clap of thunder and light in an instant, catching up Pete as he collapsed. Leo guided

Pete to the ground, a glowing hand going to his chest.

And then four impressive-looking figures—*giants*—bounded out of a spinning gray vortex that had opened up near the front entryway.

The newest arrivals were already taking action—on our side or the demon's, that remained to be seen. I got snatches of polished armor. Electrified hands. Blond hair. A towering hulk of a man with ebony skin and dark eyes stepped forward with a battle-ax in his hands.

A beautiful dark-skinned woman with braided platinum-dyed hair grabbed my father, and they disappeared into a whirling cloudlike vortex, much to his alarmed protests. *No.*

Biscuit came out of nowhere, jumping on Trevor's face, clawing at him, diverting his attention momentarily from me.

Amazingly, my cat saved my life, because Trevor let me go, and I dropped to my knees, panting, dragging in a deep lungful of air, dazed.

"*Go!*" Corinth yelled to Leo, and then to the rest of the gathered beings. "*Get them out of here! I'll get Zo!*" A megavolt of lightning spilled out of Corinth's blade, heading right for Trevor. Powerful. Wild. Deadly.

Corinth can wield lightning.

It flashed across my retinas, leaving me momentarily blinded, and reducing my vision to dazzling white nothingness. A light bloomed up bright and searing, devastatingly so, as the bolt struck something dark and shadowy that had flared up around Trevor.

I wrenched my eyes back open as the lightning Corinth had summoned rebounded off Trevor and struck my brother in the center of his chest, bowling him over backward. His wings sputtered and disappeared like a flickering flame as he slammed into Stanton—who had been standing behind him—and they both went down in a tangle of limbs and arms.

Things were unfolding in mere seconds, but it seemed like an eternity.

Leo and Peter were already gone.

My gaze shifted back to my mom, and she threw her hand out toward me and screamed, "Zoey, go!"

I staggered back to my feet and ran right as another giant, who had spiky golden hair, grabbed my mom around her shoulders.

"Get my daughter firs—"

But before my mom could even finish the rest of her sentence, they disappeared into a swirling vortex, a thunderous echo filling the entire house in their wake. And then, last but not least, the largest one out of the armored strangers, the one with the battle-ax, grabbed Jimmy, and they disappeared in a clap of thunder and a rush of air.

Heavy footfalls sounded behind me. I tensed, knowing it was Trevor, and then I tripped over something, a pillow or a body—

Larna lunged forward, as graceful and feline as a stalking panther, striking out at Trevor with both blades, one sinking deeply into the demon's torso. She hit him so hard the blade broke off from the end of her bracer; I could see the sharp edge still sticking out of his stomach. And the other blade was heading straight for his throat, but Trevor caught her arm, stopping her attack, the knife edge quivering an inch from his chin.

Then he did something completely unexpected: he crushed his body up against hers at the same time as he twisted her arm backward at an angle I knew it wasn't meant to go in. She screamed. And I saw it at the same time she did. Larna's blade sticking out of his belly … was now in hers too. The steel had pierced all the way through, skewering both of them together like meat in a shish kebab.

Larna's eyes went round in surprise and dread as Trevor gave her a grim sort of smile. "That tickles," he said in a calm, vexatious way, not bothered whatsoever by a blade being buried in his gut.

I scuttled backward on my hands and feet, horrified and transfixed as he pulled Larna roughly against him, inch by inch, forcing her arms back down by her sides, pinning them in place. She let out a guttural cry of agony.

A body came out of nowhere and flattened me to the ground, and I gasped, a surge of panic and adrenaline and fear kicking me into action again.

At first I thought it was Trevor, that somehow the demon could be in two places at once—and I was going to kill him. He was dead. Rage roiled through me. *Peter!* I struggled against strong arms, biting into soft flesh, and whoever had hold of me yelped in pain, releasing me.

Cruz.

My chest was heaving and my lungs were on fire. Even the blood in my veins felt scorched. I couldn't let this a-hole kill Larna.

Without thinking about what would happen to me, I lunged for Trevor's legs, hitting him at waist level, remembering my play fights with my brothers. With Peter. Except this was real. Brutally real.

Trevor stumbled back, losing his footing for a second, but not before tossing Larna across the room, over the card table, like she weighed nothing at all. She flew through the air, hit the dining-room table, knocking off our food and appetizers and the turkey, and then she went incredibly still, her head hanging limply off the edge, eyes closed.

Cruz threw himself on top of me, and something connected with my head, hard—maybe his boot. Stars shot across my vision. He was trying to tell me something, but I couldn't make out what he was saying. "Stay down," maybe. My ears were still clogged from the rumble of thunder and my raging pulse.

Cruz's protective weight lifted off me, and I squinted up to see Trevor holding him in a death grip. But Cruz had something in his hand, and the moment he lifted it up, I could see what it was: the shield key chain, the one Corinth had given me—and I'd just gifted it to Cruz.

A strange golden light was spilling out of it, surrounding us in its glorious intensity—

Corinth was back on his feet, and my gaze caught his. Smoke curled up out of his midsection from his scorched armor.

And before I could shout a warning, Gabriel Stanton was behind Corinth, planting a firm hand on his shoulder at the same time as Trevor let out a startled gasp and dropped Cruz, a hand going to his face against the light emanating from the shield.

Corinth lifted his dagger, his movements full of barely contained rage.

I rose to a shaky knee, and Gabriel Stanton pressed the button on that weird device thing in his hand—

The moment he did, everything went still—*peaceful*—kind of like watching the remnants of snow falling after a hard blizzard had passed.

Crimson flames shot out of the device, enveloping Corinth and Gabriel Stanton. A second later, all the light was sucked from the room—a detonation happening in reverse. The impact lifted my braid into the air, and then my entire body levitated like I had just hit zero gravity.

At this point, my mind was a complete blank.

And then after that, events unfolded in strange strobe-like flashes. Each pulse coming from the device felt like a single heartbeat. The thumping melded with the beat of my own heart—a dulled, lumbering sort of rhythm.

Thump-thump.

Thump.

Thump.

Thump-thump.

Thump.

The world around us imploded as chaos and pandemonium erupted, and then it winked out of existence altogether, swallowing us up with it into swirling darkness.

Thump.

16

ALASTAIR

Alastair writhed against his restraints. Blood ran down his wrists and ankles, but for some reason, he couldn't feel his wounds any longer. Nor his battered knee. Nor his bruised ribs. Nor the lash marks on his neck caused by the whip.

Alastair's chest ached right at his heart.

At least Stanton had relieved him of that awful razor wire. His energy had left him eons ago. He was caving to the inexorable gloom that was pulling him under. Underwater—so he couldn't breathe.

The voice had started out as a tiny scratch in his head. Now it was a full blown shout: *Surrender. You no longer need to fight. Your life is heavy. Put it down.*

He could feel whatever it was taking hold over him. Once again a tremor racked its way through his body, and Alastair's back arched up off the table he was stretched out upon. His throat was raw and achy. His fuzzy gaze traveled down to the spot where the sliver of metal had pierced the skin at his side. He was soaked in sweat, shivering; the tracery of thin black lines was inching closer to his heart.

He had to fight. To hold on. For Larna. Her name was a sweet reprieve in his mind. He imagined her telling him to hold on. He imagined her holding his hand in comfort, even though his fingers were just so numb—had been for quite some time. What had Ephrem done to him?

Give up.

Shock and pain towed him back into oblivion.

Alastair wasn't strong enough to fight this.

Who was he married to again? *Larna. You're married to Larna.* He shook his head, the inky cold clouding his mind, scattering his thoughts and confusing him. Was he married? He nodded. *Yes. You just went through this. To Larna.*

Alastair imagined her voice, and it was his lifeline as he came racing back to the surface as if he'd come up for one last, final breath of air.

Give up. Give up. Give up. Give up. Give up. Give up.

Larna. Alastair said her name again in his head, louder. *Larna.*

Just then the world around him exploded in light and sound and chaos. Was this it? He was dying. The ear-shattering pressure expanded throughout the cavern—a sulfurous smell mixed with metal and rain.

Golden showers of stinging fiery light took shape and burst into existence next to him, along with several figures who were bounding out of a churning vortex.

His vision swam out of focus. *Angels.* Blessed angels. It had to be. Corinth. *Larna. You aren't dead. Just hold on—*

"*Al.*"

Damn if that voice wasn't annoying on most days … but today, *today*, Alastair thought that voice was the most beautiful thing he'd ever heard in his entire life.

"I'm here, buddy. Hold on. I got you."

Pitch-blackness bled into Alastair's vision, and he almost succumbed to the beckoning darkness, but Corinth's words kept him rooted to the here and now.

They sounded like salvation.

There came a shocked breath, and then he felt the familiar warmth of healing flood through his veins—he knew what it felt like from previous experience—as someone, an angel, pressed a hand to his chest.

Corinth.

That blessed angel.

Someone else, a second, terrified voice, was screaming like a banshee in the background. A girl. But Alastair was all muddled and woozy, and the dark voices hadn't left his head entirely, so he couldn't be sure he was really hearing it. He could not clear his vision. The piercing sharp pains in his heart were unbearable now. It felt like someone was driving a nail into it, one hammer blow at a time.

"*There are dead bodies up there!*"

Alastair caught snippets of a third person, a guy shouting, just as high-pitched as the girl's shrill screams were. He wondered if they felt the oppressiveness of this place too. It was disturbing. Hideous.

Distantly he pondered what they were doing here, and how they had gotten here. Nothing he could help with at the moment. Alastair was in his own world of torment—dragged into obscurity, as if someone had a hold of his leg underwater and was toying with him, letting him come up for air right before towing him back under again.

There was more panicked shouting.

A flurry of motion.

After what seemed like an eternity, Alastair's sight came back to him in small increments. A patch of light here. A blur of movement there. Watercolor images taking on sharper shapes. Faces. Familiar. Troubled.

When he could breathe more deeply, and he realized someone had removed his restraints, only then did he chance opening his eyes.

Corinth was gazing down at him, worry lines cutting deep creases in his forehead and around his mouth. A warm, white light was emanating from Corinth's hand, the one he had pressed up against Alastair's bare chest.

He tried to speak, to tell his friend that he didn't feel right, but his mouth wouldn't work. His soul hurt.

"What the hell did they do to you?" Corinth snarled, his voice dripping with outrage and alarm. "You're … you're a right mess, Al. And that *leg* …" He shifted as if turning around. "Gabe, what did they do to him? You had better start talking … My patience is wearing thin—and you had better pray my family is okay …"

Alastair heard a mixture of apprehension, alarm, and fatigue in Corinth's voice. His family. *Oh no.* The Taylors had been caught up in this too. An overwhelming sense of dread filled Alastair's aching chest like a balloon. He tried to roll over onto his side, to sit up, but his limbs felt too heavy, not attached to his body. He had to help—to warn Corinth.

"He's been infected … by Ephrem," Gabriel explained. "A very powerful demon. He wants to create his own army to do his bidding—"

"Let me guess—to take over the world," Corinth cut in wryly. "Yeah, yeah, yeah, I know the master plan made by all evil douchebag's everywhere."

Gabriel laughed, and for a second, his face came into focus behind Corinth. "You don't get it, Mr. Taylor." He shook his head, exasperated. "He doesn't want to take over the world. He wants to take over *you*." That seemed to silence Corinth into submission, because Stanton continued without any interruption. "He needed Iszler. One, because he has a trace of angelic blood still in his system, and two, because he's human. He's the closest thing to a Nephilim …" Gabriel's voice drifted off. "You get it now, or do I need to spell it out for you?"

"Trevor … Ephrem … he did this to Al to get to *me*? To experiment on him?" Corinth said, sounding deeply disturbed.

Alastair could also detect a hint of guilt in there too. He tried to keep his eyes open, but the pressure started to build up in his head again. *Don't trust Stanton*, he wanted to tell Corinth. Dammit he wanted at Stanton, to wring the tycoon's scrawny neck.

"You can heal people? Who the heck are you?"

This was a different voice. Not Gabriel's. Female and small sounding, the one who had been screaming before.

Not Larna's.

Another male voice spoke up, coming from behind Corinth somewhere, speaking in Spanish, but then he switched to English. "What are those black squiggle lines on his skin? Should he look like that? Is he … *dying?* That's a lot of blood …"

There was a slight pause, and then from the girl: "Where are we, Cor? How did we get here? This place … is … it … it feels *wrong.* It feels like something evil … is trying to get under my skin. It's too dark in here." The girl's voice was shaking now. "What are you? You're … an angel? You're *not* my brother. You had wings. Can you fly? You're not my brother!" she was shouting, sounding panicked again—in shock. Alastair knew what that sounded like—he was close to it himself.

Corinth's face swam in front of Alastair's as he bent over his prone form, his brows puckered and eyes closed in concentration. "I *am* your brother, Zo." His voice cracked, but he kept his eyes screwed tightly shut. Corinth's face had a gray tinge to it, Alastair noticed. "Nothing's changed. I just can't explain everything right now. Help me patch Al up. Can you do that for me, Zo? I can't heal all of these wounds on my own. There's something really wrong with him."

"You can *heal* people?" Zoey squeaked.

Alastair knew what someone sounded like when they were on the verge of a breakdown. Zo. Zoey. Corinth's little sister. *Holy hell.*

Corinth brought his little sister with him?

Blinking, Alastair tried to concentrate on her face. On anyone's face. He'd even settle for Stanton's right now, and that was saying something.

That strange tingling warmth flooded through him again, and the fuzziness cleared, and he could see, if blurrily.

Alastair came fully awake. He tried to sit up, but several firm but gentle hands shoved him back down, and he relented, the energy already draining out of him from just that little movement.

"Easy, Al. I don't think I did much to help you … You've lost a lot of blood."

Corinth's hand was pressed to Alastair's forehead, and the other was planted against his chest.

A cool sensation traveled down his spine, like an icy surge of electricity, almost medicinal—which made his entire body itch and his teeth start to chatter.

"Dammit," Corinth muttered. "I can't portal us out of here. Where the hell are we?"

"*Taylor*," Alastair gasped, probably incoherently—he was still pretty messed up. Feverish and sick and changing. "*Larna. Where's Larna?*"

"She's—she's … I don't know. We were attacked by a bloody fast demon—" Corinth let out a yelp and jumped back as if he'd been bitten by a snake, wringing his hands in apparent pain. "*Ouch*," he muttered, frowning. "I … I don't think I can heal whatever it is going on inside you. Not here, anyway. I need the rest of the angels' help."

"What's wrong with him?" the other voice Alastair didn't recognize asked timidly.

Alastair felt something uncoil in his chest, and pain exploded in his head, increasing to an intolerable degree, like someone was stabbing him right behind his eyeballs. He let out a tormented howl, cradling his head in both his hands. *Larna.*

Dark. Malicious. Malevolent. *Give up.*

Corinth was by Alastair's side again, pressing a

clammy hand against his head, trying to pry his eyelids open. Someone else's cool hands were exploring his wounds. Gabriel's. Alastair could make out the jagged and raised scar on his left cheek.

"He's severely dehydrated. Ruined leg. Wrists and ankles mangled. And he's lost a fair amount of blood. Not to mention the … uh, transformation happening to him. Can you walk?" Gabriel asked him loudly, as if Alastair's ears had been damaged too. "I can get us out, but not from here. We'll have to get to one of three marked gateways."

Alastair had been attempting to leap off the table to go after Stanton, but his body would not obey his commands. His shattered knee buckled, and he collapsed to the ground like a sack of potatoes, screaming in agony and cradling his leg with his other hand. He'd never been in this type of agony before. His breath was coming out in shallow pants.

Above him, he could see everything in gory detail as he clung to consciousness. The leather restraints dangled over the table, smeared brown with his blood. His chest was covered in it. So were his feet and forearms. On the ground were pools of red. He rolled over, trying to stand up, but he found he couldn't even catch his breath. After a second, he steeled himself and tried again. Black splotches exploded across his vision, and he sagged back down, head drooping.

Corinth was at his side, trying to help him to his feet, a hand going under one arm, while Gabriel grabbed Alastair's other. He growled at him.

"Stop being so stubborn and let me help you," Gabriel snapped. "It's either that or stay on the floor."

Alastair didn't answer for a full minute.

Gabriel Stanton let out an exasperated sigh. "Seriously?"

"I'm thinking about it," Alastair managed to grumble, glancing dully around. When his eyes adjusted again, he focused on a familiar face. Corinth's little sister. She looked ashen in the darkness of this place.

Was he only imagining her standing there, staring at him with eyebrows drawn together in revulsion at his appearance? She moved up to him and then shirked out of her hoodie, ripped off one sleeve, and began to tear it into strips as Corinth and Stanton assisted Alastair off the ground, helping him back into a sitting position on the table. He pressed a flat palm against his chest, gasping.

"Corinth, why did you bring your little sister to a demon realm?" he said, his words almost running together.

"Well, I thought about taking her to Disneyland instead, but we both hate crowds," Corinth answered dryly, lifting his eyebrows in a mixture of concern and sarcasm.

Corinth approached Alastair, a hand held out toward him. He knew the Nephilim was going to try and attempt to heal him again. Before Corinth could touch him, Alastair knocked his outstretched hand away. "You can't, Corinth. It's a trap. The demon, Ephrem, he *wants* you to try and heal me."

"He looks pretty bad. Those cuts on his wrists are deep," Zoey interjected, and then she swallowed heavily as she reached out to Alastair. "Is it okay if I …?" She held the remains of her hoodie up to show him she only wanted to help.

He nodded his consent as she delicately took his wrist in her hand and began wrapping it with the cloth from her torn hoodie.

Alastair winced but remained still and silent as she worked. "Do we have anything to brace my leg?" he breathed through clenched teeth. "I think I can walk if I can get it braced."

Another person, only a kid, came up to stand beside Zoey and began to help with Alastair's left wrist.

He studied the kid a moment as he said, "Is this a school field trip or something?"

The boy was a bit taller than Zoey, probably around the same age, with russet hair and smooth caramel skin. He was clutching something in his other hand. It glittered like a jewel.

Corinth eyed the object in the boy's hand. "The shield. It's forged from part of my blade—it was designed to keep you safe, Zo. Fat lot of good it did though." Corinth swore under his breath and put his free hand on his head, the one not holding his blade. "Larna, hopefully, is back at the safe house in Scotland—along with everyone else. *Pete.* Dammit, Al, this is bad. Very bad. We were attacked by Trevor Malcolm. ... Ephrem, whatever ... I have to deal with that jagweed, and I'd rather it be sooner than later."

"*Trevor?*" Alastair hissed out between clenched teeth. "As in *Zoey's* friend Trevor? Her high school classmate?"

Zoey's cheeks flushed at hearing that, and she glanced away. "I didn't know he was a demon when I friended him ..."

"Oh, come on Zo, I'm not all that bad."

That voice was as cold as the dead of winter.

Everyone froze.

Alastair's eyes zipped to the shadowy alcove across the way, to the sound of the voice he would not, or could not, forget soon enough. The bastard had hurt his family. Destroyed his wedding ring. Attacked Corinth. Ephrem was standing there, looking bored—oh, and he had all of his horde of Shades with him.

"*Oh no!*" Cruz cried, pointing frantically behind them. "The demon, guys! Trevor … or Ephrem … He's back. He's here!"

Gabriel raised an eyebrow in irritation. "Yeah, not really necessary to point that out, kid."

Corinth whirled around and, in one fluid movement, threw his blade out in front of him, letting loose a concussive bolt of lightning. Thunder accompanied the dazzling blaze, sending a shock wave through the cavernous space, the ground quaking beneath them.

Ephrem withdrew a step, not looking bored anymore, as one of the Shades stepped into the line of Corinth's attack. The bolt plunged right through the thing's chest, center of mass, and it evaporated into a black mist.

The other Shades had already started ducking and dodging out of the way. Some were gathering in front of Ephrem like a shield, protecting their master.

Alastair started to leap off the table, to go after him—

But Ephrem flicked a hand out toward Alastair, and yelled, "*STAY!*"

Alastair gasped, placing his sweaty palms against his thighs, suddenly feeling dizzy. It felt like his rib cage was collapsing inside his chest. His heart was galloping like a race horse, and it was as if someone were squeezing his insides to mush.

He fell backward onto the table, his eyes clouding over for a second, his world whittling down to only a tiny pinprick of light.

Alastair shook his head, clearing his vision, as he stared dazedly up at the macabre ceiling in anguish. Vaguely he was aware of Corinth slashing at the air with his blade in broad strokes, using his dagger like a paintbrush instead of a thousand-year-old deadly weapon.

The iridescent light quickly spread out and stitched itself together, forming a protective dome over their heads and then pouring down around them, closing their group off from the rest of the demon horde in just a matter of seconds. Corinth controlled time. Alastair had not forgotten the fact that angels could control small periods of it—slow it down and speed it back up.

He wondered if demons could do the same thing. Seeing Corinth use his angelic abilities in such a display of power—the tableau he created—never ceased to amaze him.

Zoey gasped and staggered back a step, a hand shielding her face as she watched her brother work. "That ... that ... it's ... *amazing*. What in the world *is* that?"

"Alastair is one of mine now," Trevor said nonchalantly. "You're trapped, Cory. It's too late. You can't help him. You see how he obeys me already?"

Ephrem stood inches from the barrier Corinth had

erected. The shimmering wall of light made his head look strange and oddly too big for his shoulders. Ephrem's hands were crossed over his chest, and he was regarding them with what looked like all the infinite patience in the world.

Alastair had somewhat recovered, and as he sat up, he cradled a hand against his stomach.

Ephrem's robe was gone. He wasn't worried about hiding his face now. Anger sizzled under the surface as he studied the monster standing in front of him. Even though he looked strangely distorted through the shimmering light raining down around them, Alastair could still make out the demon's face in surprising detail. He had, of course, seen him before, at Corinth's parent's place.

A muscle feathered along Alastair's jawline at seeing him, appearing as if only a teenage kid but staring at him like a wolf ogling its prey. He looked to be only fifteen or sixteen at the most. And Ephrem wore glasses, had on an unbuttoned light-blue shirt with a white tee underneath, and black joggers and white sneakers. Joggers kind of like the ones Alastair wore.

He was going to kill the bloody demon.

Ephrem put his hands in his pockets and inched even closer to the iridescent wall, his eyes glittering behind the lenses of his glasses as they traveled up and down Corinth.

Alastair had met Trevor last year. The demon had been hanging around Corinth's family for an entire *year*, and somehow they hadn't detected who or what he was. Of course, none of them had been around much. He cursed himself for not visiting more. With Trevor's trim build, pale skin, and dark hair, Alastair thought he looked like a cross between a geek and a jock—he wore both hats well, and maybe that was the point. To fit in with any crowd.

"Don't worry. He can't get in here," Corinth hastily reassured everyone.

Alastair knew Corinth. He knew no one else could detect the hint of concern in Corinth's voice but him.

"Oh, I don't need to get in there," Ephrem said coolly. "Why should I waste my resources and energy trying to break down your little angel barrier when Alastair will do it for me? He'll soon be one of my Shades. Can't you see the change in him, *Cory?*" The demon gestured at Alastair's bare chest, at the mottled, inkblot skin at his side. "The darkness inside him will overtake him soon. And once he's mine, he'll do anything I command of him."

To prove his point, Ephrem snapped his fingers, and one of the infected moved up to stand beside him. The one who called itself Gray, Alastair recalled. The one with the whip. Its skin was coated in thick black ink, and the veins in its neck were silver.

Ephrem pointed at another one of his Shades that had filed up to stand beside them. "Gray, take this one's heart."

Did it used to be a human? Alastair was pretty sure it was male. Had it been someone's friend, son, father? He shuddered, thinking about turning into one of those things. No. Never. He'd make them kill him first.

Gray put its fist straight into the other Shade's chest cavity in a flicker of motion, barely perceptible to the human eye.

There was a sickening sucking sound as Gray gave a horrendous cry and then viciously yanked its hand back out, clutching a still-beating black mass in between its fingers. Alastair thought it looked more like oily sludge than a heart. He felt revolted. That was what his own insides would look like soon enough.

Is that so bad? The voice was back inside his mind: *Succumb. Give up. You are mine now.*

Alastair gasped and doubled over, clutching his side as another wave of pain washed over him.

The minion flopped to the ground without even putting up a fight or uttering a sound. Gray opened its hand and released the organ. It hit the ground with a wet thunk, and then the Shade stomped on it, reducing it to dust and ash under its foot.

"See … I will command Alastair to do the same thing to your little sister, Cory," Ephrem hissed. "I will take out your entire family—*one by one*."

Corinth stood back to his full height, squaring his shoulders, a pattern of cobalt light tracing a path up and down his forearms, igniting his veins. "Well, now I know how to kill those shadow things," he snarled. "That's it. I'm going out there." Corinth stalked toward the barrier wall, but before he could get there, Gabriel Stanton grabbed his arm and lugged him back.

Corinth slowly glanced down at Gabriel's fingers wrapped around his forearm, staring daggers at Stanton for touching him.

"We kind of need you in *here*," Stanton growled, trying to appeal to Corinth's better sense at the same time as he let go of his arm.

Corinth let out a loud growl and snarled, "If my sister and her friend weren't in here with me, I would lay waste to you right now, *Trevor*. I'm sure Gabe has told you what I did to Angela. I'm sure he's told you a lot of things."

The demon gave Corinth a terribly cold smile. "He told me everything." His eyes shifted back down to the prone form—the dead Shade.

Gabriel Stanton gave Corinth a tiny shrug that said, "Did you expect anything else?"

Was that a twitch? In the hand. There. Alastair saw it again. First a finger tic, and then the thing on the ground shuddered, and he heard an exhalation of air leave its lungs.

Did it still have working lungs?

Then suddenly the thing jerked upright and juddered, and stood awkwardly back to its feet, all jagged angles and bones, its body disproportionate and ugly, slick, bald head. *Undead.* This one was wearing dingy jeans with holes in the knees, but no shirt. Alastair swallowed past a dry throat and started to shiver, feeling worse and worse by the second. His fever was back. Zombies. He was going to turn into a zombie.

That was why Ephrem didn't care about wrecking Alastair's body. He wouldn't need it to function like a human's. He'd just keep coming back, over and over again. His breath left him in a rush. *He wants to know if this will happen to Corinth.* Alastair shivered at the thought of Corinth wielding all that power for Ephrem. He wouldn't let that happen.

"*Zombies?*" Cruz barked out, staggering back and slipping on his untied shoelace. "What more? I really, really want to go home now. I am regretting all of my life choices … This can't be happening …"

Stanton must have noticed Alastair shivering, because he shrugged out of his coat and held it out to him. "This is a four-thousand-dollar coat. Don't bleed on it."

Alastair considered freezing to death instead, but he was just so bone-chillingly *cold*. Like hypothermic cold. And then he thought of getting back home to Larna, and so he finally relented, snatching it from Gabriel without a word and shrugging into it, secretly hoping he would get blood all over it and ruin it.

Ephrem's dark eyes glittered behind his glasses as they flickered over Corinth.

He laughed and shook his head. "Why do you think I chose to infect your mother first? Of course, it turned out to be Peter instead," he said offhandedly before continuing. "Abduct Alastair. Date your sister. Lounge at your wretched house for a year."

"What do you mean, it turned out to be Peter instead?" Corinth asked slowly, stepping threateningly up to the boundary of the force field.

Zoey's face turned a shade paler. "Did he say he infected Pete?" She had her fists held down by her sides, clenched tight. "Corinth is so going to kick your ass. Right?" she murmured, glancing back at her older brother. "You *are* going to kick his ass?"

Corinth's fingers, clutching the hilt of the blade, began to crackle and sizzle with energy, the telltale sign of an angel about to use their almighty gifts. "Yes, Zo, I'm going to kick his ass."

Alastair started to feel his damp hair lift from his forehead.

"*Ho-ly crap*," Cruz breathed at the sight.

It made Corinth look like he belonged deep underneath the sea rather than on land. For the first time, Alastair noticed Corinth was wearing lightweight gold mesh armor over his shirt. A new addition. He was, of course, also wearing the holster designed specifically for his blade—made from the tip of the Spear of Destiny. The black vinyl sheath was strapped to his belt and fastened around his leg midthigh.

And then more of the demon's army lined up to stand in front of them. A lot. They filled the large cavern.

"It's tough to kill one of your own, *Cory*, especially a brother," Ephrem said. "You deserve no less for halting my plans. For getting rid of the age of vampires. For destroying someone I cared about. Now it's your turn to feel that kind of gut-wrenching pain."

17

ZOEY

*I*t's tough to kill one of your own, Cory, especially a *brother. You deserve no less for halting my plans. For getting rid of the age of vampires. For killing someone I cared about. Now it's your turn to feel that gut-wrenching pain.*

Those words kept spinning around in my head.

My world was spinning too.

A flash of ginger hair and white fangs popped into my vision again. Then Gabriel Stanton's obsidian-colored eyes. Bottomless pits. Vampire eyes I'd seen before. I wanted to question him about everything. My past. My disappearance. But I couldn't find the energy to do it.

My stomach churned at the thought of losing Peter. I tried to steady myself, still traumatized by watching Trevor impale Larna and throw her across my living room like she was a wadded-up piece of paper. And also from seeing Alastair's gruesome wounds. And then there was the ceiling of death hanging above our heads. A constant reminder of how truly evil this place was. Then the army of shadow people … I could have kept going.

Who is Corinth Taylor? Not my brother. So far, I'd learned he was an angel—he had lightning at his beck and call; he could transport himself and other people to who knew where with just a mere thought. Heal people? Vampires existed, and so did angels and demons … *Heaven and hell.*

Out of nowhere, I caved, my legs going out from under me. Fortunately, Cruz was there before I could hit the stone floor and crack my skull wide open.

He put a steadying hand around my shoulder, and we both slid to the ground in a heap, his arms surprisingly warm and gentle. Heat rushed through my face at being so close to him. He smelled like cedar and citrus and warm leaves in autumn, and his chocolate eyes were just as warm.

Cruz cleared his throat; his cheeks had a hint of red in them too. "Are you okay?"

Corinth was kneeling in front of me before I could answer, his eyes full of worry and concern. He held a hand out, but I flinched away from his touch, putting my back up against one of the legs of the table Alastair was still perched on top of.

My brother scared me, but Trevor frightened me more.

Peter was probably turning into one of those nightmarish creatures right this very second—*This is Corinth's fault.* My stomach clenched, and I felt the overwhelming urge to throw up. Like, everywhere,

Exorcist style. It was all too much. *Pete.*

I shook my head and glanced up at him. "*Cor.*" His name was a plea on my lips. "Are we going to die?"

My watery eyes flickered to Trevor, who was still gazing at me from the other side of the oddly glowing barrier. He hadn't said anything else since he'd taunted Corinth, only watched us with a hawklike gaze and a predatory sneer on his face, biding his time until Alastair changed into one of those things. Shades. That's what he'd called them.

Speaking of, his dark army hadn't moved. They all had blank faces and oil-slick skin, black ichor—unnatural—watching and waiting.

Corinth had his fingers curled around the handle of his dagger in one hand, and with the other, he reached out to touch me, but then he must have thought better of it, because he pulled his hand back. "Not—on—my—watch." He enunciated each word, to make sure I knew how serious he was.

Alastair was looking more like one of those Shade things by the minute. His skin was a bluish gray; his blond hair was matted to his forehead. The fancy-looking coat that had once been Gabriel Stanton's was partially open, revealing his bare chest. Don't get me wrong—he was still in tip-top shape, with chiseled abs, which I kept sneaking glances at, but his torso was covered in zigzagging black lines that looked like raised scars underneath his skin. He had an arm cradled against his flat stomach. Red had started to seep through the strips of material at his wrists, and his knee, I could see through a tear in his athletic pants, looked … ruined.

I was pretty sure Trevor couldn't hear us from where he stood, but he waved at me as if he'd heard what I'd just said. I had no idea if demons had superhearing.

"Cor … just tell me something … *anything*," I begged him.

Alastair spoke up before Corinth could. "She has the right to know, Corinth," he pressed gently. Then he let out a long, pained sigh before saying, "And unless you can tell me you have a plan to get us all out of here soon, you do realize you will have to kill me, right?"

"No way on earth, Al. I … I *do* … have a plan. I plan on singing Kumbaya until they all go away because of my horrid yowling," Corinth half snarled, half whispered sarcastically.

Alastair rolled his eyes. "We aren't on earth. Look, you've given me ten years. *Ten* wonderful years with the woman I love. A normal life I thought I'd never have. I'm thankful for that—"

"*No*," Corinth snarled through clenched teeth, cutting him off. "Al … just stop it. So help me … I am tired of your fatalistic attitude. You do not get to give up on me." He pursed his lips and looked up at the shimmering light raining over our heads, a wounded expression on his face. "Do you think so little of my abilities that I can't figure out a plan to fix this? I just need some time to think. Give me a minute, Al."

Alastair's head drooped so low that his chin touched his chest. "I'm not asking you to be the one to do it, Taylor." He glanced up, and his glassy eyes slid slowly to Gabriel Stanton, who was studying the device in his hands not too far away. "I'm asking Stanton to do it. Maybe you

can bring me back from the dead, like you did before …
after …"

Gabriel Stanton turned back to regard Alastair, his face a blank mask, and for the longest time, no one said anything. He just stared at Alastair.

I wondered what their history was. *Rocky at best*, I thought.

I wanted to ask twenty thousand questions, but I sensed this was not the time, and my brain was too jumbled to form coherent thoughts, anyway.

Cruz was on the other side of me, squeezing my hand as hard as he could, staring at Trevor. "I can totally believe that guy is a *demon* … but tracking your family down, enrolling himself at your school, making friends with you—all of it to keep tabs on you … well, that's all next-level messed up and insane," he said, shaking his head. "*Weirdo.*"

My eyes drifted back to Trevor, standing there with an imperious smirk, staring at me, and I shivered. "Yeah, he is."

A shadow crossed Gabriel Stanton's features as he moved closer to Alastair, bringing me out of my reverie, and my attention back to Alastair's worsening condition.

When Stanton was standing directly in front of Alastair, he said, "If you had asked me to kill you ten years ago, I would have done it without batting an eye." He pulled at the end of his fancy shirt-sleeve, tugging it down. "Believe it or not, I don't want you dead any more than Mr. Taylor does. But make no mistake, Iszler—if it comes down to it, it'll be my life I choose first."

Alastair seemed at a loss for words. He closed his eyes

and slumped back down, a hand splayed out on his abdomen, looking spent.

I pulled my hand out of Cruz's and stood up as Corinth started pacing within the confines of the dome, his face pinched and strained. When he saw me approach, he stopped and blew out a deep breath.

"The vision I keep having—of red hair and fangs." I whispered so that, hopefully, no one else could hear us. "That happened, didn't it? It was a vampire who abducted me? Vampires *exist*? And Gabriel Stanton is one of them? Who was the vampire with the red hair?"

He studied me with those big, wide amber eyes of his and, as if finally deciding something, said, "I didn't know you remembered any of it. You never said anything ... all this time. I just thought you were having nightmares ... and that it was a phase you'd grow out of ..." He hung his head as if something was weighing on him. "Yes, it happened when you were five. Gabriel Stanton ordered his people to kidnap you to get at me. The one with the red hair was working for him. Stanton *used* to be a vampire. And at one point in time, so did Larna, Al, and I. But not anymore."

"What?" I breathed. "Why would he do that?" My eyes flitted to Gabriel Stanton. "Abduct me."

"Gabriel Stanton is a douche," he said in answer. "And he's very good at manipulation."

"You used to be a *vampire*—?"

"Ascended being," Gabriel interrupted.

Cruz finally shot to his feet, his face waxy. "Are you guys kidding me? Seriously?" He looked around at each of us in turn, purple lips pressed into two thin lines before he said, "Vampires? Angels? Demons? Who the hell are you people?"

Corinth threw him a look and rubbed a hand across his own mouth. "Ten years ago Gabriel Stanton kidnapped you, Zo. To get me to work for him. To use me for my powers. I got you back, but not before Stanton used vampire compulsion to make you forget what he'd done to you—so you wouldn't remember what had happened."

Everything was starting to click into place. I rubbed at my chilled arms. I'd had to rip my hoodie to patch up Alastair, and the cold was starting to creep in. I started to shiver as I glanced at Gabriel Stanton. A vampire. I was pretty sure he was *still* a vampire. He was staring at me again with those deeply set dark eyes. Oddly enough though, I was glad to know. I finally had answers to my burning questions, and I wasn't crazy. I wasn't imagining it all.

I wanted to ask him how he managed to get me back from Stanton, but instead, my gaze lit on Gabriel, and I said, "So, then, why aren't you one now? An ascended being or whatever?"

"Ask your brother that question," he spit out. "It's his fault."

I turned back to study Corinth, noticing the animosity growing between all three of them again. "Can you really bring people back f-f-from the dead?"

"No," Corinth said firmly. "Not even full-blooded angels can do that."

"Full-blooded?" I asked. "You're Nephilim. Half human, half angel, right? What about those other really tall people who came and took Peter and Jimmy and Mom and Dad away?"

"Those are full-blooded angels. My friends. They will do everything they can to help them."

"Why can't they help us now?" I asked slowly.

Corinth sighed. "There's something blocking me from communicating with them. I can't portal out of here." His fingers crackled with a spark of electrical energy as he added, "But it appears I can still portal *within* this realm, which might prove useful."

"How were you able to bring Alastair back from the dead?"

"It's a long story." Corinth placed his weapon next to his leg as he slumped down on the floor, seemingly thinking.

After a second, he put his head between his hands, and then I joined him, crossing my legs underneath me. The floor was ice-cold even through my jeans.

"Vampires were created by a group of rogue fallen angels calling themselves the Grigori. For future reference, the Grigori are bad. The Watchers, my angel friends, are another faction of angels who came here, to earth, to stop them—they're good. Still with me?" he asked.

I raised my eyebrows but only nodded, barely following along. The Fallen. Grigori. I'd seen those names before, in biblical texts. I'd heard of the Watchers too. What did I remember about them from Bible study? A group of angels cast out of heaven because they'd sinned. That was all I remembered. Not much. Suddenly I wanted to know everything about them, now that I knew they existed.

"I ended the reign of vampires ten years ago. Angela, their leader—she's überbad—used her blood and demon blood—probably Trevor's—to create vampirism, to serve as a plague to all humankind, in order to control the world. Al used to be one of those creations: vampire."

My eyes moved up to Alastair's blood-stained chest again on impulse. "Angels created vampirism?" I was so lost. Whatever was happening to him sure looked like a plague to me now. I wondered if we'd been infected too, just by being in close proximity to him. Something told me no—it had everything to do with that glass shard Trevor had flicked at my mom.

Vampires actually existed?

I felt the truth of this deep in my bones. Somehow it made sense. My heart thudded loudly in my ears, and I opened my mouth to ask Cor a billion more questions, but he held up a finger to stop me.

"I got hurt … badly, and vampire Al stepped in to save me, but in order to do that, he had to drink some of my blood—angelic blood—which was, at the time, extremely toxic to vampires. Gabriel—" Corinth's eyes flickered to the tall stranger, who appeared to be listening intently to what Corinth had to say. "Al died …" He cleared his throat. "And Gabe finished the job he had started. Because Al still had my blood in his system, my biological father, an angel, who you know as Dave Lancaster—he was a Watcher—helped me bring him back."

"Those angels, back at the house, your friends, the ones with armor and the very large swords, they are these Watchers? Your *father* … he is one of them?" I picked at a fingernail, refusing to look at him. "So Leo … was never my half brother. *You* are? Mom did cheat on Dad?"

Corinth wrapped his hands around my interlaced fingers. "Dave *used* to be my biological father. Not anymore. He's gone. And no, she did not cheat on Dad."

I didn't jerk away this time. After a moment, I finally risked a glance back up at him. His gaze was intense, and his chestnut eyes glowed like lanterns. I felt horrible learning that his biological dad was gone. I wondered how he felt about all of this.

"Leo *is* my brother," he emphasized. "*I* am your brother. Al *is* my brother. Larna *is* my sister. Always and forever. Blood isn't the only thing that makes up a family. It's everything else. The in-between. The support. The concern. We take care of each other, right?"

A single tear slid out of my eye, and then more started escaping after that. I wiped at them, feeling tired and drained as I nodded. "Then why didn't you tell me any of this? You didn't take care of me. Why keep it a secret for so long? Mom and Dad—do they know? Do Pete and Jimmy know about all this?"

Corinth bit his lip. "They all know. Everyone except you."

I sucked in a shocked breath, and my chest constricted with the pain of betrayal. "Why not *tell* me?"

"It was my choice, Zo. I wanted to give you a chance at a normal life before I sprang all of this crazy on you—"

"*Normal?*" I scoffed. "Look around. You're way too late to prevent anything bad from happening to me now."

"She's right," Trevor pointed out again, smiling coldly back at us from the other side of the electrified barrier. "She is dead."

Fear clawed its way up my throat at hearing that.

"*I could say the same thing about you, demon,*" Corinth snarled at Trevor before turning back to me, his fists balled at his sides. "When Peter and Jimmy turned eighteen, I told them what I just told you. I was planning on telling you the minute you turned eighteen, because all this weirdness started when I turned eighteen, and I was grateful to have been given the gift of normalcy before my life changed—to *this* freak show. You were always so involved with school. I didn't want to ruin that." He opened his palm, and sparks shot out of it, and then a ball of energized light began forming, and his blade magically materialized in his grip, ringing sharp and clear as the magic faded.

He held the dagger out for me to see. I could feel the thrum of its power just by being in close proximity to him. It felt like standing too close to a downed power line. The electricity hummed through my veins, biting. I shivered at feeling its power.

It could have been any ordinary blade with a worn bronze hilt. No inscriptions or markings on it. From tip to handle, I guessed it was about twelve inches long. There was a round bronze pommel at the end and a leather grip with a metal guard.

"My biological father, Danel, worked extremely hard at suppressing my gifts for my entire life—that is, until I took possession of this blade." He held it up, and silvery-blue sparks flew off the edge of it, and I jumped back with a yelp in surprise.

"So what's so special about it?" I asked cautiously.

Maybe I didn't want to know.

He blew out a deep breath, his gaze darting to Trevor's briefly, probably unsure about what he wanted to share publicly, since apparently the demon could hear us. "It's made from the tip of the Spear of Destiny. The Holy Lance."

I heard the words come out of his mouth, but for some strange reason, I just couldn't process them or put them together. *Spear—of—Destiny. The—Holy—Lance.* My heart leaped in my chest, and my pulse slammed behind my eyeballs. God. Angels. Demons. Vampires. Hell. What else was out there, waiting in the shadows?

The Devil.

Trevor was still watching us, his weird Shade army all around him—

Alastair cried out.

He was breathing rapidly, a flat hand pressed to his bare chest. The infection was spreading. The black lines snaking toward his heart looked angrier—more prominent—now. We didn't have much time, and I was wasting it by asking questions, but I couldn't help it. I had to know everything.

Cruz eyed Corinth warily. He'd been so quiet up until now, and I'd almost forgotten he was even there. He stepped closer to Corinth and uncurled his fingers around the object he was holding. In his open palm sat the still-glowing shield talisman. "This is part of the Spear of Destiny?"

Corinth raised an eyebrow at him and nodded. "It is. I had to make sure Zoey was protected. Obviously, it doesn't ferret out demons ..."

"My mother"—Cruz cast his gaze down and his voice broke—"used to be very sick. As soon as I took this home, she somehow made a miraculous recovery. This thing … it … it can *heal* people too?"

"It … sort of has a mind of its own." Corinth shrugged as if that was all there was to it—no more explanation needed. "It brought me back from the dead. So, yeah, probably."

I gasped at hearing that, my eyes going wide, reeling. Dead. My brother had died. "*What?*" I screeched.

Corinth threw his head back and closed his eyes briefly, as if he'd just admitted something he shouldn't have. "Don't tell Mom and Dad that part, okay?" he said with a grimace. "No one else knows about me dying."

"Can it heal your friend?" Cruz pointed at Alastair, looking shaken.

Corinth shook his head. "No. There's a dark energy trapped inside him. I can feel it, but I just can't get to it. It … it feels wrong. Sinister." His concerned gaze locked on Alastair once again.

Gabriel Stanton moved up to watch Cruz with interest now, a hand under his chin.

"This shield has been glowing in my hand for some time now," Cruz said. "I can feel this strange energy coming off it. Like the whir of gears … It feels … soothing, protective somehow. Do you want it back? Would it help?"

"You should keep it," Corinth told him.

Cruz's caramel-colored eyes widened in surprise. "Really?"

"It wouldn't be glowing like that for just anyone—"

A shrill laugh rang out, interrupting Corinth, and a tremor went through me. I looked up to see Trevor, his head cocked to the side, studying us with a strange sort of glint in his eyes.

He pointed at Alastair and flung his hand out, balling it into a fist and squeezing. "I'm bored."

We all turned our heads at the same time to see Alastair flop onto his back on the table, his arms splayed out by his sides. A stricken look crossed his handsome features, and he cried out in agony as my horrified gaze swept back over to Trevor.

I didn't know what he was doing to Alastair, but whatever it was, I knew it was killing him.

"Stop it!" I shouted.

Corinth bolted to his feet beside Alastair as his body went rigid all over and he thrashed out again, his back bowing in such a way that made me think his spine might snap in half. His coat fell open, and I could now see the amount of sweat glistening on his entire midsection. His eyes, once the color of the ocean, were now coal black—as vast and dark as black holes.

Oh no. Alastair.

My heart wrenched.

"*Cor!*" I cried at the same time as his hands ignited with a divine white light. It looked like a thousand tiny electrodes fizzling across his skin, arcing across his armor, blazing. Flames erupted along the blade's razor-thin edge in his hand, and my mouth fell open at the same time as Cruz floundered back a step.

Gabriel Stanton was beside me, gripping my elbow and dragging me away from the table. "Stand back," he said, "and brace yourselves."

Corinth clapped his hands together, gritting his teeth in resolve. And then he laid those glowing hands, and also his blade, against Alastair's chest and breathed, "Hang in there, Al. I'm going to fix this right now—whatever it takes."

18

LEO

Corinth, Zoey, Cruz, the demon, and Gabriel Stanton were all gone.

The house reeked of ozone, iron, and rotten eggs; wisps of black smoke still curled in the air from the aftermath. Leo had come back as soon as possible after dropping off the rest of the Taylor family and Larna—who, though badly injured, had been healed at the safe house. The other angels had things in hand, at least until he could get back to them.

But it looked like he was too late to be of any help to Corinth.

No one was here.

Leo's sense of dread bloomed in his stomach, deepening.

He couldn't contact his brother. Their angel communication had been completely cut off. He could no longer feel their connection. This was what worried him most. He'd never lost contact with Corinth like this before. He tried to tamp down that nagging voice in his head that told him Corinth was dead.

The demon they'd encountered was *incredibly* powerful. Leo had never seen anything like it—even stronger than him, and that was saying something. Demons weren't supposed to be stronger than angels. But this one was. Trevor was something … different. Something more. Somehow Trevor had blocked Leo's ability to control objects midflight—beaten him at his own game. He ground his teeth together. *How?*

Bloody demons. There hadn't been an outbreak of them in ages. Of course, the angels had been preoccupied with an internal war between the Grigori and the Watchers for *most* of that time …

And the one who had dealt all this havoc, Trevor, was going to be eliminated by his hand if it was the last thing he did. They'd messed with his family. The Taylors had taken Leo in without question. Treated him like one of their own.

His family.

There were a multitude of demons out there, of course, but he'd never heard of or seen this one before. Ever since they'd almost gotten rid of all Grigori—there were a few out there still causing trouble—most demons had remained relatively quiet. And now he knew why: they'd been intentionally staying out of the spotlight, waiting to make their move.

Trevor had said he needed the device back from Gabriel Stanton. Maybe this device had transported them somewhere—not on this plane of existence. His guess was to wherever they were holding Alastair—that was what Stanton had been trying to tell them. The demon had Alastair Iszler. They needed him for a purpose. But for what? If Gabriel was involved, it had to have something to do with him trying to become vampire again.

Suddenly there came a noise in the dining room. Leo's hands were arcing with portentous energy, aimed in that direction, but he stopped his assault as soon as he saw what had made the noise.

The cat. Biscuit.

He was lapping up gravy out of one of the overturned dishes on the table. Leo could see a spot of bright red on one of his paws.

He approached Biscuit slowly, a hand held out in his careful approach so as not to spook him. Biscuit glanced up at Leo for a brief moment but then went back to eating, ignoring him. When Leo was close enough, he gently reached out to scratch Biscuit behind an ear. The cat swished his tail and then meowed.

Gently lifting the feline's paw, Leo inspected the wound. The cut was pretty deep. "I'm sorry you got hurt protecting our family," Leo said softly. "The least I can do is protect you too." His hand, still on the cat's head, lit up in a wash of glorious golden light. He could feel Biscuit's rapidly beating heart, feel the warm blood pumping through his veins, even sense the sting of the cut in his own hand. The connection was palpable. He closed his eyes, sending a healing warmth rushing through the cat.

Biscuit purred affectionately as Leo started repairing the skin around the wound and then, ever so slowly, pulled it closed, like psychic stitches.

A second later, Biscuit was licking Leo's hand, his paw completely healed, like it had never happened. The pain vanished from his hand too—

Leo!

The voice that cut into his thoughts was loud and filled with concern. Ikari.

What is it? he asked quickly, responding by using their angel link. He could feel Ikari's worry through their connection, and he didn't like it. Angels could access thoughts and memories, and communicate with each other telepathically. A gift that came in handy—unless you had been spirited away by Gabriel Stanton, apparently.

Come back. We need you now. Hurry.

Leo scooped Biscuit up into his arms and called up a portal, quickly vanishing in a vortex of wind and thunder and lightning.

Leo popped into their farmstead—right amid pandemonium. The minute he set Biscuit down, he was bombarded by Larna and Ikari, both of them vying for his attention.

"Were they there?" Larna asked breathlessly. "Did you find them?"

Leo shook his head as Ikari said, "This way." He led Leo straight back through the entryway toward the rear of the house, heading for the stairs that led to the second floor.

Leo turned to Larna. "Feeling better?"

She nodded, the corners of her mouth hardening somewhat, and he could hear the tension in her voice as soon as she spoke. "But I'm more worried about Peter." She ran a hand through her hair. "I'm a doctor, Leo, and I can't do anything to help him. Nothing. This is beyond Western medicine. You have to help him."

There was a flurry of activity coming from one of the upstairs spare bedrooms. He crossed the threshold right behind Ikari and sucked in a sharp breath as soon as he saw Peter. He'd gotten worse. The boy lay sprawled out across a twin-size bed. Afternoon sunlight spilled in from one of the large oval windows facing west. The soft rays washed his face in a pinkish-golden glow.

Right outside sat a stone cottage, and then beyond that, nothing but open green farmland, rolling hills, and kilometers of drystone walls. Sheep and cattle grazed the countryside. Little tufts of white and black dotted the hillsides. They'd chosen this spot in Scotland for a reason. For the most part, their neighbors left them alone. Something the Watchers had been lacking for a very long time.

Out there, it was quiet and serene. Inside the farmhouse, it was a completely different story.

Peter let out a strangled cry right as Ikari ushered Leo inside.

The room was crowded.

Peter's mother, Susan, was sitting in a chair beside his bed, clutching one of his limp hands in hers. Tears were streaming down her face. At the foot of the bed stood Peter's father, Zeke. His younger brother Jimmy was facing the window, the profile of his face looked strained.

He raked a hand through his golden locks. The gesture was so like Corinth's signature move that it sent a shock wave of anguish coursing through him. His chest tightened.

Jimmy turned to Leo and said, "Did you find Zo? Cor?"

Leo bit his bottom lip and shook his head. "Not yet. But I'm working on it."

Samyaza and Tamiel were beside the bed, kneeling on either side of him, their blazing palms flush against his chest. Peter's curly sandy-blond hair was matted to his forehead. His eyes were closed and his mouth was parted.

He was taking in slow, shallow breaths. His last breaths.

Leo glanced around the small bedroom at all the worried faces. "Larna … can you clear everyone out? We need more space to work."

Larna gave a curt nod and gently laid a hand on Jimmy's back. "Jimmy, why don't we get some hot tea? Let them work." She gave Susan a nod and then Zeke. "Please?"

Reluctantly Susan released her son's hand, and then she stood shakily to her feet. Larna moved to place a supportive hand on Mrs. Taylor's arm as she led them all out.

Zeke stopped in front of Leo before leaving and said, "Fix him." It was not a plea; it was an order.

"We will do everything in our power, Mr. Taylor," Leo said with calm assertiveness.

They filed out of the room and let the angels do their work.

As soon as they were gone, and the door was closed,

Leo rushed to the bed, kneeling beside Samyaza. His dark eyes snagged on Leo briefly. "The shard the demon used against Peter wasn't of this world. It is of hell." Samyaza's voice caught, and he looked across the bed at Ikari, whose eyes were closed. "Ikari was able to link with Peter telepathically for only a moment. Peter is changing. Evolving into something evil. We tried to slow down the process, but it only seemed to speed it up."

Tamiel lifted Peter's shirt to reveal oily black patches all over his skin, and squiggly lines near his heart. "Here." She pointed at his chest, where the infection seemed to have started. "This is where the shard went in. The infection has spread out in a branch-like pattern, inching up toward his heart." Tamiel's voice was deep and rich with her accent. "We tried to extract the poison as soon as we got back … but then Samyaza quickly discovered that if we did that, one of us would be exposed to the same type of infection. We suspect this was the demon's plan all along: to bait Corinth into healing his mother, which is who this was originally intended for." She gestured to Peter's chest. "Whatever it is he's turning into, it's evil."

Ikari's eyes popped open, and he let out a gasp, falling backward onto his rump. He swiped a hand across his sweaty brow. "I … I … can't … It's not working. It's bad, Leo. Real bad."

"What if we work together?" Leo suggested. He put a glowing hand against his brother's chest. The result was immediate. Ice spread like wildfire through his veins, heading to his extremities. His breath plumed out in front of him in a puff of white. His vision went out of focus for a moment.

The icy sensation was all over, making his insides feel bitterly cold, and he sucked in a shocked breath, pulling his hand back. It felt fifty times worse than ice burn. Angels knew cold.

His entire body was shaking—and that was just a few seconds of exposure. It wasn't just cold; it was foul. There was a dark presence inside Peter, waiting to take over. "What if we try and heat his body up, to counteract the cold?"

Ikari snapped his fingers, and a blanket appeared magically in his hands. "It's electric." He plugged it into a socket at the footboard and hastily threw it over Peter.

Leo looked over at Ikari and pulled a face at him. "Really? An electric blanket?"

"I welcome any and all better ideas," he growled.

Leo didn't have any.

So they all went to work, covering his body with blankets, trying to warm him up, and then their hands glowed golden again as they bent over Peter's body.

Maybe they could buy some time until Corinth got back. He had the Spear of Destiny. That blade was powerful. If anyone could heal his brother, it would be him. They just had to hold out a little while longer …

19

CRUZ

Things had gone from bad to worse. Zoey's brother was huddled over Alastair, his hands awash in silvery-white light, exactly what Cruz thought a halo might look like in real life. Corinth had sweat on his brow, and his eyes were closed in concentration.

Cruz had backed up so far away from them that he hadn't even realized Trevor—the demon—was right behind him, standing just on the other side of the faintly shimmering blue wall. The only thing protecting them from his massive demon horde. And it kept flickering like an old lightbulb about to go out.

Which Cruz knew wasn't good.

"I imagine it's terrifying, knowing you don't have much time left to live."

Cruz spun around to see Trevor eyeing him up and down, a Cheshire Cat grin plastered across his face. Cruz licked his dry lips and lifted his shield talisman up in front of him, hoping to inflict as much harm on the demon as he possibly could.

Trevor clucked his tongue. "That's not a cross, and I'm not a vampire. Even then, crosses never worked against vampires."

Cruz staggered away from the flickering force field right as Corinth let out a cry of anguish and collapsed to his knees. Zoey held a hand to her forehead. Wisps of her sandy hair had come out of her braid and were standing on end. Her mouth was gaping open. She looked to be in utter and complete shock, her face as white as a ghost's.

Blinding light radiated off the blade in Corinth's hand, and he was panting from the exertion of trying to heal his friend.

Underneath Alastair's open coat, Cruz could see how far the infection had spread. The black sheen covered his entire chest. Trevor was right. They weren't going to make it out of this alive. His heart sank.

Alastair reached a shaking hand out to Gabriel Stanton. "*Please.*" His eyes fell slowly to Corinth, and he nodded, his meaning clear—he wanted Stanton to finish him off. "Tell … Larna—"Alastair gasped as another wave of apparent pain rolled through him "—I love her."

Corinth shot Gabriel a look that was clear to Cruz. If Gabriel Stanton tried anything or even moved a step closer, Corinth would be the first to cut him down.

"Gabe—stay back," Corinth warned. He closed his eyes and took in a deep breath, then blew it out. And he did this several more times before shakily getting back to his feet.

Those bright and searing wings unfurled out of Corinth's back again. They looked scorched and battered, and were the color of burning charcoal. The air seemed to be sucked right out of their protective bubble, and then it thickened. Cruz felt faint, and his skin prickled all over. *What the holy …?*

Zoey stumbled back, a hand raised to shield her face. They watched in stunned silence as Corinth's eyes filled with lightning, flashing in empty sockets. *No way.*

Alastair's face was contorted in pain. He looked like a wounded animal as Corinth reached out toward him with flickering fingers. Alastair was stretched out on the table, so when he tried to sit up, Corinth laid a firm hand on his shoulder and forced him back down. Alastair was too weak to put up much of a fight.

"I'm sorry about this," Corinth whispered to Alastair as he brandished his blade, slashing out with it in a blur of motion. With no other warning, he made a small incision to the left side of Alastair's torso, near his abdomen. Alastair sucked in a sharp breath and then a moment later screamed bloody murder, writhing on the table like he was in his final death throes, clearly suffering.

Trevor was laughing now.

Corinth's dagger disappeared in a flash of light and then reappeared, holstered at his thigh. A moment later, he lifted his hand and gestured at the open wound, as if pulling on an invisible string, much like Cruz had seen Trevor doing when he'd tossed him across the room like a rag doll …

Alastair shrieked in agony again, his body going ramrod straight, and then, as if someone had pulled a cord at his back, he went limp and almost sagged off the table. His eyes were closed and his chest barely lifted.

"Hold him down," Corinth commanded, sounding winded.

Gabriel grabbed one of Alastair's arms, obeying without comment, as Cruz grabbed the other one, while Zoey braced his legs.

Corinth radiated heat like an oven, and Cruz had to close watering eyes against the onslaught. His heart thundered in his chest. He was going to die in a sauna.

Alastair bucked wildly under their grasp; Cruz had to almost lay his body across Alastair's, trying to hold him down. And then, ever so slowly, something started to glow crimson beneath Alastair's skin, radiating brightly. A tiny sliver of an object. It was moving, getting closer to the incision Corinth had made with his magical blade.

Corinth's face twisted up in concentration as he curled his fingers, beckoning and straining, pulling at faint ripples in the air. Cruz was beyond fascinated. Whatever Corinth was doing, it was definitely of a divine nature.

A moment later, something slipped out from the cut, drifting away from Alastair's side—a crystal shard the size of a thorn.

It quivered in the air, as if wanting to be let loose again.

Corinth's eyes were tiny slits as he strained against some unknown and unseen force. The wings at his back flickered like a weird visual effect on TV, and then extinguished altogether.

After that, it happened quickly.

The glowing crystal hovered in the air for a second

before turning back on Corinth, moving with the speed of a bullet. Imperceptibly fast. Cruz lost track of it, and he tried to let out a cry of warning, but by the time he started to speak, the shard had already hit Corinth square in his chest, burying itself deeply into his flesh. A bull's-eye. Dead center of mass, where Corinth's heart was located.

Zoey shrieked at the same time as Corinth doubled over and flailed back a step, a hand going to his chest where it had entered. His face was a color of white Cruz had never seen on a person before. Snow-white—like death.

Cruz reeled as he watched Corinth sink to his knees in ludicrous slowness, his magic blade in one hand somehow, and then it slipped from his fingers, striking the stone with a final-sounding clang. Zoey's brother followed behind it, falling onto his side, shuddering and gasping. Tears were streaming down his face.

And then he choked out one terrifying word: "*Run.*"

Gabriel Stanton backed up, toward the shimmering wall of protective light, his face dropping as he surveyed the situation. There was nowhere to go.

Zoey let out a startled sob and flew to her brother, her arms going around his neck as he went incredibly still and silent, splayed out on the hard stone.

For a moment, no one moved or said anything.

Except for Trevor. His loud, harsh chuckle broke the quietude, sending chill bumps popping up along Cruz's arms. To Cruz, his laughter was the worst sound he'd ever heard in his entire life. At this point, he wasn't even sure Zoey's brother was breathing. *No.*

Suddenly Corinth sat up, his body stiff, his face a

blank mask. And when he turned toward Zoey, Cruz's chest squeezed to an excruciating degree. Those eyes. They were hideous. Solid obsidian, like shiny glass marbles. Bottomless.

He shuddered.

Corinth's neck and forearms were covered in weird whorled patterns. The loops glowed like silver tattoos, and electric light raced up and down his skin.

And in the background, Trevor was *still* laughing as Corinth's fists sparked to life like matches being lit.

After that, the barrier he'd erected around them all to keep them safe flickered and waned and—*gulp*—shattered. It came crashing down around them like a giant wave hitting a seawall. A tsunami, really.

Gabriel Stanton stared up at the place where the dome had just been, and breathed, "*Oh … bloody hell.*"

"Your eyes …" Zoey was pointing at Corinth, and she'd already started to scoot across the polished stone away from him, clearly frightened.

The demon, Trevor, still behind Cruz, said, "Thank you, Stanton. Job well done. You will get exactly what is owed to you now."

Corinth's body shook as he lowered his head, his golden-brown locks falling into his eyes. A grayish light erupted out of him, which forced Cruz to back up a step.

He stuck a hand out to help Zoey to her feet, just in case they needed to run, but she didn't take it. Her attention was glued to her brother.

"Corinth, what are you doing?" Zoey whispered, her gaze darting to the macabre ceiling, and then to the legion of dark shadow thing's stalking around them. "What did you do?"

"We are so screwed," Cruz murmured.

Corinth's tall frame was teeming with electrical energy as he stood slowly back to his feet, stretching his neck from side to side. Then he rolled both of his wrists, as if testing his body out for the very first time. Like it seemed foreign and strange to him. Alien-like.

"I don't think that's your brother anymore ..." Cruz said slowly, backing up. The hairs on his scalp stood on end as a whoosh of cold air hit him.

"Gabriel Stanton—give me the device," Trevor ordered. "And I will let you walk out of here. This is a one-time offer. I would take it if I were you. The rest, Zoey and Cruz, are mine to deal with as I see fit."

Trevor's blown-out pupils met Zoey's, hungry, and this made anger swell up inside Cruz, volatile. Cruz tapped into that rage, balling his hands into fists, temper rising. He was no stranger to fighting—maybe not demons, but he wasn't going to cower in fear either.

Gabriel reached into his pocket and pulled out the round device he'd used to get them all to this horrid place.

"What are you doing?" Cruz almost shouted. His stomach gave a flip as soon as he realized Gabriel Stanton was not on their side. He had never been on their side. He was on the demon's side. The billionaire held the device out to Trevor, his eyes flitting to Alastair's still form stretched out on the table.

Once again the word *dead* popped into Cruz's head.

Alastair was dead. And so were they.

Trevor was beside Corinth, and Cruz hadn't even seen him move. The rest of his evil army followed suit, moving as one.

Zoey's eyes darted back and forth between them all, her brows furrowing in concern as she assessed their dire situation. "*Cor ... please. Help us.*"

Corinth turned those dark, fathomless eyes on Zoey, gave her a sadistic grin, and said, "Your brother is dead."

20

ALASTAIR

Alastair's eyes flew open.

He was feeling better than he had in ages. His extreme dehydration was gone; his leg and body were mended—good as new. His pulse was strong, slamming through his veins, along with something else—a heaping helping of heat and strength and adrenaline. Power. Corinth had awakened something inside him when he'd extracted that shard from his body.

Alastair could feel the energy coursing through his veins, dangerously compelling. Also, the infection was gone, and so was the dark voice inside his head.

Although *that*, he feared, seemed to have taken up residency inside Corinth now.

Alastair knew something was wrong with Corinth. His eyes were empty. No lightning. No irises the color of maple syrup. No soul shining out. Nothing. Only black. Silver light traced an inky pathway up and down his arms, looking like supernatural tattoos.

He'd seen something similar on Angela's skin way back—

Stanton was about to hand Ephrem something, but instead, he ejected two wicked-looking thin blades hidden underneath his long-sleeved shirt, slicing out at Ephrem, catching him in his side.

Ephrem's lips quirked down at the corners, and the demon slammed a flat palm against Gabriel's chest, sending him sprawling backward to where Alastair had just leaped to his feet near the table.

Zoey and Cruz, seeing Alastair back on his feet, ran to his side, their eyes wide in surprise and relief.

Alastair glanced down at Gabriel as Gabriel gazed up at him, his mouth falling open.

And Alastair did something completely out of character—he reached a hand down to help Stanton back up. Stanton's eyes went round as he accepted his proffered hand, getting back to his feet and wiping his pants off.

All the while, Ephrem never moved, only studied Alastair with a curious eyebrow raise. "This is going to be *fun*."

Stanton's hair was tousled half-way in his eyes, and he had a cut above his brow. He rubbed a hand across his forehead and said, "Do you think you can take him?"

Alastair nodded down at Corinth's unlit blade. "Without his blade, yes. Well … uh, maybe …"

Corinth stretched his hand out and pointed it at the holy blade, still on the ground. He beckoned for it, his hands crackling with a surge of dark energy—purple and black. But to Alastair's utter shock and surprise, the dagger only flickered and juddered against the stone, and then the light dissipated, winking out completely. Corinth gripped his wrist with his other hand to try and steady it—and then tried again, his face screwed up from the effort.

"What's wrong with him—?" Zoey asked, her voice wavering.

Corinth shot forward, plucking up the dagger, but as soon as he had hold of it, it started to glow red-hot, like a coal in a fire, and then he cried out and dropped it.

The clang of metal on the stone was deafening, like a church bell tolling. It slid across the polished stone and then stopped just shy of Zoey's feet. Corinth tried to call on the blade once more, his fingers splayed wide, and brows drawn together in concentration.

Nothing happened.

The weapon did not move or even flicker. Corinth pressed his lips together in a thin, firm line.

A sinking feeling hit Alastair right in the pit of his stomach. The heavenly relic was done with Corinth, which could only mean one thing: he wasn't the one in control anymore. His brother was gone. Maybe for good. *No.* His heart squeezed in distress.

Alastair glanced at Gabriel, who appeared just as stunned, probably coming to the same conclusion.

Corinth stepped toward his sister, and Alastair tensed up, ready for a fight. He didn't want this. Not like this. The infection had taken hold of *him*. Corinth had sacrificed himself for Alastair's life. Fire licked at his insides at the thought of having to kill his best friend. *Dammit, Taylor.*

Alastair's eyes shot briefly over to Ephrem. The

demon was gloating. His face was lit up with a lordly sort of smile.

The Shades surrounding Ephrem began to move, but Ephrem put his hand up to stop them. "Don't do anything until I command it."

Gabriel Stanton whispered to Alastair out of the side of his mouth. "Are you fully recovered?"

Alastair shot Stanton a questioning look. "Don't tell me you're going to actually make a stand with me?"

Gabriel straightened to his full height, his back erect and his blades held in a fighter's stance in front of him. Alastair had been in too many perilous moments to not recognize one when it was right in front of him. This was the moment right before horns blared, signaling the start of war. They were grossly outnumbered.

"I'm all about self-preservation," Stanton purred.

Alastair could see Cruz's chest heaving up and down in his apparent fright, and he looked a shade paler than normal, but there was fire in his eyes. His message was clear: Cruz wasn't going down without a fight either. *Good kid.*

The blade was closest to Zoey.

But she wasn't interested in the weapon. She only had eyes for her brother. Tears were streaming down her face as she gaped up at him. Alastair knew how distraught she must be. For all she knew, her brother Pete was dead. Her world had been shattered. Now she'd lost another brother.

He heard Cruz suck in a sharp breath and hold it in. No one moved. If Corinth went for the blade, chaos would ensue. It was too close to his sister—and Alastair couldn't let her get hurt in the crossfire.

Corinth turned to Ephrem. "What would you like me to do?"

"Who commands you?" Ephrem's cold, hard eyes glittered behind his glasses, strangely enthralling.

"Angela."

Angela? No. Alastair was pretty sure all the blood had drained out of his face. The angel who had had it in for all Nephilim—and humankind. She had hated Corinth for being the last half human, half angel. This was not good. His skin felt clammy as he turned his eyes on Corinth once again. Dammit, they couldn't get rid of her …

Ephrem pinned Alastair with a gloating glare, stepping closer to their group. There was no shield protecting them now. "You remember Angela, right?" He waved a hand glibly in the air. "The angel Corinth killed. Drained her dry, if I recall correctly, back when he was a *vampire.* She and I used her own genetic makeup, before she was … killed—I use that term loosely—to create what Corinth has become: *better.* It took us both time to realize beings as powerful as the Nephilim couldn't be controlled. Not by compulsion or demon possession, I mean—he's been protected by spiritual attacks for quite some time. But because Angela got inside his head, and vice versa, a tiny sliver of her dark consciousness still lies dormant inside him—not dormant anymore. Even without a body, she still influences him."

Alastair felt sick with dread and worry. "What are you talking about?"

"Corinth has always had darkness inside him. Don't tell me you never noticed it before. All those angels and vampires he killed ten years ago … the shard inside him only served to release that darkness. Angela made sure that when he was infected, she would be the one to gain control over his mind once again. Did you hear the voice inside your head? She is doing the same thing to this half blood—controlling him like a puppet."

This can't be happening. Corinth, you idiot.

Alastair would have been the one being controlled if Taylor hadn't stepped in. An overwhelming flood of guilt rolled over him like a tidal wave. He suddenly wished Larna were here to talk some sense into Corinth. She'd always had a way of getting through to him.

After what seemed like a considerable amount of time had passed, Alastair finally found his voice again. "Corinth, *brother*," he pleaded, "don't make me fight you. Snap out of it. You have fought against worse trash than this before—and won. You already beat Angela once. Time to rise up and do it all over again."

"You're shoeless and shirtless and weaponless, Alastair Iszler." Corinth's voice sounded dark and taciturn and distant, and it made Alastair cringe inwardly as he continued. "You don't stand a chance against me. But I can say, I've always wondered who would win in a no-holds-barred fight. You ... or me."

"And it would also appear you're weaponless," Alastair whispered. "Even the blade stands against you. It can smell when something's rotten, *Angela*." He spit her name out like a curse. "Don't let her take control, Cor. Please, see reason. Don't make me do this. What about your family back home? Jimmy and Pete? Your mom and dad? Leo? They need you now more than ever. We can end this and all go home."

Dark Corinth's gaze landed on the dagger near Zoey's feet, his head tilted to the side, glossy black eyes unblinking. "They aren't my real family. They never were. Larna married a fool. You're a fool. I've always thought it; I've just never said it. And when I leave this place, and go to your wife, I'll convince her of that fact, right before I kill her too, and everyone I—*he*—used to love."

It wasn't Angela taunting him; it was Corinth's evil alter-ego. But it sounded almost like he and she were having trouble separating themselves from each other's personality. Alastair wondered if this meant Angela was still weak. Corinth was still in there somewhere. Alastair knew that. She hated Corinth for beating her.

Alastair glanced down to his borrowed and soiled coat, bare feet, and then to his bloodstained chest, and shrugged as he shed what was left of the material on his wrists. There was no point in getting angry, but he really hated hearing his brother say he'd do harm to the woman he loved, and to his own family. "Are we going to fight?" Alastair asked evenly. "Because I've done a lot more with a lot less. And whatever Corinth did to heal me … it worked—better than I think he even realized." He held up his healed wrists for Ephrem to see. "I haven't felt this strong in my entire life. Remember, I still have a remnant of angelic blood left inside me."

Maybe that was what Corinth had been betting on when he'd restored him.

Dark Corinth inclined his head toward Ephrem, who had stepped up beside him. He was waiting on the demon's command. He cocked his head to the side as if he were listening to something, and then said, "Angela says I should do whatever you ask of me."

"Kill your sister," Ephrem said without remorse or thought or pause. "That should be entertaining. Slowly though—use only your hands … no lightning. I want to watch as you do it."

Son of a bitch. Heat flooded Alastair's face. "Don't make me do this, *Corinth*. Please."

Ephrem adjusted his glasses and let out a small grunt of satisfaction. "I like it when you beg, Alastair." The demon snapped his fingers, and in a swirl of black smoke, suddenly he was holding a leather muzzle in his hand—the one he'd made Alastair wear. "You forgot something, Alastair." He nodded at the Shades fanned out beside him. "Take Iszler alive, but make sure he watches the Nephilim kill Zoey first, and then put him back on the table. I'm not finished with him yet. And get that device from Stanton. Bring me his head," he ordered. Ephrem lifted his palm and held out another one of those needlelike shards. "Cruz, this one is for you. You will make a fine follower. At my beck and call to do all sorts of evil, torturous things—and you'll enjoy it."

"Alastair?" Zoey asked with a whimper, glancing between Gabriel and Cruz. "What do we do?"

"Do exactly what I tell you to do, when I tell you to do it," Alastair half snarled, half whispered.

"Since when do *you* obey anyone, Taylor?" Stanton breathed. "How the hell did she manage to get her hooks into you? I thought you were stronger than this … Don't you have a halo … to prevent you from spiritual attackers?"

Corinth's mouth quirked up on one side, and he

pulled his armor and shirt up for them all to see. Alastair heard Zoey suck in a shocked breath.

The patterns and intricate loops and whorls covering his entire chest and abdomen gleamed like polished silver. He ran a hand over the place where Alastair knew his heart to be. Black squiggle lines spiderwebbed outward, linking with the glowing spirals. "In order to repair me, she had to break me. Make me anew. My heart no longer aches." It came out whisper soft and sounding almost—*almost*— like the old Corinth once again. Sad. Heavy. Lost. Corinth's fathomless eyes ticked over to Gabriel as he pulled his armor and shirt back down. "Don't be in such a rush to lose your head, Gabe."

It was Corinth's voice, but *not* his voice. It sounded disconnected and robotic, and it gave Alastair the chills.

Gabriel gestured at Corinth with one of the thin blades at his wrists and raised an eyebrow. "I've actually wondered how long you'd hold up in a fight against me, Taylor. I give you two solid minutes."

Corinth lifted his hands in the air, and a clap of searing light shot out of them, and then he threw a concussive bolt right at Stanton. It struck Gabriel in his chest before he could even think to dodge out of the way.

The impact bowled him backward and sent him sprawling across the table, flat on his back, spread-eagle and unmoving.

Alastair exploded into action in a blur of motion, slamming into Dark Corinth before he could retaliate. They both went down to the ground, a clipped cry of surprise escaping from Corinth's mouth.

And then they fought.

21

ZOEY

Alastair had lied. He hadn't told us what to do. There'd been no time. Trevor had disappeared.

Now all I could do was stand there for far too many dazed seconds, staring at my brother fighting Alastair.

Not my brother.

I'd never seen him in combat before. I'd never seen him act so callous or cruel before. I had to keep reminding myself that he wasn't my brother. He was different. Those markings on his skin … they looked nasty and horrific.

Alastair moved almost as fast as Corinth did, and suddenly I realized why my parents had always wanted me to train with him. He was magnificent. All I could discern was a black blur from his borrowed coat as he hit Corinth, and they went down in a heap.

Not-my-brother threw an elbow into Alastair's jaw, and Alastair's head snapped back. But then Alastair was winding strong legs around not-Corinth's neck at the same time as Alastair grabbed one of his glowing arms and pulled it down into a submission hold. I'd seen my brothers pull that move a million times, wrestling. Alastair wasn't trying to hurt Corinth; he was trying to subdue him.

Meanwhile, Gabriel Stanton was just stirring back to life.

Something glinted off to my left, near my feet. My eyes flitted down right as a flash of bronze hit me square in my eye. The blade. It winked again, begging me to pick it up. To take up arms. Suddenly the need to hold it was all-consuming. I glanced around at the Shades, which had all started to inch closer, and realized it might not be a bad thing to have a weapon in hand.

The sound of smoke and wind whipping through the air all around us was unsettling. Cruz held the key chain out in front of him like a—well, a shield—and it began glowing golden. Protective. Enveloping.

The Spear of Destiny.

Heart racing, I bent down to snatch up the angelic blade, just out of reach of the shield's light, and felt the hairs on the back of my neck stand up straight. Breath plumed out in front of me as shadowy fingers took form, a hand with no body reaching for me—

Cruz slashed out with the tiny shield—I mean, it was the size of his palm, but it sure didn't seem like a small trinket as he bravely jumped in front of me with it held out.

I yanked the blade into my grasp with trembling fingers, and the disembodied hand vanished before it could take full form. The glorious light winked out on the blade, plunging me back into darkness as soon as I yanked it into my grip.

I gasped, almost tipping over from the weight.

I hadn't been prepared for how heavy the dagger was. All bronze and dense metal. The handle was wrapped in tan leather. My fingers tingled, and a charge of zinging energy ran up my arm, disorienting and enchanting at the same time. A deep sense of calm settled into my bones as I clutched the weapon to my chest—

Strong hands reached down and hauled me back to my feet.

And I twisted around, almost slicing Cruz's fingers off.

"*Whoa*," he breathed, jerking his hand back, not the one still clutching the glowing pocket-sized golden shield. "Careful with that thing. I don't think they like the light … Oh … *crap* …"

Things were happening very quickly now, and I didn't know how to wield a knife. How did people fight with these things? Did I just start hacking with it? That sounded like a good option.

I did just that, waving the sharp tip out in front of me, holding it with both my shaking hands as half a dozen demons started to move toward us, all dark shadows—like a death march.

Gabriel Stanton, having recovered somewhat, jumped off the table and wobbled unsteadily on his feet. I could just make out a flash of thin black armor through a hole burned into his shirt. One of his blades slid back into his sheath under his sleeve, and he slapped a hand to his injured chest, his breath hissing out between his teeth.

The billionaire's pearl-colored silk shirt was open, and a sheen of sweat stood out along his collarbone. Stanton pointed to a dark, shadowy alcove in front of us, past the place where I'd last seen Trevor standing. "Go through there." He reached into his pocket and pulled out the round device, the one Trevor had wanted so badly, and shoved it into my free hand. "Take your first two rights, and then a left, and then one more right. Find the diamond-shaped pattern etched into the wall—that's where the exit will be. Select the matching symbol on this device when you find it, and push this red button. It will take you out of this realm—"

As if sensing someone coming, Gabriel twirled around, wielding his weapons once again, right as a dark shadow swooped at him out of a cascade of black smoke. He ducked and dodged a stray fist and struck the shadow in its back with his extended blade, and I heard a solid thud as the Shade hit the ground. And then Stanton was moving away from us, leaving us behind.

There was something elegant about the way he fought, spinning, and weaving his way through the oncoming horde. It was exactly how I pictured a fencer or a knight might fight, or someone who knew how to handle a sword.

Until he disappeared in the throng of smoke and fog, thick in the air.

I shoved the device Gabriel had given me into my hoodie pocket, all the while thinking this couldn't be real. Why was this happening to me? How were we supposed to get out of here if we couldn't see the exit? What right had he said to take? I was frozen for a moment in indecision and fear.

Something came soaring out of nowhere and struck me on the left shoulder, hard. I felt a searing pain blossom, and Cruz wrapped his fingers around mine, pulling me down behind one of the table legs at the last second. It was not cover, by the way—half of my body was sticking out from behind it.

"You okay?" he whispered. "I think they can move objects with their minds … like telekinesis … We are *so, so* dead."

"Gabriel Stanton said to go through there." I pointed in the direction he had indicated to go in, noticing he'd made a hole for us. "We can make that," I said, clutching the dagger close, a swirl of apprehension and adrenaline flooding through me. "Follow me." I hopped up, hoping he was right on my heels as I ducked past several reaching hands and arms, on the move, heading toward the alcove. My fingers were already slick on the blade's handle, and I almost dropped it as Cruz pressed himself closer to me, banging his knee painfully into mine.

"I can't see them," he whispered hoarsely, cursing and limping beside me. He paused and held his hand out, stretching the light from his talisman so it would extend its reach, and gasped. "Never mind. I see them."

We were surrounded.

The shallow halo coming off the charm in Cruz's grip wasn't enough light to see by. It was still too dark to see past the horde of shadowy bodies all around us. They were ink-blots filling a black hole. I could feel them hovering nearby though. Waiting. Watching.

The shadows came out of nowhere, trying to seize us again. To separate us. I heard a hiss followed by a rush of air whooshing past my head. There were so many.

Cruz was pulled one way, and rough demon hands jerked me the other way.

"*Cruz!*" I cried out in alarm, heart thudding.

My breathing was coming in shallow pants as I sliced out and jabbed with the dagger at the forbidding darkness. A blinding flash of gold fire blazed up along the edge of the blade, catching a shadow thing's hand, and it recoiled, disappearing from view.

Another Shade darted forward—

Give me more light! I thought in frustration as something else tried to rip the weapon out of my hand, but they jumped back with a squeal as I blindly thrust the sharp edge out again, a glorious light bursting forth from it, sheltering me in its amber hue.

Suddenly I could see.

The numerous Shades holding Cruz a few feet away dropped him like a bag of stones upon seeing the light, and he landed in a stunned heap on his side. I stumbled toward him, my legs barely functioning, and our attackers squealed in rage and fright, backing up as fire burst along the edge of the blade again in my two-handed grip. The warmth coming off the hilt made it feel like it had been heated by the sun.

The rest of the Shades surrounding us cowered back, suddenly looking frightened and hesitant.

Catching on quick, I brandished the holy relic higher, the light spreading out around both Cruz and me like a blessed beacon. "Stay back!"

Cruz shot to his feet, opening his palm and the shield key chain radiated the same golden glow. He held it up, mirroring my actions. "They … they moved away," he said, sounding winded and immensely relieved. "We should keep going … to … to the place Gabriel said to go."

But I saw movement off to my left. Beyond the pale dome of light surrounding us, I could see Alastair grappling with Corinth. Alastair had an arm wound around his throat in a chokehold. Not-Corinth disappeared in a dazzling clap of thunder and a cloud of thick sulfurous smoke. *My brother.*

Alastair clutched at empty air where not-Corinth used to be, and because he'd been using his body as leverage, his forward momentum caused him to fall face-first in the same second not-Corinth landed behind him. Not-Corinth viciously kicked him in the back. I heard a snap followed by Alastair's sharp cry of agony as he fell to the ground.

While he was down, not-Corinth kicked him again, this time in the stomach, causing Alastair to flop over onto his back, his long coat flying open at the same time. There was a flash of pale skin as Alastair clutched a hand to his stomach. Not-Corinth pounced on him, straddling Alastair's prone form—a blazing hand pressed up against his jugular.

I was already running to help before I even knew my legs were moving. I couldn't let that thing possessing my brother kill Alastair.

But before not-Corinth could end him, Alastair bucked his hips, unseating him, and struck out with two quick, hard jabs to Corinth's jaw. Alastair was fast. Faster than I'd ever seen anyone move.

Not-Corinth flew backward, but I didn't get to see what happened next, because Cruz had caught up and grabbed me around my waist, and he was already dragging me across the cavern, toward the place Gabriel had told us to go to, before I could put up much of a fight.

"Zoey! We have to go!"

"*We can't leave them behind!*" I tried to rip free, to help my brother and Alastair, but Cruz was a lot stronger than I had given him credit for. Stronger than me. Maybe it was the terror and adrenaline coursing through him, because he hoisted me off my feet, carrying me now. I lifted my legs and dropped them, using all my weight to throw him off-balance—a move I'd learned from Jimmy. He let out a shocked yelp as I jerked out of his grasp and ran—

Right into a pair of black-rimmed glasses.

Cold, glittering eyes.

Cream-colored skin.

Auburn hair.

For one awfully long, stretched-out second, we just stood there blinking at each other.

Trevor.

I swallowed heavily, my heart pounding. He gave me a sadistic grin as an invisible force kept me pinned in place, my muscles screaming. I couldn't move. I couldn't even breathe.

It was unnaturally dark, but by the orange fire sparking off the metal in my right hand, I could see his eyes. They looked like the ocean at night—cool, serene, deep—and he smelled like an inferno, all smoke and ash and destruction. My knees felt shaky.

I'd never used a knife to cut anyone before—not anything resembling a human, anyway—until recently, that is. I'd never had to defend myself to the death. I was just a teenager. But every single fiber of my being was telling me I should use this blade on him right now. My blood was rushing in my ears.

In a blur of motion, he snatched hold of my wrist, the one not gripping the dagger, and twisted it back, all before I could let out a startled cry. Icy fire spread up my arm where his fingers dug into my skin. *Oh, hell no.*

The light can hurt him, I reminded myself, and as soon as I thought it, the blade flared up in almighty glory. To my intense satisfaction, Trevor recoiled, and it was enough to free me of his invincible hold once again. This time, I didn't hesitate. I slashed out at him, the light flaring up even brighter—more brilliant and divine than before.

Trevor fell back a step, out of the way of the torch, his eyes sparking with fury as Cruz came up beside me, brandishing the shield.

"Get back, demon!" he bellowed.

Trevor hopped nimbly out of the way as Cruz swept the light at him, forcing Trevor to stay well out of our reach.

At our backs, I knew there was probably a horde of his Shades waiting to pounce. I could feel their eyes on us. The air was sawing out of my throat now, and I sounded like a wounded animal, my pulse racing.

"Zo ... it's okay," Trevor reassured me, his hands

held out in front of him. His voice was soothing, and as gentle as stalks of grass swaying in the wind. "Back up." He gestured at his Shades behind us, and they obeyed, taking a couple of steps back, their presence receding. "See, they listen to me. They do whatever I ask of them. Turn the blade over to me, Zo. I'll let you go. *I promise.*" He beckoned me forward, smiling, and some of the frost left his eyes. "Just give me the blade."

"Tell them to stop fighting," I said.

Trevor lifted a hand and said, "*Stop.*"

The chaos around us melted away. I could no longer feel Cruz's hand at my back, or the dagger's comforting weight, or the heat of the hilt in my grip. No scrabbling or clawing or shouting in the background. It was only Trevor and me. No more noise.

"*Zo,*" he crooned, his voice melodic. "I'll make you a deal. You give me the blade, and I'll save your brother."

My throat burned as a sharp pang of nausea rolled over me. *Corinth.* Those solid black eyes. I shivered. I couldn't take it. I was weak. I needed my brother, and he needed me right now. I could end this. I could save his life like he'd saved mine, and Alastair's.

"You promise? You will let us all go?"

Cruz's sharp, insistent voice broke through the fog in my brain, and I could feel and hear him again. "*Zoey.*" He jerked on the hood of my jacket, insistent. "He's lying to you. He just told your brother to throttle you with his bare hands. He won't help us *or* your brother. He won't let you go. He only wants you to think that he will."

I felt Cruz push his back up against mine as he shifted and turned around, his body tensing against me. We were surrounded on all sides. Where was Gabriel? And it struck me how odd it was that I now wanted the man who'd kidnapped me to rescue us.

"Cruz is wrong. I don't want you dead. I like you." Trevor's eyes flashed behind his glasses, and then, as if by habit, he pushed them back up the bridge of his nose again. "I always have, Zo."

Behind him, just outside the reach of the light, I could see the outline of bodies standing still in the dark. Motionless. Eerie. Not even their chests were moving.

Where are Corinth and Alastair? How long can they last? Did he stop them too?

"Where's my brother?" I asked, gripping the hilt tightly between trembling fingers. I raised it up. The heavy golden light illuminated Trevor's face, throwing dark circles from the lenses of his glasses around his eyes. He looked like a ringmaster at the circus, introducing his next death-defying act. He flinched away from the light, but he was still smiling genially—and it reminded me of the first time we'd met, when I was alone in the library with him, and he'd tripped over my feet. All white teeth and awkward charm.

"Your brother is over there." Trevor pointed across the way, and I could barely make out his tall silhouette. Corinth flashed me a grin, his eyes shining. He was back. He was himself, and something inside me released, and I felt the tension slowly leak out of me.

"*Cor,*" I sobbed, and the ache of seeing him whole again left me feeling incredibly drained and relieved. My limbs and arms were so heavy.

I swung around and held the blade out to Corinth,

but he didn't come try and take it from me. He just stood there, his posture a bit off. His shoulders a little too erect. Too arrogant. And his smile seemed off too, now that I was studying him. Unnatural and forced. It didn't quite meet his eyes.

"See. He's okay," Trevor insisted.

I lifted the blade and held it out, balancing it on my open palm. "Let them go, and you can have it."

Trevor's eyes narrowed as he squinted down at me. Ever so slowly he reached out to take the weapon from my outstretched hand, but as soon as he neared, I slashed out, catching him by surprise. The razor's edge sliced through the thin material of his long sleeve, not cutting him, but pissing him off. He hissed and yanked his hand back, shaking it, his dark eyes flashing. I heard something crack in his jaw as he clamped his teeth together, enraged.

Trevor threw a hand out and wiggled his fingers at Cruz. A thin tendril of black smoke snaked out from his hands, heading toward Cruz. The next second, he was on his knees beside me, a hand clamped over his mouth, his face turning a frightening shade of red. The shield Corinth had given Cruz was still clutched in his other hand, and it was pulsing like an angry crimson flame.

"*Don't hurt him,*" I begged. "Please. I just want to go home. Leave him alone. Please!"

"Throw the dagger over there." Trevor pointed to the opposite side of the space we occupied. "As hard as you can, and I'll let him live."

My gaze sought Cruz's. He had a hand over his mouth; his eyes were pleading with me not to do it. He shook his head and tried to stand, but he fell back onto his side, curling in on himself, his legs jerking feebly.

I realized that Trevor could kill us without even touching us, by only using his mind. What was the point of having the blade? The only way we were getting out of this alive was if I gave him what he wanted. I couldn't stand here and watch Cruz die. My heart was hammering away with the dread of making the wrong decision.

"You'd better hurry," Trevor hissed. "He can only hold his breath for so long."

I took up the blade, lifted it high, and threw it as hard as I could.

22

LEO

The lone figure stood on the crest of a hill. The setting sun in the background was blocking his face from view. All Leo could make out was the familiar long charcoal-colored hair. The man's locks matched the color of his thick beard. He was watching the fading sun paint the sky a pale pink and ruby, like a grapefruit.

Corinth's mother was at the window, staring at the man, a hand to her chin, looking deeply troubled.

Outside, Larna was standing in front of the man, and they were speaking animatedly to one another.

Leo strode over to Susan. "Are you okay?"

She shook her head, and a tear leaked out from the corner of her eye. She brushed at it angrily and said, "Pete's girlfriend, Carlie, has no idea what happened. She was supposed to come over for dinner. They've been dating for a year. What do I tell her? Is she okay?"

"Zeke and Jimmy went to get clothes for your family

with Tamiel," Leo said. "They are taking care of things and will make sure she's okay. You're all staying here until we can get Pete well again."

The sun streamed in through the window, and Leo could see the creases around her eyes more prominently. She looked like she'd aged in just the few days they'd been here. Leo wanted to reach out and comfort her, but he wasn't good at that sort of thing. Corinth was the glue that held them all together, not him.

"What about Cruz's mom?" Susan asked. "She has to be worried sick about her son. I don't even know where he stays—"

"Do you know anything else about him? Something that could help us track her down?" Leo asked.

She dabbed at her nose with a tissue, seemingly in thought, and then looked up. "I think he works at that ice-cream shop a few blocks down from our house ... I've seen him in there before."

"I'll send Ikari over there to ask around. He'll get Cruz's address and then pop over there and influence her."

"By *influence*, you mean, like, compel her or something, right?" she asked. "You make it sound like it's no big deal, Leo. But it is. It's a huge deal messing with people's minds. Like what was done to Zo when she was five—to make her forget that she had been abducted ..." Her voice hitched.

Leo put a reassuring hand on Susan's arm. "Cruz's mother will not have any lingering side effects. I promise. Ikari will only plant a simple suggestion in her head ... that her son is okay, and he is staying with friends for the weekend. And that their holiday dinner was lovely."

She whispered, "But what if he's *not* okay? What then? I just feel so useless!"

"He *will* be okay," Leo promised her. "Corinth is with them." He knew it was an empty promise, but if it helped give Susan some bit of relief … well then the lie was worth it.

Again his mind shifted as he thought about where Corinth could be. Wherever he was, he hoped he could handle things on his own.

"Have you gotten through to my son?" she asked, almost as if she could read Leo's mind.

He shook his head and frowned. "No."

Another tear rolled down her cheek, but this time she didn't wipe it away, only gazed up at Leo, her jaw set. "What about my daughter, Leo? She's not trained for this … She can't defend herself … Is she with Gabriel Stanton? Because we all know what he did to her in the past … Wherever they went, it can't be good. I'm—" She broke off for a second to clear her throat, crossing her arms over her chest. "I'm worried about them. Trevor … that kid … he's not a kid … but a demon … this *whole* time. I don't know who to trust anymore. Do you know anything about him? Can you track him down? What was that thing he threw at me? I spoke to his parents—or fake parents—once …"

Leo pursed his lips before speaking, thinking about everything he had just learned. Not much. "The demon's mansion, the one he has been staying at, was cleaned out. There's no trace of the phone number he gave you to speak to his"—Leo did air quotes—"'*parents*.' I wish I had more answers for you. All I know is that the thing festering inside Peter is evil—demonic in nature. So maybe one of them knows what's going on. As we speak, Samyaza is trying to track down a demon horde near here. Once he roots them out, he'll make contact with me, and I'll join him. I only wanted to give you an update, and to check on you, but I have to get back to Peter."

"The Grigori," she said slowly, seeming to mull the word over. "The angels who were united with Angela's cause. They did this to him?"

Leo nodded and then looked down, avoiding her penetrating gaze. She knew all about Angela. Corinth had filled his parents in on everything—that Angela was Leo's mother, and that Corinth had killed Angela. It was never easy admitting he was related to someone who had caused so much devastation and harm—had killed so many—just because of her hate for all Nephilim and humans alike. He was ashamed.

Leo felt a gentle hand cup his cheek, and he glanced up to see Susan standing on her tiptoes. Her eyes were soft and tolerant as she gazed up at him. "Angela's actions are not your fault. You saved my son's life, and so did Danel."

He nodded and then turned to leave, but she put a hand on his arm, stopping him. When Leo spun around, he saw she was staring out of the window again. "Who is that man with Larna?"

Outside, Leo could see the dark-haired man still speaking to Larna. "That's Vinson."

"*That's* Vinson?" she asked, sounding in awe. "I've heard so many stories about him, but I've never had a face to put to the name. He's shorter than I expected."

Leo gave her a sideways glance. "Vinson likes his anonymity."

He wasn't too keen on eavesdropping, but he suddenly wondered what they were talking about. Even from inside, and standing in front of a closed window, he could hear what they were saying.

Larna said, "Whatever's happening to Pete ... it's bad."

Vinson growled.

They were silent for a second before Larna spoke again. "I'm worried about them. I'm going with Leo to this demon clan to get answers. Are you coming with me?"

Vinson put a hand on Larna's shoulder. They didn't say anything after that. They didn't need to.

Ikari stood shakily to his feet beside Pete as soon as Leo entered the cramped bedroom and closed the door behind him. He swiped a hand across his brow and blew out a deep breath, staring down at his dying patient.

Peter's skin was changing; it was starting to look like his entire body had been dipped in oil. His once-curly locks were gone—he was bald. Anything resembling his normal appearance was fading. Dark, thick lines snaked up the sides of his neck like vines.

Leo's throat tightened, and he found he had to clear it first before speaking. "Did you find anything else out?" he asked Ikari.

Ikari shook his head and dropped his gaze away from Leo's, suddenly looking defeated. "His mind is a jumble, filled with dark thoughts. The infection is spreading to his heart, overtaking him. He will succumb—and sooner rather than later. My first thought was that I could remove the source of infection, but as soon as I got anywhere near it with my mind, I realized that was exactly what it was engineered for: to prevent angels from healing humans, and to infect or kill the angel in the process if they do try and remove it. I tried to relieve some of your brother's pain, but …" Ikari shook his head again, glancing back at his prone form. He was so deathly still. Something indecipherable flickered across Ikari's face. "I can end his pain."

Leo balled his hands into tight fists, thinking about Corinth and his family. "Are you telling me there's nothing else we can do for him? To help him?"

"Don't you think I've already thought of everything?" Ikari said softly, gently. "His blood is poisoned. Any angel subjected to that sort of infection would be uncontainable. Malevolent. Demonic. I've never seen anything like this before. None of us have."

Leo whirled around, a hand going to his head. He just needed time to think. To buy more time. To save Peter. *Curse it all! Where is Corinth?*

The door opened, and Larna marched in, a frown marring her pretty features. Moisture filled her eyes as she crossed her arms over her chest and studied Peter. "There has to be another way to save him—"

Peter was taking in rasping breaths, and then his body seized as his back arched up off the bed. Suddenly a whirlwind of smoke filled the room, blinding them. The smell of charred wood and sulfur and soot was strong in the air.

Larna was shouting something unintelligible at the

same time as Ikari moved toward Peter, and Leo's hands ignited in a blaze of electric fire.

But it was already too late.

Pete's eyes snapped open. Through a brief parting of the pillar of dark smoke, he met Leo's worried gaze. His face was completely covered in black ichor now, and his eyes were bottomless pits. *No.* Peter gave Leo an insane sort of grin, shrugged his shoulders back, and disappeared in a cloud of thick vapor.

23

ZOEY

The blade went whizzing end over end into the darkness, a glint of bronze metal. And just like that, it winked out of sight like I'd tossed it down a never-ending well instead of across a dark cavern.

There was no clang of it striking anything solid. It was just *gone*.

And the moment I relinquished my hold on it, Trevor moved, slamming into me with such force I flew backward into a glowing stalagmite a few feet behind me. Breath left me on a rush of air, and a minuscule half a second later, he was crushing his body up against me, his arms locked around mine, inhumanly strong. Up this close, all I could see was a fuzzy blur of glasses and his infuriatingly superior grin. Had he always been this tall? This strong?

I opened my mouth, trying in vain to pull in air, winded … *I am dying … I can't … breathe.*

I'd had the wind knocked out of me before, play fighting with my brothers, but this felt infinitely worse. Like I was dying. *I am going to suffocate to death.* My back had to be one giant bruise. The smell of ash and burnt wood and a trace of sulfur was strong in my nostrils. I tried to double over from the pain and lack of oxygen, but Trevor braced a flat palm against my collarbone, forcing me to stay upright as I gasped for air.

He was going to kill me. I could see it in his eyes and feel it in his touch—the way he clenched his fingers against my chest. My stomach did an agonizing flip, and I froze, glancing down at his hand so close to my throat.

His inkblot eyes were wide and round behind his glasses.

Warm breath rustled my hair as he leaned in closer. "You really are naive, aren't you?" he hissed softly, darkly. "I thought it was cute at first—now it's just annoying."

Trevor ... Ephrem ... the demon, he was terrifying. A monster who could snuff me out with a single thought. Control my actions. My breath, even. *Cruz. Please don't let him be dead.* I couldn't stand it. Tears pricked the corners of my eyes. *What have I done?*

All the while, Trevor, or Ephrem, or whatever his name was, watched me as I struggled to draw in air, sounding like a wounded animal. Everything hurt. I wanted to break down and cry, but I reined in my emotions, determined to not give him the satisfaction.

His eyebrows disappeared into his tousled hair as if he were amused. I couldn't believe I'd ever thought he was good-looking. How had I not seen him for what he truly was? Evil. He could sense my fear, and he liked it. The way he was looking at me now made me feel like the gum on the bottom of someone's shoe. Worthless.

Shock, and also his hand at the hollow point of my throat, kept me paralyzed to the spot, but I managed to find my voice. "Get ... your ... hands off ... *me*," I spit, my voice coming out more as a croak.

My brother had been brave. Alastair had been brave. Cruz had been beyond brave. Why couldn't I be brave like them? Instead, all I could do was shrink away from his touch, but there was nowhere to go, my back was pressed up against the jutting formation so hard my feet barely touched the ground.

Everyone was dead except for me. Cruz's blood was on my hands. His death was my fault. That thought sent me spiraling, and the room spun as black bled its way into the edges of my vision.

Turning his head a little to the side, Trevor called out to someone behind him in the pitch-blackness. "*Corinth, I have your little sister. It is time to bring me Alastair so that he can watch you end her life.*"

Suddenly there was a whirlwind of fog rolling in, and a blaze of ice-blue light coalesced behind Trevor, and out of the smoke's swirling depths leaped my brother—*not* my brother—lightning crackling across his skin, chillingly so.

He isn't my brother. He is a bringer of death.

The hairs on the back of my neck began to rise as the husk of my brother moved to stand behind his master. Silent. Obedient. Rapt.

"Where is Alastair?" Trevor asked Corinth without taking his eyes off me.

"I'm working on it," the thing resembling my brother

said hotly from behind Trevor.

Alastair. He is *alive.*

"You're telling me that you can't subdue a mere *human?*" Trevor snapped. "You can control time, and you have lightning at your beck and call … I said, BRING HIM TO ME *NOW!*"

"He's a lot faster and stronger—"

"What about Stanton?" Trevor asked, cutting not-Corinth off, the tinge of anger in his voice still apparent. "I don't see his head at my feet either."

Not-Corinth shook his head in agitation. "He ran away."

Hearing that Alastair was alive gave me a sudden bout of much-needed courage. Trevor still had his head turned slightly, so I locked my arms out against his chest as hard as I could. It was like trying to move a mountain with my bare hands.

At seeing my failed attempt to push him off me, Trevor edged back a little, and his lip corkscrewed up on one side. His hand was unbelievably ice-cold against my skin. And all I could think about was slapping that grin right off his face, but when I drew my hand back and hit him as hard as I could, I knew I'd signed my own death warrant.

My hand throbbed all the way up to my shoulder, and his skewed and bent glasses fell to the stone at my feet with a satisfying clatter, the lenses breaking.

In terrifying slowness, his smirk *did* vanish—and it would have been more satisfying if such a dark and chilling look hadn't crossed his face at the same time. "Good thing those were for looks only," he hissed, his voice sounding low and guttural. There was no smile on his face as he struck out like a viper, fisting a hand into my braid and viciously yanking my head to the side.

A sharp pop of pain tore up my neck, and I cried out in surprise and anguish.

"I was going to make your death quick. Well … quick*ish* …" He tilted his head, seemingly thinking about something. "Your brother could snuff the light right out of you if I gave him the order … but now …" He licked his lips and yanked on my hair, pulling my face closer to his. "Now I think I'll make you regret that," he whispered, and then, with incredible strength, he flung me to the ground.

Before I could even attempt to try and brace my fall, my skull bounced off hard stone, and stars shot across my vision. Something wet slid down my forehead as I crawled on my bruised hands and knees, dizzy, trying to get away. But I stopped short when I saw gray Converse.

I looked up. And up and up some more, my head still reeling.

The shell of my brother was standing over me, staring with those pitiless black eyes—uncaring.

The pain in my head took a back seat to everything else as my heart thundered away, my breathing double-timing. For a horrifying moment, I thought someone was stabbing me in my chest, until I realized this was a panic attack.

Seeing my brother staring down at me sprawled out on the ground, *crawling*—and his face a blank mask, not attempting to help me—hurt worse than anything Trevor could *ever* do to me.

Not-Corinth bent down, reaching for me—

"Stop," Trevor ordered. "I have something else in mind for her now."

Not-Corinth obeyed, his hand still outstretched toward me, and I stretched mine out toward him, imploring, hoping and praying he would help me. He would never hurt me. Never. He wouldn't stand by and let this happen.

"Snap out of it, Cor, *please*," I pleaded, reaching.

But he only glanced behind me with an almost imperceptible nod, presumably looking at Trevor, and then stood slowly back up to his full, towering height.

There came brisk footsteps, and then icy fingers encircled my wrist, and I was jerked back to my feet. Trevor twisted me around to face him, his other hand gripping my elbow, pulling me close against him.

A bout of adrenaline tore through me. "*Corinth!*" I shouted, thrashing against Trevor's viselike hold, trying to turn around, to get my brother to look me in the eyes. I could convince him to snap out of it.

Not-Corinth clasped his hands in front of him and … just … he … well, he … *watched.*

"*Cor!*" I shouted, louder this time. "Don't let him do this … Please! Cor!" I kicked out at Trevor, and my foot connected with his shin, and by some small miracle, I managed to rip out of his iron grip—and ran.

"Help me—"

In that same second, Trevor vaulted out of a tower of billowing smoke that was still curling up and around his tall form, and belted me across the face.

I listed to the side, the world tilting right along with

me. I couldn't tell which way was up or down. I tasted salt and copper. My knees buckled, but before I could hit the ground, Trevor was behind me, crossing his arms over mine, pinning them against my chest like a straitjacket.

"Be a good girl," he whispered in my ear. "I'm going to take your hand, and then you're going to come with me without a fight. Did you see what I did to Alastair? You don't want that to happen to you, do you?"

One more slanted glance in my brother's direction showed me a flicker of something in his eyes ... something like anger and distress *and* ... I thought I saw him stepping toward us, his fiery hands clenched—

But then Trevor was hauling me away from not-Corinth, almost ripping my arm out of its socket. I didn't care about the fire lancing through my wrist. I planted my feet, pulling away from him with everything I had in me.

When we came to a grinding halt, my arm outstretched in front of me, wrist bent up at an unnatural angle, only then did he finally stop and face me, a dark grin on his face. He was looking at me as if I were a petulant child trying to run away. My face was pinched and strained with pain and something—blood, I thought—leaked into my eyes, stinging them.

"You're only making this worse for yourself," he said gruffly. "I could control you by using my mind ... but where's the fun in that? Hmm?"

Suddenly agony ripped through me as in one swift movement, he tugged my arm so hard my feet slipped out from under me. I gasped as I slid across the slick floor, forced to follow him like a dog on a leash—my arm the leash.

"Don't let him kill me, Cor!" I shrieked one last time. The throbbing in my head and my racing pulse melded together. It was all I could get out before I tripped, and fell to a knee, my breath sawing out of my mouth. I would make him drag me, at least.

Tired of my struggling, Trevor reached down and slung an arm around my waist, hoisting me off the ground as if I didn't weigh a thing. He trapped my arms against my sides, carrying me like a suitcase under one arm, my feet dragging awkwardly behind me.

"At first I wrote you off as boring," he admitted, not even sounding winded. "But now I see why you're *his* half sister. Defiant until the very end. I like that."

I tried to tell him to go to hell, but I couldn't breathe, and the only thing that came out of my mouth was a strained groan. Any light left in the cavernous space disappeared. I had no idea where he was taking me, but it wasn't to the steel table Alastair had been restrained on.

Pretty soon, all I heard was the sound of my own labored breathing, the scuff of Trevor's feet on the stone, and mine dragging behind me as we moved further and further away from where we'd left Cruz and Alastair and Gabriel Stanton.

He had ahold of me so tight I could feel the flexing of each of his muscles, and every time he took a step, I bumped against his chest. It reverberated through my body, jarring my ribs. I kicked out feebly, and he squeezed me tighter. The air seemed to thin out like we were in an enclosed tunnel or chamber. I couldn't get in a deep breath.

And he kept walking, on and on and on … seemingly

forever. It was pitch-black. It smelled dank and closed off, and it was devastatingly quiet.

"W-w-where," I wheezed, "are you taking me?"

"Disobedience must be dealt with by a firm hand," he said in answer.

I had a sinking feeling in the pit of my stomach. Those words were beyond sinister. I wanted to ram them back down his throat. Get away. Make him stop touching me. We were alone. Not even his dark army was following him. If I got free now, perhaps I could evade him. I realized this would probably be my last chance to escape.

Taking as deep a breath as I could manage, I bucked wildly in his grasp. He must not have been expecting it, because he loosened his grip on me and I kicked out again. Trevor stopped in his tracks to readjust his grasp, winding both arms around my middle, as if I were a fish trying to slip free of his hold.

"Where do you think you're going?" he admonished.

"*Let me go!*" I roared, kicking out with everything I had left. I would make him kill me on my own terms.

"Do you remember telling me what your biggest fear is?" He squeezed my rib cage until blotches of light erupted across my vision, and only when I went boneless in his arms did he haul me back into his one-armed grip and start walking again.

I didn't like the way those words sounded. I could hear the tinge of excitement mixed with something darker in his voice. Something primal. Like he was enjoying himself and he wanted me to fight. I'd told him what my worst fear was. A lightning bolt of shock went through me at the thought. *The dark.*

I couldn't see anything, only hear his breathing. It was devastatingly quiet other than that. I didn't know how he could see to walk. We'd entered an enclosed space, because something suddenly smelled rancid and tainted.

Trevor stepped down, and my feet hit a dip in the floor, and then a moment later, he deposited me roughly onto my rump without another word. I cradled my right arm, the one he'd tried to rip clean off my shoulder. My entire body was sore and throbbing, and I tried to blink in the darkness—but it made no difference. I was completely and utterly blind. There was nothing to see by.

Something cold clamped around my left wrist, and I almost jumped out of my own skin. A second later, a strange tingling sensation shot up my arm—something dark and sinister and supernatural. I shivered as the thing on my wrist lit up a strange electric blue for a moment, and I could see.

An iron shackle.

And then it cinched down, like a fitted glove, and I stifled a scream as my heart shot up into my throat.

I could feel icy breath on my neck, and then he was gone.

"*Wait,*" I begged. "*Don't leave me here.*"

It was as dark as space—space with no stars or moon or solar system—only death. Endless. Confining. Suffocating. I was blind. He'd left me in a dungeon with rats and rotting, venomous things that were only meant for a Stephen King novel. I should know—I'd read plenty of them. The overwhelming scent of staleness and something else made me gag.

"*Don't leave me like this,*" I pleaded, and I hated the

desperation in my own voice. *"Please. Not like this."*

There came no reply.

Only emptiness.

He knew. He knew I hated the dark.

Dread bloomed in my chest. I didn't move for a good two minutes, just tried to catch my breath and not pass out, listening to the erratic beating of my own heart. There was a twinge of spine-tingling fear right between my shoulder blades. Like eyes staring at my back. *I am still alive.*

Finally, when I thought Trevor was gone, I put shaking hands out in front of me, barely able to lift the heavy manacle on my wrist. There was an awful crick in my neck, and my ribs ached where he'd squeezed the life out of me. The iron had to weigh at least fifteen pounds—definitely meant for those who were a lot stronger and stouter than a hundred-and-ten-pound girl.

And it smelled rank, like body odor and human waste and decay. I almost choked on the denseness of it, and I started to take in short, quick breaths, imagining that this was what desperation and suffering smelled like. Death. A burial ground.

I shivered.

This was where bad things happened.

I was panicking now, but I couldn't help it. I sucked in a shallow breath through my mouth and tried to stand up, grappling with the heavy chain, using my right hand to help lift it, but I was immediately met by resistance and the sound of a metal rattling and snapping taut, which brought me abruptly crashing to my butt, my wrist pinned to the floor by the sudden crushing weight.

I let out a cry of frustration, feeling at the iron cuff. I had extra-small wrists, so I should have been able to at least slip my fingers under it, but there was no slack or give or room between my flesh and the metal. I clamped my fingers around the iron, but it would not budge. That weird icy tingling sensation seemed to increase the more I messed with it, like someone had pressed an exposed battery to my bare skin. I sucked in a shocked breath and stopped. That hurt.

Blindly, I followed the attached chain until it ended at something solid in the floor. My fingers explored further. It was large and round and cold—some sort of wide metal loop bolted into the ground. I gripped it tightly with both hands and pulled, straining with everything I had, but there was no way this thing was budging, not unless I suddenly turned into the Hulk.

He'd chained me to an anchor—a restraint meant for giants.

There was a slight decline in the floor, so I crawled on my hands and knees, the manacle and chain clanking loudly on the stone, until my fingers hit metal slats, like a grating. Just on the other side of the bar in the ground was a recess in the stone slab. Some sort of drainage system. Maybe this was my way out. A few more feet, and I found deep ruts and grooves sunk into the ground. My free hand hit something dry and crusted over.

I rubbed my fingers together, and it flaked off as an overwhelming tang of metal hit me. *What is this?*

My brain answered back: *Blood.*

I was pretty sure the stuff on my hands and knees wasn't water. I dry heaved. This was the spot where either people were forced to relieve themselves or he drained his victims dry. Neither was a pleasant thought. How long did he plan on keeping me down here?

"*Jackass!*" I yelled, my voice echoing off the enclosed space. He had wanted me to find this.

"Now that's not very nice."

Trevor's voice made me jump in fright. How long had it been since I thought he'd left? It felt like centuries. My heart crashed painfully against my rib cage as a wash of heat flooded through me. He had been watching. Probably highly entertained. Sicko. I was just so angry. Not like this. Not in the dark. I couldn't see him. I couldn't *see*.

"*The dark*," he drawled. "I thought I'd let you get acquainted with it before you die."

A feeling of helplessness washed over me so strongly I collapsed, my world shriveling down to nothing.

The dark was where monsters waited to attack. Except I'd recently learned monsters could attack *anywhere*. Even in broad daylight. I closed my eyes—not that it mattered; it was so dark—but a flash of Cor's disinterested face as he watched me being taken away hit me, and I opened them again, and my heart ached. *Cor.*

I couldn't even produce a small pocket of light behind my eyelids when I squeezed them shut. I was in the middle of a dungeon with my back exposed to who knew what terrible things. I pulled my legs up to my chest, wrapping my arms around them and resting my chin on my knees. I was pretty sure Trevor was gone. I hadn't heard a peep out of anyone for a good long while. Hours.

At some point, I realized I didn't even know if my eyes were open or closed. It didn't matter. The black was hostile. I had explored as far as I could, awkwardly using my foot to tap around. From what I could tell, I was right smack in the center of a sunken circular chamber, shackled. I couldn't reach beyond the outer step. A recess maybe, which, you know, was a heartening feeling being in the center of.

I imagined Trevor's cold breath on the back of my neck, his icy fingers wrapped brutally around my wrist again, his hands on my body—exactly how the cursed manacle felt right now: restrictive. I cringed and pulled my right hand up to my forehead, and agony shot through my shoulder. Gingerly I used my tongue to explore the cut on the inside of my lip where he'd struck me. *Asshole.*

This was my worst nightmare, and he knew it.

Once again I planted my palms against my eyes, hoping for some patch of light to greet me. The darkness had never held any sort of comfort whatsoever—it had always been the opposite—and now I wondered if that was because of what had happened to me when I was five. That feeling of being in the dark all alone had come from somewhere. And then I thought about Corinth, and a pang of loneliness struck me. My brother. He was gone. *Cruz.*

Was that the sound of something slithering behind me?

I jumped, turning around, trying to scoot across the tacky floor, petrified.

My mind felt fractured, like it might shatter into a million pieces at any given moment. I couldn't focus on any one thought at a time. Instead, a million macabre images skittered across my vision—mainly of me being attacked by something with tentacles and sharp teeth.

Disobedience must be dealt with by a firm hand.

Those words kept running through my head.

I felt Trevor's arctic breath on my ear again and jumped, turning my head from side to side, searching and listening. He wasn't there. I was alone. Maybe. It was only a matter of time before he came back for me though. I swallowed past a dry throat. How was he going to kill me? Was Cruz dead?

Disobedience must be dealt with by a firm hand.

I felt his fingers on the back of my neck, and I froze, taking in a shaky breath. He wasn't there. I was only imagining it. His hand was fisted into my braid—

And I screamed, shuffling backward across the concrete. The chain snapped taut, and I crashed brutally onto my side as the sharp iron bit at my arm, sending an icy shock wave of agony through me. I lay there, stunned, unable to breathe. He wasn't there. The sour air was too thick … My head swam. *Breathe …*

I must have passed out, because I was lying on my side, my right arm pinned beneath me, and when I shifted it out from under my body, pins and needles trickled down my hand. Everything I'd learned in just the span of a few short hours was enough to drive anyone mad. This couldn't be real. I wondered which was worse: waiting for your own execution or going through the actual execution.

I felt eyes on me and assumed he was watching, waiting.

Get a grip.

With a sudden jolt, I remembered I had my cell phone in my hoodie pocket. I sat up, overcome by a bout of dizziness, and reached inside it, my fingers hitting the smooth surface of my case. I pulled the phone out and pressed the power button. Nothing. No light or signal or battery source. Underneath my fingers, I could feel the screen had deep fissures running across it. It must have broken when Trevor threw me to the ground.

And then I found something else in my pocket—the device Gabriel had entrusted to me. The one that could get us out of this dreadful place. Trevor hadn't taken it back. Maybe, in his excitement, he'd forgotten about it, or maybe he didn't know I had it. Maybe he thought he'd just take it off my corpse. Maybe it was his way of torturing me … escape being so close, yet so far away.

I found the button and pressed it, hoping against hope that it would work. I hadn't been magically transported away. I was still sightless. Stuck in this dank hellhole.

I tugged at my wrist in irritation, once again feeling the odd tingling sensation running up my arm. The blood in my veins seemed to thicken, and the clank of the chain was deafening in the utter stillness of the room. I tried to wrench the cuff around, but my skin burned like it had frostbite.

How could this thing be so formfitting? I wasn't sure

if I could stomach pain … but I guessed if I had to choose between a mangled hand, and not living, I'd choose a mangled hand.

I clanked the chain again, harder, and screamed. And then again, and again. *Clank. Rattle. Clank. Rattle.* Over and over, my hand aching, my body racked by tremors, until sweat lined my brow, and my arms were too heavy to lift. I kept screaming until I had no voice left. Gabriel or Alastair might hear me.

I slumped over, exhausted, my head splitting. What was the point?

My head resting against cold stone, I blinked. There was a light. A torch emerging down a long shaft. The light at the end of the tunnel. This was it. I'd died.

Of course, the more likely explanation was that I was hallucinating—either that or maybe Trevor was coming for me. I knew I was half in shock, so when the golden glow got closer, I sat up. It looked like a flickering mirage. I licked my lips. Blinked again. It was closer. I threw a hand over my eyes, shielding them from the blaring light. I had been down here longer than I'd thought, apparently.

The lit orb bobbed and weaved like a disembodied ghost, moving closer.

My pulse quickened. *What is that?*

My eyes tried to adjust; they blurred and watered.

I clanged the chain again. "*Hello!*" My voice came out raspy and hoarse. "*I'm here! Help!*"

And then I stopped, suddenly terrified that maybe this was Trevor's doing, and he was messing with me. He wanted to give me hope, only so he could rip it away again. No one called out my name. If it were Gabriel Stanton or

Alastair, wouldn't they be calling my name?

The light grew steadily brighter.

I picked the heavy chain up, getting ready to move—

And then the apparition came fully into view, and I could plainly see that it was indeed a ghost, and I was dead.

24

ZOEY

The metal glowed golden, highlighting his honey-colored skin, giving him an ethereal sort of hue. Mocha eyes met mine, and that face was looking at me like *I* was the apparition—when clearly it was him. *Cruz.* I sucked in a shocked breath, still waiting for my eyes to fully adjust. My heart skipped a beat.

"*Zoey,*" he breathed, quickly dropping down to his knees in front of me, the shield key chain clutched in his hand, at the same time as I got to mine. His eyebrows creased in concern. "Are you okay?"

"I thought you were dead," I said, letting out a shuddering sob.

His face lit up with a brilliant smile. "Same," he said, sounding relieved. "I only *played* dead. Well, not at first. At first I really was dying from that Darth Vader grip Trevor had over me, but with the help of this—" he held up the still-shining shield, smiling in triumph "—

apparently, not even Trevor can touch or control someone. When I fell down and clutched the shield to me, I could breathe again. But by then you'd already thrown the dagger, and your scary possessed brother was there— and I didn't know what else to do …" Cruz glanced around, wrinkling his nose. "What's that smell? It smells like something died—"

I threw one arm around him, nearly toppling us both backward, and held onto his neck as if we were suspended in space and if I let him go, he might drift away from me forever. Or disappear like a mirage. I was crying now. "I thought I got you killed." I couldn't hold it in, and the awful tightness in my chest loosened just a tad as he let me sniffle into his shirt.

He is *alive.*

Cruz lightly patted my back, and then, as if he needed the comfort and nearness too, enveloped me in his warm arms, shifting closer to me on his knees. I could feel his necklace underneath his shirt as I squeezed him tighter.

Gently he extricated himself from my death grip to study me. "You're shaking." He lifted the light to examine my face, and then let out a soft curse in Spanish. At least, I was pretty sure it was a curse by the way he spit it out. Heat flooded his cheeks, and his eyes narrowed down to tiny slits.

"I never liked that guy, but seriously, I am going to *kill* him. When you see red flags, man …" He lifted my chin so he could get a better look at my face and head in the soft light. "I don't think it needs stitches. It's already stopped bleeding." His scarred fingers grazed my bloodied and fat lip. A fizzy, bubbly sensation rose up inside me at the way he touched my face. Cruz winced in empathy. "Seriously, I am going to *kill* him—I mean, when I figure out how to slay a demon," he reiterated, fury lacing his voice.

"Get in line," I vowed vehemently.

"I think it's a good idea we don't stick around. This place reeks, and it gives me the willies—" He passed the faintly glowing light over the ground and then paused when he saw the chain next to my legs. "What's that—?" His throat worked past a swallow. "Oh no. That's not what I think it is, is it?"

Cruz let the illumination from the key chain wash over our surroundings. I had been right, at least, in my assessment of the chamber.

For the first time in my life, I wished the light would go out.

We were right smack in the center of a sunken circle. He followed the chain with the light to where it ended at a metal bar bolted into the ground. All things I'd assessed by way of touch and smell ... but ...

His mouth fell open. "*What the ...?*"

The circle had a weird triangular pattern etched inside it, with smaller, pentagram-type symbols etched inside that.

Breath left my body in a rush of air at seeing what was smeared all over the floor. Brown. Everywhere. Like rust. The edges of the recess we sat in were spattered with it— as if there had been so much it had slopped over the sides, staining everything burgundy. Probably enough blood to fill a small pool before it had dried.

I shivered, thinking about how many people had been left down here to rot. Dozens. Hundreds. And then there were the bloody palm prints. Smeared everywhere. Fingernail markings were gouged deep into the ground and all over the walls. Deep grooves, like people had tried to dig their way out. Above us hung more chains, with manacles and restraints and sharp, pointy-looking death traps. A torture chamber.

I felt sick. Now I knew why that drain was there. At least it wasn't fresh.

"Okay, time to get out of here." He cast an anxious glance around, his voice wavering. "Let's go."

Using both hands, I hoisted the heavy shackle onto my lap, and his eyes snapped down at the sound of the chain clanking. "Can you help me out of this?"

Cruz's eyes locked onto the chain, and then they widened in alarm, his face losing all its color in an instant. He shook his head, staring at it, partly in shock and disbelief. And then something else flickered across his face: Defeat. Hopelessness. Despair.

Cruz lifted my hand with both of his so he could get a better look at the iron. "This is … really heavy." He inspected it using the light from the key chain. "Where's the lock or keyhole? Is there a latch? What are those weird swirl-like patterns on the iron? Is this carved with some sort of spell work?"

I shook my head. "I … I have no idea. Trevor or Ephrem … he … he put it on me in the dark, and I couldn't see …"

The etchings were curved and flowing, almost like Chinese calligraphy or something, I thought. It matched some of the symbols in the floor. Ancient looking. The words *ritualistic sacrifice* immediately popped into my head, and I shuddered. What did he have planned for me?

Ritualistic sacrifice.

I was starting to really panic by the time Cruz reached around with both hands and tried to jerk the metal cuff off by sheer force, working it back and forth against the hard bone on my wrist. Icy, debilitating pain tore up my arm as the metal dug into my flesh, and I inhaled, gritting my teeth against it. I tried to brace my left arm with my right as I yanked hard on it at the same time he did—

The metal crackled and lit up ghostly silver in the semidarkness, and an invisible force slammed through my entire body, jarring me to my core. My heart stutter-stopped in my chest, and the next thing I knew, I was staring up at Cruz, flat on my back.

I was aware that he was super-duper close to my face, his hands on my waist. Every inch of my skin felt like it was covered in ice crystals. When I exhaled, my breath plumed out in front of me.

"Are you okay?" Cruz asked, worry lacing his voice, his eyebrows knitting together. "What the heck was that? Dark magic?"

I nodded, grabbing my head. "Well, we're not doing that again," I wheezed, sitting back up with his help.

"Something tells me that this thing can't be opened with a key."

I laughed bitterly, folding my legs underneath me, feeling winded and shaky and weak. I'd been robbed of all my breath. I wasn't getting out of here. My heart plummeted.

We didn't speak for a long time after that.

There was nothing left to say. I thought he was trying

to think through our options, but we didn't have any left. *I* didn't have any left—but *he* still did. I knew what I had to do. But like a coward, I waited to tell him. I didn't have the nerve. I couldn't be left alone in the dark again.

Cruz stood up and moved around the room, inspecting everything by the lantern-soft glow of the shield key chain, his nose wrinkled in disgust from the awful stench. I watched him bend down and examine the strange markings and engravings, then wander the outer, raised edge of the circle, muttering to himself.

Eventually, he shuffled back over to the anchored loop in the middle of the circle and yanked on it, looking more and more drawn and irritated by the second.

He finally let out a bark of frustration and knelt down in front of me, placing a supportive hand on mine. "You're trembling again," he said, and after a second, he shrugged out of his blue parka to drape it over my shoulders.

I glanced down, enjoying the warmth of his lingering body heat on the material, inhaling the scent of spice and pine and something else—maybe hair gel.

"Aren't you cold?" I asked thickly, feeling grateful. There was a lump in my throat.

He ran a hand through his wild, curly locks. "I'm okay."

"Thanks," I whispered, tugging the coat closer and adding, "How did you find me, anyway?"

"They thought I was dead. Trevor's *un*dead, or whatever he calls them, they left me alone … They didn't want to get near the light. You and Trevor … disappeared … He … he …" Cruz paused. "He dragged you away, and

I was just too scared to move … For a long time, I just lay there. I'm so sorry, Zoey. I thought I was too late … I tried to follow him, but then I got lost."

"I'm scared too," I admitted, putting a hand over his. "But you're here now."

"I could have done more." He shook his head. "Your brother. He's terrifying."

"Whatever's gotten ahold of him … it's not my brother," I snarled, and after another beat, I added, "Cruz, I threw the dagger away. This is all my fault. I did this. I'm so sorry. We could have gotten away … I should have listened to you."

He shot back to his feet, irritated. "You were trying to save my life, and if that was my brother, I would have done exactly the same thing to try and get him back."

I felt the tears scald the backs of my eyelids as he continued.

"I searched for what seemed like hours and hours for you, and it just got darker and danker. And then I heard that banging noise, and I followed it—and then you screamed, and I thought the worst …"

"You didn't run into any of those weird … Shade things?" I asked. "There was no locked door you had to bust down to get in here? No guards?"

He shook his head, and in the soft light, I saw a lock of charcoal-colored hair fall into his eyes. He brushed irratatedly at it. "Who needs a door or guards when you have unbreakable magical shackles? Also, I'm pretty sneaky. One time, I snuck out of work early without anyone else knowing about it the *entire* shift …" He let the sentence trail off and lowered his gaze from mine.

"Sorry. I ramble when I'm terrified out of my mind."

"Cruz," I began, and then stopped. *It's true*, I thought suddenly. *Misery does love company.* And I did *not* want him to leave. I wanted to tell him that I was absolutely horrified by the idea of being left alone in the dark again. But I didn't. I wanted to tell him to stay with me. But I didn't. I wanted to curl into a ball and cry. Not yet. I wanted to tell him Trevor scared me to death. Instead, I said, "You can't be here when he comes back."

Cruz sat back and rubbed a hand across his chin, looking at me, like he was riddled with guilt. He'd thought about leaving me too. I could see the tension in his face and in his shoulders. I couldn't say I blamed him. I had gotten Cruz into this mess, and I was going to get him out. At least one of us could live. There didn't seem to be any more moisture left in my mouth. *Who am I kidding?* Trevor was going to come back for me any minute.

I fished the small, round device out of my hoodie pocket, the one Gabriel Stanton had given me, and held it out to him.

He inched closer, brandishing the key chain again so he could get a closer look at what I was holding.

"Gabriel Stanton and Alastair are still alive—at least, they were when I left them. They'll find me. *You*," I said in a throaty whisper, "can still get out. Take this." I plunked the device into his open palm without asking for permission. "Please t-t-tell my family I love them. My mom … tell her … I'm sorry I was such a … jerk to her."

After an incredibly long stretch of silence, Cruz drew his eyebrows together and curled his fingers around the device as he took it from me. "You still haven't tried my mom's cake."

That gave me pause, because it wasn't anywhere near what I'd thought he'd say. My eyebrows shot up in question.

"You and I are getting out of here *together*—so that you can try my mom's cake," he clarified. His voice sounded small now. "Even if Alastair or that weird vampire billionaire manage to find you, how are they going to get you out of that?" He pointed at the iron around my wrist. "I'm not leaving you down here by yourself. I already did that once. We'll figure something out. Just give me some time to think."

He plopped down beside me, crossing his arms over his chest as if that settled the matter. I felt a pang of regret hit me, but also something else: relief and an extreme sense of thankfulness swelled in my chest.

The golden light cast dark shadows under his eyes; he looked older all of a sudden. How had I not seen him before? I mean, really seen him.

There was a lump in my throat as I nodded, slumping back down. He must have sensed how cold I was, because he edged over and leaned into me, pressing himself against my side. Our thighs touched, and his body heat and proximity were both reassuring and comforting.

After a second, I said, "Can I take a look at that gateway thingy? I mean, now that we have light to see by."

He lifted the device and held it in his palm, handing me the still-glowing shield so I could illuminate it. There were three symbols on the device, and a toggle switch that could be flipped to one symbol at a time. A diamond, a circle with a line through it, and a symbol that looked a lot like a three-leaved clover.

Nothing happened when I toggled between all of the symbols and pressed the red button. Not surprising, but I had to try.

Cruz pointed to the cloverlike symbol first. "I think this one's called a *trefoil*. In Latin, that means 'three-leaved.'"

I gave him a sideways glance. "You know Latin?"

"I know math," he corrected, tilting his head to the side as if in thought. "It's like a trefoil knot, as in knot theory."

I shook my head. "I'm not familiar with knot theory."

"Knots appear in daily life all of the time. Shoelaces, rope, rings. Mathematical knots differ in that the ends are joined together, so that they can't be undone. Sort of like that stupid shackle on your wrist …"

"Wow," I said, my mouth hanging open. "You're supersmart."

Cruz brushed a lock of hair out of his eyes again, glancing down. "I thought it would be cool to be an architect at one point in time … before my mom got sick, I mean. But I kind of let my grades slip, so I'm not even sure I could get into college at this point."

"You're a sophomore, right?" I asked. "You still have time. I could help you study …" I glanced down at my bound wrist and let the rest of that sentence trail off. *Not now.* Neither of us wanted to say what we were both thinking—we probably weren't getting out of here alive.

"So Gabriel Stanton said to find the same diamond-shaped symbol etched into the wall and then toggle this thing to the corresponding symbol, and press the button. And presto, we're out of here."

He huffed out a dry laugh. "Sounds like lottery scratch-off instructions." When he saw the puzzled look on my face, he said, "My mom used to play a lot … before she got sick and we couldn't afford—" He stopped himself short, picking at the ring that was still attached to the shield key chain. I could see his scars standing out silver-white against his bronzed skin in the lantern-like glow. He licked his lips, seemingly deep in thought.

We fell silent again, and I concentrated on the rhythmical sound of his breathing—for I didn't know how long—until he said, "My scars. You still want to know how I got them?"

I nodded my head against his shoulder, suddenly needing the distraction of talking, and I really did want to know. "But you don't have to tell me unless you want to."

"I want to."

A tiny flutter went through me at hearing that.

He let out a soft sigh. "When my mom got sick with lung disease—when we found out it was terminal—I … I snapped. She was all I had—*is* all I have. I never knew my dad. I have some extended family in Mexico, but no others nearby. I didn't know how to deal with it. I was just a *kid*." He stressed the word. "I was angry *all* the time. I had to funnel out all of that negativity somehow … so I picked fights. With anyone I could. I didn't care who it was, as long as they hit back. And even the things that didn't hit back, like brick walls, glass windows … one time even a cement block. Plaster. Boards … Whatever I could find …" He made a fist and ran his fingers along his blemished knuckles.

A pang of sorrow rolled over me, and I felt something

wet on my cheeks and realized too late what it was. Tears. Cruz must have seen me swipe at them, because his gaze seemed to pierce right through me.

"That must have been a nightmare," I finally said. "Having to go through that all alone."

"It was."

I reached out to trace the outline of one of his scars, a bigger one on the back of his left hand, and when he turned to look at me, I could see moisture glistening under his eyes.

"It feels really good to talk about this, actually. And now that my mom is doing better—because of you and Corinth—I feel like I owe it to him to at least look out for you."

I hadn't thought about it like that. Suddenly my stomach was full of a million tiny flutters, like moth wings beating against a glass window.

He turned his head, and his hair brushed my face, feather soft, and if he moved any closer, I was sure we would be sharing the same breath. His eyes were a light, syrupy brown. My heart picked up its pace.

There was no way I was going to let him stay down here with me. No way. I did not want his death on my conscience. I'd dragged him into this. Well, technically, Corinth had.

"Look around," I said.

He did; his gaze flitted to the brown stains smeared everywhere, and he visibly shuddered. You couldn't not look at it. And that smell was rancid.

"You can take a wild guess at what happens down here. If you're here when Trevor comes back—" my voice cracked "—he'll torture me in front of you, or vice versa … and because you have the key chain and this device, he'll use me against you in order to get it back. *You have to go. Please. I'm begging you.*"

He gazed back down at the key chain clutched in his hand and nodded.

Good. He was going to leave. My stomach felt like a hot stone was sitting in it.

But instead of getting up, he gently laid the glimmering shield in my lap. "He can't touch you if you have this." Suddenly his eyes lit up as if he'd thought of an idea, and he plucked the key chain back to press it firmly against the manacle on my wrist.

I glanced down, hoping to hear the faint click of it unlocking and unclasping—popping open—but when nothing happened, he sank back down, his face falling.

"What if I find your brother's blade? It's magical … like that shackle. Maybe I can use it to bust you out of here. Magical things can counteract other magical things, right? That's how it works in the movies. Good counteracts evil, right?"

I lifted my shoulders in a small shrug. "I have *no* idea how any of this works. And besides, you would need light to see by … and possessed Corinth is still out there …" It came out whisper soft, and I held the shield out to him again. "Cruz, *please*. Go."

He pulled something out of his pocket, and suddenly a white light flared up, blinding me for a moment. He flipped what he was holding around so I could see it—his cell phone—and my heart rate kicked up another notch. "I have this. Trust me, I can run. I used to play soccer.

They won't catch me. I don't need the shield to keep me safe, but you do, in case that douche comes back."

"How much battery life do you have left?" I asked. "Does it have a signal?"

He barked out an exasperated laugh. "No signal in this hellhole of a dimension. And I have enough juice left," he added confidently. "This is going to work." He stood up, gazing down at me, his mouth puckered as if he had something else he wanted to say. There was something about the way he was staring at me. Like he might never see me again.

He might not, I thought.

"It's too dangerous, Cruz … *Please*, just take this and go. Run away." I held the glowing charm out to him, waving it like a white flag. "You can get away. No one will think the less of you."

He refused to take it. "I'm coming back with the blade. And hopefully Alastair—he seemed like he could kick way more ass than I could." He handed me the portal device back. "So you know I'm not abandoning you. Keep it safe."

And then, before he could change his mind, or listen to my further protests, he turned around and dashed out of the sunken chamber, bounding up the step, the light from his phone bouncing down the tunnel as he moved away.

He *was* fast.

I didn't even get a chance to ask him if he even knew where he was going.

I watched the light until it finally dwindled and faded into nothing.

25

ALASTAIR

The entire legion of the undead was after Alastair. And Gray, the Shade with the whip, was the ringleader. He had taken the damn demon down at least four times already, but Gray had kept springing back up like a weed.

Alastair was beyond exhausted. This was the main reason he hadn't been able to help Zoey and Cruz, to make sure they were okay. Or go after Stanton. He needed that device from him, seeing as how it was their only way out of this godforsaken place.

Who was he kidding? Stanton was probably already long gone by now. They were trapped here.

And then there was Corinth. A dark shadow of his former friend. Soulless. Brutal. Evil. Taylor fought with a ruthlessness Alastair had never seen before.

The nagging voice at the back of his mind kept telling him that he was going to have to kill him. His brother.

His best friend. And it hurt. More like it crushed his soul. Dark Corinth wouldn't stop coming for him until his orders from Ephrem and Angela had been fulfilled: putting Alastair back on that table to be experimented on. It was up to him to stop his best friend, but he had no idea how he was going to do that without killing him.

And that was what gutted him the most—the fact that he had even considered it.

A sharp pang of guilt knifed its way through Alastair, constricting his chest, cutting off his airway. *No.* He had to think clearly. Be levelheaded. Except he couldn't. For once in his life, he could not think straight. His breath came out in shallow, ragged pants. He didn't think he could do it: *Kill Taylor.* He closed his eyes, and for a brief moment, he thought it might just be easier to let Corinth kill *him* instead.

If it weren't for Corinth's little sister and her friend being lost in this demonic realm, he might have already given up. And this thought was enough to make him fight harder. Faster. He just needed to buy more time.

Alastair's eyes popped open, and he dodged lithely out of the way of another one of Gray's attempts at lassoing his neck with that damn whip. It snapped so close to his head his eardrum popped, and for a moment, all he could hear was a high-pitched ringing in its wake. The bastard was trying to take his head off.

Alastair moved in the space of a single heartbeat, appearing behind his adversary almost as fast as a flickering mirage, snapping an arm out and catching Gray across the back of its skull. The demon dropped its weapon and stumbled forward at the same time as Alastair rammed his bare foot into the Shade's back, at the base of its spine. He heard the deep crack of bone breaking, and then the thing collapsed with an earsplitting howl of rage and pain.

Gray's body shuddered; it writhed on the ground like an earthworm wriggling in the dirt as it tried to put itself back together again.

And then something unexpected happened—everything froze.

Gray's cries muted; the Shade's body went utterly still, and Alastair's heart even seemed to stop thumping in his chest. He couldn't move. He couldn't blink. He couldn't think. Only a frosty mist plumed out from his parted lips as a brutal cold raked down his spine, tugging all his warmth out of him—sort of how it might feel if he were lowered into a vat of dry ice, he imagined. There was a charged bite to the air, and a pressure at the base of his spine.

Alastair knew what it was.

Or rather, *who* it was.

He could feel their approach in his bones. *An angel*—controlling time—opening up portals. Traveling through lightning was Corinth's signature move.

There came a swirl of thick black smoke, materializing out of nowhere, accompanied by a terrible rumble of thunder, shaking the cavern walls. And then he felt the bridge connecting this world and the next opening up, swirling like ink in water.

Dark Corinth.

Before vampires had been wiped out of existence by Corinth Taylor, the last surviving Nephilim, the sharing of blood between progeny and maker had bonded them to each other. It was a feeling he had learned to resist over time when he'd been a vampire himself. And for some peculiar reason, he felt that pull now. *Impossible.* He wasn't vampire. But he had been Corinth's maker—at one point in time—he'd been the one to turn him …

Of course, Alastair had killed his own maker, Wrentmore, so that was probably why his connection had been severed. Alastair had never spoken to Larna about this. If he didn't tell her about it, she didn't have to feed into that notion. Because Gabriel Stanton had turned her, and that meant that they had been bonded, and he did not like that thought at all. Not one bit. He hated Stanton. He hated vampires.

Yet *now*, in this very moment, he'd never felt so strongly connected to vampirism. It felt like tasting blood for the very first time as a newly turned vamp— intoxicating and rich. A warm, drunken stupor. Foreign but somehow profoundly right. Feral and thrilling. His pulse thundered in his ears. *Am I turning?*

It was this very feeling that froze him dead in his tracks as Corinth bounded out of the vortex, throwing an already-blazing hand out toward Alastair in a wide, sweeping arc, wicked fast. White-hot lightning poured out of his fingertips with deadly precision.

There was no avoiding the impact—

The glare seared his eyes at the same time as a deep crack shredded the air, and it didn't so much pulsate around him as through him, rattling his teeth in his very skull. He clamped his jaws together as a searing heat ripped through his body. Bright splotches surged across his vision like he was staring directly into the sun. No, scratch that—it was as if he'd walked right on out into a solar flare.

A golden ray of light surrounded him in a cocoon of energy, and then something shifted loose and fissured inside him, then burst outward, exploding out of Alastair's chest. His lungs burned. His insides felt gooey. Everything was glowing like smelted metal. *Am I on fire?*

One second, Alastair was standing, and the next, he was gliding across the polished stone, colliding with a spiky rock formation ten feet behind him. Bits of gray powder rained down around him, and breath left him, refusing to return. At his back, the outcropping was scorched and blackened.

A hot, prickling sensation tingled over every inch of his flesh. A strange sort of newness rushed through him, like shedding an old skin. He let out a gasp from the headiness of it hitting him all at once. *Power.* This was nauseatingly familiar. Vampirism, but not. His head spun.

Alastair's mouth dropped open as he stared at the lightning crackling across his fingertips. *Holy powers.* He hated admitting that he missed possessing supernatural abilities. He had a trace of angelic blood running through him, thanks to Corinth, but he'd never truly experienced what it felt like to be an angel. Not until now.

Alastair blinked several times, trying to clear his vision, and there, across from him, lay a dazed Corinth, his arms cradled over his stomach, his back propped against a charred wall, his eyes half-closed.

Through his own hazy vision, he could see Corinth's chest rising and falling rapidly.

Alastair wondered distantly if he was Corinth's mirror image—both of them having been blown off their feet in opposite directions to each other. There were lightning-shaped whorls scored into the wall, glowing silver-white; they curled up and around Corinth's prone form, looking a lot like angel wings.

Alastair glanced up, wondering if there would be anything similar on the wall he was braced against. And unbelievably, etched on the stone behind him, was also a set of scorched wings, but these glowed red-hot instead of arctic silver. His pulse was thrumming loudly in his ears.

What in the world …?

Corinth's eyes popped open, and suddenly Alastair could see his honey-brown irises, glowing almost golden—the complete opposite of those empty sockets he'd had for eyes a few moments ago. The silver tattoos on his arms and neck had dimmed considerably as well.

The tightness in Alastair's gut eased, and an overwhelming sense of respite passed over him as he lifted his eyes skyward. *Thank God. He's still in there.*

Heeey, Al.

A slurred voice burst into Alastair's mind like a transistor radio blaring to life, loud and obnoxious. *Bloody hell.* The sudden intrusion of a foreign voice inside Alastair's mind sent a second bout of adrenaline tearing through him, and he jolted into a sitting position, a hand pressed to his bare chest, shaken.

Corinth. Am I imagining this?

Alastair would recognize that twangy Texas tenor anywhere. The voice was blessedly normal-sounding, but he could sense the agony and worry in it too. A swell of sorrow he knew didn't belong to him overrode all of his other emotions, and it felt so uncanny that his world went topsy-turvy for a second, and he sagged back down against the wall.

A psychic connection where he could feel emotions that didn't belong to him wasn't something he had been prepared for. He could barely hold his own burgeoning emotions at bay.

Relief flooded through him, so great he felt the moisture build up behind his eyes, threatening to spill over, and he wondered if Corinth could sense what he was feeling too.

Can you hear me? Corinth? You there?

Barely. Corinth whispered back almost as quickly as Alastair thought it. His voice sounded thin and hollow in Alastair's head.

Did you just read my mind? Whoa, this is weird. You can hear my thoughts?

No—I can't read your mind. You're tuned in to … our … angel channel. We're linked. You got your wings, bud. Welcome to the club, Al.

Still stunned that he was actually using telepathy to communicate, Alastair spoke only using his mind. *How am I able to … to do this?*

Corinth shook his head as if to say, "Not now," and then Alastair felt a flood of pain radiate through him, all-consuming—and he swore it felt like someone was dicing his heart. Alastair took in a sharp breath as Corinth shifted his legs, trying to get back to his feet, his face gray.

What the hell is that?

Eventually, Corinth gave up and groaned and then

stopped, clearly too hurt to move anymore. His usual wild mane of hair was plastered to his forehead, and he had managed to prop himself up against the wall using an elbow, wincing. *You whammed me good, Al*, he groaned. *Not … back. I can't hold Angela off … for long. Please … Al, I'm begging you, help my … Zo. She's in trouble … Ephrem … he took her. I can't …* His body shuddered, and he closed his eyes, his face straining from the effort of staying in control. When he opened them, they were solid black, like polished marbles, and the ink-like swirl patterns on his arms had started to flicker and grow stronger once again, and the stabbing sensation in Alastair's heart grew to an unbearable degree. He clutched at his own chest, knowing that the pain wasn't coming from him.

I'm s-s-sorry …

We don't have time for apologies, Al shot back through their psychic link. He knew Corinth was fading fast. *You fight her, Taylor. Fight her and beat her.* Alastair tried to move, to go help Corinth, but his head and heart erupted in agony, and he slumped back down. *Ouch.*

"Quit messing around, and find your little sister yourself," Alastair growled, out loud this time, squeezing his temples with both hands to get some relief from the incessant pressure at the base of his skull. That was what Vinson would have said if he'd been here. He wanted to end their connection, to make the pain stop.

I need you to fight harder, he pleaded with Corinth.

If Ephrem had Zoey, that meant she was probably dead. He'd lose Taylor forever if that monster had killed her. Corinth would give up. He'd blame himself for her death.

Where is the other kid, Cruz? It felt more natural now to Alastair; communicating like this was easier than talking.

Corinth's chest heaved up and down as he tried to regain control over his own senses once again. After an incredibly long time, his eyes churned and then changed back to their original color. When he spoke this time though, his voice sounded much feebler, and Alastair could feel Corinth's remorse and guilt and shame through their shared link. *I don't know. I ... I think he's dead.*

This kind of pain almost hurt worse than when he'd died saving Corinth's life. But it wasn't Alastair's torment he was feeling. It was a shared pain—emotional overload. Taylor was suffering.

Listen, this is important. Find the blade. You have to use it to ... carve out ... my ... heart. Only you, Al. No one else can use my blade against me. Corinth stopped speaking, most likely because he had felt Alastair's flinch and irritation through their connection. There came something akin to a dry, sardonic chuckle as Corinth said, *I'm not ... looking forward to it either, buddy.* His voice was insistent and imploring. He did feel what Alastair felt. *I'm in misery, Al.*

Corinth licked his dry lips and then flashed him a small, sad smile, and it was so him that it was enough to get Alastair back on his feet again. He laid a flat palm against the wall, trying to orient himself to the right way up once again—his world was still spiraling.

If you stab me in the heart, it won't kill me, but it will kill ... Ange—

Alastair's stomach seized, and he almost buckled to

his knees as a black bottomless pit of despair opened up inside him, and he couldn't breathe. When he tried to right himself again, he saw Corinth's eyes were all black now. No whites left. And his smile had turned wolfishly predatory.

Their connection fizzled out completely right as a dark figure hurtled out of the shadowy alcove nearby—

At first he thought the blur was a Shade or Ephrem—but then Alastair realized it wasn't a Shade at all. It was Stanton.

Suddenly Alastair was moving again, staggering forward, ignoring the deep, slicing pain in his chest, right at his heart. There was a glint of silver, and then Gabriel Stanton was standing over Corinth's form, the ejected blade from one of his hidden bracers kissing Corinth's throat.

Alastair listed to the side and almost fell as he stumbled closer to Stanton. "*Wait!*" he cried.

Dark Corinth didn't move. He was grinning like the Devil now as his black eyes slid back to him, evaluating, studying. And seeing that wide, callous grin, and those unblinking eyes caused Alastair's stomach to bottom out.

"Since when do you hesitate?" Dark Corinth asked, taunting Gabriel. "Go on. Do it, Gabe. What are you waiting for?"

Stanton turned slightly to shoot Alastair an inquisitive glare, his eyebrow arching.

"*Stanton,*" Alastair hissed, inching closer, his hand held out in front of him. "*Don't do it.* Corinth is still in there. I know how to stop Angela now, and save Corinth. *Do—not—do—it.*"

Stanton's hand was steady and unwavering as he dug the blade into Dark Corinth's jugular. A stream of blood oozed down his neck. "Iszler, I realize your superpower is compassion, and now, apparently, wielding lightning." He said the word *compassion* like it was an insult. "But this is our only shot at taking him … uh, *her* out. Angela is not someone we want running around in a Nephilim suit. Corinth would want this—"

"He won't die," Alastair said quickly. "You can cut Corinth's throat, but he won't die, Stanton." Alastair's bare feet were filthy, and he kept stepping on bits of sharp rock with each step he took toward them both. "You notice how those shadow creatures keep coming back to life?" Alastair pointed at the swirl-like markings on Corinth's neck. "He's infected. Do you think that if you slice his throat open, it will kill him? Why do you think he—she—is goading you?"

Gabriel shrugged slightly, looking unperturbed. "Still worth a try."

"You want to stop Angela for good, right?"

Dark Corinth's skin crackled all over with tiny arcs of electrical current, but he stayed where he was, still as a statue. He was waiting to see how this played out, those eerie eyes ping-ponging back and forth between Alastair and Stanton.

"You have a way to do that?" Gabriel asked slowly.

"I have to stab him in the heart with the Holy Lance—"

"*You!*" Gabriel Stanton barked out an exasperated laugh. "*You're* going to stab your best buddy here in the heart with his own blade?" He sounded more than skeptical. "Tell me you have the dagger so we can get this over with, then. Because if you don't, it would be easier for me just to relieve Mr. Taylor of his head and be done with it. It would take him awhile to piece himself back together again, at least."

"Just give me some time to find the blade …"

Dark Corinth's shrill, and exceedingly creepy, laugh echoed around the cavern's enclosed walls and carved-out death ceiling above them. It didn't seem to bother him in the least that he had a knife pressed to his throat. "You have to get closer in order to stab me, *Alastair Iszler*. Do you think you can do that?" Dark Corinth raised his head just enough to look at him from under his lowered brows. His eyes had clouded over; they looked like frosted glass, pupils and irises separated only by a thin ring of violet—like Leo's eyes but different, deadlier—and suddenly Alastair knew he was speaking to Angela. His heart shot up into his throat at the way she was looking at him—vulturine.

"I will make the Nephilim watch, held hostage by me, as I slaughter his entire family. He slaughtered mine, after all. All of them."

Angela's voice coming out of Corinth's mouth was like a punch to Alastair's gut.

"I only wanted the best for humanity. It was drowning in poverty and disease and ignorance. It needed guidance, protecting, provisions. I would have provided that. And a teenage boy took that away from me. What would you do if someone killed your entire family?" Alastair could hear the grief in her-his voice, and something else, something he likened to a desperate plea.

"The Grigori were my family, and *he* killed them. *The Nephilim killed them.* It's only fair that I end his family too. You have to see the reasonableness in that. It's already set in motion—it has been for a very long time. Ever since he inserted himself into my mind like a persistent little thorn under my skin. We have been linked this entire time."

Anger bubbled up inside Alastair like a volcano about to erupt. His breathing came out in short, shallow bursts, and he fisted his hands down by his sides. A part of him really wanted Gabriel Stanton to hurt her. To make her feel pain. "Let—my—brother—go."

"He's not your brother anymore, and he never was," she said coldly, using his lips to speak. "But he is all mine now."

Just then the room exploded into a flurry of activity as Shades spilled into the small space. Dozens of them, all black flickers of motion.

Alastair was already in his fighter's stance, ready, as he shot Stanton a quick glance, but it was already too late.

Corinth called up a portal in a split second and disappeared in a resounding crack of thunder, all before Stanton could sink his blade into his neck.

26

CRUZ

Cruz was fairly certain he was going to die.

Or be turned into one of those demon Shade things, just as Trevor had threatened.

But he couldn't leave Zoey. If he did, he would never be able to live with himself. All he needed to do was find that holy relic. He knew it would work. The magic blade would free her. He had to keep the faith.

Upon thinking that, his hand found the gold pendant under his shirt. *Where are you blade? Where are you? Show me the way.* Zoey had thrown it in the main cavern, where Alastair had been held captive. Cruz had been trying to find his way back there in the dark, without using his phone's flashlight, but he kept running into the jutting stalagmites and weird rocky outcroppings, banging his knees to bloody pulp.

The rocks looked like spikes on a dragon's back. This was exactly how he had pictured hell to look like.

Desolate. Cold. Strange. No water or food or sustenance.

Suddenly Cruz heard a scraping noise, and he ducked back behind one of the demonic-looking stalagmites he'd just run into, holding his breath, listening. *Don't look up. Don't look up. Don't look up.* If he did, he would freak out.

All those dead souls above would be staring down at him with lifeless eyes.

He shuddered at the thought.

A second later, there came the sound of soft footfalls, followed by two dark shapes passing in front of him—as silent as shadows. Not shadows. Shades. He held his breath. They were searching for something. Him. Trevor had to know by now that he wasn't dead.

Cruz's stomach gurgled loudly, and one of the Shades stopped.

Cruz squeezed his eyes shut for a second, and then opened them again. He wasn't so much hungry as sick. Right now, he was supposed to be having Thanksgiving dinner with his mother, but he was going to upchuck and give away his position instead.

After a moment, the Shade turned around and spoke to its companion in a strangely hollow voice. "Did you hear that?"

Cruz heard them moving back toward his hiding place, which really wasn't a great hiding place at all. It was more him just standing behind a tall pillar. They were going to find him. He was stealthy, but he knew he couldn't move like these supernatural creatures could. Especially since he didn't even have the shield key chain to protect him anymore.

He inched his way quietly around the column, trying

to stay on one side of it as they came around the other. His heart was hammering a million beats per minute. He feared they'd hear it.

They paused in the same exact spot he'd been standing in only a moment before. One of them sniffed, like it was a bloodhound trying to pick up the scent of its prey.

Oh, man. They can smell me.

"I'd recognize that putrid scent anywhere. It's definitely human."

He heard a second sniff, closer now.

About twenty feet ahead of him, he could make out an alcove or a connecting passageway. Maybe he could dart into it without them seeing him. He was fast. Cruz was seventy-five percent sure that was in the direction of the main cavern … or was it the opposite way? All of a sudden, he felt dizzy and confused and turned around.

Very slowly he fished his house keys out of his pants pocket. He lifted his hand to throw them in the opposite direction, then run as fast as he possibly could, but then a sudden swirl of black smoke rose up all around him—

Oh no.

There was nothing he could do but watch as a Shade's fist came out of nowhere, materializing in front of him in a millisecond. It struck him in the stomach, hard, and he let out a pained grunt as things slowed to a grinding halt.

His vision blurred and his eyes started to water as he doubled over, heaving. That hurt. A lot.

Cruz was no stranger to fighting or pain or getting punched. When he'd first learned how sick his mother was, he'd had no idea how to handle the stress that came with watching a loved one slowly dying. It hadn't taken long for that stress to morph into anger and something else: resentment. He didn't understand how such a bad thing could happen to such a good person. Cruz had been angry, and he had wanted everyone else to be angry too. So he'd picked fights. He'd run his mouth just to see how far he could push people. And some of those people weren't just kids. They were older and meaner, and he'd lost just as many fights as he'd won. Hence the scars. It wasn't about winning, though. It was about guiding his pain—channeling it into something else. Something corporeal.

He probably would have kept up his horrible behavior until he got himself killed, but all it took was one night in juvenile detention to bring him to his senses.

While he sat in detention, broken and bloodied, his mother lay in a hospital bed, clinging to life. She had almost died that night. *All alone.* After that, Cruz promised his mom that he would never fight again. And then he got a job. And met Zoey.

And now he was fighting again.

He really hoped his mother would forgive him for what he was about to do.

Cruz struck out at the Shade, but the demon grabbed his fist in midair and laughed. Even underneath all the shiny ichor on the Shade's face, Cruz could see how amused the demon appeared to be as it looked at his balled-up fist clutched in its hand.

A split second later, the Shade wrenched Cruz's hand around, and icy fire lit up Cruz's shoulder. He cried out in pain.

"Pathetic," the thing said with an amused chuckle.

Cruz, ignoring the searing pain in his arm, spun around and rammed the sharpest key he had into its eye socket. The demon clearly had not been expecting this reaction out of him, because it let go of his fist and staggered back a step, grabbing at its face, momentarily stunned.

All Cruz could focus on was the glint of silver swinging from its eyeball as he backed up and ran.

Strong hands seized his shoulders from behind, and then he was flung into the air. His stomach flipped. A tiny part of him marveled at how much strength it took to toss him like a human Frisbee.

But then he was tumbling across slick stone, and he wasn't impressed anymore. His head cracked against the ground, and then each bruising blow after that sent shock wave after shock wave through his body, until blessed adrenaline took over, and on his last somersault, he managed to leap back to his feet and take off running without missing a single beat.

Behind Cruz came more surprised shouting, followed by the thundering of footsteps as they chased after him. More than two sets of feet. An army. He could practically feel all of them breathing down his neck as he hit the entrance to the next cavern, flying. He was sure his feet didn't even strike the ground. His breath was tearing out of his throat in loud pants.

Cruz had never run this fast in his entire life. Maybe it was because his life depended on it—and so did Zoey's. It didn't matter that he could barely see, or that his head was throbbing, or that he felt snapping teeth at the back of his neck—

A sickening thought of his *madre* crying over his dead body hit him, so he ran harder, almost blind.

The corridor deposited him back out into the main cavern. If he turned around now, he knew, he'd see a lot of Shades spilling out of the passageway he'd just exited. So he stayed focused on the faint path ahead of him.

Cruz could almost feel their sour breath on the back of his neck. His heart was hammering away in his chest, and for a second, he thought the sound of it might deafen him.

He wasn't going to make it.

If he could only find the blade. *Where is it?* Maybe it would work for him. Maybe he could ward them off with it. Save himself. Banish the demons all to hell. *Where are you, blade?*

As soon as he thought it, he saw a strange pulse of golden light directly across the way. Had he imagined it? *Blade. Show me where you are.*

There it was again. Brilliant. Divine. Holy.

A blink of an eye, and you'd miss it.

Then the light flared up again, and he knew he'd seen it, so he pivoted abruptly, changing direction at the last second as a dark figure hurtled past him, devastatingly close—the air moved next to his head as the Shade almost tackled him to the ground. There was the crunch of bone and a shout behind him as he fixated on the small patch of golden light.

Pumping his arms and legs, Cruz redoubled his efforts. The weapon was lit up like a blessed beacon in the dark. A homing beacon. It called to him. It needed to be found just as much as he needed to find it.

He imagined curling his fingers around the hilt—

A thick wall of black smoke and ice-blue flame shot up in front of him, blocking his path to the dagger. It blazed up like a fire-breathing dragon. Surely someone had plucked this image right out of one of his own nightmares.

Cruz's mouth dropped open as he tried to stop himself from careening right into the flames.

Too late.

His forward momentum catapulted him right into the fire, his arms pinwheeling out to his sides as if he were stuck in a vat of syrup. He felt his eyes widen in disbelief as he rammed right into a hard chest. A tall, imposing figure wearing mesh armor, towering over him. A figure with glossy black eyes—homed right in on him.

Corinth Taylor.

Zoey's brother is terrifying.

The last thing Cruz saw was possessed Corinth reaching out toward him, an insanely intense blinding light enveloping him in its fiery—and yet subzero—embrace.

Cruz blinked several times, too stunned to believe what he was seeing. First off, he wasn't dead. Lightning hadn't struck him down. The cold had somewhat subsided as Alastair had jumped right in front of Cruz at the last second, shoving him out of the way.

Now Alastair stood there, shirtless, his long coat flapping behind him like he was some sort of caped crusader.

And whatever supernatural force or energy was flowing out of his palm was incredible. A shimmering barrier formed a protective dome shield around them, blocking Corinth's attempt at sending Cruz into the afterlife—or allowing all those alarming Shades at his back to get at him.

Cruz could see the strain on Alastair's face as he went down to a knee, hand still extended, glorious lightning shooting out of his fingertips like he controlled *all* the elements: wind, earth, water, fire. A sorcerer—no, something much scarier than that. An almighty angel.

Behind Corinth, Gabriel Stanton, one of the richest people on the planet—and probably a vampire—was battling a horde of Shades all by himself. Cruz had no idea where they'd come from. How could they move that fast? *Who are these people?* Superheroes. He was the damsel in distress in this scenario. But that was okay. He was good with that. He was still alive.

"How are you doing that?" Cruz rasped hoarsely, unable to break his focus from the wall of lightning surrounding him.

"*Grab the blade, kid!*" Alastair cried through gritted teeth, clearly straining to hold his magic together.

Cruz had almost forgotten the relic was right behind Corinth, wedged into a crack in the wall. The amber light looked like the same kind of energy that was shimmering around Alastair. The closed-in air tasted salty and metallic, and the hum of electricity in the space made him light-headed.

Corinth was surrounded by a mini tornado of fire, his eyes ablaze with fury. "Yes, kid. Come and get it. But you have to get through me first." He gestured for Cruz to come at him, a grim, challenging smile playing on his lips. Corinth wasn't a person. He was something else entirely. Half human, half demon. No angel.

Uh, no.

Alastair exploded back to his feet, squared his shoulders, and careened into Corinth with a battle cry. As they met each other head-on, Cruz didn't wait—he moved, not thinking, just reacting, and knowing he had only moments to spare.

A few steps forward, and he had his hand wrapped around the handle. The leather grip and metal underneath it felt warm. He drew in a deep breath, braced his hand against the wall, and a foot too, for good measure, prepared to heave hard—

A pair of hands clamped around his middle, yanking him backward off his feet. Luckily, the blade ripped free as easily as yanking a knife out of an apple core. The dagger was heavier than he'd expected it to be. Cruz barely had time to lift it up before light erupted off the razor's edge like a ray of sunshine. The Shade attached to him disintegrated almost instantly, vanishing into a puff of smoke and sulfur and ash.

Dust in the wind.

For a second, the heat was so intense he thought his own flesh was blistering. And then the flames softened and he could see again, and he wasn't on fire.

What the …?

When the dust finally settled, he looked around, thunderstruck. They were in a different part of the realm. They'd moved somehow. There was no one fighting. No

Shades. No black-eyed Corinth. Only silence. Everyone was gone except Gabriel Stanton and Alastair, and Cruz, of course.

The dagger had stopped glowing, but he could feel the residual heat still leaching into his fingertips from under the wrap covering the hilt, heavy and tingly. Suddenly the floor looked pretty good.

The power and adrenaline that had been coursing through him was now gone, and he found himself sinking to his knees in sudden exhaustion, his entire body shaking. His wrist ached from holding the weapon up for even a short amount of time, and he idly wondered how knights had fought with heavy swords for hours on end. Lots of conditioning. They always made it look so effortless in the movies.

No one said anything.

Cruz's gaze landed on Gabriel, who appeared to be winded—bent over at the waist with his hands braced on his knees, his hair hanging in his face. His weapons were gone, presumably hidden in the armor Cruz now knew was underneath those long shirtsleeves. He could just make out a glint of gold buckles at both his wrists.

Stanton looked up at Alastair, his face still red and sweaty from exertion. "Did you just open up an angel portal and transport *all* of us away?"

"That wasn't me ..." Alastair said, clearly perplexed as he glanced at the blade in Cruz's hand.

"Then how did we move to a different part of the realm?" Gabriel wheezed, still oxygen deprived. "And lose the entourage of demons?"

"I think it was the dagger," Alastair said, cutting a

quick glance back at Cruz. "It's done this sort of thing before. Called to people. Preserved itself for centuries. It's the Spear of Destiny … There's not a rule book on how it works. Didn't you see how it practically jumped out of Corinth's hands once he was possessed by Angela? It … senses evil …"

Cruz didn't know much about the Spear of Destiny … but he could see, just underneath Alastair's partially open coat, a black scorch mark emblazoned across his bare chest. It wasn't a wound, but it looked like a strange sort of Rorschach inkblot that appeared to have been drawn on with charcoal. He thought it resembled wings—or several dark palm prints splattered one on top of the other.

And then an image of bloody handprints rose up in his mind so vividly he gasped. *Zoey! She's still trapped!* He shuddered, thinking about her being shackled all alone in that dank prison. He had to get back to her. It was only a matter of time before Trevor came back for her.

"You okay, kid?" Alastair asked, holding his hand out to help him back to his feet. "You look pale. Are you injured?"

Cruz jumped, startled that Alastair was now standing over him. He hadn't even noticed the guy move. He nodded and started to say something but realized his mouth was bone-dry. After a second of bringing some moisture back to it, he tried again. "No. I'm okay, but I … I have to get this dagger back to Zoey. She's in trouble."

"Where is she?" Alastair asked quickly, his eyebrows bunching in concern. "Can you get us back there?"

"Trevor chained her up in some creepy dungeon,"

Cruz snarled, getting shakily back to his feet. "I couldn't free her. I thought I might be able to break the shackle with the blade, so I came back for it—"

"Very foolish of you," Gabriel interjected. "I gave you the bloody way out, kid. I thought I told you to go."

Cruz felt a rush of blood heat his face, embarrassed and angry. "If it were your family, would you leave them behind?"

Alastair licked his lips. "Stanton would, kid. But I wouldn't." And then he swore under his breath as his intense blue eyes locked on Gabriel once again, widening. "*You. You* gave them the only way out of here?" he asked incredulously. "What's the catch, Stanton? When have you ever done anything for anyone without a price tag? Why are you still here?"

Gabriel raked a hand across his raven-colored beard and looked away. "Since when do you control lightning? And what's that mark on your chest?"

Alastair glanced down at his torso, unperturbed. "Don't change the subject, Stanton. You can't be working with Ephrem … so spill it … What is it you really want?"

"I want to make amends," he said with a sigh. "This is my fault. I'm trying to make up for it."

Alastair let out a mocking laugh, shaking his head. "Now I know you're lying."

"I told you, I don't lie—"

"Can we argue later? Zoey needs us *now*." Cruz cut Gabriel Stanton off abruptly.

"Can you lead us to where she is?" Alastair asked, turning his attention back to Cruz.

Cruz glanced around, hesitating. "Maybe from where

we were earlier, but not from here …"

"Is she in a stone circle with strange markings?" Gabriel asked quietly, his eyes narrowing.

Cruz nodded, his pulse starting to spike again. He didn't like the way Stanton had asked that question. Or the way he was looking, with something akin to alarm flickering across his face.

"I know how to get us there—but we need to hurry," Gabriel said, sounding concerned.

Alastair's head jerked in Gabriel's direction. "What is it?"

"Ephrem conducts ritualistic sacrifices down there. He needs a blood sacrifice in order to contact hell and the other greater demons, like him. It sounds like Zoey could be next on his list," he said grimly.

Other greater demons? Cruz shuddered at the thought, his stomach feeling full of lead.

27

ZOEY

I tugged Cruz's coat tighter around my shoulders, taking in the heady scent of his spicy cologne, and relishing the warmth it provided. I couldn't put it all the way on, because the manacle on my wrist prevented it, but I did have one arm pulled through a sleeve. The soft lining gave me at least a little bit of comfort in this dank, desolate place. I hoped Cruz was okay. Volunteering to go get the blade to free me had been incredibly self-sacrificing—not to mention brave.

What if he couldn't find his way back here?

Even though I was still scared out of my wits, I felt better with the small glowing shield clutched in between my fingers. A sign of hope. The dim light softened my anxiety. Still, the inky shadows beyond the light's reach left me with a bad taste in my mouth.

I kept thinking about things slithering out of the dark, heading toward me. All I had to do was ignore the metallic scent of dried blood, and that putrid, rotting smell … and everything would be okay—

"Well, well, well. Look who isn't in the dark any longer."

I whirled around, my pulse slamming in my veins at the same time as my throat constricted and paralyzing fear tore through me. That voice. *Pure evil.*

"However do you think we should rectify that?"

By the faint light in my unsteady hands, I could see Trevor's dark silhouette. He was fully cloaked, and his face was shadowed by his raised hood. He was standing behind me, on the top step above the circle I sat in.

I dragged myself to my feet, the chain clanking painfully against my wrist, and held up the light like a shield. It flared up bright as if in response to my distress, and thankfully, Trevor retreated a step.

It made me feel good, seeing that the light could affect him. It was his turn to be afraid. At least I kept telling myself that, anyway, mainly because he didn't look worried; he looked angry and irritated and … highly entertained.

"Nice cloak," I goaded. "When do you leave for Hogwarts?"

Trevor's black eyes were burning like twin flames. Without his glasses, they looked more intense. Hair-raisingly creepy. I gulped at the sight as he looked down at his robe. "This," he began, "is so I don't get blood all over my clothes. Your blood."

I took in a deep, shuddering breath, trying to calm my rapidly beating heart. *Don't show him fear.*

"You think that little trinket is going to stop me from

killing you?" he asked softly, menacingly, stalking closer. "Because it won't."

Heat started to creep into my cheeks. *He can't hurt you*, I tried to reassure myself. "You don't get to touch me, *ever again*." It sounded stronger than I'd thought it would have. Assertive, even.

Trevor barked out a contemptuous laugh. "I don't need to touch you in order to hurt you, little girl." He flashed me a cruel smile that made my stomach turn over, and then he put a long, slender finger against his chin. "I guess that means I have to get creative, then."

He doesn't have to touch me to hurt me.

My thoughts strayed to Corinth. My family. Cruz. He'd found them. They'd gotten caught. He could hurt them all. He had hurt them all. Icy fingers of dread stabbed me in my gut, the sensation working its way up into my chest; it tightened up excruciatingly. *Why can't I breathe?*

"Is that your boyfriend's jacket? He left you all by yourself down here with nothing but his coat? Very noble of him."

I didn't say anything. I didn't want to give anything away. *Cruz.* My mouth felt like it was full of cotton balls.

"Where is he, Zo?"

Suddenly the tension in my chest uncoiled, and I could breathe a little deeper. Cruz was still out there—alive. Trevor hadn't caught him yet.

I gave a tiny shrug. "I thought you killed him. You're supposed to be an all-powerful demon, right? Or did a teenager get the better of you?"

Trevor's smile faded a tad at hearing that, and then

he chuckled. "Are you provoking me? That's a dangerous game." He padded closer, and I jerked back a step, the chain rattling. His grin widened. "It's only a matter of time before I do find him," he promised. "Let me guess—Cruz gave you his coat and took the device on the promise that he would go find help. What I want to know is, did he steal it from you? Or did you just give it to him out of the goodness of your own bleeding heart? I bet you gave it to him. Did you believe him when he said he'd be back to help you?" Trevor tsked. "Because he won't. It was a classic excuse to save his own skin. I don't blame Cruz … It really is quite horrible down here." Trevor stood with his hands on his hips, waiting for me to respond, his face half-hidden by the hood of his cloak, the other half lit up in his obvious delight at seeing my rising panic. I couldn't keep the emotion off my face.

"You're trembling." He sounded pleased, and then he raised his hand and made a flicking motion.

I grabbed my wrist. The iron was heavy and hard to keep holding up, and my back ached. My skin prickled where the iron touched it. I could feel the magic seeping into my veins, heightening my nerves, almost like the opposite feeling to a dose of Novocain. A cold, needlelike stitch knifed through me, constricting my breathing. My entire body felt scratchy and irritated. Exposed. It might as well have been a shock collar around my neck. *Is he doing something to me?*

I didn't want to sit down, but I couldn't help it. My legs were rubber. I gasped, sinking to my knees, feeling like every single one of my nerves had been set on fire, and I curled onto my side, clutching the still-illuminated shield to my chest, remembering what Cruz had told me he'd done.

After another unendurable second, the pain subsided, and I could breathe again. It took me a minute to clear my head of the dull throbbing sensation.

Trevor, or Ephrem—whatever—cocked his head to the side, watching me, his lips curled in obvious curiosity as I sat up, and he lowered his outstretched hand. "I guess I'll have to try a different approach. Do you like surprises?"

Just as the words were out of his mouth, black smoke churned into existence beside Trevor, shooting skyward toward the ceiling of the dungeon like exhaust from a steam engine. The chamber we occupied was cylindrical, and for a moment, it curved down the sides of the enclosed walls, filling the space until it coalesced into a shape, and then that shape took on a human form, and eventually, it became solid.

A Shade. One of his minions. Its skin was thick and oily, and at first, I couldn't see anything different about this one in particular—until it spoke.

"Hey, little sis."

I knew that voice. A searing cold spread to my extremities, leaving me feeling numb all over, and my heart skipped as a sharp pain spiked through it.

I was glad I was sitting down, or I would have folded.

Please, don't let it be his voice. Any voice but his.

A wave of misery and concern crashed over me so strongly that before I was aware of it, I was on my feet again and moving toward the Shade—*not* a Shade, my brother. But the chain brought me up short, and I gasped from shock and pain and terror. His beautiful hair was gone. He was bald. Peter didn't look like Peter anymore. But he was wearing Peter's clothes. His dark-wash jeans and a black T-shirt with the Punisher skull on it—that was how I knew it was him.

I heard Trevor's laughter in the background, but it sounded distorted and muted in my head.

Just last week, that voice had teased me. That voice had called me "chicken legs." That voice had berated me for being out too late past my curfew. The owner of that voice had helped me with my homework, even when I'd claimed I hadn't needed it. I had needed it. I hadn't told him that though. I hadn't told him I loved him … There was so much I needed to tell him. He'd tried to keep my mom safe. He'd saved her life, and he'd risked his own … My chest was heaving now, and I was insanely close to completely falling apart at the seams.

"*Pete?*" His name came out in a breathless whisper on my lips, like a prayer.

Trevor might as well have reached into my chest and wrung the air from my lungs himself. The room went all wonky. I put a hand against my stomach, trying to pull myself together—hold myself together, rather.

The key chain almost slipped out of my slick grasp, and I barely managed to squeeze my fingers tighter around it, focusing on the physical pain instead.

It wasn't him.

This isn't happening.

"*Peter?*" I whispered again, stretching my hand out toward him as far as I could reach.

The *demon*—I wasn't ready to believe it was my

brother—cocked his head to the side as if studying me, but he didn't say anything else.

I didn't want him to say anything.

If I knew the truth, it meant he was gone. And that revelation wasn't something I could handle. I would fall apart, and that was exactly what Trevor wanted. I could see it on his gloating face. The way his mouth puckered as if in expectation of my breakdown. He wanted to break me before he killed me, and I wouldn't give him the satisfaction.

Two brothers gone in the blink of an eye.

My whole life changed in less than a day.

Had he killed my entire family?

I closed my eyes for a second and then opened them again. Both of them were still standing there, gazing down at me from the top step. Together. Trevor had a look of superiority plastered on his once-handsome face as he looked down his nose at me. And suddenly all I wanted to do was kill him. I wanted to rip his beating heart right out of his chest. Did he even have a heart?

"See, I told you I don't need to touch you in order to hurt you." He said it so glibly, so matter-of-factly. "I can see the wheels spinning in your head right now, Zo, but I can assure you, this *is* your brother. I mean … *used to be* your brother. Now he is one of mine. Part of *my* family. Just like Corinth. But not you. You are to die today."

I turned to the figure standing next to Trevor and looked him in the eyes—they were black and inky and soulless. Not Pete's eyes.

"I am no longer who I used to be. I am a part of something greater," the thing sort of resembling Pete said in a chilling monotone. He turned to look back at Trevor. "Couldn't she be a part of that too?"

Trevor faced Shade Pete, a surprised look on his face. Apparently, he wasn't used to one of his subordinates posing questions like this. "She sealed her own fate the minute she fought back." Trevor tapped a finger against his bottom lip in thought. "She has the shield. Get it from her. No matter what it takes, however you have to do it. Don't kill her yet though… That's Corinth's job. I need *him* to make the sacrifice … to open the gate."

"*Sacrifice?*" My voice went an octave higher; it might have come out as a shriek.

Trevor gestured to the weird patterns etched into the floors, to the dried blood on the ground underneath my feet, and to the chains above my head. "I need a human sacrifice in order to make contact with stronger demons. The ones who still reside in hell. They want out. Your death will help secure their freedom. That's your purpose, Zo. A higher purpose. Angela and I can still open the gateway, but I would prefer it if Corinth were to do it. I want to torture the Nephilim. Take all of his family away. One at a time."

I glanced to Pete, and I held his unwavering gaze. "He won't do it," I insisted, my eyes flickering back to Trevor.

"What's that?" Trevor asked.

"Listen to you. And neither will Corinth. They're too strong. And so am I." I lifted the shield, holding it out in front of me, inching closer to Trevor. To my surprise, the light intensified and I swung it out—and it almost touched the tips of his white sneakers. He jumped back in surprise, snarling a curse in the process.

"Start with the crossbow," Trevor snapped. And then his body dissolved into a pillar of smoke and ash as he disappeared.

28

ALASTAIR

They hadn't encountered much resistance since they had lost sight of Dark Corinth. Which Alastair knew wasn't just a fluke. Ephrem knew Alastair could hurt them. They were scared. Even with that rationale at the back of his mind, as they followed Stanton deeper into the bowels of the dark realm, he started to feel more and more unsettled. It was like the evil was still seeping into his bones. He could smell the dankness and desperation, and it reeked.

He feared for Zoey's life, and that was why he quickened his pace.

Alastair glanced down at the odd mark emblazoned on his chest.

And then his gaze caught on the dagger, gleaming brightly in his hand.

Currently he was using it as a torch so they could see by it. *The Spear of Destiny.* It was strange, the way he'd been able to hear Corinth in his mind. And also strange that he had been able to defend himself the way Corinth did—by generating an angelic shield.

Maybe he could call up an angel portal. Except he had tried concentrating on Larna, thinking her name over and over again, but no matter how hard he thought about her, and home, he could not transport himself away. It wasn't like he would leave Zoey or Cruz behind … He just needed to know if he could do it. Alastair couldn't even produce a single spark of static electricity, much less call up lightning to do his bidding. Apparently, angel energy wasn't just something he could whip up out of thin air. It seemed to only respond as a defensive mechanism. No wonder Corinth had been so frustrated when trying to learn how to handle his own powers. He was starting to think he hadn't given Corinth enough credit.

Cruz had been relatively silent, following behind them both, but he had come up to stand beside Alastair now, and he could sense that Cruz wanted to ask him something.

"What is it, kid?" he asked, glancing at him out of the corner of his eye.

"Vampires—they actually existed, and you … you used to be one of them?"

Alastair nodded, squinting at Stanton's tall form in front of them, leading the way. He wondered if Gabriel Stanton could hear them. "Yes and yes."

"What was it like?" he asked in an awed, hushed whisper. "I mean, how old are you? Did you have immortality? What about inhuman strength? Did you sleep in a coffin? Drink blood?"

"I'm twenty-eight," he answered between clenched

teeth, annoyed. "And sleeping in a coffin is good for your back. You should try it sometime."

Cruz peeked back over at him, his eyes wide, probably trying to figure out if Alastair was messing with him or not. "I mean, when were you born? What year?" he pressed.

"Vampirism has wrought nothing but trouble upon this world." Alastair jutted his chin out toward Stanton. "You should ask him those questions. He cares more about vampirism than I ever did. The mess you're in right now is *his* fault. Zoey's life is on the line because he wanted to get his immortality back."

Gabriel Stanton turned around and faced them both, stopping in his tracks. "I could have left you to rot, Iszler."

"Why didn't you?" Alastair hissed. "Why are you still here? You still need something and I mean to find out what that is—"

"Shh ..." Cruz said suddenly, motioning with his hands to quiet them. "Did you hear that?"

They stopped talking. And then a moment later, Alastair could hear what Cruz had heard. A low sort of humming coming from somewhere nearby ... possibly in a chamber ahead of them.

They moved closer and the noise got louder, and he realized it wasn't buzzing at all. It was chanting. Not good. Chanting was never good. Chanting meant the Shades were not afraid of being sought out. They wanted to be sought out. And they were planning something ... malevolent, ritualistic.

"Stay here, kid," Alastair growled. "Let us check this out first."

"No way." Cruz shook his head adamantly at him. "I'm coming with you. Zoey is my friend, and I told her I would be back for her."

"Okay, well, at least pipe down and do what you're told," Alastair told him.

Slowly they crept toward the source of the noise. It sounded like the droning of bees in a hive. He could not make out what they were saying, only feel the insistent low hum of their words vibrating through his body.

The blade seemed to respond in anger, the bronze glinting bright in the dark. Alastair tightened his grip on the hilt, and a sudden rush of power flooded through him, making him feel breathless and dizzy.

They halted at the opening of a cavern, and Gabriel Stanton put his arm out to signal to them that this was the source of the noise. Alastair stealthily positioned himself next to Stanton, peering around the same corner at the same time as Stanton.

Before them was situated a giant chamber. Lit torches in sconces lined the wall at their backs, spaced around the room in a huge circle. Shades stood shoulder to shoulder, their eyes black and shiny, devoid of life, or death, or anything remotely resembling free will. Hundreds of them.

And Alastair knew what they were waiting for—*them*.

He sucked in a sharp breath, not just because he now knew they were clearly outmatched in number, but because standing in the middle of the assembly of gathered foes was his brother-in-arms—Dark Corinth—still wearing his golden mesh armor, blue jeans, and gray Converse. But his eyes looked like frosted glass, and the tattoos on his neck and arms were lit up in a strange pale and ghostly light. Alastair shivered despite himself. Angela-Corinth.

Corinth, he thought. *Can you hear me, brother?*

There came no reply.

He tried again. *Taylor, I really need you to hear me right now.*

No answer. Crickets. No voice blaring peculiarly to life inside his head.

Gabriel pointed to another shaft on the opposite side to where they stood—through all of the hundreds of bodies standing between them. "She'll be in the next chamber over, but you'll have to go through all of them in order to get to it."

Alastair swore under his breath. "Let me guess—this is where we part ways. You're not risking your pretty little head for one insignificant human life."

Gabriel flashed Alastair one of his famous smirks. "You think I'm pretty?"

Alastair rolled his eyes. "You have my permission to leave now."

Stanton raised an amused eyebrow, and his scar stretched across his left cheekbone. "You have no shoes. No shirt. You're not wearing any armor. You see where I'm going with this? You need help, Iszler."

Alastair rubbed his chin in irritation. "And you're just the person to give it?"

"Maybe I am," Gabriel said, meeting Alastair's scowl with one of his own.

"Can we disguise ourselves? Make ourselves look like one of them, maybe?" Cruz said from behind them. "Sneak past them somehow?"

Alastair spoke over his shoulder. "The Scooby-Doo approach—sure, kid. Right. Maybe if they were wearing hooded robes, but they aren't, and they have that bizarre ichor covering their skin … which kind of makes it apparent that we don't."

"Well how do we get past them, then?" Cruz whispered nervously.

"With this." Alastair held up the holy relic, and a spark shot off the edge of the blade. "We stay in the light it provides, and—"

"What about Corinth?" Gabriel interrupted. "He still has lightning at his disposal and he isn't affected by the light like the demons are—or not as much, anyway. And you need the blade to dispatch Angela."

Alastair turned to Cruz, sizing him up. "Those scars on your knuckles, you get them by fighting?"

Cruz cast his gaze down at his hands and then balled them into fists at his sides and nodded. Alastair guessed the kid hadn't thought anybody had noticed them in the dark. He was used to hiding them from people. Cruz's gaze strayed to the raised skin on Gabriel Stanton's cheekbone. His eyes went to the weird symbol marring Alastair's chest. They all had scars.

Alastair pinned Cruz with a piercing look, and the kid stopped fidgeting. "Didn't you say your mother was very sick?"

Cruz nodded, glancing down at the worn stone underneath his feet, suddenly silent.

"You aren't proud of your scars, which means you probably got into some scraps you knew you shouldn't have."

Cruz's brown eyes widened in surprise. "How did you—?"

"Takes one to know one," Alastair said softly. "Except, I can guarantee I did a lot worse in my youth than you ever did. Grief is a hard thing to wrap your head around. Grief can swallow you up whole. Grief is unbearable. But physical pain—that's something tangible. Something to hold on to. Something to dispense. Something to relish. I get it."

Cruz looked back up at Alastair, meeting his resolute stare, his eyes shining.

"You didn't back down when you could or even *should* have. You didn't run away or hide. You're not wearing the coat you had on earlier, which means you gave it to Zoey," he surmised. "That's a very decent thing to do." Gabriel cleared his throat at hearing that, and Alastair barked out a quick "Shut up, Stanton!" before saying, "You're not in bad shape. I saw how fast you moved back there. You practice a particular sport? Soccer, maybe?" he guessed. "Those scars suggest you might be able to take care of yourself. Clearly, you're not a whiner. The shield, which used to be a part of the blade—lit up for you when you touched it. Not everyone has the gift, kid, but *you* sure seem to."

"What does that mean?" Cruz asked, glancing between them both.

Alastair held the dagger out to Cruz. "It means I'll take care of Corinth, and you take care of Zoey—and then you get this blade back to me as soon as you can."

29

LEO

The Taylors were gathered around one another in the living room. Mrs. Taylor was pale and shaky and mute, but she wasn't crying. She sat perched on the arm of the worn sofa with a hand on her mouth, shaking her head in disbelief. Mr. Taylor was shouting at Samyaza, trying to get him to go into action and find Zo … to do something. And Jimmy was staring a hole through Leo, an unreadable expression on his face. *Shock.* He was in shock. His brother was gone, turned into one of those things.

All in the blink of an eye.

Leo watched them with his arms crossed, feeling both his anger and sorrow mount to a relentless degree. It curdled in his stomach like sour milk. He'd let this happen. Peter was gone. Corinth was gone. Zo was gone. Alastair was gone. Their family had been ripped apart. He could see the blame in Larna's eyes as she came up beside him, her mouth pinched.

Biscuit weaved himself through Leo's legs, purring.

"*Leo*." Larna choked back a sob. "Pete, he is … is he one of them now? He's gone. You couldn't do anything to stop it from happening?" She gave him a quick scathing frown. Blame. Shame. Dread. He saw it on her face.

Leo felt every bit of it too.

Finally he shook his head. "I don't know how to find them. Ikari and Tamiel are out searching Gabriel's offices right now, trying to dig up any information about demons or that device he had—the one that transported them away—but there's just not enough to go on … I can't reach Corinth. There's a gaping hole … an emptiness inside me. I can feel it, Larna … He's gone for … good." Leo swiped a hand down his face, feeling like his insides had been ripped out and exposed to the elements. Angels didn't get emotional. Yet Corinth was his brother. Corinth's blood was the same blood that ran through his own veins. *I* am *emotional.* Samyaza sidelined him because of this—and he knew it. Actually, he wouldn't let Leo out of his sight. The truth was, Leo didn't want to leave the Taylors alone. Not if they were still a target. He'd promised Corinth he would watch out for them.

He closed his eyes. *Corinth? Answer me. Where are you?*

When Leo opened them again, he could see a dark shadow slink in front of the window—as swift as a storm cloud passing across the sun. Danger. His blood ran cold.

There came a shout from outside—Vinson—and then a couple of sharp raps sounded from a gun firing right at the same time as shadowy figures burst into the living room out of thick pockets of smoke. Dozens. Maybe more.

Leo jumped in front of Larna right as one of those thin crystal shards flew at them, quivering in the air. His sword materialized in a blazing glory of light to rest in his hand the minute he thought of it, and he brought it up in a wide sweeping arc—

The shard pulverized into a million pieces the instant it struck his weapon.

Leo spun in the same second, slicing through the neck of one of the approaching shadow things with extreme precision. The demon staggered back, black ichor spraying everywhere as it let out a bloodcurdling scream—and then disintegrated right there on the spot by his angelic blade.

Samyaza was beside Leo too now, hacking away, trying to protect the Taylors as he threw up a rudimentary shield around them with his free hand, the one he wasn't using to swing his broadsword like a club, bashing in the skull of another screaming banshee that came flying at them.

Larna had already lunged around Leo, her thin blades at her wrists ejected. She was moving with feline grace, ducking low, narrowly avoiding several shards as they embedded themselves in the wall where she'd just been standing.

They meant to infect them all.

Rage rose inside him.

Another demon dove toward Leo, grabbing onto his sword hand right as he was about to drive it through the thing's gut. He could see its eyes up close now. They were obsidian. No whites. Demon.

Black ichor covered the thing's face and neck. An image of Peter swelled up behind his eyes, and he jerked back. *Is this Peter?* Something sharp and piercing slid into his thigh—as hot as a poker left in a fire. His shield bloomed up bright, blasting the demon backward and incinerating it in the process.

Leo lurched sideways and then called out in his mind. *Ikari, Tamiel—we're under attack!* His vision blurred momentarily as he went down hard on his wounded leg.

Five of the infected had latched onto Samyaza, two on his back, and two more at his legs, and another grabbing at his arms; they were trying to drag him down to the ground, subdue him—so they could infect him. Leo saw snapping teeth as Samyaza flailed out in vain against them. His sword was gone. The shield he'd erected around the Taylor family had shattered, but so far none of them had been attacked.

The next instant, Ikari and Tamiel appeared in a clap of thunder as two portals opened up and they bounded out of them, their hands ablaze, crackling with lightning.

Ikari grabbed hold of Jimmy and disappeared at the same time as Tamiel went for Mrs. Taylor. One of those demons sprang in front of her though, blocking Tamiel's attempt at whisking her away. She disappeared in another clap of thunder, trying to portal around the demon, but the damn thing was just as fast as she was—it vanished in a puff of smoke, latching onto Mrs. Taylor at the same time as Tamiel did. Mrs. Taylor let out a terrified wail, and Mr. Taylor, in a rage, went airborne, throwing himself at the demon with reckless abandon.

Leo tried to get back to his feet, but something was horribly wrong with his leg. He bit back a cry of agony and then glanced up to see another shadow demon bearing down on him.

In a wink of light, he had his gold knife in his hand, extended out right as the demon slammed into him. His blade slid deeply into the beast's belly—hitting vital organs—but it didn't seem to matter. The thing spit and hissed in anger like it hadn't been fatally stabbed, wrapping its slender fingers around Leo's throat. They felt like razors against his skin.

Larna came out of nowhere, throwing herself onto the demon's back, clinging to it like she was riding a bronco. She rammed her weapon into the back of the thing's throat, repeatedly and in rapid succession, spraying ichor everywhere.

It let out a hideous gasp and then started to dissolve into a pillar of smoke—trying to escape—but it still had a hold of Leo, and Larna had a hold of it, hanging on to the demon's back for dear life—and then Leo's vision slid out of focus, and faded entirely as both of them inadvertently were pulled right along with the demon … sucked into the void to wherever it was fleeing to.

30

ZOEY

Currently, my demon brother had a crossbow in his hand, resting against his thigh.

I could see him fully now, because he'd lit three sconces in the recesses of the walls, all around me in a circle. The flames were making an eerie guttering noise. I shuddered, thinking about my brother being turned into one of those Shade things. No mind of his own. Taken. A demon lurking inside him in control. Corinth could fix this. If he were himself, he could fix him—like he had with Alastair. The way he'd healed his best friend had been nothing short of miraculous. A miracle. I just needed a miracle. I squeezed my eyes shut. *God, if you could just sort of zap me back to reality right now, I'd appreciate it.* When nothing happened, I cracked them open again.

Demon Pete was still staring at me with those jet-black eyes.

The monotonous echoes of chanting bounced off the

walls around me, making the scenario I now found myself in that much more chilling. Sweat pooled under my arms, even though it was cold. The noise was coming from another chamber, outside the one I occupied.

This moment felt horribly real and final.

I kept thinking about what Trevor had said about sacrifices and demons and gateways. My head was killing me. I raised a hand up to the cut and then dragged it down to my busted lip again, wincing.

"Are Mom and Dad okay?" I asked him finally, feeling resigned. "What about Jimmy?"

"Don't make me do this," he threatened. "Give me the holy relic, Zoey."

I squeezed the shield until my fingers started to go numb. Faint light shimmered from it, forming a protective circle around me. Like standing in a salt circle. Salt probably wouldn't do any harm to a demon though. I couldn't help but stare at the man—*Shade*—who used to be my brother, feeling horrified and shocked and sick.

Maybe I could somehow convince him to change back just by staring him down. It wasn't working. I didn't know what else to say to him. Was he really gone? Was his soul still in there? His eyes were just as black and empty as those of any of the rest of Trevor's horde.

I tasted bile at the back of my throat, my eyes gliding to the crossbow again.

"I'm not making you do anything—*he is. Trevor is.* That sociopath is tearing our family apart, and you're letting him, *Pete.*" My voice cracked, and I glanced down to the dark brown stains smeared at my feet. I was just so tired.

After a while, I asked in a whisper-soft voice, "Are you going to kill me?"

A part of me just wanted him to get it over with. The other part of me was hoping he'd miraculously come to his senses, realize what he was doing, and put the weapon down.

"My name isn't Pete." As if to prove his point, he raised the crossbow and pointed it at me. "I *will* shoot you."

I sucked in a quick, shallow breath.

His hands were steady. He was going to do it. My brother was going to shoot me, and he didn't even care. He didn't care, and that was what gutted me to my core. It was at this moment that I absolutely knew he was gone, but I had to try to stop him anyway. The edges of the cuff on my wrist were smooth and dull, and I rolled my aching wrist, testing it out once again, even knowing what came next. A numbing, tingling sensation swept through me, making me feel nauseous. How long had it been since I'd eaten? Slept? Had water? At least a day. I felt frail and worn.

I glanced around, trying to figure out which way to dart if he shot that thing at me. There wasn't enough length on the chain to move very far.

"*Pete*," I began again, but my voice faltered, and I stopped. I couldn't keep it together. "You are Peter Nathaniel Taylor. Your girlfriend's name is Carlie Vintash. She's an art major—"

"Shut up." he said it quietly, but I could hear a hint of anger and something else behind his words.

"*You're an engineer.*" I kept talking, more insistent

this time. I could get through to him. "You are in college to become a mechanical engineer. You love to take things apart. Remember that time you disassembled the robot vacuum cleaner, and when you put it back together again, it would only spin around in slow, lazy circles, and Biscuit rode it around like he was king of the world? Dad was so angry at you …"

"I said, give me the artifact," he spit. "One …"

"You hate country music." I spoke quicker, clutching the key chain painfully to my chest.

"Two …"

"With a passion, and—"

He loosed the bolt.

My pulse thudded in my ears as everything came to a crashing halt. I could see the bolt slicing through the air, silent and deadly, heading straight for me in excruciating detail.

I ducked down, waiting for the impact, but instead, a brilliant and divine blaze flared up in a golden shower of sparks from the shield key chain. Suddenly the flames took on a corporeal shape and expanded outward, morphing into something solid and heavy and real—right before my eyes. A full-size shiny shield. *Whoa!* I almost buckled under the sudden solid weight as it clanged to the ground at my feet.

I dropped down behind it, quickly gripping the leather straps at the back and curling into a tight ball as the bolt pinged harmlessly off the armor.

The room filled with a heavenly light and bright spots exploded across my vision in a blur of colors, and I gasped.

For a second, I was blind again.

When I was able to blink past the pain, I could see that the searing light had been just as jarring to Shade Peter as it had been to me, because he had a hand over his face and had gone down onto one knee.

And then the fully formed shield shrank back down into a portable key chain once again; I almost fell flat on my face with the abruptness of it. My shackled wrist was burning and I couldn't hold myself upright any longer.

His betrayal hurt on a massive scale, and an overwhelming ache tore through me, rending my heart wide open, leaving behind a gaping wound that would never close or heal. My brother would never have tried to hurt me. Never. He really was gone. I prayed my parents were okay, that they'd gotten out unharmed. *What if they are dead?*

Peter's inscrutable eyes skimmed over me, and then slowly he stood back to his feet, the crossbow still clutched in his ichor-stained hands. "That was a neat trick. How did you do that?"

I gulped and then lifted the shield. "Magic. And there's more where that came from. So I wouldn't try that again."

Demon Pete craned his neck to the side and said, "Time to try a different tactic." He had the audacity to sound bored as he tossed the weapon aside. "I can't stop until you give me the shield." He spoke so softly I almost missed it. "Don't make me do this."

"What would Corinth tell you to do?" I urged.

He cocked an eyebrow as if trying to figure out where I was going with that question.

"You knew he was half angel, right?" I pressed.

"According to Corinth, you stayed at home to watch over me. Pete, this is *not* watching over me. You can fight this … I know you can. You're stronger than this. Be my big brother again." I paused, my voice breaking as I added, "I … love you, knucklehead."

There was no reaction from him at all. Nothing. Only a blank stare. "I told you, I'm *not* your brother. And neither is Corinth. He's something more, and he wants what Ephrem wants. And you will too. I promise."

He was pacing now, marching around me in slow, predatory circles, staying just out of the reach of the light from the proffered talisman. I kept having to spin around to make sure my back wasn't to him. I just needed to buy a little more time. *Think, Zo. How do you get yourself out of this? Shield, turn into a weapon*, I thought. Nothing happened. No blinding light. Goose egg. Zero. *I could really use a way out of this cuff … Free me. Turn into a key. Release me. Turn into a shield again. Anything. Please—*

"And what is that? What do they want?" I asked, when the shield did nothing. How did I get this thing to work again?

"They want control. To free more demons from hell. To make this world their own. Right now, as we speak, Shades are descending upon the safe house where your family is in hiding. I sent them there. *I* betrayed the Taylors. I knew where they were being held. If you think you can persuade me otherwise, you can't."

All thoughts of escape fled me, and I sank down onto my rear, a hand going to my head in dread. *No.* Mom. Dad. Jimmy.

The demon, no longer my brother, was nodding

now. "Soon they will all be part of *this* family. They will be like me. The angels protecting them will be dead." He held up a glass shard, exactly like the one Trevor had used to infect him. It cast a reddish hue against the dark contours of his cheekbones, making it look like blood dripping down his face instead of ichor. "If an angel is hit by one of these shards, they will die. Corinth and Alastair are the exception, because they are half human. Corinth has already been changed for the better. Like me. All humans are destined for this life."

"*You gave them up?*" I whispered, disbelieving.

Demon Peter bowed his head for a second and then suddenly threw his hand out toward me and curled his fingers into a fist like he was summoning something.

Without warning, the chain at my feet jerked and rattled and shuddered against the floor, and in the next instant, it shot forward, rushing toward his outstretched hand as if it were possessed by magic. I could hear every clink and jangle of the chain as it moved. And I realized too late what he was doing right as the iron at my wrist, which was still attached to the chain, started dragging me across the ground right along with it.

An ice-cold electric shock of pain opened up inside me as I tried to claw at the ground and stop myself from hurtling toward him.

A terrified wail escaped me, and I went numb and tingly all over as the full effects of the dark energy swelled back to life inside me, winding through my bloodstream, overwhelming my senses.

By the time I stopped, I found I could hardly pull in a breath, and I was conscious of the fact that I was lying on my side, but I couldn't move.

Everything hurt.

Forcing my eyes open, I felt something wet hit my cheeks. I blinked past the fuzziness of pain to stare up into the face of my brother—beyond my brother—at the evil compelling him now. He was crouched over me, an elbow perched on top of one knee, watching, patiently waiting for me to wake up.

Once he saw I was stirring back to life, he stood back to his feet and put a booted foot to my shoulder, forcing me flat on my back. His eyes were pitch-black and merciless.

Slowly he turned to glance at something across the way, and I followed his line of sight to the tiny golden light, too far out of my reach to be of any help now. *The shield.* My last lifeline. It must have been flung from my hand the moment he'd jerked the chain toward hm.

"It's time for your conversion," he said calmly.

31

CRUZ

Cruz could not think of a worse idea: wading out into a horde of demons. *Sure, sounds like a great plan. What could go wrong?* He decided he didn't want responsibility over the blade anymore. Or to see that look of approval on Alastair's face directed at him. He'd done nothing to earn it.

Cruz clutched the glowing blade tighter as they strode out into the cavernous space. The Shades had stopped chanting the moment they had seen them all approaching.

None of them moved, only watched with a detached sort of interest. How could this be better than his idea of trying to disguise themselves? *This is a bad idea. This is a very bad idea.*

Dark Corinth and Trevor—Ephrem—were standing in the middle of the gathered group. Corinth's hands were clasped in front of him, and his eyes looked like frosted glass. He couldn't help but notice the sneer on Ephrem's face as soon as he saw Cruz holding the blade.

Gabriel and Alastair stayed in the small patch of light beside Cruz. A nervous energy buzzed between them all. The Shades parted, backing away from the torch as they moved closer to the center of the space. A few of them hissed and snarled in anger as soon as they passed, but no one made a move to attack them just yet.

When they were a few feet away from Corinth and Ephrem, they stopped. Cruz's hands were shaking as he brandished the dagger. The Shades closed the gaps and surrounded the trio, cutting off their chance of escape. He glanced around at the sea of blank faces, and murky eyes glaring back at them.

This is a very bad idea.

"Zoey better still be alive," Cruz hissed.

Ephrem's gaze locked on the ancient blade in Cruz's hand before darting back up to meet his level gaze. "Are you sure you can handle that weapon?"

The golden halo around them increased in intensity, and a spark shot off the tip of the dagger.

"I think I got it covered," Cruz growled in response.

Gabriel Stanton stepped forward to the edge of the light, and as soon as he did, Corinth addressed him. "I'm surprised you're still around, Gabe. What is Al paying you? I'll triple it."

"I'm just here for the violence," Gabriel Stanton said with a shrug at the same time as he ejected two thin blades out of the bracers secured at both his wrists. Cruz did think he looked intimidating.

Ephrem turned to regard Alastair next. "Have you come to give yourself up?"

Alastair stepped forward, toeing the line where the protective light ended. His feet were still bare, but somehow, even without shoes, and wearing black warm-up pants and a long button-down coat, it only served to make him look more striking—or maybe it was the black mark emblazoned across his chest that did that. His eyes looked like blue flames dancing in the dark.

"Is Zoey still alive?" Alastair asked, his voice sounding full of barely controlled rage.

Ephrem shrugged and then jutted his chin out toward the opening of the next alcove behind him, and the massive demon horde surrounding them. "She's alive … for *now* … but she won't be by the time you get through me. I need her blood. All of it. And she's with her brother as we speak. It doesn't matter to me which one of the Taylors kills her first."

"What do you mean, which one of the Taylors?" Alastair's hands began to crackle with golden sparks.

Cruz could feel the heat and static and ozone thicken around them, and his heart leaped in his chest.

Ephrem gave Alastair a maddening grin. "Peter, I mean. Well, he's not Peter anymore … He's one of mine. The rest of the Taylors will follow soon enough."

Cruz's eyes widened in surprise and Corinth stepped up to Alastair—just out of reach of the light, he noted.

"*You son of a bitch*," Alastair breathed. "*What did you do?*" His eyes leveled on Dark Corinth. Cruz could see a vein pop out of the side of Alastair's neck. He looked like someone not to be messed with. "Corinth—you let this happen to your family? *Wake up!*" he shouted.

Dark Corinth's eyes raked over Alastair, but he didn't

say anything as he turned his attention back to Cruz and the dagger in his outstretched hand. "That's my blade," he whispered menacingly. "I want it back."

Cruz took a deep breath, waved the dagger in a two-handed grip, and a flash of bronze hit Corinth square in his face. He recoiled, a hand going to his cheek, and his eyes widened in disbelief and anger. There was a jagged burn mark where the light had hit him.

"You sure you want it back?" Cruz warned him.

Dark Corinth's frosty eyes flashed, and his hands flew out and exploded into twin balls of flame. He raised them up and snapped his wrist forward. No warning. No hesitation. Nothing.

Cruz barely had enough time to lift his hands as lightning connected with him—

A shimmering wall flared up at the last second, enveloping his body in its protective embrace. But the impact still blasted him backward off his feet. He slammed into something hard, and then went barreling through a wall of bodies.

Hands and feet scrabbled out of the way. A moment later, Cruz's back hit something solid and he heard a sickening crunch, followed by his world spinning around him. Vaguely he was aware of Alastair bolting into action, hands held out, gloriously ablaze too.

For a few painful seconds, all Cruz could do was clutch the blade to his chest, breathing heavily, trying to clear his head, praying the light was still protecting him. He did not want to get that close to being struck by lightning ever again, no matter what … His insides still felt like goo, and his blood tingled in his veins—he hadn't even been hit full force. After another second, Cruz clamped his jaws together so hard his neck hurt.

Eventually, his vision came back into focus, and he almost wished it hadn't, because he could now see the line of demons in front of him.

She's alive … for now … but she won't be by the time you get through me. I need her blood. All of it. She's with her brother as we speak.

Get up. Get up. Get up.

Cruz was moving too slowly, the pounding in his head too severe. The indentation in the rocky outcropping behind him was the exact size and shape of his body. He'd hit his head at least twice today already. Stumbling back to his feet, he held the weapon aloft, forcing the horde back.

Mass chaos erupted all around him as dozens of the demons scrambled to get at him, cutting off his route to Zoey. All snapping teeth and claws. *I am* so *dead.* The terrible hissing increased as the Shades tried to skirt the edge of his protective bubble. Fortunately, they couldn't cross the light—not without dusting themselves in the process.

Cruz glanced around in a haze, noticing that he was all the way back to where they'd entered the cavern. *Great.* He ground his teeth together, ignoring the searing pain everywhere, sweeping the blade back and forth in front of him, and one of the gutsier demons leaped forward, plunging directly into the light.

It disintegrated on the spot, a howl dying on its oozing lips. All that was left was a pile of ash and bone.

Cruz covered his face in disgust and horror, his heart

working on overtime now.

The rest of the demons stayed well back as he trotted cautiously around them. "*Get back*," he growled, and several of the Shades parted to create a path as he made his tedious way to the opening where he knew Zoey would be.

As he moved, he let out several more commands to "*Stay back.*"

Off in the distance, Gabriel Stanton was fighting at least a dozen or so Shades; his knives were silver blurs as he dodged and weaved, cutting and slicing with meticulous aim and precision. The guy couldn't be human. Vampire for sure.

Stanton leaped into the air and slashed down with one of his blades, cutting through the neck of a demon who'd been holding a wooden-handled spear—and in the same movement, he turned around and stabbed another one with his other blade, right through its chest, ripping his weapon back out in one fell swoop.

Meanwhile, Alastair and Corinth were fighting furiously, throwing what looked like white-hot globs of lava back and forth at each other. Cruz moved faster once he realized Ephrem was nowhere to be found.

Even though the din of battle was horrific, the cries and shouts, and metal striking metal, all he could focus on was the sound of his own swift breathing in his ears.

Get to Zoey.

32

ZOEY

I held my breath, staring up into the eyes of my killer. My brother. *Not my brother.*

The monster that resembled Peter crouched back down beside me and opened his hand. The shard was sitting in his palm, glowing red like a ruby in the sunlight. I distantly wondered if he was going to infect me with it. Turn me into a Shade. He seemed conflicted about something; his eyes zipped back and forth like a clock pendulum as he studied it.

The chanting had stopped.

Why was everything so deathly still?

"I'm trying to save you the only way I know how." His voice was still frosty and detached, the opposite of what those words should have expressed, but there was something in his dark eyes that suggested my brother was still in there. Maybe he did care.

I expelled the breath from my lungs and shimmied

up into a sitting position, using my elbows for support. The chain clanked loudly beside me, and the metal cuff dug irritatingly into my skin. I winced, expecting the pain to return full force, but thankfully, it didn't. My body still felt like it had been hit by a wrecking ball. The adrenaline had worn off a long time ago, and the effects of the last twenty-four hours had started to set in.

I raised my shackled wrist, straining against the weight. "Then let me go."

Shade Pete opened his mouth to say something but stopped as soon as someone spoke behind him.

"I'm impressed, and that doesn't happen very often."

A sinking feeling hit me right in the pit of my gut at hearing Trevor's voice.

I sought out the small glowing object across the way—my only protection down the drain, literally. There was no way I could get to it now. Not chained up. I pulled Cruz's jacket tighter around my shoulders as my *demon* brother got woodenly back to his feet.

He closed his fist over the shard before turning around to face Trevor.

"How did you do it?" Trevor asked him. "How did you get it away from her?"

"I conjured the chain, and it knocked her off-balance, which caused her to drop it."

Trevor went quiet for a moment, seemingly contemplating something before he said, "You have done very well." He moved to stand near the top step, just above Shade Peter, his gaze settling on the faintly glowing shield a few feet away.

Although, to me, it might as well have been across a

chasm. A slow, cruel smile spread across his lips at seeing me without it.

"You shall be rewarded for your efforts," Trevor told him. "Someone so clever is deserving of a name … Ari. Your new name shall be Ari."

"That's not his name," I growled. "Pete—is—his—name."

Trevor's eyes swiveled to meet mine, and I sucked in a shaky breath. I would never get used to seeing such pure evil.

I felt the heaviness of the device in my jacket pocket, knowing Cruz had left it to me, and he wasn't going to get it back. That thought crushed my soul. I put my hand in my pocket, wrapping my fingers around it. I wouldn't let Trevor have it. Not if it was the last thing I did.

In the background, there came a sudden clamor of angry shouting and scrabbling. Steel striking steel. Was that fighting? It could only mean one thing: help was coming. Hope flared in my chest.

I staggered back to my feet and gestured toward the tunnel behind me. "That sounds a lot like you losing, to me, *Trevor*."

Trevor turned wolfish eyes on me, and then stepped slowly down into the circle, his movements leisurely and deliberate.

He eyed me up and down before saying, "Ari, go and join your brother and report back. Zoey and I have some catching up to do. And by *catching up*, I mean it's time she serves her higher purpose."

My eyes darted back to Shade Peter, but he was already gone in a swirl of black smoke before I could protest, or shout, or try and convince him to help me. The sudden urge to turn around and run rose up so strongly inside me that I faltered back a step, almost tripping over the heavy chain at my feet.

"There's nowhere for you to go," Trevor said, his voice lowering considerably.

My shackled wrist was stretched straight as a rod out in front of me; standing like this, there was no give or slack in the chain. I had maybe two or three feet to move on either side. I glanced around the chamber, searching, and then threw a hand out toward the shield, desperately trying to summon it the way my brother had controlled his weapon, using only his mind to do so. *Please. Come to me*, I begged.

Trevor chuckled, raising an amused eyebrow. "You have to have angelic blood in order to perform that magic trick."

And I didn't know how he moved that quickly, but in the next second, he was already standing in front of me, that wicked grin trapping me in place. My heart rate spiked as soon as I saw a flash of silver by his side—a thin, razor-sharp knife clutched in between his fingers.

There was nothing special about it.

It was dull silver, the color of flatware. Ordinary. It looked like a knife you'd find in someone's butcher block.

I gave him a piercing glare, refusing to back down, and he flicked his wrist out. There came a sharp prick under my chin, and I froze. Every single one of my muscles tensed up as tight as a bowstring. I didn't dare breathe or move a muscle. Standing stone-still, I gave him a cold, hard glare in defiance.

"I wanted Corinth to do this part. But you see, he's busy, and I'm bored." Trevor moved the blade slowly down from my face and teased Cruz's jacket open with the knife's tip—so he could better gain access to my throat, I guessed. I couldn't help myself; I tried to dive to my left, but he grabbed the collar of my jacket, pulling me flush against him and ripping it back open. I balled my free hand into a fist and jabbed out at his stomach, but all it did was make him laugh as he easily caught my wrist and yanked me closer against him. The cold knifepoint was at my jugular, and with one arm stretched down by my side, imprisoned by the cuff, and the other pinned against his chest, I was trapped.

He was so close I could feel his chest rising and falling against mine with each breath he took.

"This blade is extremely sharp," he said, his breath stirring my hair, his cheek almost against mine. "It only takes a tiny flick of a wrist. There's no ceremony needed to open the gateway. It only needs fresh blood to activate. Simple. Easy. And then I watch you bleed out. Five minutes tops is all it'll take."

I was wearing my hoodie and a T-shirt underneath, but for some reason, I felt terribly exposed. There was no moisture left in my mouth. "You're not going to get what you want, you know." I let the hatred and sarcasm drip out of my voice, angry, scathing.

He cocked his head, seemingly curious about what I had to say next. "And what is that?"

I met his steely gaze with one of my own. "My fear. I'm not afraid of you anymore."

"I am so going to miss this back and forth with you,

Zo. I really am. But in order for me to raise an infernal demon, I have to take a life. Yours. These powerful demons wreak a lot more havoc than your run-of-the-mill demons. And they are *extremely* hard to bring into this world. That's why I need your blood—*all* of it. Yet that doesn't frighten you? Not even the tiniest bit?"

There was an awful *SNAP* followed by something unrolling and spiraling down from the ceiling above us incredibly fast. A chain. It was now at my eye level. He reached out to grip it with the hand not holding the knife to my throat. "Now the fun begins—"

I saw a flicker of movement behind Trevor.

The chain coiled around Trevor's neck and lifted him off his feet, cranking up swiftly, hauling him back up with it—and the blade left my throat.

I stumbled out of the way of his wildly swinging knife, nearly falling on my rear, but I caught the manacle around my wrist and managed to right myself at the last second, my mouth falling open.

Trevor's feet dangled inches above my head, his entire body swinging from the effort of trying to free himself of the noose around his neck. And there, standing in front of me, was Shade Peter, his arm extended out toward Trevor, his eyes closed in concentration—he was using his powers to help me.

I opened my mouth, planning to scream bloody murder, only to realize that nothing would come out. Not even a squeak.

Pete closed the distance between us, and without preamble, he reached out and clasped a hand around the iron at my wrist. He recited something indecipherable, and then suddenly it sprang open with a satisfying clink, and I was free. Finally. I stretched my aching arm out as relief flooded through me, and I swayed on my feet. It was all too much.

Peter. He still didn't look human, but his actions seemed less stilted and wooden as he put a supportive hand on my shoulder to keep me upright. There was a tingling sensation as circulation started to come rushing back into my hand.

I clutched at my injured wrist, too overcome to speak.

"I'm sorry it took me so long—" he started to say, but a solid fist slammed through his back and exited out his chest.

Time ground to an excruciating halt.

Pete had a hand protruding out of his chest.

A hand.

There was no blood or gore, like I thought there probably should be with a fist sticking out of his internal organs. A wave of nausea rolled over me so strongly I almost blacked out on the spot.

In infinite slowness, Pete glanced down to the hand jutting out of his body. It was covered in black ash and ichor, and to my horror, the fingers flexed and spread apart.

Everything went still.

The sounds of the battle in the background faded. The sound of my own ragged breathing disappeared. The chain rattling above us stopped. I couldn't even hear my own pounding heartbeat, could only feel its rapid pulse in my chest, beating like a dull hammer.

And then, in the briefest of moments, I saw him.

I saw my brother behind the mask, and how he used to be. Helpful and kind and irritating all at the same time. His eyes flickered back to their chestnut hue—not quite honey—he looked so much like Corinth now—when before, I'd never thought so. Now, I could see some of the slight resemblance in him.

"*I … love … you.*" His voice came out grating and hoarse, but decidedly *his*. My brother's voice.

My chest tightened up to a horrendous degree, and then my stomach heaved.

Pete let out a single deep sigh of relief and then collapsed into a boneless heap at my feet, lifeless.

His name tore out of my lips as if I were pulling on a broken rip cord on a parachute. "*Peter!*" I panted. "*Peter! Pete! Pete!*" I didn't know how many times I screamed his name—enough to go hoarse.

And then a rough hand clamped down on my wrist. I gaped up at its owner, my brain a tangled mess of thoughts and horror and grief, to see Trevor's amused grin. His lips were pulled back into a sneer, and this time, I knew I really was dead.

33

ALASTAIR

Alastair was doing his best to stave off Corinth's attacks, but the kid, or Angela, had more training than he did when it came to using angelic abilities. A trickle of blood dribbled down his chin, and he swiped it away and threw up a hand to block another blast of lightning aimed in his direction. A shield flared up bright, and the bolt ricocheted off the barrier in a shower of angry sparks.

Alastair felt himself waning. He could not keep this up for much longer. Off to his left, Gabriel Stanton was still parrying and moving gracefully, attacking anything that was moving. Surprisingly, he had taken out a good chunk of their opposition. But it didn't matter if they kept rising up from the dead.

Dark Corinth circled Alastair, his hands fisted down by his sides, glowing like blue flames.

"You know what I'm going to do when I get out of

here?" Corinth taunted him.

"I'm sure you're … about to … tell me," Alastair panted dryly, still winded.

"I am going to kill Larna. Nothing fancy or diabolical or well thought out. Just a swift lightning bolt to her heart. She won't see it coming, because … well, she'll think her best friend is there to love and support her. Do you think Leo will see it coming? His death, I mean?"

Rage started to boil up inside Alastair. "I know that's not you talking, Corinth, so I'm going to let that slide." He knew Dark Corinth was needling him in hopes that he would become sloppy, but that didn't mean it didn't hurt—the person who he'd worked alongside for over a decade. His brother. His comrade in arms. No trace of his witty humor left in him whatsoever.

Alastair's eyes flickered briefly over the mass of demons, looking for any sign of Cruz; he couldn't see over them. The ones Gabriel hadn't slaughtered were standing back up, keeping clear, and waiting. He thanked his lucky stars for that at least, and he'd curse himself later for admitting it, but he was also glad for Stanton's backup. What was wrong with him?

Dark Corinth lifted blazing hands and started to take aim again. Alastair was pretty sure he was depleted of all his energy. He could barely lift his arms—

Above them there came a resounding crack followed by a churning of black smoke, and then out of thin air, a body plummeted down, landing in a broken heap between him and Dark Corinth—a Shade. A second later, two more bodies dropped down out of a pillar of black smoke.

There was a flash of raven-colored hair and golden

armor. Angel. Alastair saw Leo hit the ground in a stunned heap, unmoving, right as a second figure landed beside him in an impressive crouch. A woman with dark hair. Long brown coat.

Alastair's heart leaped in his chest. *Larna.* Speaking of avenging angels. His wife was wearing her brown leather duster and combat boots. Her hair was tousled and swept to the side, and the tips of her cheeks were bright pink. She had already released the thin blades hidden in her vambraces, ready for a fight.

Larna gave Alastair the once-over, her eyes lingering on the black mark on his chest, and then on his bare feet and button-down coat. "How do you always end up with no shoes on?" she asked him, breathless, turning at the same time, her eyes taking in the fighting and gore and carnage all around them—and then she froze the minute she saw Corinth, her chest heaving up and down.

"*Larna!*" Dark Corinth shouted in desperation, and he held his hand out to her, beckoning. "Don't trust Al— he's been infected! He's one of them now!"

Alastair could tell she was trying to take everything in all at once before she acted.

"He's lying, Larna. I'm okay," Alastair said hastily. "I'm not infected."

Her eyes caught once again on Alastair, and then they flickered down to his sparking, unnaturally glowing hands—where he no longer wore his wedding ring—and then to the weird symbol imprinted on his chest.

He lifted his hands up, agitated by having supernatural powers now. She wasn't going to believe he wasn't infected now. "This is … I can explain this …"

She took a hesitant step toward Dark Corinth, but Leo staggered unsteadily to his feet and caught her by the arm. "That's not Corinth," he said firmly. "Look at his eyes."

Larna stopped in her tracks, her own eyes going wide as she noticed the tattoos all over his neck and arms; a silvery light blazed up and down his body. "Cor—" she started to say, but the Shade that had landed beside Alastair popped up like a jack-in-the-box and dove at him, growling, its teeth bared.

In one fluid movement, Larna spun around and kicked the demon square in its chest. It scrabbled backward, arms flailing at the same time as Alastair raised his already-glowing hands and released the lightning at his fingertips. His blood was zinging with the power coursing through him all of a sudden, and he got light-headed again.

The bolt caught the thing in the abdomen, and it doubled over. For a split second, he could see a boy— maybe twelve years old—underneath the black ichor, blue eyes almost as bright as his own … and then the boy disintegrated on the spot in a spray of ash and dust. Gone forever. Alastair's fault. He'd killed a boy. His gut twisted with guilt.

Leo turned to regard Alastair, his eyes widening at the same time as Larna's mouth dropped open at seeing Alastair's newfound ability.

Meanwhile, Dark Corinth was laughing. It cut right through the din of battle—harsh and cold and as brittle as the winter.

"Hello, *son*," she-he said icily. "It's so good to see you

again, Leo." Dark Corinth's eyes had a tinge of violet ringing frosty irises. Violet like Leo's.

Leo turned slowly back to face his half brother—well, technically, Angela—the one now possessing Corinth's body. She-he was standing erect, golden armor gleaming like a burning star. "Angela?" he whispered. Alastair could see a muscle feather on Leo's jaw. "How is this possible?"

Most of the fighting had stopped. That was why it was so quiet. Alastair had already dispatched quite a few demons himself. Those that were still moving were shuffling and growling on the ground, trying to pull themselves back together again, but Gabriel was doing his best to make sure they didn't get back up. The rest had probably stopped because they'd been ordered to.

Stanton moved silently up behind Corinth—Angela—his blades held out at the ready. Alastair knew what he was going to do a moment before he did it—

Stanton sliced out with his blade, aiming directly for Dark Corinth's neck. For any normal human being, their bacon would have been cooked. But Dark Corinth was Nephilim, part angel, and he'd had plenty of time to hone his abilities. Hell, Alastair had taught Corinth everything he knew about martial arts. Of course, who knew what sort of unbidden powers Angela possessed?

So when she-he fragmented in a clap of thunder in one second, and then reappeared in front of Gabriel in the next, he knew Stanton didn't stand a chance.

In slow motion, Dark Corinth pressed his palms against Stanton's chest, and blue flames erupted all around him. The inferno consumed him whole. The force of so much energy at point blank range sent Stanton skyrocketing backward, sliding across the polished stone where he fetched up against the opposite wall in a heap, incredibly still and pale.

Larna clutched her chest and screamed—a sound full of anguish and dread—and Alastair remembered the strange bond that they had shared when Stanton had turned her. Apparently that bond had never gone away, even though she and Stanton were no longer vampire.

She fell to a knee, suddenly overcome.

It felt like the air had been sucked right out of Alastair's lungs. He rocked back on his heels as if he'd been punched—he hadn't exactly liked Stanton, but he suddenly realized he didn't want him to die, either, and he especially didn't want Corinth to hold himself responsible when, or if, he came out of this on the other side.

Alastair flew to his wife's side and helped her back to her feet. "Are you okay?"

She looked incredibly pale to him, just as pale as Gabriel had looked when he'd gone down, but she only nodded once, swiping a hand down her face.

"How did you get here?" he asked.

"I rode a demon," she said, as if it were a perfectly normal means of travel or explanation.

Leo turned to Alastair. "I'll deal with Angela. Where's Zoey?" he asked.

"We need the Blood Dagger to separate Angela from Corinth." Alastair spoke quickly because he could see Corinth turning back around to face them, his fists glowing electric blue. "Cruz has the blade, and he went to help Zoey."

"The *kid?*" Leo said, sounding incredulous. "I'll stall Angela-Corinth as long as I can. You go help them."

"Let's see who will win in a fight, shall we?" Angela called out, using Corinth's lips to do so.

34

CRUZ

Cruz entered the dungeon where he knew Zoey had been imprisoned, breathing through his mouth as soon as the stench of rotting meat hit him. It felt like ages ago since he'd left her all alone. Goose bumps pebbled his flesh at the thought of returning to this horrid place. A feeling of guilt churned in his chest.

Suck it up, Cruz, he told himself.

If Trevor hurt her, he was going to kill the jerk with his bare hands … demon or no demon.

Cruz crept softly toward flickering golden light, thinking it was the shield key chain he'd given Zoey before he'd left. Except the source of the light was not coming from the talisman. It was lit wall sconces. Which meant—

A gut-wrenching scream broke through his thoughts and sent ice shooting through his veins.

Zoey.

Not okay.

Cruz was running as fast as he could toward the opening of the circular chamber, not caring who heard him coming. As soon as he saw the tableau in front of him though, he sucked in a sharp breath and froze in his tracks, horrified.

Trevor was towering over Zoey, an imperious look on his face. She had thrown herself over a prone form on the ground. Above them, a long chain whipped violently back and forth; the sound of the links clinking together was beyond eerie. Zoey was incredibly pale, and she was screaming a name over and over again: *Pete*.

It took Cruz a minute to connect the dots, to figure out that the thing on the ground was a Shade, and not a Shade—Peter Taylor—one of Zoey's brothers. Cruz knew the sound of loss, and this loss went beyond torment. He'd been turned. Trevor had killed her brother right in front of her. In that moment, he knew that she had cracked. He had been on that very ledge himself with his mother.

Cruz's heart wrenched at seeing her brother so unbearably still. And then his anger propelled him forward of its own volition. Without thinking, he went flying across the chamber, dagger brandished, his adrenaline skyrocketing.

And his intention was to take Trevor down with the burning blade—ram it straight into his chest—feel his beating heart extinguish, but that was not what happened. Not at all.

The douche was a demon who had superhuman abilities.

Cruz got within arm's reach of Trevor before the demon glanced up at him, and then disappeared into a puff of black smoke like a magician—

And Cruz went sprawling through the vapor, an intense cold washing over him as he slid on his belly across the stained concrete, the blazing blade still clutched in his hand. A moment later, he fetched up against the anchor in the middle of the chamber, and a searing pain lit up his forearm as something warm and sticky slid down his hand, coating it in red.

But his full attention was on Zoey; he couldn't get her grief-stricken look out of his head. She was on her knees beside her motionless brother, her arms wrapped around his neck, weeping.

Cruz meant to get up and help her, but he felt something cold and metallic coil around his leg and bite into his skin, and then he was being dragged across the hard stone, backward. He threw his arms out, scrabbling for purchase as he thought about giant teeth biting into his limbs. *Don't look. Don't look. Don't look.*

He barely managed to hang on to the blade right as he was yanked high into the air. His stomach somersaulted, and he let out an awkward yelp as he hung upside down by one leg. Swinging back and forth with nothing but air in between him and the floor was terrifying.

As he swayed, he could barely make out the thing that had hold of his ankle. It didn't have teeth. It was a chain. Alive. Was it moving like a snake?

The blade was slick in his bloodied grasp as he dangled by one foot, his leg burning—and the blood was already rushing straight to his head. He was going to drop the dagger; he felt it sliding through his fingers.

"Zoey!" he screeched, floundering. "I can't hold on to it!"

As soon as he said it, the blade slipped from his grasp and plummeted fifteen feet to the hard stone, landing point down, sticking straight up in a crack—well out of his reach.

Trevor glanced up at Cruz, cocked his head to the side, and something red winked into his open palm. *Infection. Plague. Zombies.* All words rolling through his head as he saw what Trevor intended to do to him: turn him into one of those things—a Shade.

35

ZOEY

My brother didn't have a heartbeat. His eyes were closed; his body was limp in my arms; and his glossy onyx-colored skin, oddly enough, didn't feel cold or sticky to the touch, like I'd thought it might. It felt hot and dry. The tears were hot on my face too. My eyes were burning. I never imagined it would hurt this much, losing someone I loved.

I'd never truly hated anyone before. I mean, I'd used the word *hate* carelessly enough under my breath when I'd argued with my mother … but I'd never felt the meaning behind it. It was just a word. But now I wanted to kill Trevor with every fiber of my being. I *hated* him. *Hated* Trevor for what he'd done to my family. He'd taken away a life. Peter's. He might have already killed my parents. Corinth was possessed, and wanted to kill me. Anger took on a virulent form as everything else melted away around me.

Cruz's distressed cries sounded distorted and far away. I knew he was in trouble, but I was too overcome by a feeling of intense loathing to help him.

Get up, Zoey, a stronger voice insisted. *Peter is dead because of you. Your best friend is about to die. Peter would want you to fight. Get up. Cruz needs your help. Are you going to just let him die after he came back to save your life?*

The dagger had landed a few feet away from me.

Take up arms.

The light coming off it blazed up in an impressive wall of fire, sending Trevor floundering back a step. Luckily, Cruz was out of the blast range, swinging wildly by one leg, his arms dangling over his head. Blood dribbled off his fingers, and it hit me on my forehead. He was hurt.

Suddenly Cruz halted in place, frozen like an inverted statue, arms blurred in slow motion.

Trevor had been in the process of shielding his eyes, his face screwed up in pain and rage, brows almost meeting in the middle. This was how a mind could shatter into a thousand pieces. This was how I cracked. I wouldn't come back from this mentally sound and intact. It was too much. All of it.

The blade called to me, whispering softly, like hot breath on my ear. *Take up the Holy Lance.* A wall of flames rose up around it. Glorious. Almighty. And I could sense the danger in it too—like, smiting danger.

And in that eternal second, I knew what I had to do, even if it killed me.

The world reoriented itself, and things started happening quickly. Trevor stretched his hand out, about to flick the glass shard at Cruz, to turn him into one of his Shades—

I was on my feet before I realized how fast I'd moved—maybe the dagger had somehow gifted me with superspeed, or maybe it was all the adrenaline coursing through my veins. Either way, when I saw the shield, still glowing softly in the drain, I reached out and beckoned to it: *Come to me.*

In a wink of light, the holy relic was in my outstretched grasp.

"CRUZ!" I shouted, turning around in the same second. "*Catch!*" I tossed the shield at him, praying he'd catch it, praying that maybe he had the gift of agility and foresight too.

And miraculously, he *did* catch it.

But it didn't turn into life-size armor like it had for me. Instead, it gleamed bright and transformed into a second dagger—a mirror image of Corinth's—except the one in Cruz's hand was pure gold, like the shield. He swung the blade, and the shard struck it, pinging harmlessly off the sharp edge, and then, astonishingly, Cruz hoisted himself up, grabbed the chain still coiled around his ankle, and hacked at it with the burning blade.

It broke in a shower of fiery sparks as soon as the knife's edge grazed it. And then he fell—fifteen feet, landing on his back, motionless, his arms stretched out by his sides, eyes closed.

Cruz!

I started to go to him but realized Trevor was blocking my path—and blocking his path to me was the true dagger, Corinth's blade.

My heart was in my throat, my pulse slamming through my veins. I had to make a decision.

Trevor started toward me, angry and undeterred, his irritation on full display as he fisted his hands down by his sides. "I'm done playing with you now," he growled.

His eyes were on fire, and they looked like glowing rubies. They flashed to the holy dagger, still wedged in the stone near his feet, sizzling and sparking.

I gritted my teeth at the same time as he sprang at me—

And seizing the still-blazing blade, I expected to immediately burst into flames, but the hilt was almost cool to the touch, and it didn't hurt me. I drew the weapon up with a war cry, ripping it free of the stone in a two-handed grip, and swung it around like a battle-ax right as he appeared beside me in a thick cloud of dark smoke, his hand going for my throat.

This time the blade felt right in my hands. A perfect fit. Not like before, when I'd held it so awkwardly. Not heavy, but perfectly balanced. My fingers curled around the leather grip right as I rammed the razor-sharp tip straight into his chest at the same time as he slammed into me.

Trevor's bow-shaped mouth dropped open in surprise, and I staggered back into the brick wall behind me, taking the brunt of his assault, his body crushed up against mine. I was hyperfocused on how the blade felt in my hands as it scraped through his tissue and bone, going right through his rib cage, burying itself all the way up to the hilt, the guard the only thing stopping my hands from slipping across the razor's edge.

Pressed up against him, face-to-face, I could see myself reflected in his inflamed eyes.

I'd just stabbed him.

I'd stabbed someone.

Oh my gosh.

A part of my brain thought it was odd how easily the knife had gone in. There was no blood gushing from an open wound. No gore. No gasp of pain uttered from his blood-red lips. Trevor's sternum moved up and down beneath my hands; I felt the vibration through the handle as his chest rumbled. All the while, I was pinned against the wall by his body. He was laughing even though his lungs gurgled like a beaker of boiling liquid in a science experiment.

"You have to have angelic abilities in order to use that blade against me, little girl." And then Trevor was lifting me off the ground by my neck, one-handed, sliding my back up the brick wall. He chuckled, squeezing the life out of me, and I gagged as stars exploded across my vision. I couldn't get air into my lungs. I kicked out at him but didn't get anywhere near striking him, and my hands slid across the hilt, slipping.

All I could do was give him a maddening grin right back. At least I was going to go out fighting, my hands still wrapped around the sunken blade in his chest.

Pale fingers encircled Trevor's neck, and then his crushing weight was gone as my savior yanked him backward off me. Trevor's fingernails raked my throat, scalding hot, and I sucked in a ragged breath and fell to the ground, landing on my bruised knees in a heap. The energy I'd possessed earlier was now completely gone. I was spent in more ways than one. He was right about me not having angelic abilities. I was only an ordinary fifteen-year-old girl. Nothing more.

I managed to glance up from my prone position on the ground to see Alastair in all his magnificent—ahem, very well defined, bare-chested—glory, shoving Trevor across the small chamber.

Trevor, not expecting Alastair to possess that sort of strength, tripped up the step at the same time as Alastair executed a perfectly timed back flip and kicked him in the jaw, knocking him flat on his butt.

Alastair apparently had enough angelic energy to take him down for the both of us. I gaped at him, riveted by the way he moved, fluid and precise and supernaturally fast. And Alastair's hands lit up in hues that I could only describe as those of an exploding comet as he took aim at the dagger in Trevor's chest and threw a bolt of lightning at it.

The energy hit the hilt of the blade still buried in Trevor's chest, and he pretty much disintegrated right there on the spot, gurgling in pain and agony—sitting on his butt—as he exploded into ash, drifting apart on the wind.

The heat was intense. I curled into a ball, covering my face as it washed over me. *Please don't let me die now.*

When the fire and smoke dissipated and the chamber cleared, and I was pretty sure I wasn't dead, I opened my eyes and looked around in a daze at the aftermath. The still-glittering blade was sitting in a pile of ash where Trevor had been sitting.

Pete's body was gone, vaporized too, I assumed, by

the intense blaze. My heartache increased tenfold, and my stomach flipped. I was going to be sick. *He* is *gone*. We couldn't even bury a body. Tears streamed down my face.

Cruz was stirring back to life, and my pulse kicked in, thumping away as I struggled back to my feet. He was alive. I dropped down beside him, patting his chest awkwardly, feeling for injuries and rubbing at the wetness on my cheeks. His forearm had a long, shallow cut on it, and he winced when I hoisted his arm up to inspect it. I still had on his coat, so I shucked it off and laid it across him like a blanket.

"*Ouch*," he mumbled, his eyes half-closed and his fingers still curled around the gold hilt of the twin dagger. I marveled at it for a moment before the weapon flashed bright and then shrank back down, forming back into the miniature shield once again. Cruz cracked his eyes open and squinted down at his fingers clutching it. "That … sucked."

"You both okay?" Alastair asked, sounding winded from across the room. His chest was heaving, and half his blond hair was in his face, and his hands were still crackling like mini sparklers.

"*Okay* is one term for it," Cruz wheezed, managing to sit upright, his coat sliding down to his waist.

"*Pete*," I breathed, gazing back at Alastair, my voice cracking, "is … is … he's … *dead*." I couldn't stand the pain flooding back in again. It hurt too much. Everything.

Alastair ran a hand across his face. "*Dammit*," he whispered, his voice full of regret and sorrow. "Zoey, I'm so sorry." He stooped to pick up the blade—the true blade—that had been lodged in Trevor's chest. "I tried—"

A clap of thunder reverberated throughout the room, and a cloudlike vortex opened up right behind Alastair. It was insane how swiftly it happened—there was no time to even open my mouth and shout a warning.

Not-Corinth appeared right behind Alastair, holding a broken spear in his hands—at least, I thought a spear was what it used to be. Now it just looked like a hunk of wood, whittled down to a sharp point like a stake, and by the time my brain connected the dots, he'd already gripped it in two hands and thrust the sharp point all the way through Alastair's back, a maniacal grin plastered across his face.

The splintered handle burst out of Alastair's chest, right in the center of his tattoo in a spray of red mist. Blood dribbled down the side of Alastair's mouth as he glanced down in absurd slowness, his fingers releasing the blade he'd just picked up. It hit the stone with a ghastly sort of clang at his bare feet.

This was twice I'd seen death up close. My brother Pete and now Alastair Iszler. Both impaled through the chest.

There was still a small part of me that didn't think this was even happening. It couldn't be happening. I tasted copper in the air. It struck me, distantly, the fact that Alastair had once been a vampire, and now he'd been staked through the heart ... as a human.

My mouth shaped the word "Noooooo!"

Cruz bolted to his feet beside me, his jaw hanging open in dread and horror. I thought he screamed too, but everything sounded muted, messed up in my head.

Corinth, what did you do?

A second later, Leo jumped out of a churning vortex, arriving nimbly beside not-Corinth. And then Larna catapulted into the chamber from the adjoining tunnel—I had no idea how either of them had gotten here. After seeing her husband's fate, though, her face went bone white.

She was staring at the wooden staff protruding out of the center of his chest, her mouth open in a silent scream.

And then Alastair crumpled, blood already pooling underneath him before we even had a chance to move.

ALASTAIR

Alastair was standing on nothing. White light surrounded him on all sides. He had this woozy, nauseated feeling in the pit of his stomach, sort of like the feeling he got when he traveled through lightning with angels. He glanced down at his bare chest, expecting to see the aftermath of carnage. When he didn't see any, only bare skin, that realization only served to make him feel worse. Alastair knew what that meant. The black marks on his chest that had looked like wings were gone. He was still in his black joggers, and his feet were bare. He felt no pain.

His best friend had stabbed him in the back, literally.

Alastair blinked back the sting of tears and dazzling white *everywhere.* Slowly he turned around in a circle, studying his surroundings, mouth still agape. There was nothing discernible but snow, like white noise on a TV. Not cold. Not cotton. Fluff, maybe. Cloudlike but not clouds. Strangely comforting.

As soon as he got back to where he had started, a boy, who appeared to be about eighteen or nineteen, was now standing right in his personal space.

Alastair let out a surprised oath and tried to step back, but he glided out into nothingness, his limbs feeling heavy and weightless at the same time. He attempted to regain his balance, arms spinning out beside him, but his body did not want to respond appropriately. It felt like the first sweet moments of falling into a drug-induced sleep, lazy limbs. Dreamlike. Surreal. He took a moment to study the angel in greater detail, letting his eyes refocus in all the flurry brightness around him.

Welcome back, Alastair Iszler.

The angel's words in his head were disorienting; they sounded disjointed and echoey as if he were shouting down from a well.

The kid had bronze-colored skin, curly dark brown hair, and wide, jade-green eyes. He wore a white leather breastplate strapped across his chest. There were matching leather pauldrons at both his shoulders, and white leather cuisses—thigh armor—were attached to each thigh. A sizable ivory sword was sheathed at his hip. Alastair could tell the armor wasn't just any ordinary armor. There was an unnatural pearly sheen to it that he couldn't quite put his finger on. Advanced tech not of his world, he finally concluded.

A feeling of déjà vu overcame him so suddenly he started to feel off-kilter, and he listed to the side like he was adrift on a dinghy in the middle of an ocean during a storm. Alastair glided slowly backward. He felt like a newborn trying to adjust to walking for the very first time.

The kid moved inhumanly fast, planting a finger against the middle of Alastair's forehead. *Sorry about this,* a voice said in his mind. *But I need to see what you've seen.*

Alastair's eyes slammed closed.

There was a tiny sliver of pressure at the base of his skull, and he felt the foreign presence of someone sifting through his thoughts and memories. An angel reading his mind. He'd felt this unpleasant sensation before. In his experience, angels rarely asked permission before they did it. But he did not get the sense that this angel wanted to hurt him.

On the contrary, Alastair knew he wasn't in trouble. He was dead. A pang of regret swelled in the center of his chest, and his lungs felt like they were full of helium. *Larna.*

A moment later, his eyes floated back open, and he was breathing like he'd just been in an all-out sprint.

The angel had the look of youthful innocence— untouched by the troubles of the world—but Alastair knew that probably wasn't the case. Not at all. Underneath all that boyish charm, he could sense danger, the threat he recognized in all angels. Ancient beings.

The kid didn't draw his sword or make any more sudden movements toward him. Actually, he did the opposite: he backed up, giving Alastair some more space.

"*I'm dead.*" Alastair spoke softly, half-closing his eyes in remorse and guilt and resentment, thinking about Larna. Guilt for not having been able to stop Angela hit him hard. Also, culpability for not having saved his best friend. It had been a rookie mistake, losing his focus like that. He had never felt Dark Corinth coming. He'd lost his edge and had paid the ultimate price. *Dammit.*

The angel shook his head. "Not dead yet—a hair's breadth away from it though."

Alastair reeled at hearing that, and his head snapped back up. *Not dead.* "There's still a chance," he said thickly. "So that means you must need something from me. What?" He eyed his bare feet. "Where am I, then?" Alastair's toes felt warm, like he'd just buried them in hot sand. But the ground wasn't solid; it wasn't anything. Only light and filament and snow. Odd.

"In between heaven and hell." The boy's voice had dropped, but his words seemed to carry immense weight, as if this meeting was not a regular occurrence. "A waiting room for the beyond. And you're right, I do need something from you."

An enormous weight lifted off Alastair's chest as he squinted past the light, wincing. "Are you one of the Fallen, Grigori, or Watchers? Or—" he drew in a quick breath "—something else entirely?" And then the thought hit him that maybe this being was a Reaper, coming to take him onward.

The kid lifted an amused eyebrow. "I am an archangel. My name is Nakir."

Nakir said it so straightforwardly that it left Alastair slow-blinking back at him in confusion. Straightforwardly was not how you dropped that sort of information. *Archangel.* Alastair knew from reading about archangels that they were supposed to be extremely powerful creatures. Michael, God's chief warrior, was an archangel. He shivered despite the fact that he wasn't cold. He wasn't anything but pleasantly warm. The blood in his veins felt thick. Angel warriors. Aside from the armor, Nakir did not look like a hardened soldier of heaven. He wondered if Nakir knew God.

"Whatever you're needing of me, get on with it." When the archangel didn't respond, Alastair continued. "Corinth, he … he needs me … I can't leave him like that, possessed by Angela. My wife, she's trapped down there in that damn demon realm. Zoey and Cruz, they need my help too—"

The angel let out a soft chuckle, shaking his head, amber curls bouncing.

Alastair couldn't tell if the kid was mocking him or not. He hated being laughed at. He was dying, and this archangel was insulting him.

"Is this the part where you tell me to go toward the light?" Alastair asked, irritated. "Because that's not gonna happen—"

Nakir put a hand on the pommel of his sword. "I only laugh because the last time we met, you said the polar opposite."

Alastair could feel his irregular pulse beating sluggishly behind his eyeballs. He still had a pulse, but it felt weird. A resonant sort of feeling, more like delayed. He licked his lips. "What do you mean, the last time we met? We've met before?"

"When you died the first time—after you gave your life to save Corinth Taylor. You wouldn't remember it. I know your history, what happened to you. How you used to be vampire. You are as impressive as Danel said you would be. It was a rare occurrence indeed when the

Nephilim managed to bring you back to Earth—*human*. You're sort of all the talk around here. It's never happened before, a Nephilim with the ability to bring someone back from the beyond. The big guy upstairs must really like Corinth Taylor."

Nakir shrugged as if this were a normal conversation taking place.

Alastair, on the other hand, felt discombobulated; he really wished he could sit down, but there wasn't anywhere to sit. He ran a hand through his hair, ruffling up his combed part, unsure what to think about all this. That was why Nakir looked so familiar to him, he realized. He'd seen him before.

"You knew Corinth's father?"

Danel was Corinth's father. Danel had died trying to save his son's life, and this archangel, Nakir, had known Danel. Alastair wasn't too surprised—there were only a handful of Grigori and Watchers left on earth. The battle in Utah had taken many casualties.

"Danel was an archangel too," Nakir said. "Why do you think his son is so powerful? That's how Corinth was able to beat you in the end. His gifts and training, combined with Angela's dark power, make him a force to be reckoned with. I saw it in your memories—how bravely you fought. But you are inexperienced in using angelic abilities. He is not. Ten years ago, you sacrificed your own life when you made the decision to turn Corinth into a vampire–Nephilim hybrid. You two share blood. Like I said, rare. It must have been a very hard choice ..." Nakir paused, cupping a hand under his chin as if in thought. "Except, it wasn't, was it? It was the clearest choice you'd ever made in your entire life. Dying for your brother. You already told me all this before. You said you were okay with dying. And you would do it all over again. You were right. Angela was able to kill you because you let her."

Alastair took in a shallow breath, still feeling winded and shaken and discombobulated. Angela, possessing Corinth, had just gotten the upper hand, hadn't she? He didn't feel like he'd let Angela win. Had he? Shared blood. He knew his connection with Corinth had been something more profound. Suddenly he found he needed to get everything off his chest. The burden was too great. Alastair hadn't known he would have to relive this moment. He didn't remember it, but he felt it. He—still—felt—it. The guilt that weighed him down even now. Giving up was easier. Maybe he had given up. He'd wanted respite.

"I …I …" Alastair swallowed heavily. "I had been alive for a very long time. Over a hundred years. I was okay with dying … back then. At the time, I thought *she* could live without me, and that *I* could live without *her*. I was so wrong. So very wrong. I'd gone out trying to save Corinth's life, and I was okay with that choice. *I was just so tired.*" Alastair put his head in his hands, feeling drained and empty. Why was he telling this stranger all these intimate details? A subject he hadn't even broached himself. Because Nakir already knew. Because he'd just read his mind. It didn't matter if Alastair kept it a secret any longer. "But things are different now. I have to go back. I have a wife who's in trouble. A wife who needs me." His voice cracked. "I mean, I need *her* more than she needs me," he corrected. "I have a brother who is suffering. I'm going to save Corinth's life. They're my family, and I need them. I'm sorry, I should have led with that first. My thinking is just … it's so scattered in this place."

"Only a true warrior, who was almost cleaved in half by an archangel, would be willing to go back and do it all over again." Nakir let out an incredulous huff. "Very courageous. And painful," he said as an afterthought. "Currently you are bleeding out on the floor of a ritualistic demonic chamber that needed a blood sacrifice to open up a gateway from hell. It needed lots of blood. Blood that you just gave it in spades. Do you see where I'm going with this?"

Alastair's pulse thudded dully in his ears, and his head throbbed in tune with it.

"As we speak," Nakir went on, "an infernal demon is leaving hell's confines to enter your world and inflict as much harm on it as it possibly can."

"*Crap*," he breathed.

Nakir lifted his hand from the pommel of his sword, and Alastair realized it looked like the head of a lion. "Crap indeed. Ephrem is an infernal demon. Angela is an infernal demon, and she has the powers of an archangel, if that gives you a reference point on how very bad this situation is. Two of them in one place would be devastatingly catastrophic."

"Didn't I kill Ephrem?" Alastair cut in quickly.

Nakir pulled a face at him that clearly said, "Please." "You banished him back to hell. He'll try and get out again. I don't need to tell you what will happen if he does manage an escape, right?"

"What do you need me to do?" Alastair asked,

understanding the consequences and suddenly needing to take action for his part in everything. No chance in hell that was happening.

"I need a ride."

Alastair didn't think the angel meant using his cellphone to call an Uber …He gave Nakir a quizzical gaze, his eyebrows going up in question.

"Leaving heaven is a tricky business. In order to get to earth, I have to piggyback on a human soul," Nakir explained. "Since you are on the brink of death, I now have a rare opportunity to go back with you. But I must have your explicit permission in order to do so. Freewill and all … It means you have to volunteer. Angels don't take, they ask."

Alastair thought differently, as he implicitly recalled the angel reading his mind without him asking. But Nakir was his only hope of getting back. Alastair's thoughts immediately went to his body being used as a vessel—like how Angela was taking over Corinth's mind, body, and spirit. Would he be used like a puppet? A meat suit? For life? An eternity? What other choice did he have?

Ultimately, it didn't matter.

They needed his help, and this angel was the only one willing to give it.

"How long will I be … uh, used? Will it be like Angela possessing Corinth? Will you at least allow me to say goodbye to Larna?"

A myriad of emotions flitted across the angel's features: relief, sorrow, gratitude, and something else Alastair likened to respect, maybe. "Angela did not get Corinth's permission to use him—she forcibly took him over," Nakir said evenly. "Which means what you'll experience won't be anything like what Corinth is experiencing. He is suffering. You will not."

At hearing that, Alastair's heart constricted.

Nakir continued. "I will be in control of your faculties, but not for long. I promise to vacate your vessel as soon as I can. I must warn you, though, it may come at a terrible price. The demon realm Ephrem has created is bad. Angels, even archangels such as myself, can't portal in and out of that place … Angela is an archangel; she created it to keep us in … as a prison of sorts. She used up a lot of dark souls to make it. There is only one way in and one way out."

"The device Stanton used to get Corinth inside?"

Nakir nodded. "Yes."

"How do you know about that?" he asked.

Nakir pointed to his forehead. "I saw it."

"Shit." At seeing the look on Nakir's face, Alastair said, "Sorry. It's just … you're throwing a lot at me here. What does that mean? How do we stop Angela?" He paused. "Wait." Alastair's gaze met Nakir's olive-colored eyes. "Corinth told me to stab him with his blade. He said the dagger would separate Angela from him, and do no harm to him in the process. Will that still work?"

"That's what Corinth Taylor told you?" Nakir's gaze darted to Alastair's before zipping away again.

"That's what he told me … yes," Alastair said slowly, "What is it?"

Nakir's hands crackled with a surge of ghostly energy. "He's not entirely wrong. I will take Angela down, and take care of the Nephilim. After that, as soon as I get us clear of the demon realm, I promise to voluntarily divest myself of your body. It'll take me some time to stitch myself back together again afterward. When I leave heaven, it'll be permanent. I'll lose my ability to fly. I am leaving everything I know behind. This is not the most ideal situation for either of us. It's risky. We could lose. I may lose. And there's something else you should know."

Alastair lifted his shoulders in a tiny shrug, feeling overwhelmed. "Go on, then."

"When Corinth removed the shard from your body he transferred some of his powers to you, but you are still human. Humans should not possess angelic abilities. Your vessel is not without its limits—case in point, why you're stuck through right now, impaled. You are vulnerable, and you cannot contain the sort of power an archangel possesses. It will overload your system. Containing archangel energy, like mine, even for a short amount of time, might leave you with debilitating injuries as soon as I exit your body."

"Can't angels heal a human's wounds? Couldn't Leo, or another angel, for instance, heal me as soon as you … uh, you know, vacate the premises?"

"An angel can heal a human's wounds, yes, but not wounds of this nature. Even angels have their limits. I'm sorry, Alastair, but there is a chance you might never fully recover."

"What do you mean, never fully recover?" Alastair breathed. "Like as in I might permanently lose my hair? Or are we talking about worse afflictions … like critical wounds? Missing limbs? Because I can live with one more scar—"

"Critical wounds. Missing limbs. Shattered mind. Catatonic state."

Great, he thought. *Of course.* Alastair pushed his shoulders back, resolute. "What about Corinth? Could he do it, using the Spear of Destiny? Could he heal me?"

"You are assuming Corinth will be rid of Angela in time to heal you … That may not happen, Alastair."

"What if I say no?" Alastair asked softly, turning away. "What happens then?"

"Then you go into the light. Onward. You have mere moments left to decide though—you can choose to die, and no one would fault you for it. Most would choose to move on. You won't be thought of as anything but heroic." The archangel's eyes flashed. They were endless and hypnotic, like watching seaweed bobbing on an ocean wave.

Alastair ran a hand down his face and sighed, thinking and trying to process everything that had been thrown at him. It always came down to the last second. One final decision. "Well, seeing as how I already have a critical wound … what's one more?" He really didn't have a choice. He had to try to save Corinth. To save Larna. It was worth the risk. "Like you said, it's risky for both of us. Maybe I'll be back here sooner rather than later."

"I'm going to need you to say it, Alastair," Nakir said in a measured tone. "Give me your consent out loud."

"You have my permission," Alastair answered a beat later, before he could change his mind.

Nakir was already standing in front of Alastair in the space of a single heartbeat, placing a finger at the center of his temple. Regret was heavy in his voice when he spoke next. "Corinth lied to you. And I know why he did it … That's why I will grant you the ability to remember this conversation, because you are owed the truth. Corinth's death will be on me. Not you, Alastair Iszler."

Alastair had already closed his eyes. Once he heard that, though, he tried to wrench them open again, to question Nakir, but he found it too difficult a task. His heartbeat slammed achingly slow through his veins—thundering—impossibly distorted and warbling. His head was spinning.

No. What did I just agree to?

"I am assuming Corinth lied to you because he knew you would not use the blade against him if you knew it would kill him. Corinth won't survive his separation from Angela. It *will* kill him. But know this—it will not be your fault. *I* will be the one to end his life. For what it's worth, I think it a brave and glorious way to go out. You are doing a merciful thing for your friend, by letting me do it. For your brother. Feel proud of your selfless action, not wretched."

Wait, what? What do you mean by that? He won't survive? Alastair didn't utter a word out loud, only in his mind, because the world around him was already dwindling into nothingness, the bright white leaving only inky darkness in its wake, like a candle flame being extinguished for good.

Stop! I don't consent! I take it back!

He tried to shout, but it was already too late.

37

ZOEY

y voice was gone. It had left me eons ago. The result of screaming until I could no longer scream. Until my throat was raw and swollen. Warm arms were wrapped around me, squeezing tight. I could hardly breathe. I smelled cloves and spice and numbly realized that it was probably Cruz holding me. Not Trevor.

Trevor is dead, I tried to remind myself.

Cruz was trying to shield me from the sight of Alastair lying in a pool of his own blood. Gone. Departed. Lifeless.

I couldn't look away.

There was so much red everywhere. *Everywhere.*

Is this what shock feels like? Cold numbness spreading through my limbs and working outward.

How could the human body hold that much blood?

I could still feel Trevor's fingers on my neck—feel the angry red marks he'd left on my skin.

"Let me go, Cruz," I whispered breathlessly, feeling trapped, and he must have heard the pain in my voice, because he did. His arms fell away from me, and a draft of cold air hit the exposed skin at my shoulder, where I'd ripped my hoodie sleeve trying to help Alastair. "We have to help him …"

I glanced back at Cruz as he licked his bloodless lips. "I … I think he's gone, Zoey."

The thought at the back of my mind, haunting me, even as Corinth stood over Alastair's body was *My brother, the person who I trusted the most in this world, murdered Alastair ….murdered … Alastair.* The blade was on the ground, bronze pommel glinting in the soft light from the wall sconces—red pooled around the blade, making it stand out harshly. For a long stretched-out moment, no one moved.

Leo's chest was heaving in his apparent shock. Larna's features had transformed the moment she'd seen not-Corinth stab her husband in the back. Her face was slack and salt white, and the spark in her eyes had winked out completely. In an instant though, her gaze filled with frost and ice and something merciless as her eyes ticked slowly over to not-Corinth and then halted. That look could kill.

Not-Corinth had lowered his head—his shoulders were bobbing up and down as if he were laughing—his gaze locked on his bloodied fingers.

In the next instant, he dropped to his knees beside Alastair, his hands bathed in a golden-blue haze of light.

Still gripped by horror and utter desolation, I watched as my possessed brother placed blood-stained hands on either side of the stake impaling Alastair's chest and, in one swift motion, yanked the weapon free.

Distantly I realized he was finishing the job he'd started: killing Alastair.

But the moment the wooden lance was extracted, not-Corinth pushed down on Alastair's chest with both hands as if to stanch the bleeding. A part of my brain thought this an odd sort of action—if he wanted to kill Alastair, why not just let him bleed out?

Not-Corinth's hands were lit up, and the same energy shone on Alastair's skin. Strangely enough, the light dissipated down into his motionless body, illuminating his inner vascular network. *Whoa.*

Larna let out a battle-cry, thundering across the chamber, both blades ejected at her wrists, aimed at the shell of my brother, or Angela, or whatever was possessing him—I just couldn't keep up anymore.

I knew Larna was going to kill not-Corinth, or at least give it her best shot—the look of pure carnal rage told me so.

She couldn't see his face—he had his back to her— but I could. Not-Corinth's cheeks were wet. *Corinth's* cheeks were wet. An alarm bell went off at the back of my mind. Corinth wouldn't be upset by Alastair's death … *if* he were still infected or possessed, or whatever, by that demon … not unless … *Oh no …*

"*Larna, no!*" Leo shouted at the same time as he threw a hand out.

He is back.

A stab of icy dread tore through me right as a barrier of light flared to life around Corinth so abruptly that Larna bounced off it, sending sparks shooting in all different directions like golden fireworks. She slid backward across the chamber floor and hit the curved brick wall, crumpling into a ball, stone-still.

Leo all but collapsed to the ground, looking drained and gray tinged.

Cruz put a hand up in front of his face, blinking past the light show. "What the—?" he breathed.

For a split second, I thought Larna might be dead, until I heard her moan and start to stir slowly back to life, but she didn't get back up.

Leo stumbled toward Corinth at the same time as a brilliant ray of light illuminated Alastair's entire body, causing him to falter back a step, a hand going to his face.

And then something Corinth said came slamming back to me: *Because Al still had my blood in his system, my biological father, an angel, who you know as Dave Lancaster— he was a Watcher—helped me bring him back ...*

Alastair, skin still radiant, suddenly came alive—

In the next instant, he sat up, snatched Corinth's bloodied dagger off the ground next to his body, and seized a fistful of Corinth's mesh armor at his collarbone, hauling him closer. The Spear of Destiny's tip rested just beneath his chin.

Corinth dropped his arms down by his sides, the energy suddenly draining out of him—and to me, he looked immensely relieved and haggard, his face slack.

Alastair seemed amazingly unhurt—I mean, besides the fact that he was covered in blood and his blond hair was matted to his forehead. His eyes were lit up like emeralds, and he had a severe, resolute look plastered across his drawn features.

Corinth's eyes, on the other hand, were warm and brown and doe-like.

The look on my brother's face was one of defeat and anguish and shame. The silvery whirlpool tattoos along his neck and arms were gone, although I did notice his throat had black squiggle lines on it, sort of like he had a blood infection.

Corinth wasn't fighting back. He wasn't pleading for his life or trying to convince Alastair that he was himself once again. Realization hit me like a slap to the face.

He wanted this.

Corinth wanted Alastair to end his life.

There was something about Alastair that gave me the willies—besides the fact that he had basically just come back from the brink of death.

And the last thing I heard before Alastair sliced Corinth's neck wide open was Leo shouting something incoherent, trying to stop him.

38

NAKIR – ALASTAIR

Nakir had taken over Alastair's vessel. His fingers were curled around the hilt of the holy relic, and he had Corinth exactly where he wanted him. One flick of his wrist, and he would end the Nephilim's life.

Nakir had to do it.

He could not risk Angela being loosed upon the world as a demon—never mind the fact that Corinth's vessel wasn't hostile right in this moment. Angela was a deceiver. A manipulator. The very best at mind control. She was not compassionate or forgiving. She was merciless. She had been a high-ranking angel and was now a demon. She would kill them all without a second thought.

Al … you're not dead. Thank God.

The tiny voice buzzed to life in Nakir's head. It was full of wonder, hope, humiliation, sorrow, and disgust. Corinth Taylor. *Not Corinth Taylor*, he reminded himself.

Angela using his voice and his body for her own wicked purposes.

A trickle of darkness swept through him as their mental connection fully opened up. It felt like something sinister swirling through his bloodstream. This was how he knew it was not Corinth speaking to him—not really.

Nakir stayed his hand, but only barely. An uneasiness churned in his gut, a sensation he didn't quite understand. Maybe it was residual feelings from Alastair or Corinth, or both combined. Whatever the case, he was having trouble ending someone's life when they were defenseless and on their knees.

It's me, buddy. The minute she made me drive that stake into your chest was her undoing. She's gone for good. Please, lower the dagger. I lied to you. I lied, Al. Nakir felt a tremor of regret—not his own—run through him as the voice continued. *I thought it would be the only way to convince you to end Angela. But if you stab me with that blade, I will die—*

Speaking of blades, Nakir nudged it closer, and the sharp point bit into the deceiver's skin.

The Nephilim flinched as sparks arced in Nakir's hand—well, technically Alastair's hand—crawling across his skin. It was only a shallow cut, but Nakir needed her-him to stop speaking. Angela was exceptional at mind control and manipulation, and her performance was *extremely* convincing.

The Nephilim closed his eyes, wincing, as a ribbon of blood threaded down his throat. A soul-crushing sensation of grief poured over Nakir like a tidal wave, incapacitating him. Then came the malicious darkness in the far inky corners of his mind. Still there. Evil.

Al, please. I … I know I deserve this. I … I … Angela made me stab you … but let me prove it's really me—

I am not Alastair Iszler, Nakir snarled, communicating through their telepathic link. *Corinth Taylor does not deserve this.* Nakir was angry at himself for being baited so easily, but he continued anyway. *My name is Nakir, and I am here to end your reign of terror. You have too much darkness inside you. I can sense through our link the destruction and power you seek. Do not lie to me, deceiver.*

At hearing this, Corinth's already-wide eyes lifted to meet Nakir's.

Where's Al? Is he okay?

Nakir felt Alastair at the back of his mind, scratching to get out, fighting him with every fiber of his being. He was stronger than Nakir had given the mortal credit for.

He tried to sink the blade deeper, but Nakir's hand froze—not of his own accord. It felt like a powerful magnet had been placed behind him, and every single one of his muscles—and bones, even—was made out of iron. The resistance in his limbs was yanking him backward. His feet slid across the slick and stained concrete as he slipped in a pool of Alastair's blood.

A tremor swept through the small space, the walls starting to tremble as the chamber gave an unsettling shudder. He had mere moments to act before hell's gateway opened up and the infernal demon was released upon this world. If he didn't kill the Nephilim now, it would be too late.

Stop fighting me, Alastair Iszler, he ordered. *Even if it is only Corinth Taylor now, he is still susceptible to giving himself over to wickedness and cruelty. I can sense it. He will turn out like Angela. He wields too much power. I must end him.*

Slowly the blade inched away from the hollow point at the Nephilim's neck.

Nakir was losing control.

Don't kill him, Nakir. That's Corinth. He is not lying about Angela. He's always had that darkness inside him— but he controls *it,* came Alastair's soft cry of alarm in his head. The mortal was haughty and defiant up until the very end.

Curse it all. Actually, Nakir had never met anyone like the human before. If Nakir didn't have a job to do, he might have admired his iron will.

Corinth's voice broke through the haze in his mind again. *Nakir's right, Al. Let him end me. It's time. I can't let this happen again. I ... I stabbed you ... It was my hand that did it. Mine.* His voice shook as he continued. *I can't get the image out of my head ... your blood spilling everywhere ...*

Nakir took in a deep breath, forcing his will to take over Alastair's mind and body again, his wings unfurling out of his back. They spread out wide and glorious, but no longer golden. They were singed and scorched— blackened by his fall to earth. They hurt. It felt like he was breathing in fire. Heat blazed up all around him like an inferno, coalescing into a cyclone above his head.

Nakir had to be careful—there were innocents still in the chamber, and he didn't want casualties if he could help it. Ideally, there would be only one death today— Corinth's.

He threw up a protective barrier around them both,

and the shouts and cries of the people around him died down considerably. Just Nakir and Corinth Taylor.

Be still, he commanded Alastair Iszler, and Nakir's voice was stronger and louder this time. He was almighty. A warrior of God. This was his mission to complete. As a soldier, you had to do some unspeakable things. *Let me finish this, Alastair*, he pleaded. *Please.* The frantic and livid residual feeling he got from Alastair all but faded into the background.

Once Nakir had regained control of his—technically, Alastair's—faculties again, he strode forward, the almighty blade dripping white-hot flames at his feet. He was standing in front of Corinth Taylor once again. The kid hadn't moved or tried to run or fight. Good. He'd accepted his fate. Nakir gripped the Nephilim's shirtfront again, placing the sharp edge under his chin again, ready to end his life.

"Don't!"

The voice was shrill and high-pitched and full of so much anguish that it caused Nakir to pause. He glanced up, focusing through the shimmering barricade he'd erected around them both to see a young girl across the way from him. His heart jolted at seeing the stricken look on her face. Her lips were parted in surprise, and her braid snapped out behind her like a whip from all the supernatural energy flowing around the cavern. The tormented look painted across her soft features threatened to drag him down into oblivion. She looked so young and fragile and sad. There was something about those rich amber eyes that pulled him in and pinned him in place— something decidedly familiar and haunting.

Nakir squinted back down at Corinth Taylor, unsettled, studying the Nephilim more closely. Then he looked back up at the girl again.

She held a hand out toward him, beseeching. This was the Nephilim's sister. *No.* An excruciating tightness swirled in his chest. A pang of regret hit him so hard he almost dropped the blade. He really did not want to do this in front of Corinth's sibling.

Nakir went tense all over, every single muscle in his body singing.

The walls fractured and brick broke apart, raining down around them all. It was happening. The gateway was opening. The infernal demon was coming.

It was now or never.

Angela could take back possession of Corinth Taylor at any second. He had to do this for the greater cause—

Alastair, what are you doing? An unfamiliar voice burst into his head, making him jerk his hand holding the holy dagger.

The razor sharp edge grazed Corinth's neck and the Nephilim cringed, but didn't pull away or open his eyes. He was giving himself over willingly to Nakir. He knew what had to be done. He probably would have liked the half angel if he'd gotten to know him. Valiant. Too bad Nakir had to end his life. *This is a worthy ending for you, Corinth Taylor.*

You're not Alastair … Who are you, then, angel? Because you're about to make the biggest mistake of your life.

It wasn't Alastair's voice in his head this time. This voice sounded like one of dissent, intolerable and angry. How many people were trying to stop him from doing his job? He felt the angel's fury through their connection, and it was beyond hostile.

Do not interfere! Nakir roared back at the foreign voice in his head.

This is Leo, Danel's son. Don't kill him. He's my brother. Corinth is not *a threat now. Look at him! He's on his knees, defenseless, for pity's sake!*

Nakir didn't look at the Nephilim. Instead, his gaze darted to the young angel with his glowing hand held out, blocking his path, just off to his left, within five steps of him. *Leo.* The angel had raven-colored hair, the palest blue irises and black pupils separated by a thin circle of amethyst. He looked just like his parents, Nakir mused. A wicked-looking gold short sword materialized in his hand in a swirl of mist and light. His breastplate was bronze and heavy looking—prehistoric, really.

So this was Angela and Danel's son. Leo.

An offspring of good *and* evil. Born of angels. Once upon a time, it had been unheard of for an angel to be conceived. Leo may have been the son of two archangels, but he was not as strong as Nakir, who had never been born—he'd been created. Nakir was ageless. Leo was not. He was only a baby.

Leo's hands ignited with a dark surge of blue electrical current, running a path up and down his arms. Nakir wondered if the antiquated armor Leo wore could actually thwart lightning. Probably not. There was only one way to find out—

Leo swung his weapon up in a great overhead arc, sensing the danger. "*Get away from my brother,*" he snarled out loud. "*Or I will end you, angel.*"

Nakir glanced back down at the surrendered Nephilim, undeterred by Leo's threats. Corinth Taylor's eyes were still closed, and his head was bowed. A trail of blood ran down his neck from where the tip of the dagger still rested under his chin.

"You are born of this world, Leo," Nakir said, and his voice sounded strange coming out of Alastair's mouth. "Therefore, your powers are not greater than mine. You are susceptible to them. We are on the same side. But do what you must, because I have to finish this …" With that, he drew his arm back, one palm pressed against the pommel, the other hand wrapped around the hilt, and he thrust the weapon toward Corinth's heart, refusing to acknowledge the final cry from the Nephilim's sister. Or the fact that Alastair's own heart seemed like it had already been cleaved in two.

39

ZOEY

A bloodcurdling scream left my lips, and I hadn't even been sure I had enough voice left to do that. The once-cold dungeon now felt like an oven. My forehead was damp and my hoodie sopping; it clung to me in all the wrong places, heavy, constricting.

Cruz had gripped the medallion at his throat as soon as he'd seen the angel's wings take shape and spread out at least eight feet in length, like a mythical creature. An angel. "Alastair has … *wings?*" he breathed.

I could only gulp in response.

Mighty and biblical and ancient—all words I might have used to describe them had I been concentrating on Alastair's wings. Instead, I was staring at the dagger clutched in his bloodstained hand, resting at Corinth's neck. A trail of red oozed down his throat, glaring against waxy skin.

He was on his knees, his eyes closed, uncharacteristically

quiet for once in his life.

And Alastair was going to kill him. An eye for an eye. I wondered if Corinth had brought him back from the dead knowing Alastair was just going to end his life a moment later …

Leo staggered forward, toward Alastair, but his leg almost buckled out from under him, and I realized in dismay that Leo must have been injured during the battle.

He let out a war cry right as Alastair let loose a spinning orb of angelic energy straight at him. It struck Leo in his breastplate, burning a giant hole right through it, and blasting him off his feet. A second later, Leo's sword vanished in a wink of light, and he crumpled onto his side, unmoving, eyes closed.

"Leo!" I shouted at the same time as my gaze landed on Corinth.

His eyes finally fluttered open, and they looked— blessedly *normal*—big and honey-colored. I heard Corinth snarl something like "If you're going to do it … then get it over with, but leave my brother out of this."

A heavy cloud settled over me, and I almost folded in on myself. *Corinth.* I couldn't lose two brothers in the same day. Why had he given up on me? On himself? My feet started to move of their own accord, before even I knew what I was going to do. I had this really insane idea of throwing myself between my brother and Alastair— before he could end his life. I had seen Alastair's hesitation.

The ground shuddered and trembled, and the massive stone circle beneath my feet began to shift and pull apart, and I stumbled sideways, unable to keep my footing as a weird grating noise started up, earsplitting and howling.

Please tell me something on the other side isn't howling

Concrete grated against metal. The anchor in the ground clanked loudly and fell into the earth, tumbling away—down into inky darkness. Above us, the chains started to swing violently back and forth, rattling like a ghoul had hold of them. Chunks of rock came crashing down over my head, and I tried to dodge out of the way, but rubble and debris pelted down from every direction. The place was quaking apart, little by little.

Cruz snatched hold of my arm and pulled me out of the way at the last second, saving me from getting crushed by falling stones. My heart was thumping away in my chest when I realized we were lying side by side, both of us breathless, almost knocked senseless.

From my prone position on the ground, I could see Alastair reach a sizzling hand out toward us, the one not holding the blade.

A moment later, an impressive-looking barrier of light flared to life directly over us, preventing another massive boulder from smashing Cruz and me flat like pancakes.

Cruz let out a startled yelp as the giant rock broke apart into a spray of dust and powder, his hands covering his face. The shield glittered like diamonds, shutting out some of the crushing heat, protecting us in the process. Another guttural rumble shook the earth beneath us.

"How is he *doing* that?" Cruz asked in amazement, glancing at the shining wall right over our heads, mouth ajar. "Did he die and come back as an angel?"

I didn't answer him—the truth was, I had no idea. All I knew was that Alastair was possessed. He had been able to do a lot of supernatural things before he'd been stabbed.

I had to save my brother—even if it was from himself—so I lurched stubbornly back to my feet, stumbling drunkenly toward them as another tremor shook the ground.

Alastair's hand stilled on the blade as soon as he saw me coming.

One wrong move or flick of the wrist and Corinth was dead.

"*Don't!*" I cried again, my voice cracking.

Alastair's head snapped around, and suddenly those eyes were hovering over me, dissecting, searching. The look Alastair was giving me was so intense, the hairs on the nape of my neck stood up stiff. His normally vivid blue eyes had been replaced by golden beams of light. It felt like I was staring directly into the sun. Soul piercing. My head hurt. Little pockets of light exploded across my retinas in a kaleidoscope of colors. A shudder rolled through me, and I froze midstride, almost falling right on my rump, dizzy with incomprehension and wonder.

That gaze. Whoa.

No, *not* Alastair. Someone else. Someone using Alastair's body. For a moment, I could see both of them, Alastair and the wispy shape of a boy's face, maybe my age, maybe older, with the most beautiful bronze skin I'd ever seen in my entire life, flesh kissed by the sun—no, *admired* by the sun. His hair was wavy, the color of golden wheat, and it was styled shorter on the sides than on the top.

I'd seen good-looking people before—hell, Alastair was about as hot as they came—but this creature … I wasn't going to lie—it almost hurt to look at him. I thought I even stopped breathing for a second.

Nakir. The name was on my lips, and I had no earthly idea how it'd gotten there, so I took a chance. "*Please, Nakir! Don't hurt him!*" I choked out.

The boy's eyebrows snaked up into Alastair's hairline, a look of surprise washing over his handsome features.

And then the world around me tilted and spun, and the ground started to open up as a deep yawning crack appeared next to my foot; it looked like it was smiling diabolically up at me as I was gazing down at it.

Vaguely I was aware of Cruz struggling to sit up as the stone circle split apart between us. The floor shifted and tilted and cracked wider. Before Cruz could stand up, he was rolling in the opposite direction, thankfully away from the gaping hole in the ground, screaming.

Down far below, I could see crimson flames and sweltering darkness and pitch-black emptiness. An overwhelming sense of dark curiosity and something else surged up inside me. *What is down there?*

My teeth started to clack together.

So cold.

Suddenly I was spellbound by what could be down there. I had to know. I mean, the rational part of my brain knew the answer to that question: Bad things. Lots and lots of bad things. But somehow I'd gotten separated from everyone else, and the crack was now big enough to fit a human body through it—

Cruz was shouting something.

A gust of preternatural wind funneled up out of the pit and around me: thunderous, monstrous, demonic.

Above me, the chain mysteriously froze in place, halting its wild swinging. The ground growled like a volcano about to erupt, and the shower of rocks pelting down from above now looked like tiny glittering jewels caught in a net.

Cruz was way on the opposite side of the crevasse. I could just make out his face through a thick layer of black smog billowing up out of it in a tall pillar. He looked horrified, his face incredibly pale as he motioned for me to jump the gap.

I could make it. Maybe with a running start … It looked to be at least ten feet across. Corinth needed me. I couldn't see him now.

I ran to the far wall, putting my back up against it. I could feel it trembling as bits of brick and rock stung my face. I took off, sprinting, my arms and legs pumping, right as another colossal quake shook the entire foundation to its core—

My foot connected with something solid, and I tripped at a breakneck pace, falling toward the yawning pit.

My heart stopped, and a single helpless cry escaped my lips as I careened out into the open space—and gravity took hold, plunging me down into the abysmal hole.

Fingers clamped around my wrist, viselike, and my face and chest slammed into the side of the chasm, practically shoving my rib cage up into my throat. My shoulder jarred painfully in its socket, and fire lit up my elbow. I let out a shrill, terrified shriek, my legs dangling out into open space with nothing down below me but darkness and howling winds and—probably the Devil …

"Hold on!" Came a gruff cry from above. "I got you!"

There was a flash of blue and gold, and then a strained face came into full view, looking down at me. I let out a surprised gasp. Alastair. Not Alastair. Nakir. Both of them. His irises flickered like a dancing flame inside a lantern—twin halos, two different-colored eyes: one startling blue and the other golden. I could see them, Alastair and Nakir, trying to work in concert to save me.

The very angel who'd only a minute ago held a dagger to my brother's jugular. Those same hands had probably killed my brother. My throat constricted. His wings had disappeared and I'd really hoped he'd be able to fly us both out of here.

Nakir-Alastair grabbed my wrist with his other hand, half his body now hanging over the ledge, from his chest up. White-hot currents of electrical energy crackled across his skin and arced onto mine, and an electric jolt went through me at the contact. "I'm trying to portal us," he gasped in frustration, clearly not speaking to me. "Would you *stop* fighting me, Alastair?"

A guttural hissing came from down below. A loud,

scary hiss. The noise made my skin crawl, and I couldn't help it—there was something down there that made me glance down.

Whatever it was, it sure wanted to get at me.

There were odd, frenzied black shapes slithering and stirring against a crimson backdrop in the distance. And then, out of the black smoke, something hooked onto my ankle, biting into my skin, cold and hard.

A scream tore out of my mouth as I was yanked further into the pit. Whatever had hold of me was preternaturally strong, and it hurt—bad.

And that awful hissing sound was followed by sharp, angry snarls, which gave me the visual of snapping mandibles and supersharp teeth. This was hell. I was looking into the bowels of hell … I squeezed my eyes shut, breathing in terrified, ragged pants. An overpowering scent of sulfur and dreadful burning, like flesh, hit me.

The fingers around my wrist dug painfully into my skin, but I didn't want Nakir or Alastair to let go. I was terrified he—they—would drop me. I didn't want to look down either. If I did, I'd see what was clinging to me.

But we were both slipping now, and I was taking him with me. I opened my eyes.

"I can't—" Nakir-Alastair licked his lips "—portal you topside with that thing still … *attached* to you." He grunted in pain. "Don't look at it," he told me, his mismatched eyes going wide. I knew he was staring at the thing that had hold of me. "Let her go, *demon*!" he shouted. "*Or I'll cleave you in half.*"

But I knew he probably couldn't cleave the thing in half if he was using both his hands to keep me from falling.

The thing at my ankle snarled something in response and decidedly did *not* let me go. Instead, it jerked on my leg harder, determined to pull us all down with it.

"Aah!" I screeched as we dropped a few more feet, Nakir coming right along with me, his waist now hanging precariously over the ledge. My heart was now in my throat.

He let out a harsh exclamation in another language, struggling to hold me up, his hands clammy against my skin. "If you fall, I fall," he said in a firm but tense voice. "I won't let you go. I promise."

"Good," I managed to half pant, half wheeze. The pain in my arm and ankle was unbearable now. "Because I really, *really* ... don't ... want to have ... to kill this thing all by m-m-myself ..." I was freaking out now, thinking about him dropping right along with me. Of course, I wasn't going to tell him to let go.

Nakir-Alastair's eyes fixated on the monster, and then they abruptly darted back up to meet my troubled gaze once more. The hard creases around his mouth smoothed out, and his face turned into an inscrutable mask. *No.* His hand slipped on my wrist until he was clutching only the tips of my fingers.

And I knew, in that instant, that we were going to fall.

A cold trickle of terror washed over me as I glanced down on a pure gut reaction.

Glowing yellow eyes met mine.

It had the head of a bull, the body of a man, and the claws of a bear. All I could concentrate on, though, were those wide, flaring nostrils and the protruding tusks at the corners of its mouth. The beast hung one-handed—well, mainly all claws—by my ankle.

Distantly I wondered why it hadn't ripped me to shreds yet. I assumed it didn't want to kill me; it wanted to use me to free itself from hell. Oh, and it also had horns. Freaking sharp-looking horns. And by the looks of how big this demon was, I was surprised the beast hadn't dragged us both into the depths of hell by now—

Famous—Last—Words.

The beast raised its free arm and, with considerable strength, hooked onto the back of my hoodie and yanked on it, hard.

"Gaaawck!" I squawked as it choked me. I could feel it at my back, its body rock-solid.

Nakir made good on his promise. He fell with me.

I squeezed my eyes shut, but before we could plunge to our deaths, we lurched to a shuddering halt. The thick material at my throat ripped, strangling me in the process as the monster let out another ear-splitting howl of rage, still hanging on to me like a tick.

I kicked out and struck it across its jaw, and the thing gave a throaty howl that made my scalp prickle, and I looked up. Nakir-Alastair still had a hold of me. But it was who had a hold of *him* that had my mouth hanging open in complete and utter shock.

I'd recognize that headful of dark, messy hair anywhere. Gold mesh armor glinted bright, and then warm, syrupy eyes caught mine. They sparked with light and life, and my chest swirled with hope and relief.

"*Cor!*" His name was a sob that bubbled out of me. *He is not dead.*

"Hold on, Zo!" Corinth's arms were wound tightly around Alastair's middle. He had one leg propped against a deep groove in the cracked earth, his knee practically buckling under the pressure, as it was the only thing keeping us all upright for the time being—until my hoodie ripped and the monster lost its grip.

It swung around, using my leg like a rope, and I screamed in a mixture of agony, fear, and panic, sure that this was how I would lose a limb or worse. There came a searing heat as the thing's claws burrowed into my flesh, but adrenaline was pumping me full of all kinds of pain-blocking good stuff, and I only felt the warmth of blood oozing down my leg.

A blaze of supernatural energy exploded across my brother's skin, and a second later, his dagger was hovering in the air near his head—*vertical*. Fire blazed along the edge of the relic, matching the same kind of strange light crackling across his own skin. Magical.

Once again the blade was answering his call.

A flash of bronze and steel zipped past me.

The dagger struck the demon's left side, and it let out a gurgled cry of surprise, relinquishing its hold on my leg, and then, in absurd slowness—like cartoon slowness—it tumbled back down the way it had come.

I watched it fall, horrified and strangely enthralled as the dagger disappeared from its side in a wink of light.

My gaze flitted to Corinth above me. The contours of his cheeks were shadowed by the flickering smoke and fire. He screwed his face up in concentration, let out a huge battle cry, and then heaved us both up using nothing but brute strength. Superstrength.

All the while, Nakir-Alastair's grip on my fingers never loosened—and once he was up and over, they grasped my arms and hauled me the rest of the way back up to the surface.

I fell flat onto my back, a hand clasped to my chest, eyes closed, listening to the *thud-thud-thud* of my galloping heartbeat, willing myself to stay conscious.

It was a valiant effort, but it didn't work.

The world went blurry, like I'd just opened my eyes underwater. I was light-headed, and I couldn't quite catch my breath. People spoke around me, but their voices sounded faraway and incoherent. My leg was burning something awful. It felt like the claws were still hooked into my skin. I was afraid of seeing the damage, so I didn't look. Would I even have a leg left?

A hand reached into my hoodie pocket, and someone's voice broke through the haze of my stupor. "This is it—she had it …"

Everything melted away after that. I caught snippets of people and faces as they swam past me. Someone's hand was at my waist, their warm arm supporting the backs of my thighs. I smelled mint and copper, like blood and sweat.

Corinth, I thought distantly. *Don't leave me. Peter. Pete's dead.* I tried to tell him this—he could fix it. But I wasn't sure if it came out at all. My body felt like it was splintering apart, and then sinking. There seemed to be an urgency to his movements now. The sharp, shooting pain in my leg was relentless—killing me.

My head bounced against a chest, and there was a blinding flash of light, and an overwhelming sense of warmth flooded through my veins. Like puffy, perfectly fried sopapillas dusted with powdered sugar and drizzled with warm honey. And I didn't really remember anything after that.

40

CRUZ

Gabriel Stanton had come out of nowhere to help Cruz back to his feet. The guy had to be immortal. There was a deep gash across Dracula's—he would always be Dracula in Cruz's mind—left brow, and his chest was singed right down the middle of his thin, fancy-looking armor. His expensive shirt was shredded too.

"Can you walk?" he asked Cruz, his eyes scanning the chaos around them. The chamber was collapsing. It was looking more and more like a dilapidated Roman coliseum by the second.

Something had escaped from the pits of hell, and whatever it was—it was bad.

Cruz could feel the icy darkness crawling across his skin, gripping his heart, stealing his nerves away. This was what pure malevolence felt like. And it smelled like fire, charred wood, and sulfur. He hacked, trying to clear the soot out of the back of his throat. They needed to get out of here fast.

"Where is Zoey?" he asked, panic squeezing his chest as he got back to his feet. Pain shot through his forearm and he laid a hand over the wound, ignoring the fact that his entire body hurt. Nothing mattered except finding Zoey. "*She fell in,*" Cruz said, whispering softly. He cut a horrified glance back at Gabriel.

Gabriel Stanton didn't offer up any sage advice, only gazed out at the expansive grime covering everything like a blanket, and the gaping black hole in the ground, his eyes hooded. The faint scar on his cheek stood out harshly. "We need to go. Now. Where's the device?"

The rumbling under their feet was increasing in volume. Cruz was pretty sure this whole place was going to implode.

His heart gave a tormented lurch. The way she'd wailed when she'd fallen in … had been … *awful. Noooo!*

He scanned the edge of the precipice again. "*Zoey!*" he screeched, cupping the sides of his mouth, his voice raspy and choked. "*Zoey!*" *She can't be dead. Please, Lord, don't let her be dead.*

There came another low growl, deep from within the pit, as if in confirmation of that fact. Dread bloomed in him, just as wide as the hole in the ground.

"We need to get out of here," Gabriel repeated. "Do you have it? The device?"

Cruz shook his head, feeling shaken, his gaze fixated on the gap in the ground. "Zoey … she … she had it," he said, barely above a murmur, knowing he meant the device to get them all out of this dreadful place.

"I knew I shouldn't have entrusted our only way out of this realm to two teenage—"

Gabriel started to say, but a sudden flash lit up the darkness around them, and two figures bounded out of a thick parting of gray smog that looked like a rotating funnel cloud.

Stanton jumped in front of Cruz at the same time as Cruz's heart rate spiked, and he stumbled backward, suddenly terrified that it could be more of those dark demons after them. But once the swirling mass dissolved around the shadowy forms, he could finally make them out. Corinth and Alastair.

And then Cruz's breath stuck in his throat as soon as he saw Zoey's brother carrying someone in his arms. His eyes were drawn to the ugly red gash across her calf.

"*Zoey*," he breathed in relief and concern as soon as he saw her torn hoodie and dark blond hair. "Get your hands off her!" he shouted, and tried to rush around Dracula, determined to beat Corinth to a bloody pulp if he'd hurt her—

Corinth pressed his lips into a firm line, his face pasty, but before Cruz could tear him apart, Alastair stuck a hand out, barring him from getting any closer.

"It's okay. She's okay," he said thickly, his voice sounding off. Alastair was still shirtless and shoeless, but he didn't have the black marks singed into his chest anymore. It was just smeared with blood. There was something different about him though, Cruz thought. He had two different-colored eyes. One blue and one gold.

But as soon as Cruz's gaze fell on Zoey, all other thoughts fled him. She was unconscious in Corinth's arms.

"*Dios mío!*" he exclaimed in Spanish.

Corinth gently placed Zoey on the ground and crouched down beside her, along with Alastair. They laid glowing hands on her shoulders. A soft bluish hue pulsated out of Corinth's hand, and a strange glittering energy flickered across her skin.

Alastair's eyelids fluttered closed, the same sort of energy billowing out of his hands too, the light dissolving down into her body.

Cruz's hair started to stand on end, and an overwhelming metallic zing filled his nostrils.

"What are you doing?" he shouted, rushing toward them again, anger spiking through him.

Gabriel placed a firm hand against Cruz's chest, preventing him from getting any closer. And Cruz was really starting to get annoyed with Dracula, until he pointed down at Zoey's prone form and said, "They're trying to heal her. Look."

As Cruz watched, the inflamed and swollen cut on her head slowly closed up, her skin miraculously stitching itself back together again. The bruise on her wrist changed from a gnarly shade of plum to yellow and then vanished completely, and the swelling of her fat lip receded. Most all of her cuts and bruises healed over and disappeared— all of them except for the strange claw marks on her leg. Those were barely stitched together—blood oozed freely out of the open wounds. Cruz was going to be sick. It looked nasty.

Zoey took in a deep, shuddering breath. Despite her leg, she did look better. Her cheeks were now a healthier shade of red; some of the coloring had returned to her face.

Alastair let out a huff of irritation and then shook his

head, making eye contact with Corinth. "This will take time for me to heal. Time we don't have right now."

Corinth's gaze scanned the crumbling and dilapidated chamber. He closed his eyes for a second, and Cruz could see his eyes moving under closed lids.

Eventually, he said with a relieved huff, "Leo is okay. He says he got knocked out and that he just needs some time to build his energy back up."

Cruz made the sign of the cross as his wide eyes traveled over Corinth. How in the world did he know Leo was okay? Did he possess other powers, like telepathy? He did think Corinth looked to be back to his old self, relatively speaking. There were no inky, preternatural tattoos running up and down his arms, like before. No vacant, hollow eyes—only dark brown ones—although they contained a hint of golden glimmer, like sun dapples on water. No scary lightning on display.

Cruz noticed the magic blade was back in its holster, strapped at Corinth's thigh. He didn't know if that was a good thing or a bad thing. Probably good, since Corinth wasn't currently attacking anyone.

But Cruz had gone well past his limit of handing out his trust to just anyone, especially demons who could possess people.

There was a glint of bronze and steel at Corinth's side as he picked Zoey back up and cradled her safely in his arms once again.

"We have to get out of here—" he said started to say, but Larna came lunging out of nowhere, her blades ejected, heading straight toward Corinth. She must not have seen Alastair standing behind them yet. Otherwise,

Cruz thought, she probably would have at least paused to acknowledge that her husband was still alive. Apparently, she only had eyes for the one who'd stabbed her husband in his heart with a wooden stake.

Leo appeared out of a funneling vortex, leaping between them, his sparking hands held out in front of him, directed at Larna. "Larna, don't!"

There was a tense standoff moment when Cruz was sure Larna was going to try and rip Leo in half for getting in the way, but then her eyes hovered over the small form resting in Corinth's arms, and then a moment later, she blinked once, twice, three times. And then *finally* she seemed to come rushing back to her senses.

"*Zoey*," Larna breathed. She regarded Corinth cradling his sister so gently in his arms, and then she spoke in a restrained sort of whisper. "Corinth, are you ... back? Her leg needs to be looked at, and I'd prefer it if you handed her off to someone else."

He nodded and glanced down at Zoey, refusing to meet Larna's accusatory glare. "There is nothing you can do to help her right now," Corinth said quietly, gazing down at his sister's slumbering form in his arms. "She was attacked by a demon. Demon attacks take longer to recover from. As soon as we get away from here, I can finish healing her. And just for the record, I *am* back. Angela's gone."

"Let me take a look at her," she snapped at Corinth anyway, clearly still cross with him.

Cruz had almost forgotten she was a doctor. Even with her husband in apparent danger, he thought, it was incredible that she cared to think about others. But that was what doctors did. They healed first.

Leo's wide eyes flashed to Corinth. "Merciful heaven, I thought I'd lost you back there … What happened? Angela, is she really gone for good?" His voice broke, and he finally stopped, swallowing hard.

Alastair stepped right out of the hazy shadows behind them all, and as soon as he did, Larna's eyes locked on him, her mouth falling open. She dropped her clenched fists back down by her sides, retracting the blades into her armor at each wrist.

For a moment, no one spoke as she stared at Alastair.

She looked incredulous and confused and shell-shocked. And then she staggered forward on wobbly knees and wound her arms around his waist, planting her head against his chest. But Alastair did not share the hug—all the emotion he showed was a slight twitch of his cheek and a tightening of his jaw. After an awkward second, he pulled back from her embrace, looking uncomfortable.

Larna blinked back at her husband, her eyebrows drawn together, hurt and confused.

Leo put a hand on her shoulder, bringing Larna up short as her eyes locked on his hand on her arm with laser-like focus. "That's *not* Alastair, Larna."

Leo ground his teeth together as if he were in pain. A fine sheen of sweat lined his forehead, but his hands still crackled with that strange surge of supernatural energy.

"Angela …?" she started to say, but Leo shook his head.

Alastair stood stone-still and said evenly, "I am not Alastair Iszler."

Larna's eyes darted back to her husband's, her

expression revealing she was unsettled and worried. "Who are you, then?" she asked, on the defense again. "If not Angela, who?"

"An archangel," Leo answered for him. "He tried to kill Corinth. You can't trust him—"

"He saved Zoey's life. We can trust him."

Everyone's head swiveled toward Corinth as they gave him their full attention. He had been relatively quiet up until now, and Cruz found he really wanted to hear what Corinth had to say ... but above ground first, well away from this hellhole.

"Like hell we will," Larna snarled, but she clutched a hand to her chest, right over her heart. She looked pale, and Cruz could see her wedding band on her finger flash like a warning. "None of us are going anywhere until you explain who you are and what you've done to my husband. Your silence is scaring me, Leo," Larna breathed. "Alastair ... he's ... he's possessed? Like Angela possessed Corinth?"

Her hardened eyes flickered down to the blade at Corinth's hip and then flew back to Leo. "The pit— something flew out of it ... something evil. Should we be concerned about letting it loose on the world? If that thing follows us out ..." She licked her bloodless lips, nodding back at Gabriel Stanton as if the two of them had their own secret unspoken language.

"We really should be going," Gabriel Stanton muttered, stepping up behind Larna.

The earth tilted and swayed under their feet; a much deeper rumble resounded throughout the chamber. It sounded like something cracking deep underneath the surface. Like monsters tunneling their way through the sod. The entire place was coming down.

Whatever that a-hole Trevor had conjured up was certainly going to kill them all, Cruz thought.

He stumbled, trying to regain his footing, while Corinth listed to the side, Zoey's head lolling limply against his chest. Cruz's heart clenched at the sight.

"A vessel," Corinth corrected. "For Nakir."

"Nakir?" she asked quickly, concern filling her raspy voice. Even in the dark, Cruz could see her suspicious squint aimed at Corinth.

"Nakir is an archangel. Your husband volunteered to be his vessel, of his own free will. Angels ask permission. Demons don't. Alastair made some sort of bargain with him," Corinth clarified.

Leo cut her a quick glance again, and she shook her head, giving him a small, grim smile. "Of course he did." Dark shadows played across her cheeks, and something wet and shiny stood out on them. Tears.

"How else do you think he was able to come back after that grievous injury?" Leo interjected gently.

If she believed Leo, she didn't comment on it. Instead, she gave a jerk of her head in acknowledgment, and her silence seemed to stretch on forever until she said, "Nakir, Alastair … is he—" her voice cracked "—gone? For good?"

Cruz could feel the pain and anguish rolling off her in waves.

Nakir spoke in a firm, loud voice. *"Angela's gone. Corinth Taylor defeated her the moment he stabbed Alastair Iszler."* Everyone's eyes flickered to Corinth and then back to Nakir as he continued. "Your husband still has a chance—if we hurry."

Larna's face went a shade paler at hearing that. "What do you mean, he still has a chance? Why don't you just stop possessing my *husband* and leave him be?" Her voice was filled with ice and steel.

"I will as soon as we've gone topside," Nakir promised. "The infernal demon has been loosed upon your world already. I meant to stop it, but I was kind of busy saving the girl instead." He nodded at Zoey, still clutched tightly in Corinth's arms.

Cruz turned to study Corinth. He didn't know Zoey's brother that well, but Cruz knew he would be devastated losing a loved one. Maybe Corinth's silence was born of guilt. He blamed himself for everything that had just happened.

"There's nothing we can do about the demon now except survive to put it down at a later date," Leo snapped from behind Corinth.

Larna opened her mouth to question him more, but a huge chunk of concrete broke apart over their heads and plunged down, proving his point.

The angel possessing Alastair moved as if he owned stock in time, throwing both of his now-glowing hands high above his head. In a brilliant burst of light, the falling debris and rock hit it and fragmented apart in a cloud of dust, preventing all of their skulls from getting bashed in.

Ash and soot covered every inch of their skin. Cruz was coughing uncontrollably now. There was too much of it in the air, choking him. Dizziness overcame him, and he sank to a knee. Someone gripped his arm tight and pulled him upright. Gabriel Stanton. Dracula. Cruz was ninety percent sure the guy was still a vampire.

His stomach bottomed out like he'd just hit a pocket of turbulence on an airplane, and he felt the queasiness start to rise up inside him like a geyser. He was going to puke in front of all the superheroes. *Great.*

"He has my vote," Gabriel rasped. "I'm all about survival. Let's get out of here."

Corinth turned to Gabriel Stanton. "Can you lead us back to the gateway? Because we need to go. *Now.*"

Gabriel nodded, turned and, without another word, took off, with everyone following right on his heels.

41

LEO

As Leo made his way through the expansive, never-ending chambers, he could feel the thorn tearing at his skin, still embedded deeply in his thigh. All he wanted to do was stop and cut it out. Make the unbearable burn of evil stop spreading through his veins. *Stop.*

He slowed to a trot, limping behind everyone else, his eyes blurring. The infection was killing him. He'd gotten hit by one of those shards at the safe house. Too late. Some things were always too late. It was okay though. His brother was alive. Leo had fulfilled his angelic duties. Angels die. It was just his time.

His eyes stayed locked on Corinth's back; it was a dark blot against the inky blackness around them. As they hurriedly moved toward the exit, with Stanton in the lead, Leo stewed about his brother. Corinth had changed. The light of life in his eyes had been extinguished. Now his shoulders were slouched, and he was quiet. That was not like him. Somber did not suit his brother one bit.

That was the only thing still tying him to this world: his brother. He had to help fix him.

Corinth.

Leo felt the familiar buzz start up as soon as he spoke, his angel telepathy opening up between them. He kept his voice even and low, holding his emotions at bay so he wouldn't give away his own badly deteriorating condition. Not yet. He just needed a moment. One moment to just be. Corinth was strong, Leo knew, but he also knew news about his dying would devastate him.

Corinth. I know you can hear me.

There came no reply, only a sort of strange white noise. Leo could feel Corinth's forlorn detachment coming through their connection. Shared emotions. Except Leo was really good at hiding his own. He'd done it for eons in preparation for his final battle with Angela— his mother. Being connected through a telepathic link was not exactly all rainbows and kittens and happy thoughts. In fact, his emotions were about as far away from happy as they could get.

Up ahead of him in the narrow corridor, Leo could see Corinth's profile, his jaw tightened, and a muscle jumped out as he turned his head slightly.

There was an attack on your family. Your brother Pete … he … he was turned by one of those ill-begotten shards. I couldn't prevent it from happening. Corinth, I'm so sorry. Larna and I lost him. I haven't seen Pete in this realm yet, but there's a chance he might be here. Corinth, Pete may need our help. I'm staying here. To find him—

Peter is dead, came the short, clipped reply in his head. There was a pause before Leo heard Corinth speak again, and it came through softer this time. *There's nothing you can do, Leo. Thank you for coming after me, brother. The rest of my family, are they okay?*

Those words slammed into Leo with the full force of a wrecking ball. Corinth's inner voice was so flat and bleak. Leo lurched to the side, his shoulder scraping against the wall of the tunnel. He collapsed against it, feeling gutted. The Taylors were his family. These last ten years, he'd gotten to know them quite well. Guilt writhed inside him. He should have done more ...

They are okay—

Everyone except Peter ... Corinth reiterated, his voice hitching and then drifting off.

There was no blame that Leo sensed, only remorse and regret and a simmering anger.

A tremor worked its way through the tunnel. Rocks broke loose and crashed down from above, sending yet more dirt and soot into the already overly polluted air. Ahead of him, he heard wheezing from someone— probably Cruz. Leo's gaze flickered disconcertingly to the high ceiling as an overwhelming sense of grief rolled over him, making him gasp from the agony of it all. *No.*

I thought ... he began, trying to contain his rising emotions. *Corinth, I thought we had time to ... to save him.*

Leo quickly cut the connection with Corinth. There was pure and carnal dread in the pit of his stomach, and he doubled over. The infection was working its heinous way through him, up toward his heart. He'd never been sick before, but he'd been around enough humans to know what it probably felt like—this. His entire body ached, and he was chilled to the bone.

Larna came up beside him, looking worried. "You're limping," she noted, sounding out of breath. "What's wrong? Should I be concerned? Do you want me to take a look at that?"

From somewhere up ahead of them, they could hear Nakir's disembodied voice say, "Quickly, now!"

He gave her a fleeting glance and shook his head. "He's dead," he whispered in misery. "*Peter.*" For a moment, all he could do was let the residual feelings of grief wash over him.

Larna went incredibly still and stiff by his side. After a second, she laid a supportive hand on his shoulder, her face contracting in dismay and shock. "Are you sure?" Her troubled gaze shot to Corinth's dwindling outline way ahead of them. "Does he know?"

"He's the one who told me," Leo said.

Her face fell, and she swiped a hand under her nose. "Dammit," she swore under her breath. "Damn Trevor to hell."

Leo could sense a low growl of warning coming from below the demon realm. They had to get out now. Leo pushed off from the wall, and Larna grabbed hold of his arm, throwing it over her shoulder as they hurried on, both of them silent. They didn't need to say anything else.

Dear merciful Father, please take care of Peter.

They stood in front of the wall, the diamond-shaped

symbol etched into it, like Gabriel Stanton had said it would be. Corinth brushed a lock of hair off Zoey's forehead, but other than that, he stayed still.

"Is she okay?" Cruz asked him.

Corinth's face darkened as his gaze settled on Zoey's soft features. "Not if we don't get out of here."

A shudder went through the earth at their feet as a resonant cracking sound came from the other side of the wall. That seemed to hasten everyone closer into a tight circle.

Cruz rubbed a hand over his sooty face, glancing up, looking apprehensive. "It feels like days since we came down here."

Gabriel clutched the device in his hand, his thumb hovering over the button, but Nakir spoke up before he could push it, turning to Larna. "You asked about your husband."

She turned to Nakir, giving him her full attention. Leo wondered what was going through her head right now. She had to feel conflicted, knowing someone else was in control of her husband's body.

"As soon as we're on the other side—away from this demon realm—I will leave Alastair's vessel."

Larna cradled a hand against her stomach, looking more noticeably relieved, until she saw Nakir look away and purse his lips, as if getting ready to give her bad news.

"I'm sorry, Mrs. Iszler. You should be prepared," he began. "Mortals can only contain an archangel's essence for so long. There will be considerable damage upon my exit of his body. His injuries will be substantial—"

"What?" At hearing that, Larna moved to stand in

front of Nakir, the angel who looked just like her husband. She ground her teeth together in frustration and fisted her hands down by her sides. "You're just going to use him up and run, huh? Too busy to help save someone who gave up their freedom to get you here?"

Nakir grimaced. "I … I will need time to adjust to your world, so I won't be able to stitch myself back together again in time to be of any use to anyone."

Larna crossed her arms over her chest, her cheeks mottled and eyes red-rimmed. "Do you know anything about our world?"

"I know enough," Nakir answered.

"Well, know this, *angel*: I love him. Do you know what that feels like?"

"I understand love," Nakir said evenly, coolly.

Larna shook her head and barked out a derisive laugh. "This isn't about your understanding of love. It's about *vengeance*. If he dies, I will kill you for your part in it. Do you understand?"

Leo could see Gabriel Stanton behind Larna. There was an indecipherable flicker of emotion on his features, and the ghost of a smile flitted across his face and then disappeared. Stanton wasn't exactly an upstanding citizen, and seeing his reaction to her threat of violence only served to enrage Leo more. A bolt of anger tore through him.

"What do you need me to do, Cor?" Leo's leg was burning. He was worried. Worried that he wouldn't have the strength to help. Of course, he'd die trying.

"*Leo.*" Corinth said his name with such tensioned weight it gave him pause.

Leo turned to regard his brother in the dim lighting

of the cavern. Dark shadows contoured the half-moons under his eyes. He looked exhausted and worn down, while Zoey looked youthful and fragile in his arms. He knew what Corinth was going to say next, and Leo was cross with himself for letting him.

"This is my fault. I put Al in this mess. I'll do whatever I can to get him out of it." Corinth cleared his throat. "I can't have your death, or hers, on my hands too." He spoke louder as soon as he saw Leo start to open his mouth to argue. "Take Zo back home. I have to know she's safe. You can come back with the rest of the team, but *please*, Leo, just get our little sister back to her parents." He averted his gaze as he deposited Zoey's small form into Leo's arms without waiting on his response. "In the meantime, Larna and I will do our best to save Al's life."

"Me too," Cruz said loudly over their group, surprising everyone. "I may not have superpowers, but I know how to put pressure on a wound. Let me help."

"This isn't going to be pretty, kid," Gabriel piped up from behind him, a smirk on his face. "You sure you can handle it?"

Cruz cocked his head to the side and swallowed hard. "Uh … pretty sure. What about you, Dracula?"

42

GABRIEL

The moment Gabriel Stanton switched the toggle on the transport device to the diamond, they all disappeared in a blinding flash of light to land in one of the three places he'd designated to be his exits: London. Inside a warehouse, situated in a well-cordoned-off area with high security in place.

They had landed in a heap in front of a large oval stone in the middle of the empty warehouse. Well, empty except for the giant sarsen stone. The symbol etched into the rock was a matching diamond. The demon Ephrem had helped Gabriel design three spots he would have access to, which he knew would have to be controlled and monitored. He owned major corporations in Beijing, London, and Mumbai.

He would have to have them all shut down.

As soon as possible.

If Ephrem was still out there, he would come seeking

his revenge—here and any place he knew Gabriel Stanton owned or operated property out of.

Dammit.

Alastair Iszler was *supposed* to be his sworn enemy.

But Larna… she … she was not his sworn enemy. She was different. Even after ten long years, he could still recall her memory—now his—as he'd experienced it through Larna's eyes. A simple kiss she had shared with Alastair Iszler, and how it had made Gabriel feel. Awful. Certainly not sweet. Not at all … *yet* … He tried to shake the odd feeling of contentment out of his mind. Gabriel did not relish human emotions.

At the beginning, after he'd lost his strength, slow aging, and superhuman abilities, he could think of nothing other than hurting the one person who had taken all that away from him: Corinth Taylor. That's the feeling he needed to retain. Having rivals was so much more fun than having friends. Payback was even better.

Yet he didn't think he wanted payback anymore. That begged the question: What *did* he want? His eyes flickered to Alastair Iszler. Well, technically, the angel possessing Iszler. Nakir. He was on his feet, barely, and his body was starting to glow like a burning star about to collapse in on itself. Alastair or Nakir, he couldn't figure out who, screamed in agony, and Gabriel's throat tightened. *Damn it all.* Somewhere along the line, he'd grown to respect Iszler. He actually wanted to make his pain stop.

What is wrong *with me?*

Gabriel's people had heard the ruckus and come running as soon as they'd appeared out of thin air. Their expressions were all tense, filled with concern and fear. They all wore white lab coats, and were holding tablets in their hands, hastily pecking at their screens as they moved closer. Behind the scientists, came his security team, rifles held at the ready. They wore black suits, and it only took them a moment to surround their group as they waited on his orders.

Corinth staggered to his feet, a hand going to Alastair's head as Alastair screamed bloody murder again, dropping to his knees, his hands fisted at his sides. His entire body was filling with a blazing golden light, just as bright as the sun, Gabriel thought. And those eyes. Like lasers were shooting out of them.

One of Stanton's employees, a woman with white-blond hair and pink square-rimmed glasses reached out to help Gabriel to his feet. He brushed his war-torn clothes off. "Blanca," he said her name by way of greeting.

There was a ghastly burn mark in the center of his gear, and the minute she saw it, she gasped. It had cost him an arm and a leg to get his hands on this material. It had done its job and saved his life, but he was still irate about losing it.

"*Sir?*" she breathed, speaking to Gabriel but eyeing Alastair up and down with one eye closed against the bright light emanating from his body. "Do you need medical attention? Does *he* need medical attention? What should we do? I ... I've never seen anything like that before."

Leo still had Zoey's limp form in his arms. "I'll be back as soon as I can." He gave Corinth a quick nod before leaping into an already-dwindling vortex of wind and vapor, and there was a devastating clap of thunder. Gabriel's security team raised their weapons, expecting an attack, or for something else to come rolling out of the cyclone—but they were already long gone.

Blanca recoiled, almost falling on her face she was so flabbergasted by Leo's sudden disappearance.

The kid and Larna were on their feet now too, both stunned, inching as close to Alastair as they could get without being turned into crispy fried nuggets. The space around them was starting to feel like an oven, and Gabriel's hair was standing on end from all the static in the air.

Alastair was going to pop like a balloon.

"Lower your weapons," Gabriel barked at his security team. "Enact protocol Descend."

His head of security at this location, Kiefer, stepped forward. "Code word?"

"Eliana," Gabriel snapped.

Kiefer spoke into his earpiece. "Evacuate everyone now. Destroy everything."

There was a flurry of activity around him as the rest of his team went to work, a high-pitched alarm starting to wail in the background.

"Sir, we have your chopper ready and waiting. Follow me," Kiefer said.

"I'm staying."

Kiefer looked like he wanted to argue and knock some sense into Gabriel, but he knew when not to argue with his employer. He gave Gabriel a curt nod, waving at his team to obey the issued orders.

They all took off at a trot as Kiefer said before leaving,

"You have your radio?"

Gabriel tapped his ear, where his almost-invisible earpiece was inserted. "I'm good. I'll call you if I need anything."

Corinth regarded Gabriel with one of his annoying eyebrow raises. "Why aren't you running for the hills right now? Something's not right here …"

He rolled his eyes. "Do we need my medical staff on standby, Mr. Taylor?"

Corinth wrung his hands out. They were glowing golden blue, dripping energy like sparks on a welder's torch. "No. They'll just get in the way. I'll try and stabilize him, with Larna's help, until I can transport him back to the safe house, where she has a make-shift operating room set up."

"*Corinth!*" Larna cried, shielding her eyes from the light. She had stripped out of her father's old duster, and she sounded terrified for her husband's well-being.

Gabriel felt a twinge of remorse wriggle in his gut. This was partly his fault. He could see the dark shadows like rings standing out under her eyes, and he could also see the bowstring tension in her body—the hard line of muscles rigid on her back. She was incensed with Taylor, but she also needed his help. Conflicted. Maybe this would be their undoing. Gabriel could only hope.

Corinth threw up a barrier around Alastair, gritting his teeth from the increased heat. Smart. He was containing Alastair's energy instead of trying to protect them all from Alastair. Gabriel knew Taylor still had his limits. Everyone did. Even half angels with bloody biblical daggers at their disposal.

Plus, the kid had changed. He was a shell of his former self. A piece of him had died, and Gabriel couldn't figure out why. Those feelings usually came from the loss of a loved one. Gabriel was intimately familiar with that kind of pain. He'd been alive for over two thousand years. That kind of pain sent you to dark places you couldn't crawl out of. Places that devoured you, chewed you up, and spit you out—leaving you to rot.

He'd been rotting for centuries, although now that he had a timetable for his inevitable demise, maybe a little less so.

Welcome to the club, Mr. Taylor. Members only.

Alastair let out another ear-shattering bellow—and then what looked a lot like fire to Gabriel exploded out of his body, fracturing the barrier Corinth had erected around him to keep them all safe.

A jagged line, like splintered glass, fissured down the sides of the magical dome, and Corinth's entire body shuddered as he took a knee, struggling to maintain the shield he'd erected. Gabriel could see the blade at Corinth's side radiating the same type of energy that was spewing out of his hands.

And then, just like that it was over.

Alastair's body was no longer ablaze or glowing—it didn't even show the tiniest bit of illumination. He was utterly slack, on his back, his hands stretched out by his sides, face ashen. For a moment, no one moved.

Gabriel thought they all looked just as shocked. There was no way someone could live through that. No way.

Larna was the first one to move, and then she was

assessing his injuries—professional, calm, controlled. Gabriel had been burned beyond recognition in the past. Pretty much eighty percent of his entire body. Those injuries had been grievous, but he'd been able to heal from them because he had been an ascended being. Alastair could not heal from these wounds. His body was wrecked.

Corinth rushed past him in a blur and slid down beside Alastair, his glowing hands already pressed to his bloodied chest like paddles on a defibrillator.

Gabriel crouched beside Larna, assessing Iszler as well. "Is his foot supposed to be turned in that direction?"

"We start with the worst and move on from there," Larna ordered. "Here. Put pressure on his wound." She tore at a ripped seam in Alastair's pant leg, exposing a deep laceration on his upper thigh. "Right there." His workout pants were soaked through with red. "Cruz, can you use your belt as a tourniquet? Tie it off just above the injury."

Gabriel did as instructed. Cruz yanked off his belt without hesitating, although Gabriel noted he did look rather pale.

All the while, Corinth tried to use his powers to heal his best friend … his brother-in-arms. The golden light sank down into his body, briefly illuminating veins and ligaments. "Can you get a better look now?" he asked her. "This is …" Corinth swiped at his sweaty brow, looking utterly drained and exhausted already. "Bad. I need help …"

Larna gasped at seeing the extent of her husband's injuries from the inside, all lit up like a map. "No. No. NO!" she snarled. "I need an OR, gloves, sterile equipment, blood …"

Behind him, Gabriel heard the thunder announcing the arrival of the rest of the Watchers. They were giants, and it didn't take much effort on their part to shove Gabriel out of the way so they could work their divine healing magic.

Gabriel was pretty sure it was futile at this point, though, as he stood back and let them try and heal Alastair.

43

ZOEY

I came to, my head still muddled from sleep, remembering horns and yellow eyes and sharp teeth.

Sitting upright in a panic, I clutched at my chest, feeling my heart hammering away. It took me a full minute to figure out that the demon wasn't still attached to my leg. I yanked my arm up, terrified that the iron might still be clamped around my wrist. It wasn't. The restrictive feeling came from being tangled up in a blanket, covers wrapped around my midsection. I rubbed at my wrist, examining it, blinking dully in the extreme daylight, letting my senses come back to me. No bruises. No swelling. But a small part of me could still feel the phantom tingling in my arm after being chained up for hours on end … I shivered.

I was lying in a twin-size bed, *alive*, but terrified and relieved at the same time. *I am safe.* A sense of elation and liberation flooded through me, so great I felt light-headed.

No chains. No darkness. No blood. No rank odor. No Trevor.

I rolled both of my ankles, expecting to feel the sharp, piercing pain of being clawed by that demon, but there only came the faint sound of my joints popping. I finally managed to get my pulse to even out. Nothing hurt. I was only bone-tired. Throwing the covers back, I examined my leg where the beast had clawed me, but noticed there was nothing there to examine. No marks, only smooth skin.

Sunlight streamed in through an open window, and billowy white curtains swayed in a gentle, albeit cold, breeze. I closed my eyes for a second, taking in the fresh air, and clean-laundry smell of the sheets—*freedom*.

Maybe none of it had happened. It was only a nightmare. I glanced down to see I was wearing long-sleeved black-and-red-checkered flannel pajamas.

For a moment, all I could do was sit there and reorient myself to my surroundings. It was exceedingly bright after I'd been stuck in the dark for so long. I squinted past the sunshine, my eyes glazing over with moisture.

Outside the window, the countryside was rolling green hills, bloated clouds, and a stone wall that seemingly went on forever and ever. There was a gray cobblestone cottage sitting on the crest of a hill. We weren't in Texas. We weren't in the demon realm. I quailed. Now it felt like a lingering nightmare, but I knew it wasn't. It had been real.

Peter. Corinth. My family.

I sat up, ramrod straight, gripped by anxiety and

paralyzing fear all over again.

There was movement out of the corner of my eye, and I twisted around to see a prone form slumped in a chair, arms crossed over his chest. Corinth. His head was propped up against the wall at an angle that looked like it was going to leave a crick in his neck. He was sleeping, and he looked about as peaceful as I'd ever seen him. His floppy hair was hanging half in his face. He was wearing a cream-colored thermal, black camo-style pants, and his usual gray Converse. He wasn't wearing his blade or sheath, or if he was, I couldn't see it.

He is okay.

The tight feeling in my chest loosened just a tad, and I let out a long sigh in relief. And then I was assaulted by concerns for the rest of my family: Mom. Dad. Jimmy. *Pete. Does Corinth know?*

A horrifying vision of a hand sticking out of Peter's chest assailed me, and I started panting, unable to pull air into my lungs fast enough. They felt deflated and empty. I had started to extricate myself from the constricting covers, freaking out, when Corinth stirred back to life.

His eyes popped open and met mine.

He saw me flailing and was on his feet before I could flop out of bed like a wounded fish. "Are you okay? Don't get up, Zo," he chastised, easing himself onto the bed beside me, gently pushing me back down. "You're still weak. You need massive amounts of rest. Demon attacks are no joke—I found that out the hard way. Do you need anything? What can I do to help?"

"*Peter.*" My voice cracked, full of raw, unbridled emotion. "I need Peter, Corinth. You brought him back, right?" I couldn't hold the tears at bay now. "With your angel powers. Just like you did Alastair. Tell me you saved him, Cor."

Corinth stiffened all over, and then his bright eyes dimmed, and I felt like I was watching him break right in front of my very eyes. *Oh no.* Bright red, feverish splotches appeared on the tips of his cheeks. "*Zo,*" he breathed. "That's not how it works."

"Why not?" I almost shouted, and Corinth flinched, like I'd slapped him across his face. "You're ... an angel, right? You healed me. Why can't you fix him? Bring him back. He's ... he's ..." And then I was sobbing uncontrollably as the dark and vivid memory of his death hit me all over again. I'd been there for his final moments. "Peter ... saved my ... life." I couldn't stop crying now. Pete was gone.

A small part of me blamed Corinth, and the other part, the bigger part, blamed myself. I was the one who had let Trevor in the front door. I'd introduced him to our family. Everything hurt. The pain was constant and everywhere. Like a strong undertow in a river, I could feel it pulsing through my veins, merciless, unending.

He reached across and pulled me into a tight embrace, resting his chin on the top of my head, mumbling something—which I was sure was reassuring— but I had no idea what he was saying, because I was beyond being consoled. I'd lost a brother. And my half brother—*Corinth*—I was terrified of. He was an angel. Not my brother, really. Something deadlier. I imagined his cruel smile aimed at me, and I jerked out of his embrace, easing away. He took some of his warmth and body heat with him as he gazed down at his hands.

He looked like he didn't want any part in having them attached to the rest of his body.

Peter is dead.

The voice at the back of my mind practically shouted at me, reminding me that I should shatter all over again. Ruined. That was what I felt like. I was never going to hear his voice again. Never going to play fight with him again. Never going to get his help with my homework. My chest squeezed to an excruciating degree, choking the life out of me. Every single one of my nerves … *ached.*

After what seemed like an eternity, when I was sure I didn't have anything left inside me, I managed to glance back at Corinth through swollen eyes.

His face was dry, but he was so pale and withdrawn—distant. Riddled with guilt. I hated seeing him so lost. I could see the fault and blame in his eyes, but I had nothing left inside me to try and comfort him. He didn't deserve it. He needed to be just as tormented as I felt.

"I was almost responsible for killing you. *Pete*—" A visible tremor worked its way through him. "I *am* responsible for his death … His blood is on my hands, Zo. This is my fault."

I didn't say anything. I only felt incredibly pale.

After a while, he reached across to the nightstand beside the small bed, and picked up a cup of water with a straw and then handed it to me. I took it from him without comment and drained every last drop, feeling like I needed more. Lots more. My mouth was so dry.

"What about Cruz? Mom? Dad? Jimmy? Leo?" I finally croaked.

"They're all okay. I tried to take Cruz back home, but he's stubborn. He didn't want to leave your side. He's currently eating everything in the kitchen—even the frozen fish sticks. Not exactly the Thanksgiving dinner he had expected …"

I felt my cheeks start to redden at hearing that. "Cor … what about Alastair? The angel Nakir … I saw his true face, like, under Alastair's visage… I knew his name—it just came to me. How is that even possible? Your blade … it responded to me. I'm not an angel or even half of one. What does that mean? We aren't blood related through your angelic side … What does any of this *mean*?"

He met my wide-eyed gaze. "The dagger kind of has a mind of its own. It must have sensed Angela possessing me, and it knew the dangers of her wielding it, so it sought someone else out … someone a lot stronger than me, apparently—*you*."

I gulped at hearing that, and a tiny part of me was filled with warm pride, but the feeling didn't last long, it was replaced by a hollow pang of desolation all over again.

"Al is hurt. I don't know …" Corinth ran a hand through his hair, his eyes shining. "He's alive … but he's not out of the woods yet. Larna, she's okay, and understandably hates my guts, even though she tells me she doesn't—I can see it in her eyes. Leo is, well … he needs time to recover."

He got up and shoved his hands in his pockets, gazing out the window, suddenly transfixed. I could feel his grief from all the way across the room, and I rubbed my arms because of it.

"I should have seen this coming," he said softly,

reprimanding himself, shaking his head. The draft was no longer comforting; it was cold. "Zo, I am *so, so* sorry. For *everything*. All of it. I almost *lost* you. I never thought what I did all those years ago would catch up to me … I thought we were okay." I heard him choke on the word *lost* as he turned back around to face me.

I swallowed hard and then got to my feet, feeling woozy. "No." My stomach was empty; I was starving, and his shame wasn't helping me stay calm. I stepped toward him and then gently laid a hand on his arm. He flinched. "That wasn't you, Cor. You were possessed. You *literally* weren't in control of your own body. This is my fault too. I brought Trevor … Ephrem … whatever … here. I trusted him. I should have asked you how you were feeling. You look … awful."

"None of this is your fault. It's all on me. I mean it, Zo. I keep seeing myself *not* helping you … I couldn't *help* you." He let out a shuddering breath. "What that demon did … and … and …" He stopped, seemingly at a loss for words, overwhelmed.

I could see in his face he was reliving it all over again. He remembered being possessed. I shivered. That was a torment I wouldn't wish on anyone. I wanted to take away his pain, but I also couldn't forget how Trevor had left me all alone in the dark. It haunted me. And so did Cor's blank face as he let Trevor carry me away. I hated the lead feeling in the pit of my stomach. I didn't quite know how to process my confusion, and Corinth was the source of most of it. I couldn't figure out what else I needed to ask him, even though a lot of stuff was distantly nagging at me.

He opened his mouth to speak, but there was a flurry of activity outside the closed door.

"*I said, open the door, now ... That's my daughter in there—*"

"We're not waiting any longer ..."

Corinth strode to the door and swung it open. Standing on the other side, just at the threshold, was one of the scariest men I'd ever seen in my entire life. He had jet-black hair, a beard equally as dark as his hair, and extremely pale skin. There was a dangerous scowl plastered across his face. He wasn't exactly tall, but he was imposing. He let out a low growl of warning or something as soon as he saw Corinth.

"It's okay, Vin. You can let them in," Cor told him.

Mom marched past the scary bearded man as soon as he dropped his arm down from the doorframe. Behind her came Dad, and then last, Jimmy. They filled the small room, tension buzzing between us all.

Mom looked like an angry pelican. She was flapping her arms in distress, and her strawberry-blond hair was sticking up. She angrily glared back at the creepy man still standing in the hallway.

As soon as she saw me, she let out a strangled cry and flew at me, her small arms going around mine, trapping them down by my sides as she hugged me in a tight embrace. She felt bony and frail, like she'd lost ten pounds in a short amount of time.

"That man wouldn't let us in," she breathed into my ear. "Or I would have been by your bedside this entire time. He said you needed rest—and so did Cor. I was about to lose my mind." She gave a huff of defiance and threw a disapproving glance back at the stranger, her face flushed.

The scary man didn't say anything in response, like he was used to getting that evil-eyed stare from people. He only shrugged.

Corinth, on the other hand, reached a hand out toward the bearded man and waited. The guy eyed Corinth's extended hand with a frustrated frown. Part of me thought he might kill him, but then, surprisingly, he clasped forearms with him as if they were brothers.

Dad looked rumpled and worn. His flannel shirt was wrinkled, and so were his khakis. He had a five-o'clock shadow going on, which was odd because he was meticulous about shaving, and his brown hair was a shaggy mess, like Corinth's. Jimmy's eyes were red-rimmed, and the expression in them was almost enough to make me drop like a stone. Peter and Jimmy. They were close—they had been close. Dark splotches exploded across my vision. He looked haunted. Vacant. They'd been like twins, almost inseparable.

He knew Pete was gone. They all knew.

My family surrounded me—all of them except Corinth—at the same time, pulling me into a tight embrace. We were all hanging on to each other as if we might get separated again at any moment. It was too constricting, all that intermingling body heat and those mixed emotions coursing through us. Suddenly I felt faint, and I had to back away from everyone, giving myself more space.

Corinth turned around from the open window, straightening to his full height as if getting ready for

Mom's barrage of questions. "Mom … I'm … I would have come to you sooner, but I just … I didn't know how to tell you. Pete … I couldn't get him back … I tried …" His voice drifted off, and a lone tear escaped, leaving a track down his skin. His voice sounded so thin and dark. "This is my fault. All of it."

It wasn't lost on me that he hadn't joined in on the group hug. He crossed his arms over his chest, looking uncomfortable. Like he knew something terrible was about to happen.

Mom turned to face him, and so did everyone else as they all regarded Corinth in restrained silence. No one said a word for quite some time.

Eventually, Mom moved to stand in front of Cor, her arms hanging loosely down by her sides. She stared at him, her face going slack. And then she raised her hand and slapped him across the face.

I gasped at the same time as Jimmy yelled, "*Mom!*" He sounded horrified.

Dad stood back, his teeth gritted, too stunned to say a word. I could see how utterly he had been affected by Peter's death. Fear and grief had crippled him.

Corinth's entire body went taut, and he took a faltering step back, a hand going to his cheek, his expression one of complete shell shock. An angry red handprint was standing out on his skin.

Another tear slipped down his face.

She gripped her now-injured hand and then fell to pieces, almost collapsing, but Dad caught her around the waist before she could hit the ground. She was weeping uncontrollably. It was all too much. This was why the scary dude, Vin, hadn't let them in the room to speak to us. I understood it now. The anguish. I put a hand across my stomach, feeling sick. *Peter.* My breath seemed to have left me eons ago. He really was gone.

Dad helped Mom to the door, casting a troubled glance back at Cor. His eyes flickered with emotion: anger, remorse, and dread. "I need to talk to you, son," he whispered softly. "Don't leave, please. She didn't mean it. She doesn't blame you. Okay? She just lost a child."

Corinth's jaw clenched tight. He dropped his gaze away from Dad's, and then he lifted one hand, made a weird flicking motion, and a millisecond later, a brilliant clap of thunder rolled through the small room. I squeezed my eyes shut against the wind roaring past me, lifting my hair, and when I dragged them open again, Cor was gone.

Maybe for good.

44

ALASTAIR

Alastair awoke feeling woozy and warm and muddled—heavily medicated. Not bad, since he'd basically been ripped from the inside out by an archangel. He knew the disconnected feeling between his brain and body was probably not a good thing. The scents of plastic, rubbing alcohol, and iodine hit him.

The small room he occupied had plain white walls, hospital-grade equipment, and a cushioned chair. Alastair knew he was at the safe house. He'd been here plenty of times in the past, when Larna was setting it up. Her brilliant idea. Even with a household full of angels who could heal humans, they thought it best to be prepared—and they'd been right.

His wife's face came into focus in slow increments. *She's safe.* Beautiful golden-chestnut hair was messily pulled back into a bun at her neck. Some of it curled around her ears. She had on blue scrubs, a white coat, and a stethoscope was wrapped around her neck. *She is breathtaking.* There was a freckle right under her collarbone that he really wanted to explore in more detail. A tiny frown line appeared in the middle of her forehead as she closely analyzed a beeping monitor nearby.

"Hello, *Doctor* Iszler," he slurred, trying to move his hand toward her, but something jerked it back, restricting his movements, and he winced, feeling annoyed.

Larna smiled, and he knew it was because of the way he'd said her official title. With adoration and just the right amount of flirtatiousness. Seeing that he was awake, she immediately rushed to Alastair's side, a hand going to his arm. "Don't move." There was a tremor in her voice that almost sobered him right up. Relief. Fear. Anxiety. "This rigging is designed to keep your arm stabilized. It was fractured in three places. If you keep moving, you'll mess up all the hard work the angels and I have been putting into patching you up." She pointed to several wires and a sling holding his arm up, positioned at an angle above his heart.

He huffed out a laugh. "You're bossy."

His wife raised an exasperated eyebrow, looking amused and weary at the same time. "And *you're* loopy. How's your pain level?"

"Non-existent." His voice sounded garbled in his head, and his thoughts were scattered. He knew he should be worried about something, but he just couldn't remember what it was.

"At least the pain medication is working."

Alastair glanced down to the tube and needle taped to the back of his wrist. *Bloody hell.* A pressure cuff was wound tightly around his left arm. He was shirtless, and a thick bandage covered his chest. Larna moved to the foot of his gurney, pulling his scrub bottoms up to inspect his right ankle. There it was, her doctor's face—all business, no emotion—but Alastair had known her long enough to learn how to read *all* of her facial expressions, just like she'd learned how to read his. It was the face she made when she had to give someone bad news. Really, really bad news.

"Ahhh, darling." His words came out sounding muddled together again. "Don't look so glum."

Larna pressed her lips together into a firm line, and the full weight of her eyes on him made him feel suddenly uneasy.

She opened her mouth to speak, but before she could get anything out, Ikari came marching into the surgical room. His spiky faux-blond hair was glittering with hair product. He wasn't wearing his usual armor; he was wearing sweats and a baby-blue sweater that offset those dark eyes of his.

"That looks a thousand times better," Ikari said optimistically, his tall form towering over Larna's as he inspected Alastair's ankle. Ikari's gaze caught his for a second. "Hey, dude, glad to see you awake. We were worried there for a second. It looks like you'll have a few new scars to add to your collection. This one is the coolest though." Ikari cocked his head to the side. "Looks like a starburst, doesn't it?"

Alastair glanced down to see an indent in his ankle where a hunk of muscle was missing; it looked like a shark had gotten ahold of his foot. His flesh was white and raised, standing out against tanned skin. It didn't look like a recent injury; it looked old. This was one they'd already managed to heal—to the best of their ability, anyway. He lifted his leg slightly, to get a better look, and a wave of intense pain and nausea washed over him, ripping the breath from his lungs. His vision blurred.

Somewhere at the back of his drug-addled mind, he was dimly aware that the mark looked more to him like an asterisk than a starburst. *Ouch.* Now he felt the pain. It was flooding back in, debilitating. For a moment, all he could do was try and breathe. His mind was starting to clear too, and those horrid memories were taking him to places he did not want to revisit.

Like the feeling of losing that much blood so quickly.

He remembered his conversation with Nakir in painstaking detail.

"Didn't I kill Ephrem?"

"You banished him back to hell. He'll try and get out again. I don't need to tell you what will happen if he does manage an escape, right?"

He shuddered and let out a small gasp.

"Easy now," Larna whispered. "The angels did what they could to heal you, but they had a lot of work to do. You're still recovering. You have forty-three stitches in your chest. Your femoral artery"—she lifted both her eyebrows—"ruptured, and you almost bled out. I've never seen anything like that type of injury before. Corinth worked all night to help heal you. He only stopped when he collapsed. Your foot ..." Larna swallowed hard. "It's going to need lots of physical therapy, and even then, I'm not sure how much range of motion you'll have in your right leg. I'm sorry. I'm so sorry, Alastair … You won't be able to run."

He coughed and then said in a husky voice, "I … I … knew what was at stake, Larna." Guilt hit him full force, and he looked away from her heated gaze. *Too much.* Nakir had warned him, but still …

The room had gone quiet while he'd been lost in thought. Eventually, he said, "Where's … Corinth? I need to talk to him." Alastair wanted to tell him it was okay. He needed to warn him about Ephrem. He knew it hadn't been Corinth's doing. It had been Angela's. But if he was having nightmares about being stabbed, he knew Corinth was probably having the same ones, just from the other point of view. A startling vision of the wooden handle sticking out of his chest almost had him gasping for air again.

"He's with his family," Ikari answered for Larna, bringing him out of his reverie. "They just got the news about Peter. They need time to grieve over his death."

Ikari was standing beside Alastair's bedside, and Alastair had no idea when, or how, he'd even gotten that close. The angel gazed down at him, giving him a pitying stare. Alastair did not like that look he was giving him. He didn't want anyone's pity. Alastair knew the decision he'd made.

Corinth's brother is dead. He liked Pete. He had taught him self-defense. He'd spent every year at their house during the Thanksgiving break. The backs of his eyelids felt hot.

Another wave of guilt rose up inside him, twisting his gut into intricate knots, making him feel raw and exposed.

"Can you ...?" Alastair cursed, suddenly feeling humiliated and angry and upset that he had to ask for help. He just needed up—out of this bloody bed—and he couldn't even go to the bathroom without assistance. He started struggling, pulling at the blood pressure cuff on his arm. He just needed fresh air. A burning pain engulfed him, but he ignored it, trying to jerk his arm out of the sling. "I need out of here." A vision of him being tortured by Ephrem hit him full force. The gag covering his face, restricting his breathing ... and a wave of dizziness brought him up short.

Larna reached out to stop him from moving, but that only made him want to pull harder, to struggle more. "Hey, hey now. You're going to injure yourself further."

His breathing was coming in shallower and shallower. "I ... I think ... I'm going ... to be ill. I just need air. N-n-now."

"You need me to help?" Ikari asked evenly, his fists already glowing blue.

"Can you give us a minute?" Larna asked him.

Ikari gave a quick nod, understanding lighting his eyes. And then the angel quickly left the way he'd come, giving them space.

"You're having a panic attack," Larna explained. "Take slow, deep breaths, Alastair. Easy. I've got you."

He watched like a wounded animal as she reached over to his IV and adjusted his pain medication, and then she eased herself onto the bed beside him, avoiding all the wires and tubes attached to him. His intuition to fight wasn't completely gone, but her warmth was comforting, so he went still. She was so warm against him.

"Look around the room. What do you see? Can you name five things that are blue in this room? What are they?"

Alastair wanted to tell her to stop patronizing him, but his vision was rapidly darkening around the edges, and his arms were tingling. He'd never had a panic attack before. He'd never felt this out of control. He'd always been in control. Not anymore. "I ... I see the blue clockface on the wall." He licked his lips and opened his eyes, trying to concentrate on something else. Anything other than the memories of dying—and worse, coming back. His eyes flitted from the beeping monitor to the table tray near his bed, to the chair against the wall. "Your scrubs ... they're ... they're blue."

"That's good. What else?" she insisted, pulling his free hand into hers. She kissed his knuckles, his signature move on her. Her breath felt soothing against his heated skin. He was panting now.

After another minute, Alastair's heartbeat slowed, followed by his breathing. The pain eased a bit, and the tension started to slowly drain out of his body. All he wanted to do was sleep. He was so exhausted. He closed his eyes, letting the drugs lull him under.

"*Alastair.*"

Larna's soft voice seemed to drift to him from faraway, and it took him another minute to respond, but he could sense her worry as she laid her head on his shoulder, so he didn't go away completely.

"Mm-hmm?"

"I know you're trying to be strong, like you always are. But I just want you to know, with me, you don't have to be strong all the time. You can … just *be*. Vulnerability is *not* weakness. You got that? You're going to be okay. I love you. No matter what happens. We're going to get through this together."

Right before he succumbed to slumber, something uncoiled in his chest, and he thought, for once in his life, he might not be able to.

45

LEO

Tamiel and Samyaza—his most trusted allies and team—held their illuminated hands over Leo's leg as he sat on a barstool in the separate guesthouse. It was a small two-story gray rock cottage with three bedrooms, only a half kilometer away from the main house, where everyone else was located.

Crieff, Scotland, was beautiful. Rolling hills. Lots of trees. Green valleys. Tons of privacy. It was a good place to set up base, without a lot of prying eyes and neighbors asking questions. He'd wanted some privacy. Not everyone knew he was dying. Corinth certainly didn't. If his brother had known, he'd have been trying everything in his power to heal him, and then he'd have got himself possessed—*again*—or worse, killed. No sense in anyone dying on his behalf.

They were currently trying to use their combined angelic energy to inspect the damage that had been wrought by Ephrem's Shades. Their combined energy was palpable. Leo was wearing nothing but his boxer shorts. Being in a state of half undress in front of his fellow angels didn't bother him. He wasn't human. His body was merely a vessel. Nakedness wasn't something he was bothered by. What bothered him was being without his armor—he felt defenseless. Angels weren't supposed to get maladies or abrasions or have flaws. They were supposed to be invincible. Until now, that is. Of course, Leo wasn't like ordinary angels. He was born of this world.

Maybe that was why he was dying so slowly.

The thorn wriggled under his skin, burrowing like razor wire down into his flesh, cutting an agonizing path through sinew and muscle. He screamed, clutching the back of the stool, trying not to instinctively pull away from their incessant examining. His breath was coming in deep, ragged pants. They both stopped their progress, looking more than concerned for his well-being.

"Why'd you stop?" he wheezed, his chest heaving up and down. "Keep … trying …"

The angels had been working for over two hours, and Tamiel was starting to look just as bedraggled and worn as he felt. Beads of sweat stood out on her forehead, and her usual dark, silver-rimmed eyes were glassier than normal; her black skin was ashen. She swayed slightly on her feet, swiping a hand down her face. "The more we try and extract it, the deeper it digs in—"

Samyaza's steely eyes met Leo's again, and he let out a frustrated bark, yanking his hands back as if he'd been burned. "This is what it must feel like to have frostbite," he muttered. "I don't think we've made any more progress. We only seem to be making it worse. I think it's engineered to repel angelic energy."

The wound looked festered and angry; ink-black squiggly lines stood out against Leo's cream-colored skin and snaked all the way down his thigh to his calf. His entire leg felt like it was on fire. He sucked in a sharp breath and stood up, grimacing from a new bout of pain. And he just managed to catch himself on the countertop before he toppled over.

Tamiel reached out to help steady him, but Leo shook his head at her, begging her off. "My thanks for your aid, but there seems to be nothing left to do. How long do I have?" he asked Samayaza, his teeth chattering. His fever had started to come back.

Samyaza shrugged tiredly, casting a worried gaze down at his feet. "I don't have a clue. Could two weeks or two months ... but that doesn't mean we're going to stop trying to figure this out. We still have time before the infection runs its course. I think the Blood Dagger—"

"No." Leo snapped his fingers, and sparks shot out of his fingertips, into the air—and then fizzled out like a flame being extinguished. Nothing happened. His brain felt fried. He turned his head slightly, annoyed. His clothes were still folded neatly on the dining-room table and *not* on his body. Even his powers were dwindling. *Great.*

Slowly he shuffled over to the table and tugged his dark-wash trousers on—the old-fashioned way—and then he threw on his light-green knit sweater. Angels couldn't make something out of nothing, but they could manipulate and rearrange matter in human-made objects.

At least, he used to be able to do that.

Leo lifted his right hand and made a flicking motion. A purple bolt of lightning shot out of his extended hand and formed the shape of a sword, the supernatural light snapping and sizzling until it finally solidified into metal, the pommel resting in his closed fist. "Where's my armor?" he asked quietly, already knowing the answer. It had been burned to a crisp by Nakir in their battle.

"It's ruined, Leo," Tamiel explained gently. "There's nothing to salvage. It will take time to find the proper steel to forge more. You need to rest." She put a hand on her hip. "Does he know?"

By *he*, Leo knew she meant Corinth. He shook his head, refusing to meet her accusatory glare.

"You should tell him. He will want to know. You're his brother," Samyaza interjected.

"Corinth has enough loss to deal with right now. As you said, we have time. Please don't say anything," Leo said.

Samyaza sucked his bottom lip through his teeth. "We will stay silent … for now."

"You have my gratitude," Leo said, and then he left, using the door this time.

46

ZOEY

In the kitchen at the cottage, I sat at the table, contemplating eating the corned beef sandwich in front of me. It smelled like it could quite possibly be the tastiest thing I'd ever eaten, but I didn't have the stomach for it yet. I knew I really needed to eat; I just kept thinking about the slap. And then the devastated look on Corinth's face after my mom had hit him. Really, the only reason I'd come in here was to find Cruz, but he was nowhere to be found, and I had been so famished.

"You should eat something."

I flipped around in my chair to see Dad and Mom coming through the kitchen doorway from the living room.

My dad had been the one to speak. I noted he looked like he could use a million years' worth of sleep. Mom was wearing a rumpled blouse and loose-fitting jeans, her hair in disarray, like she'd been constantly running her fingers through it.

She joined me at the table while my dad pulled the third chair out and sat too.

"Where's Jimmy?" I asked.

"He's sleeping," Dad answered, his voice low and tired sounding. "He hasn't slept since we got here. Larna had to give him something to help him fall asleep … He hasn't been himself since … well, understandably …" His voice drifted off as I noted he could use some much-needed sleep too.

My chest ached. I felt so empty and hollow. None of us were ourselves. *Jimmy.*

After a moment of contemplative silence stretching between us, I reached out and picked up the sandwich and tentatively took a bite. It did taste heavenly. My stomach rumbled in pleasure, and it clenched up with a hunger cramp, so I took another bite, and then another, until I'd finished the entire thing in about two seconds flat. I didn't know how long it had been since I'd last eaten. I wiped my mouth, feeling marginally better, yet my stomach felt a little unsettled.

"About keeping you in the dark for so long …" my mom started. And then she seemed to rethink her choice of words, because she glanced over at Dad and said, "We're sorry. We want to tell you all of it. Everything. If you'll let us."

I shoved the empty plate away from me and then rubbed the cold from my arms, even though I was wearing flannel pajamas. "About time," I grumbled.

A million different thoughts flitted through my mind, with a million different ways I could handle this moment with my parents. My heart felt like it was in my throat. I knew exactly what I wanted to say to both of them. It had been a long time coming, and it was very important that I get it out, now more than ever—especially since I'd almost died.

"No, Mom, I'm sorry." A flicker of relief and regret crossed my mother's features as I said, "My entire life, you guys were just trying to protect me. I … I thought Mom had cheated on you, Dad, and I took it out on her. On everyone. I've been angry for so long. I thought you were just being overbearing and overprotective … horribly unfair parents. But you weren't. You were doing the best you could with an impossible situation." I squinted down at my hands clasped in my lap, trying not to cry for the four thousandth time today. "But that doesn't mean I'm not mad. I mean, I am … I'm *unbelievably* mad at you both. At Cor. At our situation. P-P-Peter's gone." My voice cracked. "But it's not your fault. And I don't think you should have taken it out on Corinth the way you did, Mom."

I chanced a quick peek back up at my mom to gauge how she was handling what I'd just confessed to her. She had this strange, pinched expression on her face, her eyebrows almost touching in the middle, and her hands were clasped tightly together on top of the table.

She nodded. "You're absolutely right, Zo. I should never have hit him. I've tried to find Cor since then, to apologize, but … we … can't seem to get ahold of him yet. I fear I've gone too far—"

Dad settled a hand over hers, and surprisingly, a tear leaked out of the corner of his eye. I'd never seen my dad cry before. It was startling, and it made my heart clench in empathy.

I sat up straighter, concerned about my brother. "Give him some time. Corinth gets it. I know he does. We've all been through so much. We just need time to grieve in our own ways."

"When did you … get to be so … grown-up and wise?" my dad finally asked, swiping a hand down his pale face.

I shrugged as another swell of grief rolled over me, threatening to tow me under and drag me away into its undercurrent forever. Would this feeling ever go away?

Eventually I said, "Will you start at the beginning? Tell me everything?"

My dad nodded and got up from his seat. "I guess I better fix us some coffee, then. It's a long story."

47

CRUZ

Cruz found himself outside, wandering the property. He was in *Scotland*. And he hadn't jumped on a plane to get here. He didn't even have an up-to-date passport. He'd been magically whisked away by angels. That was amazing in and of itself, but everything else he'd been through in the last day had been absolute hell. One of the tall angels had healed his injuries. *Healed them!* It was beyond miraculous. He'd also been told that one of them, Ikari, had found his mother and somehow convinced her to think he was spending the weekend with friends. A feat he thought was even more miraculous than healing … At least he knew his mother was okay, and he wasn't going to be grounded for, like, ever.

Cruz's fingers grazed the cool metal of the shield in his pocket. *Hello, shield. Thank you for saving my life. Uh, can you turn into a dagger again? That would be cool.*

Nothing happened. No answer. No weird hum or whirring of gears … or weird biblical burning bushes nearby … and he was starting to feel really silly talking to an inanimate object, so he pulled his hand back out of his jacket and wandered the property, thinking.

Cruz had been out of the United States a couple of times before, to visit extended family and cousins in Mexico City, but Scotland was nothing like Mexico City. Mexico City had a vibrancy and hustle and bustle of a big city. Overcrowded streets, vendors selling tortas, huaraches, barbacoa, and sopes. The shops there were filled with all kinds of colorful trinkets and pottery and clothing.

In Scotland, it was rainy and green and quiet—oh, and cold! Much colder than in Texas. A breeze cut right through the thin material of his parka, and he shivered. White sheep dotted the landscape, grazing on the hillside nearby. He did not think this much green could exist in one place. Was it going to snow?

Another cool gust lifted his hair, and he swiped a hand through it, combing it back down. This place smelled of livestock, and something sweet he couldn't quite place his finger on—probably fresh air. Crisp and clean.

His mind kept replaying the horrible events of being down in that demon realm. Cruz really hadn't had the chance to process the existence of angels and demons and … and other, worse things that went bump in the night. A part of him just wanted to go home. But a bigger part of him really wanted to know more about those creatures. Vampires. Maybe he was still in shock. Something akin to unease, wonder, reverence, and a modicum of fear fluttered through him at the thought of meeting real angels.

If he hadn't seen it, and experienced it with his own eyes, he would not have believed any of the recent events had actually happened.

Zoey's screams came vaulting back to the forefront of his mind though. Okay, maybe he was ready to go home and never think about this ever again.

Cruz had planned on talking to Zoey but had given up the minute he'd heard the argument between Corinth and his mother. A twinge of guilt pricked at him. What could *he* do? The sound of the slap had been brutal to his own ears; he couldn't imagine how it had felt. He just needed to clear his head.

A white stone path led to a koi pond and a garden filled with carefully arranged rocks that looked like ripples in water. The shrubs and trees were all neatly pruned and trimmed, and several small wooden bridges adorned the trail. He had seen something like this at the botanical gardens back home.

At the end of the stone path sat a large wooden structure. Cruz found himself drawn to it, and without thinking, he walked through the open doorway to get a closer look inside.

A bamboo mat lined the entirety of the floor space. The room was sparse and barely furnished. Fastened to opposite walls were racks full of what looked like training weapons: wooden staffs and swords and knives—a bow. Someone's workout room.

Right across from him, in the middle of the space at the far wall, stood a tall figure.

Cruz gave a start, afraid he'd intruded on someone's private quarters, only to realize that the figure wasn't actually alive.

Feeling dumb, he moved closer, discovering he'd mistook an empty suit of armor for a person. It looked like it belonged in a war museum. Ancient. Antique. Awesome. The first thing he noticed about it was the black helmet. A thick, dark mane of hair was sticking out of the top—maybe horsehair. The matching body armor was immaculate and shiny; he counted eight iron plates patterned to look like fish scales. Shoulder guards, shin guards, thigh guards, and chain mail. *Cool.*

He left the armor alone, trying to tamp down the feeling of needing to try it on, and wandered over to a rack against the wall to pick up one of the wooden knives. Even though it was only made out of wood, it still felt heavy in his hand, awkward, like the blade had at first. He didn't quite know how to hold it. He jabbed out anyway, slicing at the air, pretending it was Trevor's face—

"Does Ikari know you're in here messing with his stuff?"

So surprised at hearing the voice, Cruz dropped the training weapon, and it hit the mat with a solid thunk. He twirled around, unsure what to do with his hands now that they were empty. He settled for putting them in his pockets. *Oops.*

Standing in the archway was Corinth. His eyes shimmered like a flame as they studied him, sharp and full of secrets.

Cruz shivered despite himself, remembering the way Corinth had gone after Alastair. The way he'd stabbed

Alastair right through the chest with that wooden spike …
There had been so much blood. And those wings … He
shivered again as a chill went down his spine. The guy could
transport himself to anywhere in the world by using magic.
What would Cruz do with that sort of power? Anything.
Everything. Transport himself into every single baseball
stadium on earth … Corinth could wield lightning.

"Uh, sorry … I was just—"

"Playing with the weaponry," Corinth said evenly as
he entered the training room, hunching down to get
through the doorway.

"You're part angel?" Cruz blurted, unable to keep the
awe out of his voice. "And those other … really tall
armored people are … angels too?"

"Yes and yes." Corinth glanced at the wooden knife on
the ground, a frown marring his face. "Trevor … Ephrem
… he's not dead. I thought you should know that."

Cruz's fear kicked up a notch, and his heart rate
spiked at the mention of Trevor being still alive. *No.* "*He's
not dead?*" Cruz squeaked. "I thought Alastair killed him."

"No. He only banished him to hell. Ephrem might
not escape, but I have no doubt he'll try."

"Can a demon possess me?" Cruz asked, suddenly
sick at the thought. "Like how you were possessed?
Because I never want that to happen to me. *Ever.*"

Corinth's eyes darkened a little as he pursed his lips,
seemingly thinking about what he wanted to say next.
"What happened to me is not going to happen to you. But
demons *can* possess humans. If you strengthen your faith
and keep the shield with you, in theory, you should be
okay."

"'In theory'?" he said. "'Should be'? I don't like the sound of those words."

"I wish I had a more definite answer for you, kid. You got dragged into an extremely dangerous situation. This isn't a game."

Cruz felt his face start to heat up, suddenly flustered. "I … I know this isn't a game," he mumbled under his breath. "Almost dying a few times has made me extremely aware of that fact."

Corinth's golden eyes narrowed down to tiny slits as he studied Cruz. After a moment, he scooped up the wooden blade from the bamboo mat and said, "That is exactly why I'm taking you home."

Cruz's gaze landed on the training weapon in Corinth's hand, and his throat closed up at the recollection of him stabbing Alastair in the back. "But I have to talk to Zo—"

"She doesn't want to see you." His voice was flat, devoid of all emotion.

That stung.

Cruz, feeling slightly unsettled, fished the now-pocket-size shield out of his parka. "This relic. It turned into a dagger for me when I needed it the most. I was able to wield it. What does that mean?"

Corinth's looked down to the tiny trinket in his hand. "It means you're worthy, kid."

A crinkle in the middle of Cruz's eyebrows formed as he pulled them together in disbelief and confusion and something else—a trickle of pride. The talisman felt heavier now. More vital. Cruz didn't feel worthy to carry it around, but he also believed something had led him to be here. Healed his mother. God, maybe. Something else more divine. Maybe that was his approval.

"So teach me how to use it," Cruz said firmly, glancing back up at Corinth, a bout of rare courage coursing through him. "I mean, I've tried to make it work again, and nothing is happening …"

Corinth's eyes snapped up to meet Cruz's. "What did you say?"

"If Trevor … or Ephrem, is still out there, I need to be able to defend myself, right? Teach me how to use that." He pointed at the wooden blade still in Corinth's hand, suddenly determined. "All of it. I mean, I want to learn how to defend myself."

"I appreciate everything you've done for my sister. I really do. She does too. You fought bravely on her behalf, and you're handling all of this way better than I did when I first learned about the supernatural, but it's time to go, kid. This isn't your fight—and trust me when I say this: you do *not* want it to be."

Cruz swallowed hard, thinking about everything he'd been through. Basically, hell. A lot. He'd never been complimented in that way before—but he had been dismissed before. Many times. And he knew what that felt like. This.

His throat felt raw, and when he spoke next his voice sounded husky in his ears. "This is my fight too."

"How do you figure?"

"Trevor tried to turn me into one of those *things*. A Shade." He lifted his hands up, a tinge of anger bubbling out of him now. He had always had a problem with his temper. "Ephrem or whatever, targeted me just like he targeted you. Several times, actually. And I survived. I mean, isn't this everyone's fight? You can't be responsible for the entire human race. Those were some scary demons. Did that one infernal … demon … get loose? Won't you need help? Will those Shades be back? Will they come looking for me?"

Corinth raked a hand through his dark hair, mussing it up on top, and then he stepped over to the rack, gently placing the wooden knife back into the slot Cruz had taken it from. His shoulders tensed, and Cruz could see the outline of hard muscle underneath. He knew the guy worked out.

After another minute, Corinth turned around and strode up to Cruz, within arm's reach of him. The ghost of a smile flitted across his features, and then vanished so quickly Cruz thought he'd imagined it.

Corinth pulled something out of his pocket. A watch. One of those cool-looking, high-tech smart watches that probably cost a fortune. He studied it for a moment before saying, "Yes. The infernal demon is still out there. Are you volunteering to track it down? You want to be a superhero? Because you'll only find those in comic books and movies. They don't exist here. Everything and everyone you know and love will be tested. Taken away from you. You have a mother waiting for you back home, right? You saw what Trevor did to my family. You want that to happen to yours? Are you prepared for that?"

Cruz glanced away, knowing where Corinth was going with this line of questioning. Maybe he was right. Cruz did miss his *madre*. He wanted her to be safe. Was she a target? His stomach twisted into knots.

Speaking of mothers … Cruz's eyes flickered over Corinth's cheek. There was no mark, but Corinth must have sensed Cruz's gaze halt on his face, because he quickly turned away. The guy had lost his brother. He must be devastated. Cruz didn't know what to think about Corinth's praise or being called brave, because he sure didn't feel brave now. He felt tired and ready to go home. He needed to check in on his mom.

"I didn't think so," Corinth said gently. "But I am going to give you this." He handed Cruz the watch, and Cruz accepted it, looking down at the flat, square face, feeling … well, he didn't know how to feel. *Holy cow.*

Corinth edged closer to him, and then he reached out to touch the screen. The watch lit up as soon as he touched it. *Nice.* There was a clock on the face, of course, but beside the clock was a folder, like an app—the only one on the digital readout.

Corinth tapped on the image, and it pulled up a picture of a red phone. "Push this button only in emergencies. And by *emergencies*, I mean *only* demon attacks," he clarified. "I don't do social calls or party tricks. Also, you break it, you buy it … Got it, kid? And for the love of all that's holy, please keep all this supernatural stuff to yourself. Don't even tell your mom."

Cruz nodded, speechless.

Corinth said, "If you know what's best for you and your family, you'll stay away from Zoey and hers—and protect yours. Am I clear?" And then, in an oven-hot flash of light and thunder, they disappeared, spirited away into a vortex of wind and fire and nothing.

48

ALASTAIR

Alastair was alone, sitting in a wheelchair, staring out the living-room window of the cottage in Scotland, watching the snow just beginning to dust the field outside. The flurries were darting all over the place in the blustering wind, erratic, unsure of which direction to go in. Which was kind of how he felt right now. Biscuit lay curled on his lap, sound asleep. Alastair didn't mind the little fur ball keeping him company.

His broken arm was shoved into a tight cast, and his injured ankle was propped up on the footrest for elevation. There was a long vertical cut all the way down the center of his chest, but it was bandaged up. Every time he moved, he could feel the wound stretch, and a twinge of pain would shoot through him. All things considered though, he knew he was lucky to be alive.

He was on all kinds of painkillers, which he had almost refused to take, but the constant discomfort had been too overwhelming to endure for long. His body was wrecked. It was odd: his ankle was fully healed, but the chunk of missing muscle and flesh made it difficult to walk—not that he'd really tried. He wasn't too enthused to start that journey quite yet. With a typical injury, people had time to heal and rehab and acclimate—to get used to the damage. Alastair would have to learn how to walk all over again, probably with the assistance of a cane or a walker. This thought had put him in a sour mood.

"Are you going to stand there lurking in the hallway all day?" Alastair spun the wheelchair around using his one and only good hand.

Corinth clutched the strap of the duffel bag at his shoulder, looking drawn and haggard and uncomfortable, standing in the doorway.

After a brief pause, he strode all the way into the room, stopping next to the cream-colored sofa to prop his hip against the armrest. He dropped his bag down by his feet, breaking eye contact with Alastair to stare out the window.

Alastair thought he looked far, far away, to a distant galaxy.

"Do you think we can skip the back-and-forth apologies? You know, for trying to kill one another," Alastair asked in somber resignation.

Corinth gave him a sideways glance and nodded, his eyes swimming.

"Going somewhere?" Alastair prodded when Corinth didn't say anything else. He decided he didn't like stoic Corinth.

"I, uh … am just cleaning some of my things out—"

he lowered his gaze "—and contemplating disappearing forever," he added, sweeping a hand through his untidy mop of dark hair, looking crestfallen.

Alastair's own hair was probably in as much disarray as Corinth's, but at this point, he really didn't care. He predicted sweatpants and tracksuits for his foreseeable future. He let out an amused grunt and scratched the cat behind one of his ears, thinking.

"What?" Corinth asked, pursing his lips as he watched Alastair pet Biscuit, looking both puzzled and annoyed at the same time.

"You won't leave."

It was a statement, not a question.

Corinth quirked an eyebrow at him. "What makes you so sure?"

"Because I know you, and I know how you feel about family. Yours is way too important to you for you to just up and leave them all behind," Alastair reasoned. "The threat is too recent. Too imminent now."

Corinth's face darkened, and he swallowed hard before saying, "That's *exactly* why I need to leave." His voice wavered. "*Pete* … his death *is* on me. My entire family was attacked because of *me*. You were grabbed because of *me*." He spit out the word. "I stabbed you in the back, and I can't get that image out of my head. I can't look at you the same way ever again. I'm ruined, Al. I want to make them all *pay*. There's something wrong with me. The darkness is back with a vengeance. My mom won't even look me in the eye anymore … There's so much loathing inside me. I just want it all to end …"

"Congratulations, Taylor," Alastair said evenly,

understanding Corinth's plight better than anyone else ever could or should. "You're more human than angel. And for the record, that's exactly what I expected you to say. None of us are immune to heartache or anger or darkness. Grief is no different from physical wounds. If you don't take care of yourself, if you let it fester, it'll take over. The *true* way to mourn the dead is to take care of the living—including yourself."

Corinth let out a frustrated sigh and slumped down to the couch, putting his head in his hands.

Alastair eased the wheelchair over to the sofa and put a reassuring hand on his brother's shoulder.

Finally Corinth lifted his head. Tears were streaming down his face, and he nodded once in thanks to Alastair.

"You know, your sister was very brave down there in that demon realm. I saw her stab Ephrem with your blade, straight through, no hesitation. And Cruz could have left her behind, but he didn't … He stepped up and took on an infernal demon all on his own."

Corinth's brows furrowed as he swiped a hand down his cheek. "Really? Zo did that? She *is* brave, isn't she?" He looked more in awe now as he considered what Alastair had told him. Eventually, he said, "I don't think that makes me feel any better though. It just makes me feel worse. Like I should have done more to help her. You. My family."

"You're only one person," Alastair said. "Besides, the shield answered to them both—sort of like how the dagger responds to you."

Corinth took in a deep breath and then let it out before saying, "What are you trying to tell me?"

"It chose them. You need to train Cruz and Zoey," he whispered. "Prepare them for what's to come. This isn't over. Don't leave them in the dark like Danel did to you for all those years."

"No, absolutely not," Corinth snapped, sounding hurt. "I … I can't. Zoey deserves a normal life … I'll research angelic warding and ancient artifacts to keep her safe. Leo and I will protect her—we'll start guard duty if we have to. I'll teach at her high school. Besides, she'll have a smart watch … I'll come running if she needs me—"

"At least give her the option," Alastair said gently. "And Cruz."

"No, Al." Corinth stood slowly back to his feet and laid a hand on Alastair's shoulder. A moment later, a glowing warmth flooded through him, sweeping sweet relief through his veins, and thickening, until he started to feel like warm jelly. The laceration on his chest seemed to close together just a tad more. It could have been a few minutes or a few hours, but when Alastair opened his eyes again, his sternum felt infinitely better—only it itched a lot, like it was starting to scab over.

Corinth swayed unsteadily on his feet, and he gripped his own chest, gasping, his eyes glazed over with pain.

Alastair clasped Corinth's wrist to stop him from toppling over, noticing that Corinth now looked gray and sickly, and Alastair was angry at Corinth for overextending himself, and not asking his permission before trying to heal him.

"Are you okay?" Alastair asked, concern and ire filling his voice. "Dammit, Taylor, stop doing that."

Corinth cracked his eyes open and nodded, visibly

shaky. "I'm okay. I just couldn't leave you like this … without doing more."

"It hurts?" Alastair asked. "When you heal me?" And his heart constricted, which had nothing to do with his physical injury. "You felt it … didn't you? My injury."

Corinth nodded. "Only the more severe maladies … the ones caused by demons or angels." He reached down and grabbed his bag and moved to leave but stopped, turning back around. "Al, take care of yourself and my family for me. I don't know when I'll see them next."

And with that, Corinth disappeared.

49

GABRIEL

Gabriel stood in a small patch of sunlight, staring up at the cloudy sky, his gloved hands on his hips. Of all the things he hated about being human again, this was not one of them. Everything else about being a mortal, he detested. He couldn't remember ever enjoying the warmth of the sun like he did these days. The sleet-bloated clouds were just watery enough to allow the rays to poke through and warm his cheeks. It wasn't quite freezing outside, but it was cool enough for a heavy coat. Just the way he liked it.

Curse it all. He should be gone by now.

But there was something holding him back. *Someone*, rather.

He needed to talk to her—explain himself—which was very unlike him.

Except he could feel Larna. Feel her distress and despair all the way across this damn ugly field.

As an ascended being, Gabriel Stanton had been one of the oldest and strongest of his kind. Some used the term *vampire*. A term he had always rebuked. When he had been an ascended being, created by angels and demons, he had been the one to turn Larna. And even though he was human *now*, they still shared a bond with one another. It was both vexing and exhilarating. He'd turned others before, of course, but Larna had always been different. One of a kind.

She exited through the front door of the two-story cottage, her chestnut-colored hair gleaming in the sunlight like a crown. A queen. She was wearing her father's jacket. It billowed out in the wind behind her in a cold draft of wind. Underneath the brown leather duster, she wore blue scrubs. The jacket for her father. The scrubs for her mother. *How cute.* She wasn't tall, skinny, or blond, like models on magazine covers. She was curvy, muscular, and short. Not generally the type of person Gabriel found attractive. But there was something about her that drew him in. A quiet self-assurance. An aloofness he couldn't quite put his finger on. Something deep and rich and complex. The feeling he got when he was around her was akin to trying to hold on to a kite as it fought to fly away in the wind. All he wanted to do was reel her back in. Collect her. Own her. Lock her away forever.

Gabriel Stanton, the tycoon, found it exceedingly frustrating that he could *not* have her. *Alastair Iszler has her.* Anything Alastair owned, Gabriel felt he should own too. He had all the money and status in the world, and he could not buy the one thing he really wanted. Family. Maybe the real rivalry was with Alastair, he thought distantly.

As she drew closer, he remembered the way she had touched his scar. So gently. Her eyes had been so warm. No one else had dared do such a thing in all the two thousand years he'd been alive. He would have killed anyone else on contact if they'd tried that. But the warmth of her fingers on his raised skin still lingered, even after ten years …

As soon as Larna Iszler saw Gabriel standing on the hill a short distance away from the cottage, she made a beeline for him, her lovely bow-shaped mouth turned down at the corners, wary and cautious. She was looking at him now as if he might turn into a dragon and start burning the village down at any second.

Gabriel grinned at that thought. He didn't blame her. Their relationship had been more than complicated. Hell, he might have burned everything to the ground by now if he were still an ascended being. Humanity had softened him—weakened him.

He liked that look Larna was giving him now. Cagey. Disturbed. Guarded. She stopped a few feet away, her eyes ticking over him; her mouth twitched up at the corner as she fixed him with a glower.

A flutter of excitement and challenge rolled over him—and also the awareness of how close she was to him.

Silence pressed in around them, but it wasn't uncomfortable. For a moment, all they did was study each other.

"If you want to say something, say it," she finally said.

Ah, so she was angry. *Good.*

"How is lover boy?" he asked, needling her. It was too easy, and he found himself slipping into his old routine.

"I'm sure he's okay. He has that survivor's grit … Tell him he owes me four thousand dollars for my ruined coat."

He practically heard teeth grind together as she hissed, "You call Alastair that again, and I'm going to make a mess of that expensive tailored suit you're wearing. And why do you care? You got him in this mess in the first place."

She looked so ashen, and worried, so all thoughts about being his usual snarky self quickly melted away. For some reason, he found he did not like that heavy feeling sitting in the center of his chest. *Her* anxiety, not his. He wondered if she could sense his emotions as well. *Yes*, he thought, *she can*. "My apologies, Mrs. Iszler. How is your husband doing? How is Mr. Taylor handling the death of his sibling? He has my condolences, by the way. Tell me you didn't see the day coming when Corinth and Alastair would go at it. Those two have always had a thing for you."

Gabriel had done it again. He couldn't help himself. He hated Taylor more than he did Iszler.

Larna's eyes went a shade darker, and her voice came out sounding like steel. "It's *Doctor* Iszler—but don't tell me you actually care, considering you did all of this … to … to him … to Corinth, to both of them." Her voice trembled in fury. "For what? To be a vampire again? Something else? Revenge? I should kill you right here where you stand." She tugged at the sleeves of her coat, where Gabriel knew her blades were hidden. Again, it was weird seeing her in medical scrubs and armor.

Would they fight today?

"Ascended being," he said insolently. Gabriel would have preferred violence to having this conversation any day of the week. He nodded, feeling the beginnings of a smirk curve his lips. He really did like her. "Mr. Iszler told you?"

She pursed her lips together, and then spoke so softly, menacingly, that he almost had to lean closer to hear her over the sudden howl of wind. "He told me *everything*. Tell me why you did it, you son of a bitch."

Gabriel let out a tiny breath, his heartbeat picking up a tad, which was an odd feeling for him. The swirl of green and brown in her eyes reminded him of leaves in early autumn. He did not feel guilt, yet this was as close to it as he thought he would ever get. "I'm not sorry for the choices I made—I did that because Corinth took something very precious from me, and I need to get it back. He stole my way of life, *Larna*. My family. Surely you understand that." Dammit, it was out of his mouth before he could pull it back in, her name soft on his lips. "I am sorry for hurting you."

He did not say her first name lightly, and she knew it. She seemed shocked, because her eyebrows went up into her hairline, and she stepped back slightly, a hand going to her chest. His own heart ached in the exact same spot she pressed her hand to.

"It seems to me," she said, "that you need to find a new family."

"Are you volunteering?" Gabriel asked with a smirk. "For years, I could think of nothing other than my revenge for what Corinth Taylor did to me. What he did to thousands of our kind without so much as giving us a choice. I'm not the only one who still thinks this way, Larna. He has a target on his back. I was approached by

Ephrem, early on … while he was still working with Angela. I was livid after the Nephilim took my near immortality from me." Gabriel sucked in a shallow breath, unsure why he was sharing this information with her. He touched a finger to the scar on his left cheek. He had to get this out. "My … my mother … I hadn't had thoughts about her in ages—you dredged up those old memories that I'd shut away for so long. That was a gift. You are special. I know you care about him, so this is my warning to you. But I also have a proposal for you. Come work with me. I'll supply you with whatever you need—"

Larna let out a derisive laugh. "Surely you must be joking. Why would I ever work with you?"

"To create ascended beings again, of course. But this time, we'll do it the right way. With you by my side. No one gets hurt … No casualties. Only volunteers. I know you want to be something greater again. Think of the power it will bring you. The strength. The status. Wealth. Family."

"Do it the right way?" She sounded incensed, and her cheeks were flushed rosy. "Gabriel … if you do this, you will make an enemy out of Corinth and the angels. They'll come after you."

Gabriel lifted his eyebrows in challenge, crossing his arms over his chest. "So, that's a *no?*"

"When will you give this up?" she asked, her voice full of frustration.

"Never," Gabriel said. "But that doesn't mean you have to tell Alastair or the angels about this conversation. It can stay between us for now. I'm not going to hurt anyone."

"Are you a friend or foe, Gabriel?" she snarled. "Because if you try and bring vampires back, you will definitely be hurting people … and we will be at odds."

"Well, then," he answered swiftly, smoothing his tie out with one hand. "Foe it is."

TO BE CONTINUED.

Join the adventure for the latest book updates, freebies, and also to support your very grateful author here.

Sign up for our mailing list to keep in touch: **http://eepurl.com/dg029j**

Come join me on Discord for an online book club—I pop in and chat quite often, and I'd really love to see you on there too. Come say hi at:

https://discord.gg/UYGXNTJ. Love this book? Please think about rating/and or reviewing it. It means the world to me to hear from you.

Social Media Links:

https://twitter.com/MistyGH_

https://www.facebook.com/TheBloodDaggerSeries/

https://www.instagram.com/mistyhayesofficial

https://www.goodreads.com/mistyhayes

https://www.amazon.com/author/mistyhayes

https://www.bookbub.com/authors/misty-hayes

ACKNOWLEDGMENTS

This year. This year. This year.

As I sit and type this, grumbling to myself, it is late November 2020. I swear this has been one of the most challenging years in which to sit down and write a book in. And with schools being out everywhere, people out of jobs, people still working and risking getting sick—and the general uproar of society—well, it's a wonder this book ever got finished. With that being said, this is exactly why it is so important to profusely thank my inner circle for their support. They are an integral part of keeping me sane. First and foremost, thank you so much to Christy Leonard, who gave me the idea of writing in Zo's POV.

Also for her never-ending encouragement, and excitement to read this new book in the spin-off series. To Amy Tillery and Stephanie Hancock, for the memories in NOLA.

Leonora Bulbeck, editor extraordinaire, *you*, as always, never cease to amaze me. Your expertise, professionalism, and all-around grace get me through the tough times. Thank you for your tireless work and input into my writing craft.

Thank you to Mark Reid, my cover designer, who is the best mind reader out there. Your covers are brilliant. Thank you to Lorna Reid, my formatter—always there for me and wicked fast and always professional and magical.

Thank you to Becky Pruitt—always. My guide. My adviser. My sister. I know you would have proofread this book—had you not decided to get cancer and then *BEAT* said cancer all in the same year. #Goddessgoals. #StrengthInSpades.

To my family and all of their unyielding support and guidance. My father, Robert Hayes, for teaching me to give it my all. To my little sis, Sherry Daugherty, you are strong and brave and kind, and you worry too much. Keep your chin up, and learn to trust yourself. Love you, gorgeous! To Jeremy Daugherty and Paul Leonard, and to "Big" Oscar and Susen Pruitt.

Thank you to Misty Spitzer—my writing partner and Ambassador of Quan. Getting together, clacking at the keyboards with you, listening to music, and sometimes getting work done is something I always look forward to.

Thank you to Stephanie Hancock for pushing me to get my butt in gear—in all aspects of life. I wouldn't be writing or into film if you weren't in my life. XO.

Thanks go out to Juan Arriaga for giving me the inspiration for Cruz Saldivar, and thank you to Michael Smith—historian, professor, and travel companion— This year's road trip adventure was off the hook. Hitting the road was the ultimate ode to *Supernatural* and its finale this year. It gave me a lot of time to think and process and *not* have a mental breakdown. And also to *have* a mental breakdown.

An extreme, huge THANK-YOU goes out to my beta readers: my mom: Annie Hayes, June Owens (Momma #2), and Christy Leonard, and a HUGE thank you to Shannon Knight, for all your notes and incredible support.

To my readers, you supply me with an endless bounty of grit to keep writing. Thank you. Thank you. Thank you. And one last thank-you.